I0612924

TWICE CURSED

ANNIVERSARY EDITION

Coventry Press Ltd.

TWICE CURSED

CURSED BY BLOOD SHIFTERS

MARIANNE MOREA

Coventry Press Ltd.

Somers, New York

ISBN-13: 978-0-9884396-0-3

First Edition: Coventry Press Ltd. 2014

Printed in the USA

For Bill,
The Love of My Life

PROLOGUE

NEW YORK CITY

Four a.m.

"Damn! It's cold," Detective Ryan Martinez muttered, blowing on his hands. He stepped lightly, picking his way through the shattered glass and wood covering the street. Even to an untrained eye, it looked as if the bar had exploded from the inside out.

He shook his head, his lips pressed together in a grim line, watching as CSI began their initial investigation inside what was left of the bar. Most of the victims had their throats ripped open, and there was so much blood and debris, it looked like a gangland war zone.

Outside, three victims lay prone on the sidewalk, their bodies bent and unnatural in the dirty snow. The red glare of flashing patrol lights gave the grisly scene a surreal appearance. Nobody in their right mind wanted to be out tonight, least of all for a mess like this.

Patrol had already cordoned off the area, but the ghastly scene attracted rubberneckers even at this ungodly hour. God bless the city that never sleeps, he thought grimly, while uniformed personnel busied themselves with crowd control.

Martinez caught sight of his dour faced superior. Detective Sergeant Michael Shaw flashed his badge and crossed the police barrier, nodding to the uniformed officers operating the perimeter. He crouched under the yellow police tape, stepping carefully to avoid the frozen footprints dotting the sidewalks like potholes. With a grunt, he stood up, straightening his coat. "Whatta we got, Martinez?"

The young detective flipped his notebook open, his breath puffing out in clouds of wet smoke. "Multiple homicide, Sergeant. Nine bodies, six inside the club and three out on the sidewalk. Injuries appear to be severe with possible D.O.A.s. Triage paramedics are still calling it."

Wind gusts cut down the street like a razor, slicing into the back of his neck and setting his teeth to chatter. He turned his collar up and brushed the snow from his hair and shoulders, leaving his shearling suede coat dotted with damp splotches. Melting snow had mixed with freezing rain, turning most of the East Village into a gray, slushy puddle. Plummeting overnight temperatures had left the normally vibrant streets coated in black ice. If the cops weren't careful, some of their own would head to the hospital along with the victims from this latest bloodbath.

Inside what was left of the bar, the CSI unit sifted through the rubble, recording evidence, and a thick tension pressed down on everyone while they waited for additional ambulances to arrive. It was a sure bet a call was put out to more than one EMS Corps based on the look of things.

"Any witnesses or statements yet?" Shaw asked, stepping over broken glass and bodies, careful not to step in any of the blood. Dark smudges were evident under the Sergeant's eyes, despite wind-reddened cheeks and at least a day's worth of stubble. His mud brown hair looked as if frustrated fingers had raked through it a hundred times.

"No, not one, and the bartender's dead too. No security camera either. It's as if someone came in and went postal on the whole damn place, then disappeared without a trace. Inside, it's tore up pretty bad as well, blood everywhere except in each vic…" Martinez stopped short.

At Shaw's raised eyebrow, Martinez cleared his throat. He wasn't being a wiseass, nor was it mere speculation. He *knew* the victims had been drained dry. The young detective frowned, wincing a bit at what Shaw would think after the medical examiner's final report confirmed what he let slip. How would he explain himself? A good guess? He didn't think so.

Martinez's hand went to his mouth, and he gagged slightly. Christ! What the hell was that stench? He knew it was more than just the blood and gore. It was happening again. There was something underlying all this, something beneath the obvious that didn't seem to register with anyone else.

Hunches were nothing new in police work. Most detectives had a blue sense, a gut feeling when it came to solving difficult crimes, but Martinez's uncanny abilities went way beyond hunch. Things had been curious on and off for the last six months, ever since he made detective. He had been one of the youngest officers promoted to the squad in quite some time, and from that point, his sixth sense, or whatever it was, had shifted into overdrive. Sometimes it was a blessing, like when his squad located that missing six-year-old last month. Other times, not so much.

Either way his extrasensory revelations made certain members of his squad a bit nervous. They already thought of him as half a freak, referring to him as *the dog* behind his back because of the things he could sense. However, unlike bounty-hunter and reality TV star, Duane 'Dog' Chapman, it wasn't out of respect for his skills.

The hair on Martinez's neck and arms stood on end, but there was no way he was saying anything else to Shaw about what he sensed. He'd heard it all before. "Hey, Martinez, maybe you should put in for the canine unit... we heard they add a lifetime supply of dog chow to your bennies when you retire!" Ha. Ha. Ha. No, thank you.

Remarks like those taught Martinez to keep his cards close. Tall and handsome, with piercing green eyes and dark wavy hair, he carried himself as if he could own the world if he wanted, but the truth was, he was a loner, and preferred it that way.

The shrill sound of sirens shook him out of his passing reverie. The ambulances had arrived along with the Medical Examiner. As the man stepped out of the car, Martinez's eyebrows shot up. Their Duty Captain had clearly called in the big guns. He watched as the man greeted the chief M.E., calling Shaw over to give the brass a run through of what they had found so far. The M.E. nodded, before heading inside with his team. As per protocol, the injured were assessed and then transported to the nearest hospital, with D.O.A.s going directly to the main morgue at Bellevue. Of course, Martinez already knew there were all dead.

A uniformed officer pushed past the others and walked toward him. Urgency written on his face. "Detective, you'd better come with me. CSI found another victim. He's still alive, if just barely," he said, pulling Martinez's attention back to the scene.

"Where?" he shot back, shoving his notebook into his breast pocket.

"Behind the bar," he answered.

The man led the way through the blown-out door, his face pale against his blue uniform. His underlying green pallor made his rookie status patent, and the poor cop kept wiping his nose and mouth with the back of his hand.

The two moved past CSI photographers, to stand just behind the crisis unit, as the medical team prepped the victim for transport.

"Can he talk? I need a word with him before you take him," Martinez asked, leaning over the EMT lieutenant as he worked.

The lead EMT shook his head. "I doubt it. His throat's pretty torn up, and he's lost a lot of blood. If there's any chance at saving him, we've got to move now. Either talk as we walk, or ride with us to the hospital. Your call, Detective."

The victim's hand shot out grabbing Martinez's arm. His eyes were wild, and he clawed at the oxygen mask over his nose and mouth.

"Take that thing off his face!" Martinez yelled, but no one moved to take the mask away.

The man's fingers clutched at the Detective's coat, his mouth working beneath the clear plastic trying to form words.

"It's going to be all right, sir. We're taking you to the hospital," the EMT said, shooting Martinez a dirty look. "We've got to go, NOW!"

The injured man wouldn't let go of Martinez's coat. He opened his mouth again, his eyes pleading, but a series of gurgled rasps were the only sound that escaped.

EMTs pried the man's hand from Martinez's coat, and then moved like lightning out the door, loading him into the waiting ambulance.

Shaw walked back. "Did he make a statement?"

Martinez's gaze followed the ambulance's flashing lights as it turned the corner, the telltale whoop-whoop of its siren echoing in the air. "Yeah. It was garbled, but I managed to make out what he said."

"Well?"

The detective took a deep breath and turned to face his superior. "He said it was the devil," Martinez answered, his eyes trained on the sergeant.

The corners of Shaw's mouth pulled down, and a disgusted sound escaped his lips. "Great. Just what we need, another crazy complete with hallucinations," he said, stamping his feet for warmth. He shoved his hands into his pockets again. "It's gotta be drug related, either that or he's psychotic. Lowlife mutt probably knows he's gonna die and is panicking about paying the devil his due."

Martinez frowned. "Maybe. Except it didn't look like drugs or psychosis to me. The guy was terrified. Whoever or whatever did this scared the crap out of him."

"Look, I'm sorry for the guy, but it doesn't really matter. Unless he spouts something that will actually help, I'm not wasting man-hours collecting gibberish. You know how I feel about that kind of supernatural claptrap."

Martinez nodded, but kept his mouth closed.

Sticking a piece of gum in his mouth, Shaw shook his head at the bloody mess mixed with the dirty snow around their feet. "Heard from dispatch on the QT that this case follows the same profile as two others this month. Been talking to the other squad leaders, and there's a pattern to these homicides, Martinez, at least that's what headquarters is thinking. In my eyes, the fact that O.C.M.E. brass is here tonight, confirms it. I don't see how they're going keep the lid on this much longer, and the captain's already breathing down everyone's neck about not having any leads. Don't know exactly how we're going to handle this."

Martinez wrinkled his nose and coughed. He had no idea either.

CHAPTER
ONE

"Y ou really didn't have to come with me, Jack," Lily Saburi crossed the street in front of One Police Plaza with the werewolf in tow. "This is my town. I can handle myself."

"I know, but Sean wants me close. We left Maine so you could get your head straight. I'm just following orders."

"Get my head straight?" She stepped onto the curb before fixing the wolf with a look. "Is that what he told you?"

Sean Leighton was the Alpha of the Brethren of Shifters, and despite evidence to the contrary, the man she loved and couldn't live without. The man she voluntarily left behind so their future together would carry no questions, no whispers, and no doubt.

"*Uhm*, no, he didn't say that exactly. I just assumed."

Her fixed look changed from skepticism to dismissive. "That's why there's a saying about people who assume. Next time, just ask."

"I'm not stupid, Lily. If I'm stuck here until you and the big guy figure things out, then you need to meet me halfway. Not treat me like I'm an idiot. I get enough of that from—"

She paused on the sidewalk at Jack's deliberate clip. "Enough of *what* from whom?"

"It doesn't matter. You're my charge as long as you choose to stay in this stinking asphalt jungle."

"It may be an asphalt jungle, but it's not that bad, Jack."

He sniffed, wrinkling his nose. "Easy for you to say. Just be grateful Sean only marked you. If he had made you a full shifter, your senses would be under assault, same as mine. The whole place smells like a public toilet."

"I get it. The city can carry a distinct pong. I guess I didn't notice, not with the temperature in single digits. I apologize for the affront on your delicate olfactory senses, but city stink has nothing to do with you following me like a puppy."

"Puppy." He shook his head. "Look, you're agitated, and I'm agitated. I have a job to do, and you really don't have a choice. Sean wants me here. Just in case. So let's call a truce, okay?"

"In case of what? Do you honestly think Edward Parr or one of his blood purity minions has infiltrated the NYPD in the last twenty-four hours? C'mon Jack. Police headquarters has at least two levels of security before anyone even gets into the building. After that, there are other buffers. I'll be as safe as kittens, to use Sean's words."

His face softened, but just a hair. "Fine. I have to follow Sean's orders, but I can do so at somewhat of a distance. YOU need to stay out of trouble, though I doubt hosing you down with holy water would help accomplish that."

"Seriously?"

"Am I wrong?"

She gave him a conciliatory half grin. "No, but it's not like I go looking for trouble."

"*Uhm*, who was it that stormed the council meeting and nearly impaled Edward Parr with a six foot lance?" His raised eyebrow was more for emphasis than mocking. "That's right. It was YOU."

Hmmph. "I was making a point."

"You think? You've got balls, Lily, I'll give you that, but you're also impetuous, and that's why I'm here."

For such a small word, *why* carried enormous subtext in this situation. Why she met Sean in the first place? Why she wasn't with him now? Every layer of the word traced its origins to one fateful night. The night Lily's best friend was killed by a rabid wolf.

Except that wolf wasn't a garden variety predator. It was a wolf shifter infected with a virus that degenerated its body and mind, leaving it feral and vicious. That night left Terri dead, and Lily a vengeful basket case hellbent on tracking the beast and putting a bullet through its head. Instead, it nearly killed her, too. If not for Sean. He saved her life. That night introduced her to a world she never imagined existed, and a love she never dreamed could be true.

The attack left more than physical and emotional scars. It left trace amounts of the virus in her blood. Enough for her body to fight, producing antibodies that saved the shifters from a fate worse than death. So why was she miles away from the man she loved, and shunned from the people she helped save?

That *why* had a name. Edward Parr. A slippery politician who believed in blood purity, despite Lily's service to the shifters he claimed to want to protect. The man who did everything in his power to derail her acceptance by the pack, and Sean's ability to claim her as his mate.

There was more to Parr's scheming than rules and traditions against fraternization with humans. His machinations had tentacles. The question was how deeply they had taken hold and was it too late to bring common sense back to the shifter community.

Letting Edward believe he had the upper hand in forcing their separation was the perfect way to buy time without suspicion. Time Sean needed to investigate, proving Parr to be the tyrant he so cleverly concealed.

Was it easy being that far away from the man she loved? The

man she craved? Of course not. The answer to keeping that craving at bay? Lots of phone sex and keeping herself busy.

"Lily, are you listening to me?" Jack waved a hand in front of her face.

She swatted him away. "How could I not? You're like a bad audio loop."

"Who is this Mark Phillips guy? And why does he need to see you asap?" He shook his head, scanning the area. "Couldn't this have waited until I had the chance to settle in and get the lay of the land?"

"We're not pioneers, Jack. There's no thieves hiding in them there hills." She pointed across the river to New Jersey. "That's Hoboken. All you'll find there are high rents and good food."

He crossed his arms at his chest, not budging from the sidewalk.

"Fine. Mark is a colleague. He's the NYPD Bureau Chief, and if you ruin this for me by making me late, I swear I'll tie your tail in a knot the next time you shift. Ever since I started working as a profiler, I've been waiting for a high profile case to come my way. You'd think my psychic abilities would be a plus, but they're not. Shifters aren't the only ones who suffer from narrow minds. Meeting Mark here tells me this is it, and opportunities like this don't knock twice."

Jack simply nodded. He didn't comment, but he walked with Lily until the two stood outside the main grounds. "So this is your police station." Clearly impressed, he took in the building and its surrounding gardens. "I'll grant you this much. You'd never guess this was a precinct."

"It's not a precinct, Jack. It's the hub of New York's finest." Lily glanced at the main entrance and then back again. "Hey, do me a favor. Go get a cup of coffee. Take my car and play tourist. If you need to sniff around Battery Park to satisfy your wolfy sensibilities, then go for it. I'm not sure how long I'll be, and I don't want you skulking around, waiting."

Jack crossed his arms in front of his chest again.

Obstinacy was as much a shifter trait as the need to race the moon. Still, Jack's perspective wasn't quite as one-sided as Sean's, and Lily hoped that would make him a little more reasonable. There was no winning this argument, and loitering around was the quickest way to draw the wrong kind of attention. The last thing either of them needed was a stint in the slammer.

He exhaled, finally, blowing a cloud of warm air into the frigid morning. "Fine. I'll take a walk around Battery Park and sniff the grass and whatnot. You have my cell number. Give me a buzz when you're done or if you change locations. I need to be close, but at this point the argument is moot. You never listen anyway."

"Glad you finally see reason. I'll call you when I'm done." She hiked her bag over her shoulder and then headed down the heavily salted pathway toward the main doors. She didn't turn around. She knew Jack watched, yet the feel of his eyes felt off somehow, and she mentally counted the days until the next full moon.

Passing through a series of metal detectors, a set of officers searched her bag at each location before she reached the lobby. A pretty blonde in a pert, navy suit sat at the central reception desk. It was clear she was administrative, and not a member of the force.

"May I help you," she asked with a bright smile.

"Yes. I'm Lily Saburi. I have a ten o'clock appointment with Chief Phillips."

"Certainly. One moment please."

The woman picked up the phone, and Lily guessed it was yet another buffer. Something was up, she'd felt it the moment she'd walked into the building. This level of scrutiny was more than the average day-to-day of dealing with New York's criminal element.

The woman hung up and smiled again, handing Lily a building pass. "Go ahead up. Seventh floor. He's waiting for you."

It had been a while since she'd been at police headquarters, and the lobby was just as busy as she remembered. Visitors to One

Police Plaza often expected something resembling the set from NYPD Blue or CSI New York.

The fact was the building functioned not only as headquarters for one of the largest police departments in the country, but it was also the polished face of the NYPD. The people who walked its halls possessed the same hard edges screenwriters try to give their actors, but here those characteristics were hard-earned. The grit may have been spit-polished until it shined, but it was still there underneath.

As she got into the elevator, the underlying unease she'd noticed at security ratcheted up a notch. She knew the feeling wasn't hers, and as the elevator climbed, the uneasiness grew until it practically jumped out at her when the door slid open on the seventh floor.

She stumbled out of the elevator and dropped her purse, the sense of foreboding gripping her full force.

An overweight man in an ugly brown suit looked up from behind half-moon glasses at his desk to the side of the elevators. "May I help you?"

People milling around turned in her direction, and three sets of eyes, each one more quizzical than the last, inspected Lily as she steadied herself. "Yes," she said, straightening her jacket. She bent to retrieve her purse. "I'm here to see Chief Phillips. He's expecting me."

The man checked her I.D. and her building pass, then hefted himself out of his seat. "This way, please."

He led her down the corridor to an office in the back, sweating and red-faced from the exertion. He knocked on the door, and a muffled, "come in" echoed from the opposite side.

"He's all yours. If he needs anything right now, he'll have to call downstairs. I've got my break. Union rules."

"Thank you," Lily muttered, watching him trundle back to his desk.

She'd worked many cases for the Chief of Detectives, but she had never been to his office. So why the invitation now? Her guess. The brass had insisted. They needed someone to pull something out of a hat and she was the magician. Based on the volume coming from the opposite side of the door, they were desperate.

Glancing over her shoulder to floor security, the guy in the ugly brown suit was gone and no one else sat at the desk. That gave her plenty of time to eavesdrop. For shits and giggles, she homed in with her senses, wincing at the onslaught of thought that rivalled the booming voices echoing through the door. She recoiled, this time turning down every other sense to watch like a fly on the wall.

"What do you mean you have no leads?" Police Commissioner, Stan O'Neill, yelled as he paced back and forth behind his desk, his normally ruddy complexion getting redder by the minute. Sweat glistened beneath his receding hairline and his usually impeccable appearance was unkempt, his suit as rumpled as his demeanor. "I thought we found a survivor. Is he able to talk? Why hasn't his statement been taken?"

"He didn't make it, sir. He died while in route to the hospital," Shaw said, drawing a meaty hand across his forehead.

"This is a nightmare, a fucking nightmare. I didn't spend thirty years of my life being all about the job to have this sort of thing happen on my watch." Rubbing his temples, O'Neill exhaled.

With his back to his deputies, he faced the windows, his hands folded across his chest. One Police Plaza and the grounds of Park Row had always been a symbol of the interconnectedness of the NYPD and New York's five boroughs. But even the river, steel gray in the distance, seemed to mock that this morning. Instead, it mirrored the anxious faces of the men sitting around the office.

Shifting in their seats, no one spoke. They had all been summoned, pulled from every source to get a handle on what was happening in the city. His city. The best of New York's Finest— Intelligence, Strategic Initiatives, Operations, and the office of Legal Matters— all were staggered by the situation.

"Please, sir, if I can—" Mark Phillips, began, only to be cut off in midsentence.

"I don't want to hear any excuses! Do you have any idea who I have screaming about this? Threatening me with things you don't want to know. Senator Ned Kelly. That's right. Senator, I-own-everything-in-this-country, Ned Kelly. His cousin's kid just happened to be one of the victims at this latest bloodbath down in the 9th precinct."

"A Kelly, huh? What the hell was he doing at a dive bar off Avenue B? If he's anything like the rest of them, five will get you ten it was off the charts kinky," Deputy Tom Fay snorted.

Phillips's head jerked left. Everyone knew Fay was a first class asshole, but now wasn't the time to be missing a filter. Still snickering, the dickhead didn't even pretend to look embarrassed. Deputies were usually political appointees, but O'Neill had been hardcore when it came to the people with whom he surrounded himself, demanding they all spent time on the job. Fay's wiseass remark made it clear *he* was a political favor.

O'Neill stopped pacing and slammed his hands on his desk. Glaring, he eyeballed everyone in the room. "Who the hell cares why? Perhaps he was a fan of slumming it. The only thing that matters now is that we don't look like a bunch of incompetent idiots. This stops now! We need to get a handle on this and pronto! So, gentlemen, any suggestions?"

The silence in the room was deafening and even Fay kept his trap shut for once. Phillips looked around. Most of the men here held shields for many years, but it seemed years of being suits had dulled their blue instincts, either that or they didn't want to risk their cushy jobs to O'Neill's anger. Well, screw that.

Phillips was still close enough to the job to want to get his hands dirty, and this shit stunk to high heaven. "I have an idea, sir, but it's a little unorthodox," he offered, mentally steeling himself for what he knew could be career suicide.

16

O'Neill slumped down into his chair and loosened his tie. "At this point, I'd be willing to listen to just about anything. We've had three major incidents in the last month leaving seventeen people dead, one the relative of a political powerhouse. The press is on the verge of a feeding frenzy, and we have absolutely no leads. It's a miracle we've been able to keep a lid on this thus far. I have no fingers left to plug up the leaks, so for God sake spit it out Phillips. I'm all ears."

"We could bring in a psychic."

"Come on, Phillips, you can't be serious? This is enough of a freak show without us intentionally adding to it," Fay interjected.

Phillips ignored the expected sarcasm, keeping his eyes on the Commissioner's silent expression.

The man's face was a mask. O'Neill said nothing, yet his eyes narrowed, drumming his fingers as if weighing the options. Leaning forward, he pointed at Phillips, fixing him with an ice-cold stare. "Do you have someone specific in mind, Mark? This better not be some hokey, spoon bender that comes complete with a lunatic fringe."

The two men eyed each other in utter gravity as everyone else in the room slowly came to realize this was no joke.

Phillips nodded. "I know someone, sir. We've worked with her before, and she's the best. Very credible, and extremely discreet," he paused, "—and I already called her. She'll be here any minute."

"Her." O'Neill's gaze narrowed, questioning.

Mark didn't blink. "It's Lily Saburi, sir."

The commissioner almost smiled. The man wouldn't know Lily if he fell over her, but her reputation was another story. That was all she needed to make her entrance. Without hesitation, she turned the knob and opened the door and all eyes turned.

"Lily." Mark Phillips came around the end of his desk to take her hand. "It's good to see you. I hope you got my note about Terri. I'm so sorry."

She shook his hand. "Yes. Thanks. It's good to see you, too." The minute her fingers clasped his, she knew his words were genuine, and she gave his hand a little squeeze. "So, what's so important you couldn't bring me up to speed on the phone?" She already knew, but played dumb anyway.

The room was large, with black leather and chrome furniture, and a wall of frameless glass windows overlooking the grounds. Besides the Commissioner and his Chief of Detectives, there were two other men in the room. Talk about home court advantage. She took a deep breath and steeled herself. Bring it on, baby.

"Please, take a seat, and let me introduce you to Commissioner O'Neill, as well as Detective Sergeant Michael Shaw, and Detective Ryan Martinez. The detectives will be working closely with you on this case. Should you choose to take it."

Lily nodded to each. "Pleased to meet you."

Phillips leaned his butt against the front edge of his desk and exhaled. "I'm not really sure where to begin." He gestured futilely. "We've had three separate, multiple, homicides in the past month. That's a lot, even for a city this size. What's worse, each one was a veritable bloodbath. The first took place about a month ago near the Roosevelt Island Bridge. The next was in Hell's Kitchen a couple of weeks later, and the latest down on Ninth Avenue in the East Village. All less than savory locations. If you know what I mean. We're really up against it this time, Lily."

"What Chief Phillips means is we are at a dead end," the Commissioner interrupted. "In each case, we found only D.O.A.s, and the crime scenes didn't provide much in terms of leads, or evidence."

Lily didn't miss the look that passed between Shaw and Martinez. Shaw was a skeptic, and probably had balked at the idea of having to work with her. What else was new?

That one look told her both detectives had more up their sleeves than they were willing to share. It was rabbit-pulling time, and her magic hat was primed and ready.

She leaned back and crossed her legs, her elbows on either arm of the chair, and her fingers laced together in front. Detectives were specialized, trained in the art of interpreting body language, and reading between the lines. Lily wanted it clear, if unspoken, that she had nothing to fear and nothing to hide.

"One doesn't need to be a profiler, gentlemen, to see there's more here than meets the eye. You've gathered hard facts about this difficult case, and as Chief Phillips has explained, you are to be commended. You are seasoned veterans, and doubtful about me and what I can bring to the case. That's understandable. What I do can't always be quantified. I, myself, don't always understand how I know what I know."

Lily paused, waiting for someone to interject, but no one said a word. The hostility coming from Shaw was palpable, and her earlier suspicions ratcheted up a notch. The man wasn't just skeptical. He would derail her entire role in this case if he got the chance.

On the other hand, Martinez's curiosity was piqued. Unlike Shaw, whose body language was closed and defensive, Martinez leaned forward in his chair, his eyes trained exclusively on hers.

She glanced up at Mark, and at his nod, continued.

"Regardless of whether you choose to believe it or not, the truth is, I see things, feel things, hear things, and know things others don't. It's called parapsychology, and I understand how hard it is to put faith in anything labeled beyond normal. Profiling goes hand-in-hand with psychic ability. However, that doesn't mean I want to be a one-woman show. I want this to be a team effort."

Shaw's face looked as if he'd sucked on a lemon. He cleared his throat, and with a grunt, shifted in his seat. Phillips was resolute, regardless, and the look on the Commissioner's face said he was in total agreement. No matter how much the Detective Sergeant resented the idea, they were between a rock and a hard place. The hierarchy of the police department was a political hornets' nest, and perhaps that was the reason for his overblown opposition. His authority had been subject, and subsequently overruled.

"What can we do to help?" Martinez asked, obviously ignoring Shaw's disapproving cough.

Lily ignored him, as well. "I'm a purist, as Chief Phillips will attest to, and prefer you not tell me the specifics. The only thing I need is a jumping-off point. That way, there won't be a question about what I learn versus what you've told me. It's the way I do things. Allowing for us to work together rather than against each other, or God forbid, have the situation become a battle of one-upmanship."

She knew the bare bones based on her fly on the wall stunt, but there was much more to this than they let on. Their earlier bickering was more about preserving their jobs and their reputations, not the nitty gritty of the case.

Phillips's face was a full-on smirk. "I see your leave of absence hasn't tempered you one bit. I'm glad, because we're going to need every ounce of that infamous tenacity to solve this case."

Lily couldn't help but smile. She should have known Mark would have her back. "Besides having little evidence and only D.O.A.s, was there anything about the crime scene, anything unusual that might give me a place to start?"

"Take a look for yourself," Phillips said, gesturing for Martinez to hand over the case file and the Medical Examiner's report.

"I thought you just said you didn't want specifics," Shaw objected, crossing his arms in a huff.

Lily shot him a look, taking the file from Martinez's hand. The detective's fingers brushed hers in the transfer, and a rush of disjointed images and thoughts spilled into her mind. She sucked in a breath and locked her narrowed gaze on his.

Phillips pushed himself up from the edge of his desk. "What? What just happened?"

Lily's eyes didn't leave Martinez's as she answered. "I need to get to the morgue. Now."

"The elevator doors slid closed, and Martinez pushed the button for the ground floor. He looked straight ahead at nothing, though the weight of Lily's stare was heavy and intent.

"How did you know each victim had been drained dry?"

Martinez's head whipped around, and his mouth fell open. She couldn't have stunned him more if she suddenly grew scales and swallowed a live rat. Still, she stood unflinching, with her arms crossed in front of her chest and her eyes fixed on his, almost daring him to lie.

"I don't know what you're talking about."

Lily exhaled. "You know exactly what I'm talking about, and don't tell me your theory was just an educated guess. You knew. I saw your thoughts." Her finger jabbed the air between them.

In a heartbeat, she had gone from teamwork cheerleader to a dagger-eyed complainant. He hadn't said a word to anyone about what he had sensed, and he certainly hadn't included it in the police report. What was her game?

His guard way up, Martinez pressed his lips together, collecting himself before he started an all-out war. "First off, don't point your finger at me. It's rude, and I don't appreciate it. Secondly, lose the accusatory attitude or this conversation is over. Shaw may doubt your specialized set of talents, but that doesn't mean I share his skepticism. I asked what I could do to help. Remember? He's the one who wanted to keep things hush-hush until he was satisfied you weren't some kind of a kook. I'll be the first to admit there's more to this than what we're seeing, so why don't you back the hell off?"

Now it was his turn to stare *her* down. Angry, he shrugged into his overcoat, stretching out the tension in his shoulders and neck. Neither said a word as the elevator opened onto the main lobby.

He never lost his cool. Not even when he dealt with the rat squad over at Internal Affairs. So why was he allowing this woman to get under his skin? The chief wanted them to work together, so he'd play nice with the psychic, even if it meant biting his tongue until he tasted blood.

"Since I've been appointed designated driver, I suggest we take one car. Traffic is a mess down here no matter what time of day, and parking is bound to be an issue. My car is in the municipal lot next door, unless you'd prefer to follow me over. The D.O.A.s for this case are being held at the morgue at Bellevue Hospital."

Lily shook her head. "No, it'll be easier if I go with you than take my own car. I can always catch a cab home from there if we're not needed back this way. If you'll excuse me, I just need to make a quick call." She walked away, already scrolling through the numbers on her cell phone before Martinez could object.

He watched her expression change from resolute, to irritated, to sarcastic and back again, before she hung up and walked back toward him. Great. She was a veritable mood-swing acrobat. Did Phillips say psychic or psycho? Play nice, Ryan. You said you'd play nice.

"Ready?" she asked.

The two walked in silence across the frozen sidewalk, taking the outside elevator to the second level of the parking garage.

Rows of patrol cars and other official vehicles were parked diagonally across from the elevators. "This way." Martinez gestured toward a jet-black Camaro parked along the far wall. A telltale chirp echoed through the concrete structure as he unlocked the doors. "Get in."

Lily buckled her seatbelt as he put the car in gear and backed out of the space. "I'm sorry, Detective. I apologize for being so abrupt. Images come unbidden sometimes, and when you handed me the file..."

She let the sentence drift, and Martinez glanced at her in the passenger seat. "It's okay. I get it. And it's Ryan."

"Ryan?"

"My first name. When we're alone, we can forego departmental formalities since you're not exactly personnel," he said as they headed down the exit ramp and out of the parking garage.

"All right. Will you answer my question then, Ryan? How did you know about the victims?"

"I haven't the faintest idea how I know what I know." He leaned over the steering wheel, watching for an opportunity to merge into traffic.

Lily raised an eyebrow. "None?"

"Nope. I just know. It's been that way for as long as I can remember. Maybe that means I'm a bit psychic, too," he answered, pulling out into the street.

"Detective Sergeant Shaw will be so impressed. I'll have to remember to put in a good word for you with special services."

"Are you always this pleasant to work with, Ms. Saburi, or is it just me?"

Lily exhaled sharply. "I'm sorry. I'm not usually this prickly. I don't appreciate having to work against a stacked deck. Phillips' word should have been enough. If you know what I mean." She paused. "It's hard doing what I do without having to deal with attitude, as well as red tape."

He smiled. "Understood. But let's remember who's on which team, okay? That way we keep friendly fire to a minimum. This case has thrown everyone for a loop, and I, for one, hope you're able to shed some light on what happened. You talked about needing a jumping off point. We have dead bodies and a cold crime scene. That's it. Anything you can give us—location, descriptions of faces, vehicles, anything— it would help a lot."

"I'll certainly do what I can."

Martinez glanced at the petite honey blonde in his passenger seat, watching again as her face showed everything. For a psychic and a NYPD profiler, she certainly wore her emotions on her sleeve. Not that it mattered much.

The buzz around the department said she was formidable, and not just on the paranormal side. She had the reputation for being deadly. A triple threat: Smart, beautiful, and as good with a gun as she was with the weird shit nobody wanted to touch.

He inhaled. God, she smelled good.

"Have you always been psychic?" he asked, redirecting his thoughts.

"No. I woke up one morning after my parents died and *voilà*. People said my ability was a gift from God. A way to still talk to my mom and dad, but I never could. My talents never ran as far as that, until recently."

He looked directly at her. "What do you mean? Like channeling the dead?"

"Yes and no. I'm sure you've heard about what happened to my partner. She was killed quite suddenly, and for a little while, I was able to see and talk to her."

"No shit! What about now?"

"No. She moved on. Went into the light, or wherever it is spirits go. Since then, nothing. Not that I'm upset about it or anything. The last thing I need is for my life to turn into a ghost town with me as mayor."

"Sounds like it could be pretty cool. Talking to stiffs would certainly make my job easier."

Lily smirked. "Yeah. Try living it sometime."

Martinez chuckled, pulling the car up to a red light. He glanced sideways, but rather than finding the amused sarcasm he expected, Lily's expression was pensive, and he wondered what shadows stirred behind her beautiful eyes.

"I get impressions. Strange smells and such," he added, pressing a bit. "I hear things, too. Faint sounds too low for most people to perceive. But even that hint of the unusual has more than a few people freaked out. Believe me, I've caught flack about it."

He looked at her face, surprised at the empathy he saw. So, the hard-ass paranormal investigator understood what it felt like to wear a label. No big surprise there, all things considered.

"So, Phillips mentioned you're pretty handy with a gun."

"And reading between the lines," she shot back. "I bet you're dying to ask why and how, right?"

"Very perceptive, and since you brought it up..." he chuckled. "Your level of skill isn't exactly commonplace, especially for a woman, not unless you're a covert Special Ops Agent."

She smiled. "No, nothing as glamorous as that. My parents died when I was ten. After that, my best friend's family took me in and raised me. My foster dad was a real outdoorsman. Hunting, fishing, camping, you name it, and the rougher the conditions, the better. He was the original Survivorman.

"He believed girls should know how to protect themselves, but Terri, his daughter, and my best friend, she wasn't really into the whole Annie Oakley thing. I loved it, though. He taught me how to shoot— guns, rifles, bow and arrows— the crossbow was a favorite of his. He taught me to be wicked-quick with a hunting knife, too."

Ryan caught himself staring at her, watching her mouth as she spoke. It was warm in the car, and she had unbuttoned her coat. His gaze traveled from her face and the curve of her jaw, down to where her cleavage peeked out from beneath the décolleté of her blouse.

Her chest rose with each breath, her full breasts unconsciously pushing against the thin fabric. From nowhere, his fingers itched to sample the creamy silk of her skin, and an image of her straddling him, her back arched and breasts heaving flashed into his mind. He felt himself grow hard. He blinked, giving his head a shake. What the fuck?

"You, okay?" Lily reached out, touching his forearm.

His cock jerked at the feel of her soft fingers, and heat rushed into his groin. An almost uncontrollable urge to grab her and force her into the backseat, to take her, violently, with or without consent washed over him. He yanked his arm away, causing the car to swerve in traffic to the blare of car horns and expletives from other drivers.

"Stay out of my head, Saburi. You were brought in to investigate the stiffs, not me." A fine sheen of sweat broke out across his forehead. Never had he felt such a callous rush where women were concerned.

Lily pressed her lips together. "Saburi? What happened to first name basis? I thought we were on the same page here. And just for the record, I don't trespass in people's minds just for the hell of it. You looked freaked out for a second, that's all."

"I'm fine." His words were clipped and tight, and he ran the back of his hand across his forehead, as much to clear his internal tension as clear away his sweat.

She unnerved him, and for more reasons than he cared to admit. Thank God, irritation had trumped her powers of perception for the moment, and she sat with her arms crossed, waiting for him to answer. He took a deep breath, but kept his eyes trained on the traffic.

"We are on the same page. However, if you want us to stay that way, I suggest you keep those antennae of yours pointed away from me."

A confused frown spread across Lily's brow. "Have it your way..." She stopped and looked over at him. Ryan tensed. If she got even a sniff of his little fantasy, it was game over.

Pokerfaced, he turned to meet her gaze.

"Detective, whatever it was you sensed, you're going to have to share it with me at some point," she said softly.

Again, her expression didn't match what he expected, and it wasn't lost on him that she'd caught herself and dialed it down on the boss lady bit. She acted as if this was routine. Same shit different day, but maybe it wasn't, and her over the top attitude was just a cover. He unclenched his jaw and exhaled quietly. Either way, it didn't matter. He was here to observe and to make sure she played by the rules.

"Sorry," he mumbled. "I get touchy when it comes to talking about things I sense on the job. I'm sure you can understand why."

"I do. Believe me, you're preaching to the choir. I've been queen of the freaks for more years than I care to count. Not that I think you're a freak or anything."

He gave her half a smile. "No harm, no foul. Let's take this step-by-step, okay? We still need to get through your initial investigation at the morgue. How about we make that our jumping off point into the world of weird, okay?"

"Deal."

His police radio chirped, and dispatch interrupted in what sounded like a rush of crackling static. Ryan squeezed the side button on his radio. "Ten-four," he answered.

"What was that?"

He shrugged. "Central just confirmed with the deputy M.E."

"Confirmed what?"

"Our meeting with him at the morgue."

She leaned back in her seat and turned to face him. "Now? But we're almost there. What if he wasn't around to confirm our meeting? Don't they care about wasting taxpayer money, not to mention our time?"

He grinned. "And how long did you say you've been away?"

She exhaled, shaking her head. "Too long."

CHAPTER
THREE

They parked on the street outside Bellevue Hospital and got out of the car. The morgue was located in a separate building, adjacent to the main hospital. Martinez flashed his badge at the entrance, and reception buzzed them in immediately. He knew the way like the back of his own hand and led Lily through a set of double doors and then down the back corridor toward a set of elevators marked employees only.

The facility was situated on the lower level, and the elevator doors opened onto a stark white hallway. "This is still a police matter, so let me do the talking, okay?" he asked, stepping aside to let Lily pass. "Once we're in, you can take over from there."

The fluorescent lights added to the already sterile, empty feel of the place, and as they walked, the sound of their footsteps echoed in the corridor. Martinez stopped just outside another set of double doors.

"Just so you know, the bodies were tagged and bagged at the scene, but the deputy M.E. should have pulled some from cold storage for us to start with," Martinez said with his hand on one of the doors. "Ready?"

"As ready as I'll ever be," Lily said, trying to squash the creepy feeling edging its way up her spine.

Martinez knocked before pushing the doors open. The two entered and stood, waiting just inside. The facility was a large rectangular shaped configuration, opening directly into an area housing row after row of mortuary-style refrigerated units. Forensic examination tables lined one side of the room, each compartmentalized into individual operating suites, complete with surgical lights and attached to stainless steel counters, together with sinks and hoses.

Microscopes and medieval looking instruments, skull saws and rib crackers, gleamed in the overhead lights next to what looked to be deli slicing machines and grocery scales.

Lily swallowed hard against the sick, *Sweeney Todd*-like feeling that lurched in her stomach.

A man in a bloodstained lab coat looked up from behind one of the stainless steel examination tables. "May I help you?" he asked, his hand resting on top of a body half covered with a blue sheet.

"Dr. Weaver?"

The man nodded. "What can I do for you?"

"I'm Detective Martinez. Homicide," he answered, flashing the man his badge. "This is Lily Saburi. Special Services. I believe Detective Sergeant Shaw called to let you know we were coming."

"Yes. Right this way." He led them to the far end of the refrigerated units. Lily shot Martinez a questioning look, but he ignored it.

The deputy M.E. swept his hand toward the stacked squares at the end of the row. "The drawers pertaining to your case have been marked with post-its. Please take your time, but I ask that you don't disturb the bodies or remove them from the cadaver trays. I have to head to pathology, but I'll be back shortly."

Martinez nodded. "No problem."

The doctor headed back toward the double doors where they

had first come in, and Martinez looked at Lily. "Ladies choice," he said with a sideways nod toward storage units.

Lily took a cleansing breath to ground herself and center her focus. The underlying smell of disinfectant stung the inside of her nose, and her stomach flip-flopped as memories from the morgue in Portland where they prepared Terri's body to ship back to New York, rushed back.

Holding her breath, she swallowed, forcing herself to focus. "That one," Lily said, pointing toward the first drawer on the bottom left.

Martinez pushed the lever down and slowly pulled open the square, stainless steel door. Cold air drifted out from the opening, along with a deep sense of foreboding. The cadaver tray slid out from the refrigerated unit without a sound, a narrow gurney on drawer glides. Lily shivered. The body was covered with the same blue sheet they'd seen on the one prepared for autopsy across the room.

He pulled the sheet back, exposing the victim. The body was that of a young man, no more than eighteen or twenty years old. Even with the medical examiner's handiwork, it was easy to see his throat and his chest had been ripped open prior to death. The typical "Y" incision used in autopsies had navigated through the ravaged and missing flesh. Martinez whistled low. "Wow. This one is definitely 3D," Martinez said, wiping his hands on his pants. "Definitely Done Dancing."

"Oh, God." Lily's hand went to her mouth, her stomach turning again. Her vision swam as a wave of lightheadedness gripped her, and she clutched onto Martinez's arm for support.

"Some NYPD Profiler you are if you can't stand the sight of a stiff," he joked, steadying her on her feet.

Lily swallowed hard. "It's not that," she said shooting him a dirty look between gulps. "Can't you sense it? It's absolute terror. Christ in heaven, it's practically radiating from the body!"

She dragged in a deep breath and placed her hand on the victim's forehead. Immediately, images flooded Lily's mind. He'd been out for a good time with friends. Rich boys slumming it, out trolling for drugs and illicit fun.

"I'm sorry...I'm so sorry..."

Lily jerked her hand back, her eyes losing focus. "What?" She blinked, turning her perplexed gaze toward Martinez. "Did you say something?"

He shook his head. "No, why?"

She frowned, peering at him from across her shoulder. Maybe her brain was on overload, and it was nothing more than a leftover auditory impression. *Or not...*

Lily froze. "Oh, God," she muttered and turned slowly back around toward the body.

"What? What is it?" Martinez asked, but Lily didn't answer. She kept her eyes trained dead ahead.

"Remember when I said I wasn't sure if my talents ran toward channeling?"

"Yeah..." he answered cautiously.

"Ding. Ding. Ding."

Martinez took a step forward and stood next to Lily. "Here? Now?"

"Yup."

Lily slid her eyes to the side expecting to see the detective's face blanch. Instead, he looked quizzical.

"Are you all right? Do you hear something too?" she whispered.

His shook his head, again. "Not a thing."

"Hey! I'm over here, there's no need to whisper..."

Lily slid her gaze back to the front. The ghost stood next to the cadaver tray, a young man, his face pale and translucent white. He was so young. It broke her heart. Way too young to have been involved in all this. *"Um... Who are you?"*

"Patrick Quinn Kelly."

Lily sucked in a breath. "It's the Kelly kid," she whispered to Martinez, and felt him stiffen beside her.

She took a step forward, keeping her movements slow and non-threatening. Outside of Terri, she didn't have much experience with talking to the dead, but the kid looked scared and as ludicrous as it sounded, she didn't want to frighten the ghost further.

"Patrick, can you tell us what happened in the bar? Can you remember?" Lily's heart clenched at the regret that shadowed his pale, translucent face. His wounds were raw and puckered, even in his ethereal form, but the terror that had hit Lily in the gut earlier was gone. There was no trace of physical pain, either, only a pervasive sadness and regret.

"Tell my mother I didn't mean it," he said, flickering in and out. *"I never meant to hurt anyone...it...it got out of control."*

"Didn't mean what? Patrick, wait," Lily said, reaching out as if she could touch him, help him.

"What? What's he saying?" Martinez's eyes flicked back and forth between Lily and the blank space on the other side of the gurney.

"Please..." The ghost said, placing a hand on Lily's forearm, making the hair on her arm stand on end. *"I don't know what I'm supposed to do where I'm supposed to be..."* he trailed off, his face a mask of fear and uncertainty.

"Tell my mother I'm sorry. I should have listened to her...I never did. Tell her I love her..." He dropped his head. A glistening tear dripped from his cheek, disappearing into nothing as it fell toward the gurney.

The fluorescent lights above them flickered and popped, and the air crackled subtly with electricity. The ghost turned abruptly, and Lily's gaze followed his toward the back of the room. *"Something's coming..."* His voice cracked with panic. He took a step and then turned back. *"Don't forget,"* he said, and then vanished.

"No!" Lily yelled, banging her hand down on the stainless tray.

"God, I hate when they do that! One magnanimous, all-encompassing statement and then poof, they disappear."

"He's gone? For good? Did he say anything about the attack?"

Lily shook her head, raising her hand in frustration. "I don't know."

"What does that mean? You said, 'an all-encompassing statement'. Does that mean he told you who did this?"

Lily shook her head.

"Then would you mind telling me exactly what he did say?" Martinez asked, his voice rising.

Lily's shoulders slumped. She turned to face him, knowing full well he expected more than what she was about to tell him. "He wanted me to tell his mother he loves her."

Martinez blinked. "You're kidding me, right?"

"Detective. He was just a kid. He's disoriented. I'm not even sure he knows he's dead, let alone where he is, and I'd bet dollars to donuts he doesn't remember what happened—at least, not in any kind of cohesive way."

They stood in awkward silence for a moment. Ryan nonplussed, and Lily not knowing what else to say.

"Doesn't matter, anyway," she said, shoving her hand through her hair. "Ghosts are historically unreliable. Their perception is skewed by their own personal unfinished business, and you can never tell if the clues they give you pertain to the questions you ask, or to some random memory." Exhaling, her breath fogged out into the cold from the open refrigerated unit. "It's better if we do this the old fashioned way."

Lily rested her hand on the body's "Y" incision, just above the heart. Immediately, her shoulders hunched, and she gagged, her senses overwhelmed by the smell of booze and blood. Disjointed images flash through her mind: Patrick sliding a c-note across to a bartender, a private room, drugs, sex and...

Lily's eyes flew open, and she jerked her head around toward the detective's waiting gaze.

"*Jesus Christ*, what now?"

Lily's gut matched the apprehension she read on Martinez's face. If what she sensed was true, they were in for a shit load of trouble. Her eyes met his. "We need to go to the crime scene. Now."

CHAPTER
FOUR

"Lily looked at Ryan's profile as he wound his way through midday traffic. The man had high cheekbones and a strong jaw, with a tiny cleft in the center of his chin. Two dimples graced his cheeks whenever he smiled, crinkling the area around his green eyes. He was dark haired, and olive skinned, a model for the cliché of tall, dark and handsome. He was the complete opposite of Sean in every way, except for an unwitting sex appeal they both wielded with ease. She couldn't put her finger on it, but there was something familiar about the young detective, and it nagged at her every time he looked at her.

He clicked the directional and glanced her way as he switched lanes. "You gonna tell me what spooked you so bad back in the freezer section?"

Lily blew out a breath. "Not until I get a better handle on it. It's too vague, but I'm hoping the crime scene will give me more precise residual impressions. Right now, I can't be sure of anything. Images are often muddied. Besides whatever impressions I'm specifically looking for, I sometimes get snippets of entirely unrelated thought."

He shot her a look, taking his eyes off the road for a moment.

"Are you saying there are variables that can skew the images you get from a victim's corpse?"

Impressed, Lily cocked her head to one side. "Very good, Detective, succinct and professional. But not to put too fine a point on it, yes. I once caught flashes from a movie a victim had seen with his girlfriend only hours before he was murdered. It made my job very difficult, to say the least, trying to sift through what memories were his and what belonged to the film."

"Jeez."

Lily exhaled softly and rested her head back against the seat. "Exactly."

They drove the rest of the way in silence. Lily looked out the window, watching the lunchtime throng fill the sidewalks despite the cold. They were just people going about their daily business, unaware of the darkness lurking in the shadows, waiting for nightfall. Two months ago, she had been just as innocent. Unfortunately, if she was correct in her assumptions, the detective was in for just as rude an awakening.

Horns blared as traffic merged past roadwork further choking the already congested streets. Lily ignored the noise. If her gut was right about what she sensed, then they were all in deep shit. She chewed on her bottom lip, weighing the options.

What she thought would be an easy distraction from second guessing her leaving Sean behind, now had the makings of a nightmare. How was she going to tell the cops she believed a vampire was at the root of all this mayhem? She knew vampires existed—but the average person? Not outside books and movies.

According to Ryan, his boss wanted to make sure she wasn't some kind of a kook. If this went badly, Shaw would have a field day, and she'd lose all her hard-earned credibility. This had the potential to be a lose-lose situation all the way around, but she'd be damned if she would allow that to happen without a fight.

Blood bath. Phillips didn't know how close to the truth he might be, and she prayed her gut was wrong. If what she suspected was even remotely true, then she needed to keep things quiet—at least until she called Sean. In the twist of a moment, her two worlds were entwined, and not the way she expected nor wanted.

Ryan pulled his car to the side of the street and double-parked. Though CSI had finished its initial investigation, the length of sidewalk outside the crime scene was still marked with yellow police tape, including the small section of asphalt covered in debris from the blown out bar. Uniformed officers were still on traffic patrol, directing cars away from the scene and keeping pedestrians moving along on the opposite side of the street.

Lily opened the passenger door and squeezed out between the parked cars. Without so much as a nod, Ryan took her by the elbow, steering her across the street.

"I don't think I need to remind you how bad it would be for you to spout off about ghosts or other weird shit at this point. For the time being, we keep this just between us." Raising both eyebrows, he dropped his chin slightly. "Got it?"

Lily blinked, tactfully disengaging her arm from his grip. "Detective, I'm a professional. In my line of work, discretion is not only good business, it's a necessity." Her answer was soft, but to the point.

Outside the bar, officers manned the perimeter, but from what she discerned, there were no other detectives on site. Ryan flashed his badge, and the two crossed the police barricade.

Lily's breath puffed out in front of her as she took in the exploded frontage and scattered debris.

"Where do you want to start?" Ryan asked.

Lily was silent for a moment, and then slowly shook her head. "The answers aren't out here, that's for sure."

She took a step toward the darkened bar, peering through the shattered doorway. A wall of stench hit her as soon as she stepped through the threshold, sending her body's alarm systems into overdrive and her trace amount of shifter blood racing through her veins, intrinsically registering the stench as dangerous.

Ryan came in behind her. "CSI has been through here already, but they've asked that you not touch anything or disturb the scene. I suppose they'll have to sift through all this again at some point if we come up empty."

She regarded him, her expression deadpan.

"What?" When she raised one eyebrow at the essentially rhetorical question, he blew out his breath. "Okay, I get it. Just try not to touch too much. There's a box of latex-free gloves in the squad car, if you want," he said, raising one hand toward the door and letting it drop.

Ignoring him, she walked further into the room, fragmented glass crunching under her boots with each step. She moved slowly, her attention pulling her across the room toward a pile of broken chairs. She squatted down, her reflection fragmented and distorted in the shattered pieces of the bar mirror lying amid the rubble.

The silvered glass was jagged-edged, and clearly, razor sharp, but Lily picked up one of the larger shards, resting it gingerly against the flat of her palm. She curled her fingers over the edge and closed her eyes. The image of a young girl, her face, sharp planed and her body thin to the point of being gaunt, flashed through Lily's mind. She was heavily made-up, and despite her youth, the girl's eyes held a desperation so profound it made Lily's heart clench. Pain, sharp and quick, raced up Lily's arm, and she knew. This sad teenager was a heroine whore.

She dropped the shard from her hand, letting it clatter to the floor, taking the image of the girl with it. But it was too late. She had opened the channel. Violence had left an imprint on the room so deep, that images bombarded Lily's mind one after the other, hitting her like uppercuts to the stomach. She wrapped her arm around her middle, biting back on the feeling of vertigo.

"Are you okay?" Ryan asked, putting his hand on her back.

She sucked in a deep breath. "Yeah. It's just a lot to process at once."

He frowned, pulling his hand away from her back. "This is nuts," he mumbled, raking his fingers through his hair. "First, the freezer section freak show, and now this." He pressed his lips together and glanced toward the exit. "We're outta here. This isn't working, and I'm not standing around with my thumb up my ass while you make yourself sick or whatever it is that's happening to you."

She dragged in another breath, holding it for a moment as she composed herself. The detective was doubtless a Type A personality. With his jaw clenched, he looked as though he was ready to bolt. "Just give me a minute. I'll be fine."

He made a face. "Maybe you just need a break, a cup of coffee or something... some fresh air," he said, glancing toward the exit again.

Lily moistened her dry lips, a ghost of a smile tugging at the corners of her mouth. Type A, definitely. "Trust me. I'm good. I just need to find my center."

Looking at his drawn expression, she couldn't help but feel for him. He was completely out of his element, unfortunately, the only thing she could do was reassure him. "There's no other way to do this, Detective, and besides, a hazmat team couldn't clear away what I sense and smell." She studied him for a moment. "You smell it too, don't you?"

He hesitated, giving her a cautious nod, before turning away. "I thought so," she said, straightening up.

Lily regarded him. He seemed upset, as if unsure of what he'd just revealed. So, she waited, not saying a word, and when he turned back, his professional veneer was once again in place.

With a nod, she took a deep breath through her mouth and exhaled. "Let's get to work."

Careful not to touch too much, she picked her way through the bar. A green clock in the shape of a Heineken bottle dangled precariously above the dirty outline where the mirror had once hung. It was the only thing left untouched in the entire place. Lily stopped, equidistantly from where it hung, turning left, then right. "This room is not the epicenter. What happened here took place after the fact."

The stench of old blood and an underlying bitter tang, she knew but couldn't place, grew stronger as she headed toward the back of the bar. She moved slowly, her stomach roiling with each step. The feeling of vertigo hadn't subsided, and bile rose in her throat.

Lily lurched forward and gagged, swallowing back on the sour taste. She gulped down air to quell the nausea, but the scent permeated everything, and she grabbed the edge of the broken bar for support.

As soon as her hand made contact, the image of a fat man in a stained t-shirt, with a limp dishtowel tucked into his dirty apron, shot through her mind. Missing front teeth showed through a wheezy chuckle as he palmed money from the bar and signaled for two girls—one of them the same young girl from Lily's previous vision. He watched, leering as the teenager coated her lips with bright orange lipstick, before slinking through a side door marked as private.

"There." Lily pointed from her half-hunched position. "That's where it started."

Whatever remained of the private entrance now hung suspended by a single broken hinge. Ryan pulled on a pair of leather gloves and carefully maneuvered the door open for Lily to enter first. She stepped through the ruined threshold into what looked like the backroom to an illegal social club.

Echoes of illicit partying and sex for hire lived in the air like noxious fumes. Amid the wreckage, a pool table sat dead center of the room splintered in half, its green felt shredded, and covered in dried blood and chalk dust.

A slick coating now congealed to a red gelatinous state, covered the floor. It didn't take much to envision the kind of blood loss necessary to saturate the floor to that point.

Beads of sweat formed on Lily's forehead and between her breasts. Ryan called to her, but his voice was thick in her ears. The room was spinning, and she gagged again, more bile rising to the back of her throat.

With her hand over her mouth, she held her breath, searching for an unobtrusive place to vomit. The last thing she wanted was her DNA mixed up with anything CSI might yet find.

"Here," Ryan said shoving a plastic bag her way.

She grabbed the baggie and turned away, retching, until there was nothing left but dry heaves. Her back was to him while she waited for the last wave to pass.

"This place is pretty ripe, despite how cold it's been," he said, handing her his handkerchief. "Sorry about that."

She wiped her nose and mouth. "Thanks," she muttered, glancing back over her shoulder. Head down, she sucked in a ragged breath. "I think I threw up everything, including my dignity."

"It's all part of the job," he said with a shrug.

Lily frowned, sealing the top of the zip-lock bag. "I suppose. This has never happened to me before. She glanced down at the contained mess in her hand and sighed. "Is it common practice for detectives to carry zip-locks around in their pocket? Not that I'm not glad you did."

His lips formed a lopsided smirk. "A lot of detectives carry them, for evidence or whatnot," he said, lifting one shoulder and letting it fall. "But, don't be so hard on yourself. You're not the first rookie to lose it at a crime scene, and you won't be the last."

"So, you think I'm a rookie? And here I thought experience was the key."

He laughed, folding his hands in front of his chest. "It is. That and how many times you've vomited behind the yellow tape."

"Ha! Leave it to men to quantify skill through bodily emissions," she mumbled, resting the baggie on the floor by the door and wiping her hands once more on his handkerchief. "...and on that note, we've still got work to do."

Lily walked to the center of the room and stopped. She took a single cleansing breath and turned her body slowly, sending her senses out like a web. Images darted through Lily's mind at high speed, but this time she was ready for them.

Laughter. Drinking. Loud music. The room was in shambles, and its story played out in time with the kaleidoscope of color and noise that flashed its way through her mind.

Along the wall, a wide rolling bar had been turned on its side, its chrome edges bent, and its frosted glass countertop and LED panels smashed. She reached out and slid her finger over what was left of the counter, bringing it to her tongue. A rush of euphoria flew through her veins, and she was numb. In a flash, there were crack pipes and methamphetamines, or Ice, as it was known on the street, piled high across the bar. The scenes were sordid, filled with images of drug-induced sex.

Lily turned toward the far wall and the broken couch pushed against the chipped paint. Her skin grew cold to the point of shivering, and panic bit into her gut. The images in her head turned even uglier, and she cried out, covering her face as she felt each blow, the tearing between her legs and warm blood flowing along the inside of her thighs.

It was the young girl with the orange lipstick. Paid for, beaten, raped.

Her head whipped around as rage, white hot and deranged poured through her from behind. As if compelled, Lily turned toward the tiny window to the side of the small bar. Shattered glass covered the floor beneath the twisted metal window casing.

"This is where the perpetrator entered the room." With each step, Lily's body shook against the storm of rage that flooded her body. Her words pushed past clenched teeth as she moved toward the window. "I'm positive. This is it."

Ryan stood to one side. His arms still folded across his chest. However, instead of the casual stance he affected before, now he just looked defensive. "Lily, what the hell is going on here? A blind man could see you're getting a reading, but you haven't said a thing, despite all your gyrations. You gotta cut me some slack. I'm out of my element here, and I don't like it one bit."

Was he for real? Lily just looked at him.

He exhaled. "CSI didn't find anything to support a point of forced entry besides the shattered glass. No fingerprints, no blood —other than from the victims—no fibers, no epithelial tissue, no hair. So what do you see that they didn't, or couldn't?"

Lily didn't answer. The closer she moved to the window, the more the anger raced through her mind—red, black, and craving vengeance. She fell to her knees in front of the hollowed out square, glass biting into her skin through her jeans. Hands at her temples, her pulse throbbed beneath her palms as her fingernails raked her scalp.

She was in the perpetrator's mind. The taste of blood, metallic and slick coated her tongue, and the taste wasn't as she expected. It was heady and thick, like honey. She ran the tip of her tongue over her own teeth, but the sensation was that of razor sharp fangs.

Her vision narrowed, and a veil of red descended across her line of sight. She scrambled to her feet and into a crouch, her head jerking from side to side and her nostrils flaring.

"Lily! What the fuck?" Ryan said, taking a step toward her, but jumped back when she snarled low in her throat like something feral. She was out of time and place, looking through the vampire's eyes as events unfolded.

Her head whipped around again, the scent of fear making her mouth water. Through the vampire's eyes, she saw the boy, Patrick, standing over the girl, his friends laughing as another rode her hard, biting her breast so hard he drew blood. The girl cried out in terror and agony, and the vampire smiled as it coiled to attack.

The image shifted, and Lily watched as if in a trance. The window shattered, and the vampire landed on its feet in a spray of glass and concrete. Covered in blood, the vampire ripped the boys to shreds, choking on bits of broken bone and cartilage as it drank, the bitter tang of their absolute terror scoring its throat.

Lily tried to free her mind, but the vampire's gnarled thoughts wrapped themselves around her perception like mutant vines—its thought processes saturated with one word. Kill.

Savoring the last of them, the vampire lifted its gaze toward the mirrored wall, its bloodied visage reflected back like a nightmare. A face so white and so thin, the cheekbones looked as if they would rip through the pallid skin, yet stark against the dark red smears streaked across its mouth. Fangs, long and dripping with yellow saliva, were stained with blood and pieces of gore.

As if shocked, the creature's hand rose to touch its hair, the long, dirty strands hanging from a white scalp, like a corpse. A vicious screech echoed through Lily's mind along with the image of a beautiful woman, tall and elegant, with long, lustrous blond hair and pearl white skin...the only thing shared with the creature in the mirror was that she too had fangs.

The vampire's mind was a swirl of incoherent thought, but one word escaped through the haze of rage and murder. Why? And for one lucid moment, the vampire's mind held the creature and the woman superimposed, and Lily knew. The two were one and the same, and the question now begged, not only why, but how?

FIVE

"If you don't tell me what the fuck is going on, I'm calling it —game over, got it? I'm not here to scrape you off the ceiling, or the floor for that matter," Ryan shouted, his arms hooked under her armpits as he dragged her to standing. "What gives? And I want it straight. No more dancing around and telling me you're not sure."

He dragged his hand across his forehead, his face furious. This was not what he'd expected when he said he'd take this on.

"You have two minutes, so start talking," he said, folding his arms across his chest again. This time it was neither casual nor defensive, the move was pure self-preservation.

"Ryan...I..."

"No. If I wanted tap dancing, I'd get assigned to the Broadway beat. I want answers. Now."

Lily took a deep breath, rummaging through her pockets. "Okay, Ryan. But I'm telling you right now, you won't believe what I have to tell you."

After what he just witnessed, he didn't doubt it. She was still fishing through her pockets, her face beautiful, but drawn. She probably needed a cigarette. After this, even he wanted one, and he didn't smoke.

Whatever Lily smelled, he smelled it too, but you didn't need a degree in psychology to know that she not only smelled it but saw whatever it was that had caused this. He took a breath and exhaled. "Come on. Let's get out of here and go somewhere we can talk."

She picked up her baggie full of puke, and the two walked out onto the street. She dumped it in a trashcan near the corner where Ryan was double-parked. Wiping her hands on her slightly blood-stained knees, she stood on the sidewalk waiting for him to finish with the uniformed patrol.

"Where to?" she asked.

"It's almost four p.m. and neither of us has eaten. Let's grab a sandwich. I know a good bagel place not too far from here. We can talk while we eat."

Lily shook her head. "I appreciate the offer, but after this, food is the last thing on my mind."

"Okay, then we can head back toward One Police Plaza. Your car is there, right? We can talk upstairs."

Lily frowned. "No offense, but with what I have to say, being anywhere near your office is not exactly a bright idea. Listen, it's late, and I'm drained. Why don't you drive me home and we can talk at my place? I'll have a friend pick up my car."

He didn't answer. His eyes were riveted as Lily rolled her shoulders, her full breasts pushing forward through the front opening of her coat. The move was harmless, especially after what she'd just been through, but it left his groin thickening and he forced himself to look away.

"Shall we?" she asked, her hand on the passenger car door.

Martinez nodded. "Sounds good." He cleared his throat and slid into the driver's seat, covering the telltale bulge in his pants with his jacket. "Where to?" he asked.

"Jane Street. Westside."

He put the car in gear and pulled out onto the street. Neither one said a word. It was like they were both lost in thought, only he would bet her thoughts occupied the mystery surrounding the crime scene. His were occupied with her. Period.

She smelled unbelievable, even despite her puking her guts up. Every move—from the way she pushed her hair back from her face, the tilt of her head, the sway of her hips as she walked around the crime scene, even when she snarled at him, all he wanted to do was throw her on the ground and fuck her.

Keep your head in the game, stupid...

Problem was, she was in the game with him, and that made it even more intoxicating. She was a bitch and a fighter, and yet he had seen her face cloud over with compassion more than once today. As hard as she was, she was still a soft touch. *Soft.* He groaned inwardly at the thought of how she would feel beneath him, what her mouth would taste like, the softness of her skin and the sharp edges of her nails across his back.

Ryan reached into his pocket and pulled out his cell phone. At a red light, he scrolled through and pressed Shaw's number. It went straight to voicemail. "Sergeant, it's Martinez. I've just left the scene with Ms. Saburi. I'm not really sure what Ms. Saburi found, if anything yet, but I'll be at headquarters later to fill you in, if I can at that point." He pressed end and put the phone down in the front cup holder.

"I wish you had told me you were going to call him," Lily said with a frown.

"Why? He's my superior. I need to check in with him, or did you forget this is a police investigation?" Ryan ran a hand though his hair, feeling himself scowl.

"I already KNOW this is a police gig, detective. That's the third time today you've felt it necessary to remind me of it, and it's seriously getting on my nerves, so quit it! You are not the only professional here. I merely wanted the opportunity to tell *you* what I saw before I have to tell everyone else. I already warned you."

"Warned me? About what, huh? What is it exactly that you think I can't handle?"

Lily didn't answer. She stared out the window, her arms folded in front of her chest.

"Now you clam up? *Jesus*, woman, a homicide investigation is no place for head games. If you've uncovered pertinent information, I need to know."

"Pertinent information? Listen well, because if you or anyone down at police plaza think you stand a chance at solving this after what I saw, you're nuts. This goes way beyond any nightmare you could ever dream up. It's going to take a collective effort, and I'm going to need to call in reinforcements of my own."

He looked at her, his face incredulous. "Reinforcements? You're joking, right? Do you know what Phillips had to go through to get the commissioner to allow YOU on the case? What? You have some kind of ESP army at your fingertips?"

Lily just looked at him, her lips pressed together. "You know, at some point during all this, you are going to thank me. And I'm going to take extreme pleasure in saying I told you so."

"Yeah, right. Let's just hear what you have to say, first. Okay?"

"Whatever you say, Detective." She chewed on her lip. "Just not here. I need to think."

His face was a mask. "Fine. I'll take you wherever you need to go to *think*." He put the last words in bunny quotes with his fingers.

"Fine. Take me home."

They got in the car and drove in silence, Lily's mind racing the entire time. When Ryan turned the car onto Jane street, she nodded toward the crowded stretch of curb.

"Pull over anywhere you can find a spot. I'm in the red brick building over there." Lily pointed across the street.

Her car wasn't back, so Jack was still out playing tourist. He didn't sound too happy when she had said she wouldn't be home until after five p.m., but he did offer to pick up a pizza, so he couldn't be that pissed. Besides, she was working, so too bad.

Ryan hadn't wiped the scowl off his face since they argued. Crosstown traffic didn't help the situation either, doubling the time it took to reach her apartment. He was annoyed, and Lily had to stifle the urge to sneak a peek into his thoughts as to why.

She'd caught him looking at her cleavage a few times and wondered if it was just him being a typical guy, or if it had something to do with her shifter blood and the proximity of the full moon. Ryan was human, but that didn't mean a thing. Hadn't the word lunatic derived from the supposed effect the full moon had on human behavior? On the other hand, maybe he was just like any other red-blooded American male when it came to big boobs.

Regardless, they were here now, and she no longer had a choice. It was curtain time.

"I'm on the top floor," she said, unlocking the vestibule door. "It's a walk-up. Sorry."

He shrugged. "No problem. I'm not exactly a donut shop cop."

His eyes may have wandered south to her cleavage, but his long, muscular legs and hard six-pack hadn't escaped her notice when he steadied her, earlier. What had Jack said? Fine full moon fun? Yeah, right.

Ryan followed behind as they climbed the stairs. Creaking floorboards and Spanish music playing softly in the background were the only sounds cutting the awkward silence.

Lily glanced back over her shoulder. "You said you were hungry. I've got fresh cold cuts and rolls from the deli across the street."

"I'm not really hungry anymore, thanks," he said, his voice clipped.

Lily had to bite her tongue. If he was this irascible now, how the hell was he going to hear what she had to tell him?

They got to the top level, and Lily unlocked the door. "Come on in, I'll just be a second," she said, and went ahead to snap on a few lights. She took off her coat and hung it on a hook by the front door, doing the same with his. Standing in the hallway, she shoved her hands in her pockets, rocking back slightly on her heels. "So, you said you weren't hungry anymore, is that true, or are you just trying to be polite despite yourself?"

He shook his head. "Whatever. I just want to get down to it."

Lily regarded him for a moment. He was clearly uncomfortable, and his body language screamed, "Let's get this over with."

"Okay...I'll make some coffee, and we can get to it."

Ryan sat at the table, while Lily went about filling the coffee pot and setting it to brew. The minute it started to drip, she grabbed two mugs from the decorative hooks above the sink and set them on the counter, along with some milk and sugar. From the drawer to the right of the stove, she took two teaspoons and laid them on a couple of paper napkins. She pushed the drawer closed with her hip, and turned, leaning back against the Formica, her arms crossed in front of her chest.

Ryan hadn't budged or said a word the entire time, but now he sat back and sniffed. "So, what's so bad that you're still procrastinating? If I didn't know you to be a top profiler, I would think you were hedging to keep your job."

Lily unfolded her arms, resting her hands on either side of her. Her fingers curled around the right angles of the countertop. "I'm not hedging. I just don't know how to tell you what I need to tell you. What I saw—what I *know*."

He leaned further back in his chair, his elbows on the armrests and his fingers clasped together in front of him. "Like Nike says, 'Just do it'."

"Vampire."

"Huh?" His brows knit together, clearly not quite processing what she'd just said.

"The perp. It's a vampire, and no, I don't mean a sanguinarian or some freak with dental implants or filed teeth. A real life, honest to God, vampire."

Ryan leaned forward and exhaled. "Okay, I get that I've been acting like a prick. You made your point. Ha, ha. Now why don't you tell me what you really found?"

Lily just looked at him.

Realization dawned, and the detective's eyes widened, his skepticism screaming. Yeah right, and the deed to the Brooklyn Bridge is in your pocket, too. He pushed himself to standing, and took a step forward, his mouth open and his expression unconvinced. "You're serious, aren't you?"

Lily still just looked at him.

"No. No way. How the hell am I supposed to go back to Shaw and report that a bloodsucking fiend, straight out of a Hollywood horror flick, is responsible for all the latest death and destruction? A vampire? Come on, Lily. You yourself said there were variables that could skew what you 'see'. I think maybe you think a vampire is responsible for this, but I think you've seen the *Twilight Saga* one too many times."

Lily stiffened, tightening her grip on the edge of the counter. "This is no romance novel, Ryan. And there wasn't one thing remotely Young Adult about what I saw. It was more like Bondage meets Triple X, but you can either choose to believe me or not—I saw what I saw—it's your call.

"But I warn you now, if you don't believe me, and don't help me do what needs to be done, then the bloodbaths will continue, and not just in out of the way dive bars. This creature is crazed. Something is wrong with it. I'll have to track it, in order to stop it and prevent any more bloodshed, but for all we know, it could have already created more of its kind."

Ryan threw his hands in the air. "More? You really are a nutcase, aren't you? And what's worse is you take me for a fool as well, thinking I'll buy this load of crap because of what I told you about my sixth sense. What I want to know, is how you got so far in Special Services without anyone realizing you're batshit. Profiler, my ass!"

Lily pushed herself away from the counter and with a single step was nose-to-nose with Ryan. "Listen to me you sarcastic sack of shit, if I wanted to, I could do a tap dance all over your mind, dig up any sordid little secrets I want and then use them against you. I could even mentally bitchslap your ass if I wanted, but I won't, because I know how hard this is to believe. Hell, I didn't believe it myself, at first.

"Supernatural beings exist, Ryan. Period. They live in a subculture that operates under the human radar, and they do a damn good job of policing themselves, usually. Something is wrong, here. I don't know too much about vampire culture, but I know they do their level best to share this world with us. Those who choose to live on the fringe of that philosophy are exterminated, either by their own kind, or by people like me."

Lily took a step back, watching as Martinez tried to process all she'd said, his eyes narrowing in disbelief.

He took a breath, rubbing his mouth with his hand. "People like you...you mean psychics?"

"No. People like me, as in vigilante. I'm a hunter, Ryan. I hunt rogue supes...supernatural beings that decide to play outside the rules."

His hands went to his hips, pushing his suit jacket back exposing his sidearm. Lily's eyes flicked from his face to his holster and froze. He was carrying a Guncrafter 50GI semi-automatic, the ballistics of which was the equivalent of carrying a small canon on your hip—not the kind of weapon you normally see on a cop. With bullets three times the size of a standard police issue 9mm Glock. It made her wonder.

Ryan turned his face away, clearly unsure as to what to think.

But when he turned back, his face was questioningly defensive. "Hunt. What are you talking about, Lily?"

"Why should I go into any more detail, when you haven't believed a word I've said so far?" She grabbed her mug off the counter and filled her cup, feeling Ryan's eyes watching her as she added milk and sugar. With a quick breath, she turned back to face him.

"It's obvious to me this conversation is going nowhere," she said, drumming her fingers on the side of the mug. "We're at an impasse. You can't wrap your head around what I'm telling you, and I have a rogue vampire I need to kill. I could try and explain, but I think you've had enough revelation for one day." She paused. "At this point, the only way I can see us clear, is for you to do whatever it is you need to do, and I do whatever it is I need to do."

Lily looked down at her mug and frowned. "Tell Shaw whatever it is you need to tell him. It's not going to affect me that much." She lifted her chin, shifting her gaze to meet his. "I know what I have to do."

Ryan was quiet. Doubt and suspicion still warred in his eyes, but they had lost their defensive glare. His forehead creased, and Lily could see him mentally gauge the probabilities. Unfortunately, nothing in his training had prepared him for this. He sat down again, his forearms flat on either arm of the chair, while his hands curled and uncurled around the edges.

Lily watched as he grappled with reasonable explanations and came up empty. "Are you okay?" she asked, taking a tentative step forward. But he put his hand up, and she stopped.

Annoyed with herself, she exhaled through her teeth. Mouth almighty strikes again. She had pulled the rug out from under everything he knew, or thought he knew, about this world, and then told him to suck it up. How else did she expect him to react?

You went on a vigilante rampage, remember? Terri's voice was sharp in her mind. Turning back toward the counter, she opened the cabinet and took out a glass and a bottle of Jamison's, pouring him two stiff fingers of scotch.

"For what it's worth, I know exactly how you feel," she said, placing the glass on the table in front of him.

He picked up the glass but then set it on the table again. Looking over at her, he hesitated, "Lily...I can't," he said shaking his head.

She put her hand up, considering him for a moment. "I know Ryan. Just do me a favor and don't assume that I'm crazy. Someday I'll tell you about how I came to know what I know. It wasn't exactly a walk in the park. Although ironically, that's where I did a lot of my hunting."

Ryan picked up his glass, giving her a quizzical look.

"Never mind. That's a story for another time," she said with a dismissive wave. "Drink your scotch you look as if you could use it."

His gaze softened, and he gave her a faint smile. "Rose-lipped maidens, light foot lads..." He lifted the glass in a quick salute and then shot the drink back. Swallowing hard, he winced, coughing a bit. "What about you, or don't you need one?" he asked, tilting the empty glass toward her.

She shook her head. "No. I need to keep my wits about me, just in case I get another visitor."

He looked at her strangely, and then it dawned on him what she meant. "You mean visitor, as in the *goes bump in the night* kind?"

"Exactly," she answered, picking up his glass, exceedingly aware of his eyes on her. "I've never heard that toast before, but I like it. Where's it from?"

"Talk about changing the subject. It's from a poem. A. E. Housman's *Shropshire Lad*, 1896."

Ryan put his hand on the doorknob, but turned back, his eyes questioning. "What you said before, about tap dancing through my brain—you weren't kidding, were you?"

Lily shook her head, regret biting into her gut at the reminder.

"No," she answered softly. "But then again, I wasn't kidding about any of it. I just hope you see that before it's too late."

She crossed her arms in front of her chest, expecting something, but he left without another word. The door closed behind him, and the sound of his feet on the stairs vanished almost immediately. Lily turned back toward the kitchen, an empty feeling welling up inside her chest. Did they accomplish anything today, or as usual, did she just make things harder than they had to be? The question didn't need answering. She had the power to fix this, and unlike the last time she went hunting, she wasn't alone. She had Sean.

CHAPTER
SIX

"Jack got out of the car and walked around the block toward the house. "Crowded, crazy city," he mumbled, stepping up onto the curb, juggling a pizza and a bottle of red wine. He stopped as a black and white cat raced out of the alley between the buildings and skittered to a stop in front of him. Its hackles rose, and it hissed, before taking off across the street and disappearing behind the dumpster next to the Korean market.

He shook his head. No self-respecting wolf had any use for the feline set, except as hunting practice. He glanced back over his shoulder, watching as the cat sat perched on top of the dumpster like it was king of the hill. Jack chuckled to himself. The full moon was only a couple of days away, and...here kitty, kitty.

He opened the vestibule door and pressed the buzzer next to Lily's name on the call box in the lobby.

"Who is it?"

"It's Jack the Ripper, who else?"

"Ha. Ha. Don't flatter yourself. Did you remember the pizza?"

"Yeah, yeah. Buzz me up, will you?"

The buzzer sounded, and he jostled the door open and headed

up the stairs. "Pizza Man!" he shouted, surprised to find the apartment door unlocked. Lily must be seriously hungry, considering how she'd reamed his ass about leaving the door half-open his very first day.

Lily came out of the living room, her iPod playing in the background. She looked tired. "Oh, man, that smells great!" she said, taking the box from him and heading straight into the kitchen. "...and you need to open whatever bottle you have hiding in that brown paper bag, 'cos I could use a drink."

Jack put the wine down on the table and took off his jacket. He wrinkled his nose and sniffed. "Was somebody here?"

"Yeah. Detective Martinez. He's working the case with me—or he was, at least. He drove me home, why?"

"Whoever he is, the boy left a funky smell in the air, that's all," he said, coming into the kitchen. "Hey, do you by chance own a cat?"

Lily looked up, licking her fingers, a confused look on her face. "No. And even if I did, I've been gone for the past two months, Jack. Do you think I'd be that neglectful a pet owner?"

He smirked. "Nah, just checking. This cat raced out of the alley just before, and with the full moon and all, I thought I might have a little fun with it...you know." He waggled his eyebrows, his meaning crystal clear.

Lily stopped, her fingers holding stringy mozzarella cheese halfway to her mouth. "Oh, no you won't, Jack. I mean it! This is not Maine, and these are not wild animals. That cat probably belongs to someone, and I won't have you terrorizing the neighborhood pets."

He just looked at her, the smirk still on his face.

"Jack? I'm serious. Don't make me call Sean."

Hmmph. "Party pooper. Just wait until you're a full shifter, then come talk to me about being PCC."

"PCC?"

"Pet politically correct."

Lily burst out laughing. "Talk about comic relief after the day I've had! You seriously need to go on David Letterman. Come on, open the wine, and have a slice of pizza, there's a lot going on that I need to tell you about."

Jack stiffened. All humor gone. "What?"

Lily put a slice of pizza on a paper plate and held it out toward him. "Stop right there. It has nothing to do with Edward Parr or wild, horny Shifters chasing me down. So sit down and I'll tell you."

Eyeing her, he took a corkscrew from the top hook of the side-board and sat down. "Then spill it already, or I'll be the one calling Sean," he said, pointing the sharp edge of the corkscrew her way. He didn't mention Sean had already slammed him with a telepathic inquisition, wanting to know why Lily's mind was in such a logjam. Now both men were suspicious, and whether she wanted to or not, she was going to tell them what was going on.

He took the plate from her hand and put it down on the table, reaching for the bottle of wine. He cut the thin metal casing away from the cork while he waited for her to start talking.

"After you dropped me off this morning, I met with the chief, and two of the detectives involved with the case," she said, getting up to grab two wine glasses from the cabinet.

"You're not telling me anything I don't already know. What happened after that?" he asked, twisting the corkscrew into the top of the bottle.

"I got a small glimpse of what happened at the crime scene the minute Detective Martinez handed me the case file. From there I asked to go to the morgue."

"And?" Jack prompted, pulling the cork from the bottle.

"There was a Shade at the morgue."

Jack looked up from pouring the wine into the two glasses. "A Shade? Like Terri?" he asked, pushing one of the long stemmed glasses toward Lily.

"Yup. One of the victims."

Jack didn't say a word he just stared at Lily with the bottle still poised over the other wine glass.

"Don't worry. I'm not being haunted or anything. But from that point, the images that followed made it imperative I see the crime scene."

He put the bottle down on the table. "For *Christ* sake, Lily! Land your plane, already! Stop giving me minor details and get to the point. What happened?"

She took a sip of her wine. Just thinking about what she had seen and smelled made her hands shake. "The crime scene was destroyed. It was worse than if a car bomb had gone off. But the horrific images from inside the building told me there was no way a human was responsible."

Jack finished pouring and took a sip of his wine, his eyes locked on Lily. "A shifter, then?" He pressed his lips together. The taste of the words sour in his mouth.

"No. Vampire."

Jack opened his mouth to say something, but then mashed it into a thin line. He put his glass down on the table and pushed himself up from his chair. "Are you sure? I mean, you've never actually had any contact with the undead." Standing with his hands flat against the table's smooth wooden surface, he leaned forward, his gaze locked on Lily's face.

"Yeah, I have. Whom did you think I was hunting before I headed back to Maine to track Jerard? Like you said, I cut my teeth on things way hairier. I guess you didn't realize that included the fanged set, as well."

Staggered, Jack just stared back at her. "You hunted vampires? Sean never said anything about that. Are you fucking crazy, or just plain stupid? Vampires are more vicious and bloodthirsty than any shifter you'll ever encounter. They kill without provocation, just because they can."

Lily shrugged. "You were the one who found the crossbow

among my things while I was unconscious after Jerard's attack. What did you think it was for?"

Jack took a deep breath and blew it out slowly. "Lily...this is bad. Have you told Sean yet?"

Lily shook her head. "No. I haven't had time. Things got a little hectic this afternoon."

No shit, Jack thought. "How many?" He needed to know, especially if Lily was going to be involved, and knowing her, she was probably already up to her ears in it.

"What do you mean?"

"Now's not the time to play dumb, Lily. Was it just one bloodsucker, or was it a pack? Vamps don't usually hunt together like Shifters. They prefer a more solitary existence, especially since they don't exactly play well with others, if you know what I mean."

"Just one. But there was something bizarre about it," she said, shoving her plate away.

"How so?" he asked. As if having one of the undead as the perpetrator wasn't bizarre enough.

Lily chewed on her lower lip. Her face pensive as if struggling to find a way to phrase it. "It was as if the images were trying to tell me something, I mean other than who was responsible. There was something underlying it all, Jack, and I can't help the nagging feeling that I'm missing the mark."

"Can you tell me what you sensed, what the vamp showed you?"

Lily nodded. "Yeah, but finish eating first or trust me, your appetite will take a hike along with whatever's in your stomach."

"You do realize you're going to have to tell Sean, because if you don't, then I will." After Sean's telepathic tirade earlier, he wasn't taking a chance on a lie of omission. He liked his pelt where it was, and he planned to keep it that way.

Lily exhaled. "I know. And don't worry, I won't put you in the middle, or make this difficult. I just want to give it another day or so. I need to see if I can narrow things down. I know what happened, but I don't know why."

"Why? Who cares, why? The vampires have their own protocol for dealing with things of this nature, and as supernaturals, we're obligated to inform their council—especially since the police have been sniffing around. With you involved, it makes the situation even more imperative."

"Me? Why?"

"Because, technically you're a shifter."

"So?"

"So? Lily, there are rules to handling cross-supernatural incidents. In their eyes, you're a shifter, but one of little significance. You being involved and working the case in conjunction with the human authorities will only give them grounds to accuse us of infringement and collusion. As our alpha, Sean is the only one who can approach without provocation."

Lily pressed her lips together. "No. We are not calling Sean, at least not until I get a better handle on things. If the vampires have a council, then they probably know what's going on. If I'm technically a shifter in their eyes, then don't you think it makes more sense for me to gather as much information as I can, before we let the vamp out of the bag? One day, that's all I'm asking, Jack. Just give me one more day. I promise I'll call Sean."

He took a big gulp of his wine and then pointed the edge of his glass her way. "Okay. But it's your ass, not mine if he starts growling."

She smirked. "Don't worry. I know exactly how to handle Sean when it comes to my ass," she said pushing herself up from the table, giving Jack a little *Baby Got Back* wiggle, as she sashayed with her wine glass toward the sink.

Red wine spewed across the table, and Jack coughed, wiping his hand across his mouth. "Trouble, that's what you are, and that's what I'm going to be in, I know it," he said, trying to mop up the mess with his napkin.

Lily bit the inside of her cheek to keep from laughing. "Aw, come on, Jack, don't be that way. I'm sorry." She grabbed a handful of paper towels, handed half to him, and then with the rest, caught a thin ruby line before it trickled off the table.

"Tell you what dinner is on me tomorrow night. Anywhere you want to go in the city."

He looked up, still scrubbing his shirt. "You're on. But I should warn you, I'm not a cheap date."

She laughed out loud. "The good ones never are."

"Martinez downed the last of his beer, the butt of his glass thumping against the scuffed oak bar.

"Wanna another draft?" the bartender asked, wiping up a spill from his last order.

"*Nah.* I think I'm gonna head home, Arnie Thanks anyway."

The bartender nodded. "Too bad," he teased, his lopsided grin making his broad face seem even broader. "The brunette sitting at the table in the corner has been eye-fucking you for the last hour, but then again, you've been too busy stacking matchbooks to notice."

With a raised eyebrow, Arnie cocked his head toward the full-figured beauty pushing her way past the crowd in their direction. Chuckling, he gave Ryan thumbs up and quickly made himself scarce.

"Leaving so soon?" the woman drawled, her eyes sweeping Ryan's face and chest.

"I was."

She pouted. "Too bad. And here I was, ready to ask if you'd like to join me for a drink."

Ryan's eyes took in her full length, from the top of her frosted head to her wide blue eyes and full mouth, and every curve the rest of the way down. Her makeup was a bit over the top for his liking, but she seemed eager, and after the day he had, he was more than ready to lose himself between a pair of long legs.

"What's your name, sweetheart?"

"Charlie. My mother named me after her favorite perfume...you know, the one that was so popular back in the late seventies?"

"Nice," he said, but had no clue what she was talking about. "What'll you have?"

The brunette climbed up on the barstool next to his and leaned forward, her tight blouse one deep breath away from a wardrobe malfunction. "Whatever you're having."

Ryan signaled to Arnie for two more drafts, then swiveled his stool to face hers. "I haven't seen you in here before. Are you new to the neighborhood?"

She giggled, running her fingers through the length of her hair. "Yeah, I guess you could say that."

Arnie brought the drinks over, giving Ryan an encouraging nod. Not that he needed encouragement. Women came easy for him. Problem was none of them ever seemed the right fit. He thought he stumbled upon something special with Emily, the tall blonde he met in Boston on his way back from testifying in the Callahan case. She rocked his world that weekend, leaving possibilities open for the first time in his life. The long distance relationship worked for a little while or so he thought, but one visit left that possibility as cold as the stiffs he saw in the morgue.

Squashing the errant thought, he raised his glass to hers. "Sláinte," he said, clinking the side of her glass with his. No poetry necessary for this one.

"Swedish, right? I just love when guys talk another language. It's so sexy," she giggled again, swirling the foam at the top of her glass with her finger.

74

He raised an eyebrow, as he took a sip of his beer. Okay, so she wasn't exactly the sharpest knife in the drawer. Nothing at all like Lily. He frowned, pushing the Freudian thought away, focusing instead on the leggy girl practically sitting in his lap.

The brunette held her beer, running her long, red fingernail delicately up and down the frosted glass. She took a sip, and the condensation dripped from the bottom of the glass to her chest, its wetness trickling in a tempting line toward the deep cleft between her breasts.

"Here," Ryan said, handing her a napkin.

She took his hand, guiding it to just above her cleavage. Her mouth parted, and she licked her lips in obvious invitation, sliding the napkin out from between his fingers.

Her skin was warm to the touch, and his fingers didn't hesitate, dipping well beneath the low cut scoop of her blouse. She was braless, and her nipples hardened through the thin fabric at the simple touch.

Ryan slipped his arm around her narrow waist, bringing her closer. With a practiced move, she tilted her head, arching her back so her chest pressed against his. He bent to nuzzle her neck, expecting the same intoxicating feminine scent he had smelled on Lily all day. Instead, he got a nose full of cigarettes and cheap perfume.

The dirty ashtray smell settled on the back of his tongue, and he cleared his throat. Reading the sound as a groan of consent, the brunette slid her hand over the bulge in front of his pants. She lifted her mouth to his, murmuring a soft sigh into her kiss. She drew her tongue along the edge of his bottom lip, teasing.

He didn't care that they were in a public place. Her body was soft and supple, and she was just what he needed after being torqued up all day. His hand splayed across her décolleté, and his fingers dipped again into the deep cleft between her breasts. He feathered kisses along the tender skin beneath her jaw, her breath fanning across his ear, her low moans inviting him to explore more.

Ryan closed his eyes, but the fantasy playing out behind his lids didn't include the brunette in his arms. The starring role belonged to another woman, the one whose lush curves and delicious scent had taunted him all day.

His eyes snapped open. Get a grip, Martinez...what the fuck?

He grabbed the brunette by her hair and crushed his mouth to hers. As anticipated, he tasted a mix of cigarettes and beer, but ignored it. Inhaling deeply, he tried to catch the taste of her wet arousal. If his sixth sense had taught him anything, it was how to judge when a woman was ripe for the taking.

But the telltale scent wasn't there. Instead, the taste of her mouth coated every nerve ending with the residual scents from a host of other men.

Pissed off, he put his hands on her shoulders and shoved her away. He worked the little muscle in the corner of his jaw, biting back on his own recklessness and lack of discretion.

"Take your little bag of tricks and leave. Now." he said, leaning forward so she could read the severity on his face.

"But..."

"I know what you are, and I know what you're trying to pull. I'm a cop. And unless you want to spend the rest of the night in jail on a solicitation charge, I suggest you take my advice and scram. My offer expires in one minute."

Her eyes narrowed, and her mouth fell open for a moment before she pressed her lips together in a thin line. Ryan could see the skepticism in her face as she toyed with the idea of starting a scene. She sat there, almost daring him to make good on his promise, but her smug look disappeared the minute he opened his wallet to pay for the drinks, his badge as clear as the fear blooming on her face.

Truth was, he had no proof, only his trust in his sixth sense. But she didn't have to know that.

She unceremoniously slid from the barstool and grabbed her purse from the bar. With a sniff, she sidled off toward the door without as much as a backward glance.

Ryan wiped his mouth on a napkin. He downed his beer and ran a hand through his hair. Arnie walked over, wiping his hands on a bar towel, a quizzical look on his face. "Guess she wasn't your type, huh?"

"Not in the least. And I better not find she's anyone else's type either or my friends in vice will be paying you a little visit."

Arnie's mouth fell open. He threw the towel over his shoulder and leaned forward on the bar. "A pro? *No shit!* In here?"

Ryan nodded. "Yup. Hopefully, I scared her enough she'll rethink her choice of profession."

The bartender shrugged, pushing himself back. "Can't save the world, Ryan. All we can do is have faith," he said, grabbing a couple of shot glasses and filling them with Jameson Irish. Pushing one toward Ryan, he lifted the other. "Sláinte."

Ryan lifted his and shot it back. All we can do is have faith... Jeez, when Arnie gets it right, he seriously gets it right.

He wiped his hand across his mouth. For him, faith had always been something in short supply.

Aging out of the foster care system in California, he had headed east as soon as he'd turned eighteen, putting as much distance as he could between himself and his past. After everything he had gone through growing up, he joined the NYPD in hopes of finding some answers—but seven years later, he was no closer to knowing anything more about himself than he had then. All Martinez knew was that he was different, and until he figured out why, he was better off alone. Not exactly a trait conducive to a job where trust is crucial for survival.

Especially of late. He exhaled sharply, his thoughts drifting back to Lily. How could one woman fuck with both his head and his cock so much, in such a short time?

Vampire, my ass. It was bullshit. That was all he'd chalked it up to. But the same sense of foreboding that bit into his stomach the minute Lily uttered the word, twisted in his gut once again.

Grabbing his coat from the back of the barstool, he headed for the door. There was only one way to find out if there was any truth to what she claimed, or if he was just as crazy.

He pulled his car out onto the street and headed south. Patrol had manned the crime scene round the clock for the past seventy-two hours, but now the department had no choice but to turn the place back over to the landlord. CSI had done all they could, and Lily...well, that remained to be seen. It wasn't that late, but the cold had left most of the streets deserted, and he easily wound his way toward the east side.

He maneuvered his way down Avenue B until he found himself face to face with the crime scene. The place was deserted, trans-formed into more of a hollowed shell in just the seven hours since he and Lily had left the premises. Remnants of yellow police tape flapped in the wind, like so much shredded ribbon. Plywood covered the windows and the front door, and it looked as though someone had swept the glass and broken pieces of wood from the sidewalk.

Ryan parked and got out of the car, buttoning his coat against the wind. A wide sheet of graffiti covered pressboard, blocked the entryway, nailed into what was left of the original door jam. He pulled on his leather gloves and searched around the edges for a weak spot. Finding a small gap on the side, he gently pried the wood back, just far enough so he could slide in behind it.

The interior of the bar was pitch black, and Ryan fished in his pocket for his xenon tactical flashlight. He clicked the base, and immediately a narrow swath of light cut through the darkness.

The room was unchanged, and in the silence, the glass crunching beneath his feet echoed like a train wreck. He moved toward the backroom, the place where the images had supposedly been the most vivid.

Holding the flashlight in his teeth, he yanked what was left of the door from its hinges, laying it on its side against the wall. The knowledge that he was now guilty of breaking and entering, not exactly lost on him.

He moved through the doorway, shining his light through to the center of the room.

"Jesus Christ!" He jerked back, drawing his gun. In a crouch, he fanned the light across the floor, catching his own distorted reflection in the bent chrome of the rolling bar. "Great. The crazy bitch has got me jumping at shadows now" he muttered, holstering his gun.

No matter how he tried to deny it, Lily's words and her resolute certainty had unnerved him. Annoyed at himself, and annoyed at her, he stood in the freezing darkness.

What did he think he was going to find? He wasn't a psychic. The best he could do was register the funky scent that permeated the place.

He moved toward the ruined couch. Even in the constrained light, it was easy to see where dried blood had crusted over surface fabric. The putrid scent was stronger here than anywhere else in the room.

Pulling on a pair of latex gloves, he took his penknife from his pocket. With a ragged breath, he leaned forward, grabbing hold of one of the seat cushions, and jabbing the edge of the blade into the center. He half cut, half ripped a wide swatch, swallowing hard against the fetid stench.

He straightened up, closing his knife before sticking it back in his pocket. "Here goes nothing," he whispered, taking a step back from the broken piece of furniture and raising the foul piece of cloth to his nose.

Ryan closed his eyes and inhaled, his stomach roiling in protest. Nothing but his own nausea registered, and he forced himself to inhale again, this time moving the fabric even closer. He gagged, the sour taste of whiskey rising to the back of his throat, and he dropped the shred to floor. His knees buckled, and he caught the edge of the couch. As he moved to get up, his head reeled with olfactory images racing through his brain. He couldn't see, but his other senses took over.

Like a jigsaw, the one foul stench separated into distinct scents, each one registering in his mind. Sweat, sex, feces...but his mouth watered when he zeroed in on the blood. He inhaled through his mouth, the smell coating his tongue, and he moaned in visceral pleasure.

Ryan lurched forward, his fingers clutching the flashlight as he struggled for the door. He crashed his way out onto the sidewalk, and once again fell to his knees, his body recognizing the truth in Lily's words, even as his mind revolted.

God in heaven, what do I do now?

CHAPTER

EIGHT

L ily opened her eyes, wincing against pressure throbbing behind her lids. Sunlight streamed through the bedroom window, making her squint at the clock on her nightstand. *8:30 a.m.* Another bright winter day, in the city that never sleeps because the nightmares are real.

Her bedroom was overly warm, and she kicked the covers off her feet, freeing her legs. The baseboard heat hissed quietly in the corner, the sound grating on her already throbbing head. She hadn't slept a wink. Fragments from the day before plagued her mind, a cavalcade of terror haunting her dreams like a horror film looped on replay.

Muffled sounds from the kitchen and the aroma of fresh-brewed coffee told her Jack was out of bed, but the thought of getting up to join him left her even more exhausted than she already was.

The phone rang, and she rolled onto her back, draping one arm over her eyes, the counter pressure offering a modicum of relief as she listened to the answering machine pick up in the other room.

"Jack!" she shouted, wincing again with the effort. Her lips were dry, and her tongue tasted like sandpaper spackled to the roof of her mouth.

His footsteps echoed, getting louder until the bedroom door opened, the scents from the kitchen entering along with him, making her stomach turn over. "You bellowed?" he asked, wiping his hands on a dishtowel.

"Don't be a smart ass," she snapped, cringing as she tried to sit up. "I feel like crap."

"Well that's what happens when a human consumes half a bottle of Jamison's and an entire bottle of merlot in one evening."

"Liar. I did no such thing." Pain exploded behind her eyes. Okay, maybe I sort of did. "I heard the phone ring. Was it Martinez?"

"The machine got it, but I don't think it was him—not unless he woke up this morning as a soprano. It was some woman named, Beverly. She left a message for you to call her back."

"Beverly?" Lily slumped back against the pillows.

"That's what I think she said."

"Hmmm."

He looked at her strangely. "Is everything okay?"

"What? Um, yeah...sorry. I'm fine. I just didn't sleep much last night," she answered, but he still eyed her with suspicion.

"You sure? Perhaps there's something you want to share with the class?"

Lily couldn't help her smile. "No. I'm sure. I just need a cup of coffee to clear the cobwebs. Give me a sec, and I'll be right out."

"All righty, then..."

"Uh...Jack? Did she say anything else?"

He stopped, giving her another weird look. "Why don't you just listen to the message yourself?"

"Hmmm," she said again with a nod. "I'll be out in a sec."

Jack shut the door behind him, and she rearranged her pillows before turning over onto her side. Beverly. Her phone call meant she and Carl knew she was back in town. Lily hadn't seen or spoken to them since Terri's funeral—just left them a quick note saying she was going back to Maine, and she'd be in touch.

Of course, that never happened, and a pang of guilt shot through her chest knowing she could have called but didn't. And why hadn't she got in touch with her best friend's parents, the people who took her in as a child? Because, despite all her bravado, she was a chicken shit when it came to family.

Beverly and Carl Hess were the only two people, besides Terri, who could force her to face things she didn't want to face. In the past, she'd always had Terri as a buffer. Now she'd have to deal with them alone. What was she going to say when they asked where she'd been all this time?

Chicken shit. Definitely.

She pushed her covers back the rest of the way and jammed her feet into her slippers. The room may have been overly warm, but hardwood floors in New York in February were ice cold. Grabbing her robe from the end of the bed, she slipped it on, and headed into the bathroom to wash her face and brush her teeth.

"You look like shit," Jack said, looking up from the paper. "Can I get you anything?"

"Two Advil and a cup of coffee."

"Pain killers and caffeine. The breakfast of champions."

"I'm in no mood, Jack, so leave off, okay?"

"Okay...*jeez*. I know you had a bad night, but I've seen you more bandaged up than The Mummy and still have a better disposition. What's going on with you?"

"Beverly is Terri's mother. I haven't spoken to her since before Jerard attacked. I'm going to have to go there today and seeing them is going to bring it all back—for them and for me."

"Why haven't you called them? The Compound has a communication system that rivals NASA. Surely, Sean would have let you make one long distance call?"

Lily shrugged.

"Bock, bock, bock," he said, crooking his arms in an elegant chicken impersonation.

"Jack..."

"Sorry. But I still don't understand why you're apprehensive? Just tell them you went back to hunt down the animal that mauled Terri and ended up mauled yourself. I mean, you have the scars on your throat to prove it, if you have to. Say you ended up with temporary amnesia or something. Just leave out the supernatural stuff."

"It's not that. They know me. Going off on my own is not something out of the ordinary. They know it's the way I cope."

"What, then?"

"Terri was an only child until I came into the picture. After my parents died, the Hess family treated me like their own, same as Terri. I was the one who held back, especially after realizing my psychic ability, always thinking I would eventually be able to channel my parents, talk to them. Terri thought so, too. As a kid, I wanted to believe my gift was akin to a celestial long distance phone plan. My hotline to heaven."

"So, what's wrong with that? I bet a lot of kids would have felt the same way."

"There's nothing wrong with it, except it got in the way of my ever feeling like Terri's parents were anything more than just that, Terri's parents. It hurt them, even though they never said a word to me about it. Now that Terri's gone, I'm afraid they blame me. Not because I made Terri go with me to Maine, but because when Jerard killed her, he took me away from them too. In essence, they lost both of us. Now I'm back, and I'm afraid I won't be enough. That I'll hurt them all over again."

"Lily, how you choose to handle this is just that...your choice. Either you can continue to run, or you can step up and be their daughter. It's obvious you love them. And from what you've said, they obviously love you too, though God knows why. Just let that be enough. The rest will come, if you put in time and effort."

Lily considered him for a moment. It was no surprise Jack had earned admittance to Sean's Hunters at such a tender age, or that he'd won a place in Sean's heart. They were so much alike. Wise, patient, and loyal to a fault.

Lily turned right at the end of the exit ramp and merged onto the rural highway heading toward North Salem. This area of Westchester County was horse country, with miles of grazing pastures traversing multiple townships and two state lines, each separated by weathered, split rail fences, and dotted with stables and equestrian jumping courses.

She hadn't been this way since August. As the road twisted, she watched the landscape unfold across her line of sight. Once lush acres lay fallow, buried under snow, and the surrounding trees seemed melancholy in their hues of gray and brown. Lily sighed, hoping the bleak colors weren't an omen of how her visit would go.

The road was rough from all the snow and ice as she turned onto the long common drive Terri's parents shared with one of the local breeders. In the far paddock, a few horses pawed the frozen earth, their beautiful manes shining in the chilly afternoon sun, falling in a silken cascade across blankets covering their flanks.

Beverly and Carl expected her over an hour ago, so she shifted into low gear and headed toward the private drive, almost hidden behind the leafless hedgerow across from the barn. A quarter of a mile later, she was at the house.

Putting the car in park, Lily quickly checked herself in the makeup mirror, double-checking her dark circles were properly concealed. Beverly was part bloodhound when it came to sniffing out if her girls were taking care of themselves, and the last thing Lily wanted was for their visit to begin with maternal instincts blaring.

As usual, Carl had cleared the driveway down to the blacktop. Lily knew the owners of the neighboring horse farm always plowed the roads, but Carl was a typical male when it came to his 'toys'. Give him a reason to fire up his snow blower, and he was a happy camper.

From inside the car, she could hear Cookie barking. The chocolate lab was a better lookout than Buffalo Bill, and that meant everyone knew she had arrived. Flipping the visor back up, she grabbed her purse and got out of the car.

From her vantage point, she could see the entire yard. The large oak tree off to the side of the house still held the chair swing where she and Terri used to sit for hours, talking and laughing. She closed her eyes, and for a moment she was twelve years old again, helping Carl carve their names into the trunk of the tree.

Beverly's planters were still in their place on either side of the slate walkway, iced over and barren, but Lily knew come Mother's Day they'd be overflowing with impatiens and begonias.

The house itself was an old groundskeeper's cottage, modest by comparison to the sprawling acres and large farm homes surrounding it. But what it lacked in size, it made up for in charm. Red brick, with a double peaked, grey slate roof, it looked as though it belonged on the pages of a fairytale. In the spring, an English wildflower garden graced both sides of the yard, attracting butterflies and hummingbirds by the score.

On the outside, nothing had really changed. But Lily didn't need her psychic ability to guess how things had changed on the inside, and that's what worried her.

Taking a deep breath, she shoved a few stray strands behind her ear and started up the front path. What was she going to say? Did she still own the right to just breeze in as if this was still her home, as if she still belonged here?

With her hand on the brass doorknob, she bit her lip. Just one quick peek... She shook her head. No. The truth might hurt too much. With a deep breath, she reached for the doorknocker, instead. *Tap. Tap. Tap.*

Cookie barked madly behind the door, and Carl's deep voice resonated from the other side for her to sit and be quiet. The front door swung open, and there he stood, unchanged and smiling.

"What are you doing standing outside in the cold? Get in here and give me a hug!" he said, opening his arms.

Lily's breath hitched, and her throat tightened against a sudden urge to cry. She walked into his arms, breathing in the familiar scents of peppermint and cherry pipe tobacco that always clung to him. A million memories flooded her mind as he gave her a squeeze before leaning back to kiss her cheek, nuzzling his salt and pepper beard against her chin, as he did when she was a child.

"How's my wild girl?" he asked, when he finally stepped back, allowing her the rest of the way through the door. He scrutinized her as she shoved her gloves in her pocket and took off her coat and hat. "You okay?"

"I'm fine, Carl. How about you?"

He slid his arm around her shoulder and steered her towards the kitchen at the back of the house. "Better now that we know you're home and safe."

Lily cringed inwardly. It was about as close to a verbal admonishment as he would give her, but translated it said, *'Your mother was crazy with worry, and I had to deal with her for months. Is a simple phone call too much to ask?'*

Carl was a big man, about six foot, three inches, and Lily looked up at him across the wide expanse of his flannel shirt. "Yeah... I'm sorry about that. I guess I should have called."

"Hmmm. Well, you're here now, and that's all that matters," he said, depositing her at the kitchen table and moving toward the coffeepot and mugs Beverly had obviously set out. "You want to warm up with a cup of coffee or do you want to head upstairs and see Beverly first?"

Lily instinctively glanced through the kitchen door towards the hall stairs. "Why is she still upstairs? It's almost noon, is she sick?" There was nothing upstairs except the two bedrooms, the upstairs bath and the tiny staircase that led to the attic.

Beverly was never one to lie down during the day, and she always made sure the beds were made, and the rooms picked up before she came downstairs in the morning. Immediately worried Lily pushed herself up from the kitchen chair.

"Sit down, Lily. Bev's fine. She's just in the attic looking through some things she thought you might want to have. That's all."

He wasn't telling her everything. The attic was as cold as hell this time of the year, and there was no way Beverly would be up there unless...

She didn't wait for him to elaborate. Guilt slashed across her chest making it hard to breath. It was obvious. Beverly was losing herself in the attic among the things she had saved from Terri's life, from her life. Hence, the memory box left for her in the apartment.

Beverly was stuck, and Lily had left her alone in her grief, with no one to cling to, no one to help ease her pain except Carl. Lily had taken herself out of the family equation, too obsessed with her own selfish quest for revenge. Shame, heavy and suffocating, descended on her, and Lily's mind replayed the same words over and over again. Thoughtless, Self-centered.

Lily took the hall stairs two at a time, purposely ignoring the family pictures hanging on the wall. At the top, she headed straight for the attic door, left partially ajar. As she climbed the narrow stairs, the wind whistled, low and moaning through the attic eaves, and the temperature dropped significantly the closer she got to the top.

"Beverly?" she called out gently. "You up here?"

"I'm here, dear. In the back by the trunks. Watch your step, Carl still hasn't gotten around to fixing those loose boards."

Lily walked over to where Beverly sat cross-legged on an old remnant of carpet, a thick throw blanket wrapped around her shoulders, and fingerless gloves on her hands as she sorted through items in one of the trunks.

"Bev, for Christ sake, it's got to be twenty degrees up here. What are you doing sitting in the freezing cold?"

The older woman looked up, waving Lily off with one of her gloved hands. "Oh, honey, I don't feel the cold when I'm all wrapped up like an Eskimo. And let's not forget about my hot flashes. So, don't worry. I'm as toasty as can be up here in my little perch."

The corners of her eyes crinkled as she smiled up from her spot on the floor, but the telltale signs of where she'd grown careworn were there, despite her attempt at humor. The light had gone out of her eyes, and Beverly's voice had lost the lilt of easy laughter.

"Why didn't you make Carl carry all this downstairs for you? If you're worried about his back, between the two of us I'm sure we can shimmy it down the stairs. We'll put it in the old bedroom, that way you can look through everything without risking frostbite."

Beverly just blinked. "No. I like the solitude up here."

"Well, Carl doesn't like it and neither do I. You may think you're fine sitting up here in the freezing cold, but even in this dim light, I can see your fingertips are blue. This is nuts! You've had time enough for solitude..." Lily stopped herself, suddenly conscious of the annoyed tone to her voice. This was not the time for her habit of masking concern with anger. When it came to appropriate ways of dealing with emotions, who was she to talk?

Her chin sunk to chest, her cheeks hot with self-reproach. "...and so have I," she added softly. "We've both been alone in this for too long. I've been alone in this for too long." Her voice caught, and she looked away, not wanting to upset Beverly any further.

The older woman stood, pushing down on the lid of the trunk with her hand to steady herself. "Oh, sweetheart...don't. You did what you had to do," she said, taking a step towards Lily. "We all deal with grief differently. I found my place of peace up here with my memories." She paused, as if afraid to ask. "Have you found yours?"

Lily hesitated, and then slowly nodded. What else could she say? It was the truth, even if the truth was more farfetched than any legend or folktale. She had found peace with Sean, with his entirely unreal reality.

Would she ever be able to tell Beverly about Terri, and how she stayed for a while as an earthbound Shade? Probably not. It would hurt the woman too much if she knew she could have said goodbye to her daughter, yet not been given the chance. No. This was one secret that needed to stay buried.

"Come on. Let's both get warmed up, and then Carl and I will bring whatever you want downstairs," Lily said, changing the subject.

"I..."

Lily took her elbow, steering her toward to stairs. "Sorry, but I'm not giving you a choice. I want a nice, long visit, and I'm not doing it up here in the tundra. You're coming back downstairs, and I don't want to hear another word about it."

Chuckling, Beverly slid her arm around Lily's waist. "When did you get to be so pushy?"

Lily leaned into her, the warmth of being home flooding her body with peace. "I learned from the best.

CHAPTER
NINE

"Lily and Beverly sat on the floor of the spare bedroom, sorting through the trunks Carl had dragged, one after the other, down the stairs. He refused any help, yet red faced and out of breath, mouthed the words, thank you, to Lily as he left the two women to their task.

The room had changed so much in the four years since she and Terri had moved out. But the feeling of belonging, of coming home, permeated the walls and a weight lifted from Lily's chest. No matter where she went, this was home. Reaching into the trunk, she took out a stack of photographs and flipped through them. Most were of Terri as a baby, but one picture stopped her and left her staring.

"What's the matter, honey?"

"Where did this come from?" Lily asked, holding up a picture of Beverly at their town's Halloween parade. Terri was in her stroller, in a pink onesie with bunny ears and eyeliner whiskers. In the background was Lily's own mom, with Lily in her arms dressed as a bat.

Beverly peeked over Lily's arm and chuckled. "Carl took that picture our first year in North Salem. It's funny that the four of us are in that picture I didn't even know your mother at that point. You know the story—we didn't meet until we enrolled you girls in the community center's Mom and Tot music class. You and Terri were just two years old at the time.

"Your mom and I took one look at each other and knew we'd be friends. She was the only down-to-earth woman in that entire group! Talk about your bunch of wannabes."

Lily held the photo, running her thumb over the curve of her mother's face. In the photograph, her mother was about the same age as she was now.

"You look just like her, you know," Beverly said softly.

Lily nodded, and with a sniff, placed the photo back in the trunk. "Lucky me," she said with a shrug.

"Sweetheart, you should keep the photo. It was a good luck omen then, maybe it'll be a good luck omen now," she said, placing it back in Lily's hand.

Lily shrugged again. "Stranger things can happen. It's funny though. Even as babies, Terri was all in pink and I was all in black."

Beverly smirked. "Only you would think of that."

Lily opened her mouth to say something else, but stopped, watching Beverly pull a blue and white receiving blanket from the last trunk. "What's that?" she asked. "I don't remember seeing that before." The blanket looked old and worn, and it certainly didn't look like anything Beverly would have put on Terri as a baby. It had an institutional feel about it.

"This is the blanket that Terri was wrapped in when the nuns brought her to me." Beverly held the blanket up and Lily saw the Good Samaritan Hospital stamp across the back.

"Nuns? Don't you mean nurses?"

Beverly shook her head. "No, sweetie. They were nuns." She lifted her eyes, and they were full of nostalgia and regret. "We never told her, or you." She paused. "Terri was adopted."

Lily was speechless, but her face must have spoken volumes because Beverly's crumpled a bit.

"Oh, honey, I don't defend not telling her. We always thought the right moment would present itself, that we had all the time in the world to find a way to break it to her gently." Beverly's eyes misted over, and her voice cracked. "I even wrote her a letter. I bet you think that's pretty chicken shit, huh?"

Lily just blinked. Hadn't she used those same exact words to chastise herself for not calling? Guess emotional avoidance was a learned behavior. In this family, anyway.

Except for Terri...

Beverly reached into the trunk and pulled out a flat rectangular jewelry box. She lifted the lid and took out a small stack of papers and official looking envelopes. "It's in here, along with her adoption papers," she said, handing Lily the stack. Lily took them from her hand and placed them on the carpet next to her.

"Can I see that for a moment?" she asked, extending her hand toward the receiving blanket.

Beverly nodded. To anyone else it may have seemed an odd request, but not in this house. The girls had kept Lily's secret just between them until they graduated from college. When they decided to open a paranormal investigation company, they knew the idea would raise more than just eyebrows. Beverly and Carl were going to want an explanation. And boy did they get one.

Lily took the blanket from Beverly's hand. The woman's grief, mixed with her apprehension at what Lily might see, passed along, as well.

She gave the woman a reassuring smile, and then closed her eyes, wrapping her fingers around the faded fabric. Images formed slowly, incongruous at first. Lily focused her concentration on Terri's essence, her strong life force, willing the hazy images to clear and align.

Frames resembling an editor's reel, choppy and flickering, played across her mind—a woman straining, her feet in stirrups, nurses by her head and one next to the doctor at her feet, counting down the contraction time.

"Push Teresa...come on, work for your baby. One more big push!" Lily's lips curled in a soft smile as she watched the scene play out. *"It's a girl,"* the doctor said, as the baby slipped into his hand, covered in blood and a white, cheese-like substance. Wailing, her tiny, puckered face turned red and purple as nurses took her, cleaned her and wrapped her in a blanket, before placing her in her mother's arms. *"Seven pounds, two ounces and nineteen inches long. She's perfect. But don't get too comfortable, Mommy, you've got one more to go!"*

The mother placed a kiss on the baby's head, but her weak smile suddenly turned agonized as an unexpected contraction tore through her. Her back arched, and she screamed, blood gushing from between her legs.

"Take the baby!" the doctor yelled.

"Christ, that was fast..." one of the nurses said, but before she could finish her sentence, another painful contraction hit right on top of the previous one.

Nurses scrambled back and forth, one taking the first baby, and the other trying to keep the mother quiet and immobile.

"Keep her still," the doctor commanded.

"Teresa, I know it hurts, but you need to stay calm so Doctor Bennett can see what's happening. Squeeze my hand, small breaths..."

"My baby! Save my baby!"

"The placenta separated, she's hemorrhaging," Bennett said, pushing the instrument table aside, shouting instructions to the nurses.

"Blood pressure is 60/40 and dropping," one of the nurses said. *"Respiration weak and thready. FHR variable.*

"Start an I.V... saline, lactated ringers and get an oxygen mask on her! Call the O.R.! Tell them we're on our way, stat! Tell them to have a supply of O Negative ready...and somebody notify the NICU. You—get that other baby to the nursery!"

"She's crashing! I can't find a pulse!"

"We're losing her! Move people, move!

Lily opened her eyes and exhaled, her fingers relaxing their hold on the blanket.

"What did you see?" Beverly asked, unease lacing her tone at Lily's daunted expression.

Not sure where to begin, Lily folded the blanket and placed it on the floor next to her. "Bev, did the adoption agency ever tell you Terri was a twin?"

"What?"

The look of disbelief on Beverly's face said it all, and Lily simply nodded. "Based on what I just saw, it's true. Although I can only assume the other baby died along with Terri's birth mother. I believe her name was, Teresa."

Beverly's hand went to her mouth. "It's true then." Hands shaking, she picked up one of the envelopes from where Lily had put them on the floor next to her. Opening it, she removed a sheet of paper and unfolded it, handing it to Lily. "Terri's birth mother's name was Teresa Garcia."

The paper had everything listed—birth date, weight, height, ethnicity, the record of the mother's death and the medical explanation why: Blood loss due to placenta abruptio—everything, except a father's name and no mention of it being a multiple birth. There was no next of kin listed either, so perhaps it wasn't something included on the birth record if the twin didn't survive.

Beverly looked numb, and Lily reached out to take her hand. "I don't know Bev, but based on what I saw, neither Teresa nor the other baby survived. Terri was lucky to be born first, it's the reason she lived."

Tears dripped down Beverly's cheeks. "I'm just grateful we were there for her. I don't want to think about what life would have been like if we weren't."

Lily pulled her into a hug but didn't say another word. A sense of peace settled over her, knowing Terri's biological mother had loved her and wanted her, and what happened was just a sad turn of fate. Somehow, she knew Terri knew it too.

"Knock, knock..." Carl said, standing in the doorway. "I don't know about you two, but I'm starving. Can we take a detour off memory lane for a bit and have a late lunch?"

Beverly wiped her face, and sucked in a deep breath, holding it for a moment. "Perfect timing," she said. "I think we could all use a break."

Lily put her hands on her thighs and sat back. "Sounds like a great idea. I have dinner plans later tonight, so a late lunch would be perfect."

"You have dinner plans?" Beverly asked, wiping her nose with a tissue she fished out from her shirt cuff. "You never eat out unless it's those dirty water dogs from the cart vendor on the corner. Does this mean you've met someone?"

Lily laughed. "Nice. You make me sound like a social misfit. I do have a life, you know—but, yes, I did meet someone—although I'm not having dinner with him tonight. My plans are with a friend."

"A friend, huh?" Carl chimed in, waggling his eyebrows. "Maybe we just might get a chance at grandkids yet, Bev."

Rolling her eyes, Lily made a face. "Seriously, guys?"

Carl crossed his arms in front of his chest and glanced at Beverly, neither moved, their expressions letting Lily know they weren't budging until she gave them details.

"All right, since you'll only bug me from now until forever, his name is Sean. He's from Maine. But if you must know, things are kind of up in the air for us right now. I don't want to get into it, but my life is pretty complicated at the moment. Adding a long distance relationship on top of everything else—well, let's just say we're taking it day by day," she said with a shrug.

Carl flashed a warm smile then winked, before sticking his hand out to help Beverly up off the floor. "That's the best any of us can do, sweetheart. Take things day by day."

Lily rocked back onto the balls of her feet and pushed herself to standing. Her head came up, and a warm glow spread through her chest at seeing Beverly tucked under Carl's arm the same way she always remembered. "I know. And I didn't mean to sound dismissive, or anything. It's just...well, it's complicated."

Beverly slid her free hand around Lily's waist and gave her a squeeze. "You'll figure it out, honey. I have faith in you. And when you're ready to introduce your young man to your family, we'll be here."

They turned to walk out, and Beverly let go, her hand trailing in Lily's as they stepped through the door.

 Words sprang to mind from nowhere, probably from some long forgotten English class. *Beauty is truth, truth beauty—that is all ye know on earth, and all ye need to know.* Nevertheless, in that moment they rang true as Lily watched her parents together.

"I love you guys," she murmured from behind.

Carl grunted. "Yeah, yeah, we love you too. Can we eat now, please?"

Lily threw her head back and laughed. Things had changed, but then again, they hadn't. Terri would always be with them, and Jack was right. It would be enough, as long as she allowed it. She always have Terri, and she'd always have Beverly and Carl... but most importantly, she had Sean.

Suddenly dinner wasn't what she wanted. She needed to get back. She needed to tell Sean she was wrong. Wrong to leave. Wrong not to stand by his side against Parr. Wrong not to trust their love was strong enough to see it through.

"Lils!" Carl called again. "We're waiting, and if my stomach growls any louder the neighbors will think we're harboring a wild animal."

If he only knew. Lily grinned, putting the memory of Sean's low growl out of her mind. Dinner with the parents first. Then Sean. Always Sean. Forever Sean.

"I'm back!" Lily called from the hallway, dropping her keys on the credenza against the wall next to the closet.

"I'm in the kitchen," Jack answered, above the clatter of dishes and the sound of the refrigerator door opening. "How'd it go?"

She hung up her coat and stopped in the kitchen doorway, Jack's butt greeting her as it peeked out from behind the open refrigerator door. "Are you cleaning the shelves or just taking inventory?" she said, leaning on the doorjamb and crossing her arms in front of her chest.

Poking his head up, he flashed a quick smile. "None of the above," he said, closing the door with his foot, his hands full of sandwich fixings. "By the way you're looking at me, I guess everything went okay today."

"Yeah, everything went fine," she answered, shaking her head as she watched his elaborate set up at the kitchen counter. Eight slices of bread, stacks of pickles, lettuce and tomato were all paired neatly across the Formica. "Jack, what are you doing?"

"I'm hungry," he answered with his mouth full.

"I can see that," she said, as he peeled off layers of sliced turkey and stuffed his mouth, while at the same time, piling thick layers onto four slices of bread. "Is this your way of telling me, you don't want to go out for dinner tonight?"

"Depends on where you're taking me."

Lily smirked. His back was turned, but she knew his face held the same wry smile, despite the soft rustle of plastic wrap as he wrapped and unwrapped.

"We're going to Peter Lugar's. It's one of the best steakhouses in the city. Well, actually, it's in Brooklyn, but it's the best."

"Terrific. I can't wait," he mumbled, turning around, and shoving half a sandwich into his mouth.

Lily grabbed a bottle of water from the fridge. "Tell me the truth, are you really that hungry, or are you just bored? Because you've been doing nothing but eat, lately."

"You make me sound like a chick with PMS," he said, taking a sip from his own water bottle. He took another bite of sandwich, shoving a stray piece of pickle into his mouth, and chewing slowly.

"This city of yours may not be much in terms of fresh air, but it certainly has its diversions." Tilting his bottle of water her way, he winked. "So, definitely not bored."

Waving her hand at him, she shook her head. "Let's not go there, okay? I don't need to know what diversions you've found to keep yourself busy." Cracking her bottle of water open, she considered him. "Could it be because tonight's the first night of the full moon? I mean, you've been cooped up here with only me for company, and let's face it, I'm not much fun when it comes to shifter-related activities."

He chuckled. "You could be."

"Jack."

"I'm just saying. Sean would supply the right bite in a heartbeat if you said the word."

"Yeah, well. Let's not go there either," she said dryly, placing her water bottle on the table.

She glanced back up as Jack stacked the last two sandwiches together and took a couple of bites. Just the mental image of lengthy incisors left her shivering, and she unconsciously slid her hand around the back of her shoulder where Sean had marked her.

The spot tingled under her fingers, and a rush of warmth spread through her lower belly. Lily pictured him in her mind. His blue eyes as they burned with desire, his long, lean body and wide shoulders, and the way the smooth, hard muscles of his chest and belly felt under her fingers. In that moment, her body craved his and the miles between them suddenly seemed like vast oceans.

What was it he'd said about the full moon and uncontrollable urges? The sky was dark, but the moon was absent from its blackness. Moonrise was still hours off, yet here she was panting on the inside like a bitch in heat. How was she going to get through this so far away from Sean?

Jack's eyes were on hers as he finished eating, watching as if he could smell her inner arousal. He cleared his voice and wiped his hands on a napkin.

"I don't know if the moon has anything to do with my excess appetite," he said, deftly shifting the conversation to neutral, and away from the dangerous ground they both sensed. "Could be, but I don't really have a frame of reference. I've never been away from the pack during a full moon."

Grateful for Jack's tact, Lily exhaled, stilling her mind, and pulling herself together.

"Back home, the Hunter's usually go for a run on the first night," he continued. "...and Sean likes to include a ritual hunt at some point during the cycle. I missed last month's because Sean had me and a couple of other newbies helping out at the research clinic. With the viral outbreak and the panic afterward, the nurses needed us to help keep things moving smoothly, although Doc Volkmann seemed to want us there about as much as we did."

Residual tension throbbed between her shoulders and Lily rubbed at the nape of her neck, careful not to graze the edge of Sean's bite mark, again. "So, you've been stuck doing grunt work rather than joining in the fun, huh?"

"I wouldn't say grunt work, but yes, Sean put our skills on ice at times. A shifter needs to exercise his inner animal, or else..." His eyes wandered the length of her, from the top of her honey-blonde head, over the swell of her breasts, to her feet and back again. "...he suffers."

"Ah, Jack?" she said, taking a step backward. Either she was right, and he had sensed her passing spike in heat, or she wasn't the only one affected by the approaching moonrise.

He exhaled, rubbing his face with both hands. "Yeah, yeah. I'm okay. Or at least I will be. Give me a big, juicy steak, the rarer the better, and I'll be right as rain. That and a quick jog before we go," he said, grabbing his jacket from the back of the chair.

Lily moved out of his way as he went past. "All right but be back in an hour. Our reservations are for eight-thirty, and they won't hold them if we're late."

With a quick wave over his head, he was out the door. Lily turned back to the counter to wrap up what was left of Jack's sandwich mess. If this was the first night of the full moon, what was in store for her over the next two days?

As EXPECTED, the restaurant was crowded. Weeknight or not, it didn't matter, Peter Lugar's was a landmark, almost as famous for their gleaming wood interiors and true gentleman's bar, as they were for their porterhouse steaks.

They walked in from the street, and a wall of warmth, thick with delicious scents, met them by the coat check. Busy wait staff carried trays back and forth from the kitchen to the dining rooms, the sizzle of steak following in their wake.

Jack handed Lily's long, leather duster to the coat check, and then met her next to the hostess stand. Inhaling through his nose, he raised his chin, a silly smile on his face. "You get thumbs up on this one," he said. "My mouth is watering already."

"Good, because I had to call in a favor to get us this reservation."

The maître d' coughed, and then raised his arm gesturing toward the stairs. "Your table isn't quite ready yet. Please, feel free to wait in the private bar upstairs, and we'll call you when all is prepared."

Lily winked at the man, and then followed Jack up to the bar to wait. Sometimes being psychic had its advantages.

"What can I get you?" the bartender asked, as Lily slid onto the smooth, high-backed leather stool.

"Merlot, please," she answered, placing her bag on the counter.

Jack grinned, swiveling his seat around to face hers. "Hair of the dog, huh?"

Hmmph. "Not even close. And the whole canine thing is your gig, not mine. Remember?"

"Ha! Keep telling yourself that," he said, swiveling back around to face the bar, signaling the bartender with a quick lift of his chin. "I'll have a Sam Adams. Winter Lager if you have it."

The bartender nodded, giving Lily a quick wink before he went to get their drinks.

"What's with all the winking? First the guy at the door, and now the bartender, do you know these people, or is this just part of your natural charm?"

The bartender put two napkins down on the counter and then placed Jack's beer on one, and a red wine glass for Lily on the other." You want a frosted glass with that?" he asked while pouring Lily's wine.

"No, I'm good with the bottle."

The man nodded once, putting the cork back in the bottle of merlot. "I couldn't help but overhear," he said to Jack, gesturing toward Lily with his head. "Your friend here is a very special lady. She really saved our ass last year, if you'll excuse my language."

Jack looked from one to the other, his eyebrows high.

The bartender put his hand up, his face as serious as a heart attack. "You have no idea. I never believed in that sort of thing, you know, ghosts and whatnot. At least not until I got the royal shit scared out of me one night after closing. From that point on, to say things got creepy around here is an understatement. Whatever it was, spirit, entity...whatever...it raised unholy hell almost every night after closing, so much so, the owners didn't know what to do. We all thought they should call in an exorcist, but they didn't want to risk bad press."

Jack raised his beer bottle in salute. "So, they called you, instead. Nice work," he said, a ghost of a smirk at the corner of his mouth.

The bartender shook his head. "Hand to God, my friend, I don't know what she did or how she did it, but it worked," he said, giving Lily an appreciative smile. "And don't let her fool you. She may be tiny, but then so is an M-80."

Lily patted the bartender's hand. "I was glad to help."

The bartender nodded, sliding his hand out from beneath hers. "You're okay in my book," he said, before turning to help customers at the other end of the bar.

"Does Sean know about how you 'clean house'?" Jack asked, taking a sip of his beer.

"Yes, he does, but we don't really talk about it much. The past couple of months have been...strained."

Jack's gaze softened. "That's an understatement, but I wouldn't worry. Things have a way of working themselves out, even if it's not how you planned. You just have to leave yourself open to change."

"Change, huh."

"Yup."

Lily considered him. Leave yourself open to change. Yeah, okay, Jack. You're about as subtle as my .45.

The whole question about her transformation to full shifter was off limits, and he knew it. In the last two months, she'd had enough change to fill a lifetime, thank you very much. It was hard enough wrapping her own head around the idea, let alone trying to explain her hesitance to Sean and Rissa. Why all of a sudden did Jack feel the need to add his two cents worth? Well, she wasn't taking the bait. Until further notice, off limits meant off limits.

Swiveling her seat around to face the room, she glanced out the tall windows at the darkened street and the light rain shimmering in the glow of the streetlights. She took in the antique sconces set into the original brick walls, the polished bar, and the wide planked floor. The place never changed, seemingly at home in the modern world as it was back in 1887 when the restaurant first opened.

In her peripheral vision, she watched Jack sip his beer, tilting the bottle up, and then absently running his thumb over the condensation-wet label. A shadow crossed his eyes, and for a moment, he wore the same expression she'd seen on Sean's face when he was brooding. Perhaps there was more to Jack's idea of accepting change than she thought. *It's not always about you, Lily.* Terri's voice interjected at the back of her head.

"Ms. Saburi? Your table is ready," a waiter interrupted.

Jack threw twenty dollars on the bar and waited for Lily to grab her purse. They followed the waiter downstairs to their table at the back of Driggs dining room.

Conversation filled the cozy setting, a low buzz hovering just above the sound of clinking silverware and tinkling glasses. The dining room's rich, warm décor created an inviting ambiance, but despite its welcoming appeal, an edgy tightness had settled between Lily's shoulders. They ordered their food, and though Jack managed to shake whatever it was that temporarily preoccupied him, she, on the other hand, couldn't shake the feeling of unease that crawled its way up her spine. Her Spidey senses, as Carl liked to call them, were tingling.

The house sent a bottle of merlot to the table, and Lily did her best to smile as the sommelier opened the wine, but even its smooth bouquet and fruity peppery bite couldn't ease the tense feeling. Something was up, only she couldn't put her finger on it.

"You okay?" Jack asked, watching her face.

"Yeah, I'm good. I just have this knot between my shoulder blades that won't loosen up," she said, rolling her shoulders for effect. "The weather always seems worse on this side of the river, especially in winter. Maybe it's the wind."

Jack snorted. "Right, because it's so much colder and wetter here than on the other side of the bridge."

"What's that supposed to mean?"

The waiter brought a basket of bread and put it on the table with a small silver container of garlic butter. Jack took one of the long seeded rolls and broke it half. "It means that comment made you sound like a typical Manhattan snob. *'I can't move to Brooklyn, even cabs won't go there!'*" he said in a high falsetto voice.

Lily's mouth fell open, and her eyebrows shot almost to her hairline. "Tell me you didn't just quote Miranda from *Sex in the City*," she asked, tilting her head to the side in amused disbelief.

Biting into his roll, he gestured with the bread in his hand. "Hey, if the high heels fit," he said, chewing.

Oh, no he didn't! Pulling her foot back, she kicked him hard under the table.

"Ow! What was that for?" he said, dropping his roll on the table.

At his stunned look, Lily burst out laughing. "You're kidding me, right? Sticks and stones, Jack, but a swift kick works like a charm when you want to shut someone up. And, by the way, I am not a snob!"

"Not cool, Lily," he said, wincing as he rubbed his shin.

She chuckled, picking up her wine glass. "Cool? I don't know, Jack," she said, shaking her head. "I don't think guys are allowed to use that word once they can quote scenes from chick flicks."

He straightened up and picked up his beer. "Are you done?"

She raised an eyebrow at him. "Are you?"

The waiter interrupted, bringing their salads. "Your steaks should be out soon. Is there anything else I can get you? Some fresh ground pepper, perhaps."

"No, thanks. We're good for now," Jack replied, watching Lily's amused face. "How's your neck, by the way?"

Lily stopped with her wine glass halfway to her lips. Straightening her back, it cracked a bit, but other than that, her muscles were as loose as noodles. "Well, well, well..." she said, smirking.

"Nothing like a little adrenaline rush to help you forget about muscle tension, eh?"

Lily picked up her fork, shaking her head. "Nice. I can only imagine what you'd do if I needed to scare away a case of hiccups."

They sat in relative silence while they ate. Jack's humorous detour may have helped relieve the knots at the back of her neck but did nothing to alleviate the feeling of dread that seemed to seep from the walls.

Whatever it was, it lurked on the periphery of her second sight. With a feather's touch, she sent her senses out, tendrils spreading from her consciousness. In New York City, criminal behavior was never in short supply, and with that in mind, she searched for anything out of the ordinary. She could feel the weight of what lurked like a set of watchful eyes but couldn't find its source. Who was watching, and why was it watching her?

The waiter returned, carrying a large tray, and Lily reeled herself back in. She'd have time again to feel out what was eluding her for the moment, but right now, the tantalizing aroma and telltale sizzle of porterhouse steaks rose along with the steam from the top of their plates.

"Bon Appétit," the man said as he placed the last side dish on the table.

Wine glass in hand, Lily took a sip, watching Jack dig into the aged beef, so large it hung over the edge of his plate. "Enjoying yourself?" she asked, still centering herself.

"Mmmm."

"Good, I'm glad."

Jack swallowed, then picked up his beer and took a sip, watching her from across the amber colored curve of the bottle. "You've barely touched your food, what's the matter? You said things went fine today with Terri's parents."

The waiter filled their water glasses, and Lily smiled up, when he asked if everything was okay. "Fine, thanks." The man put another roll on her bread plate and with a nod, moved to another table.

"Well?" Jack continued.

Lily picked up her butter knife and slid it into the corner of her roll. "Things went great. In fact, better than great. Bev and I had a long talk and we both realized how much we need each other in our lives," she answered, breaking the roll in two with her thumbs.

Jack tilted his head, pointing the tip of his beer in her direction. "You mean *you* realized."

Lily shifted slightly in her seat. "Yes, Mr. Know-it-all...I realized," she said, reaching for the small silver butter dish, and scooping some of the creamy yellow with the edge of her knife. With a couple of quick swipes, she spread the butter, lifting her thumb to her mouth to lick the excess from her finger.

"Glad to hear it. But if that's not what's bugging you, then what? And don't say it's nothing, because the scent of anxiety is coming off of you in waves." He dug his fork into his baked potato, bringing the steaming, sour creamed deliciousness toward his mouth.

She put the buttered roll down on her bread plate, and then

smoothed her fingers against the starched linen napkin resting on her lap.

Sean picked his hunters well. Jack was smart and almost as perceptive as his alpha, but she wasn't about to say anything about what she sensed. She may have picked up on a flutter in the atmosphere, but it was much too premature to do anything about it yet. Telling Jack would only turn him into an overbearing wolf.

Sean would be so proud.

She'd given Jack enough of a heads up already. Perhaps what she sensed was nothing more than a by-product of full moon fever, and it was her turn to have sensibilities go haywire. She still hadn't forgotten how Jack had looked before he left for his run.

"I don't know what's wrong with me. Maybe it has to do with what we talked about earlier. I know you took my head off for calling you a babysitter a few days ago, but after what you said, I can't help but feel like we're back at square one."

"Square one? What did I say?"

She frowned, her brows knitting together as she looked at him. "Jack, you said, and I quote, 'Sean puts my skills on ice at times'. That sounds an awful lot like disgruntled, and I can't help but wonder if it has anything to do with you being here with me, instead of up at the Compound," she said, lifting one shoulder and letting it drop.

"I didn't say *my* skills. I said *our* skills. Sean is the Alpha, and as members of his hunters, each of us is obligated, by more than just loyalty, to obey."

"I understand the political maneuvering going on in your world right now, and with the way you said it, it makes me think you'd rather be in the thick of things up there, instead of down here with me."

A small smirk spread across Jack's mouth as he leaned forward with his forearms on the table. "You know, for someone so smart, you can be really dumb sometimes. And what's with the, *your world,* crap. Last time I checked we were both a part of that world, or does that mean you changed your mind about Sean in the last few days?"

Lily picked up her wineglass but put it down again. "Now, look who's wearing the dunce hat? I never said that, not even close," she shot back with a huff. "But since you're obviously trying to change the subject, it must mean I hit a nerve. Answer my question. And what's all this bull about you being obligated by more than just loyalty? Are you trying to tell me Sean forces you to do things against your will?"

Jack nodded. "Yeah, that's what I'm saying. Not that he ever has, or will," he hesitated, "...only that he can. At least that's what I'm told. As to putting our skills on ice, I was referring to the bedpan duty Sean gave us last month," he answered with a matter-of-fact frown. "It's not exactly the hero-hunter role I looked for when I joined the Hunters. But I get it. I'm one of the newest to join, so shit rolls downhill. "

She raised one eyebrow. "Pun intended, I'm sure."

He chuckled, taking another sip of his beer. "You got that right."

Lily gazed at him still unconvinced. "You still haven't answered my question, though. What about now? Is shadowing me the equivalent of a Hunter on bedpan duty?"

Jack's smirk spread into a full on grin. "Other than you being a royal pain in the ass? No. I volunteered for this assignment. I mean, hey, what better way to move up the ranks then to guard the Alpha's girl?" he added, waggling his eyebrows. "Besides, somebody needs to keep track of what you're up to."

"Me? And what am I up to?"

"Oh, I don't know, how about hunting rogue vampires, for one?"

"Hmmm. And let's not forget the cynical cops I've been hanging out with, and my almost non-existent credentials by the time this is all over, and the fact that Sean is still stuck playing political Russian roulette with a power hungry sociopath."

Jack tapped his fork lightly against the side of his plate, a frown creasing the area between his eyes.

Exactly.

Lily exhaled, picking up her knife and fork. "Who could blame either of us for being distracted? Hell, but this is progress, as far as I'm concerned," she said, gesturing with the utensils. "If this was a couple of months ago, I'd be almost postal."

She sighed. Dramatic much? Count your blessings, things could be much worse. Her stomach clenched. There it was again, that uneasy ripple along her sympathetic nervous system, making her pulse quicken. "Maybe I'll join you the next time you go for a jog. Might take the edge off for me too."

"We could always walk home."

She choked, swallowing a piece of her steak, hard. "From Brooklyn? Are you nuts?"

He pointed his fork at her, bouncing slightly up and down. "Hey, we took the subway across the Williamsburg Bridge, with you insisting the entire way that I needed the whole New York experience. So, once we cross back over the river, why don't we walk home from the Delancy Street subway station instead of taking a cab back from that point?"

Wiping her mouth, she considered him. "You do realize that means walking almost completely across town?" She waited for him to say something, but he just shrugged. "At night," she added to reiterate her point.

Jack shrugged again, picking up his water glass and signaling to the waiter for a refill. "It's only about two and half miles, I clocked it in the cab over from the apartment. Maybe, we can go barefoot in Washington Square Park, like in that 60s movie with Jane Fonda and Robert Redford."

The waiter poured ice water into both of their glasses and topped off Lily's wine. She cut another piece of steak, and dipped it into Peter Lugar's famous steak sauce, letting the combined flavors melt in her mouth.

"I'm starting to wonder about you, Jack. First quotes from *Sex in the City*, and now classic movies. I don't know whether to be impressed or suspicious," she said with a chuckle. "But as to walking back, I suppose we could do it. That is, if it's not raining."

Savoring the taste of the food on her tongue, she mulled over Jack's idea. Maybe it wasn't as dubious a suggestion as she first thought. Plunging herself into the thick of things worked best these days, and perhaps it would give her a better bead on what was making her senses erratic.

Fork and knife in hand, he leaned forward to make his point. "Come on, with your stress levels and my usual peccadilloes compounded by the full moon, we need to head out on foot at some point tonight. So eat up. You're going to need all the energy you can get."

The dessert cart passed, and Jack rubbed both hands together, like a kid. "As for me, I've got my name all over one of those 'Holy Cow' hot fudge sundaes and a piece of New York cheesecake."

Lily raised an eyebrow. "Can you say WerePiglet?"

"Oink, oink."

The two walked up Broadway, past New York University's *Tisch School of the Arts*. The famed university comprised whole area, with student and faculty buildings surrounding the park and its environs. They crossed onto Washington Square Place, two blocks from NYUs *Arts and Sciences* building and the park entrance at Washington Square East.

The unease rippling along Lily's nerve endings had subsided by the time they had finished dinner and left the restaurant. But when they got off the subway and started walking, the feeling of being watched came back with a vengeance. It crawled up her spine and over her shoulder, and the closer they got to Washington Square Park, the louder the warning bells clanged in her head.

She tried to shake it off, but profiling was akin to speaking another language—if you don't use it, you lose it. Except for the few hours she'd spent with Martinez, she hadn't really worked in months. She was out of practice and could almost smell the thin metallic coating of rust on her deciphering skills. Odds were, what she sensed was no more than the average aura of menace hanging like smog over dark corners of the city.

"The Arch is just around the corner. Do you want to head into the park here and walk over toward the fountain, or do you want to head over to University Place and the north entrance?" Lily asked, as they stopped at the corner. Shifting her weight in her boots, she winced.

"Don't tell me your feet hurt, because I know you've tracked creatures for longer than we've been walking."

With a grimace, she shot him a dirty look. "That's easy for you to say, you're not wearing heels. If I had known we'd be traipsing all over lower Manhattan on foot, I'd have worn my shit-kickers."

"You're the one who's supposed to be the psychic."

Grimacing again, Lily toed off her right boot, scooting back to lean against the scaffolding in front of NYU's Silver Center. "I knew you were going to say that. I'm psychic, Jack, not the Amazing Kreskin," she grumbled, rubbing the ball of her foot.

A high-pitched howl cut through the empty street, jerking her back to attention. The sound came from somewhere down University Place, and Lily jammed her foot back into her boot, her senses moving into overdrive. It was a definite cry of pain, but the sound was anything but human.

"I knew it!" she hissed through her teeth. Rusty skills my ass. Grabbing Jack by the arm, she tugged on his jacket. "Let's go."

When he didn't move fast enough, she shot him a look and took off at a run, crossing the street and sprinting down the block in the direction of the arch.

Another agonized wail echoed through the adjacent trees and the flat expanse of the ornamental circle surrounding the park's central fountain. Shit. What the hell has she got pinned? A shifter? She'd never heard a shifter make a noise like that and wondered how many other kinds of supes there were out there, that she'd yet to come across. With the way her life had been going lately, she'd bet the Grimm brothers an entire fairytale full.

Jack came up beside her, his yellow-gold tie fluttering behind him as he ran. "What the hell are you doing?" he asked, grabbing her elbow and pulling her to a stop next to the wrought iron fence surrounding the park's perimeter.

"It's here, Jack. I can sense it," Lily answered, hoping her look told him loud and clear to stay out of her way.

Eyes narrowing, he tilted his head to the side. "Who? The vampire? Here?"

"No, my Aunt Susie. Yes, the vampire. I was in its head at the crime scene, Jack. Remember? Even if the images were residual, it feels like the same imprint. I know it. I can feel it. Tell me that howl didn't raise the hackles on the back of your neck."

Jack let go of Lily's arm and straightened. Exhaling, he put his hands on his hips, pushing his suit jacket back.

"Of course, it did, along with raising the gooseflesh up and down my arms to match. I thought I sensed something when I went out for my run. Things were too quiet." He shook his head and sniffed, wrinkling his nose. "There are supes all over this city, but I just chalked the muted signs up to the garbage and funky smells you all seem not to notice."

His eyes narrowed, and he crossed his arms in front of his chest. "You've been feeling it all along, haven't you? Despite your little tap dance back at the restaurant when I asked what was bothering you."

Lily lifted her chin a notch. "Well, I guess that means we both need to stop second guessing, but that's not what matters now. The vampire is here and based on that pitiful sound I don't think it came to play."

Jack peeled his jacket from his arms and loosened his tie, slipping it over his head and shoving it into his breast pocket.

"Why are you stripping?"

"If I need to phase, I don't want to ruin this jacket. I just bought it."

Lily looked at him and blinked. "Seriously? We've got a

deranged supe in the park across the street from crowded NYU dorms, and you're worried about your outfit?"

With his black slacks, a black shirt, yellow tie and a black sports jacket, he must have gotten his idea of New York chic from watching reruns of the *Sopranos*. He couldn't have looked more Mafioso if he tried.

"Pretty sharp, huh?"

"Like a knife," she replied dryly. "Are you ready?"

"You talkin' to me?"

Lily pressed her lips together. "Don't make me shoot you, Jack."

"What? My Robert De Niro impression making you a little twitchy?"

"Yeah, but only my trigger finger." Ignoring him, she continued down the street, moving at a fast clip, while Jack shadowed her every step. As she approached the north side, she slowed, stopping just short of the ornate, gas style streetlamp outside the entrance to the park.

The arch stood just inside the north gate about twenty-five feet from the sidewalk. Fashioned after the *Arc de Triomphe* in Paris, it was a landmark, despite the ever present homeless sheltering in the gardens to either side.

With a practiced eye, Lily surveyed the area, checking for anyone who might end up as collateral damage, but thankfully, the cold had left the park deserted tonight. A silhouette moved around the base of the tall structure, away from the street side view, scooting behind the far statue of George Washington.

The park was mostly in shadow, despite the light from the full moon, but Lily spotted the figure as it dragged its prey toward the children's playground off to the right of the entrance.

She held her finger up to her lips and motioned for Jack to follow. Sliding her hand into the hidden gun compartment along the outside of her purse, she drew her 9mm. Not that it would do much good against a vampire, but it was better than nothing. The ability to stun and run can sometimes mean the difference between life and death in a business like hers.

Stashing her cell phone, cash, and thin leather credit card case in her other boot she then placed her empty purse under the closest bush.

She shoved the 9mm into the back waistband of her pants and motioned for Jack to stop. Her adrenaline level ratcheted up a notch at the feel of the cold steel against her back, and her focus narrowed even as she expanded her senses. Cold steel or not, it would not do to get blindsided by another predator sniffing around the scent of fresh blood.

She squatted down behind the winter-dead shrubs, thankful again for her choice of black clothing. With her left hand, she slid her boot halfway off her foot and removed two thin, sharp-edged stakes from an inside flap.

Jack's eyes widened when she handed him one of them, but he shook his head, reaching for his belt buckle, instead.

"Don't shift, yet." Lily's voice skimmed across his mind. *"I need to get close enough so I can pick her brain...or what's left of it anyway. I want to try and get a bead on where she's made her lair. If we approach together, the distraction of two attackers might give me just enough of an edge."*

"Man, having your voice in my head feels weird. I've only communicated like that with other Hunters. Kind of sexy..."

"Head in the game, Jack..."

"On three, then?"

"Yeah, but approach with stealth, not like a screaming banshee. Got it?"

"Strength of the wolf is in the pack. After you, alpha-girl."

"Wait! One more thing..."

Lily reached into her pocket and pulled out what looked like a tube of lip-gloss. Dragging the goopy applicator wand over her lips and under her nose, she then handed it to Jack.

"Vicks. It'll help manage the stench."

"How the hell..." he started to ask, but then held up his hand, wand and all. *"On second thought, I don't want to know."*

He smeared the Vicks exactly as instructed, then handed the tube back. Lily shoved it back into her pocket and with a single nod, unfolded herself but stayed in a defensive crouch. Jack did the same but let her take the lead. What did he know? She was the one with all the vamp experience.

She moved out into the open, the stake in her right hand, flattened against her outer thigh. As she walked, its sharp edge dug into her skin through her pants.

Jack flanked her. They were barely five feet from the vampire and its victim, yet still in shadow. Jack's nostrils flared, and he looked at Lily, his eyes puzzled.

She took a step closer, joining the vampire in the reflected light from the streetlamp at the edge of the playground.

"Holy mother of God!"

The female vampire stood over its victim, its lips pulled back over yellow, saliva-coated fangs, horrific in their cold symmetry.

Its victim lay half in shadow, half in the ambient light. *"Lily, if that's what I think it is, then she's feeding on her own,"* Jack's voice was tight in her mind.

Gurgling sounds came from the vampire on the ground, its throat severed almost to its backbone.

This was what was wrong in the atmosphere. Like feeding on like. It didn't add up. Vampires fought, even killed each other for various reasons, but never did they hunt and feed off each other like prey.

The vampire turned and hissed at them. Claw-like fingers, as bloodied as its mouth, swiped at the air, its nails, jagged-edged and caked with gore and dirt.

"Is it female?" Jack said, revulsion clear in his voice, even as it choked through Lily's mind.

"Yes. It's not the same vampire from the crime scene, but she's definitely related."

Just like the vampire from Lily's visions, this one's hair hung in ragged strings, but it was more from dirt and dried blood than from rot.

This one was redheaded, and she was young, both in human years and in vampiric terms. It was obvious she hadn't been a vampire long. Lily shook her head almost imperceptibly. There was something wrong with this vampire, beyond the average 'what's wrong with this picture,' notion of a human turned bloodthirsty predator. This creature was sick, and in the same manner, Lily sensed in the vampire from her visions at the crime scene. Reaching out with her senses, she registered only partial coherence in its thoughts, but blind anger and its craving for blood overrode even that.

It hissed again, shocking Lily back to the present. The vampire took a step toward them, but stopped, sniffing the air. It whirled around, its stench wafting toward Lily and Jack as she turned. Jack gagged, despite the scent of Vicks helping to mask the smell, his eyes widening in shock.

Lily didn't move from her spot, keeping her eyes trained on the vampire and a tight grip on the butt of her stake.

The vampire straightened out of its crouch, its body language still tense, but no longer defensive.

A moan from the injured vampire on the ground broke the silence, pulling the redhead's attention back to its prey. It stood as if torn, wanting to feed, but something else pulling its attention.

"Why isn't it attacking?"

"I don't know. It can see us, it smells our blood, I'm sure of it, but something else has it enthralled."

From the shadows, thick with the stench of rot and old blood, another vampire walked into the moonlit patch of playground.

Lily tensed her grip so tight on the stake, her knuckles looked as if they'd rip through her skin. *"It's her,"* her voice shrilled in Jack head. *"...the one from my visions. She must be the redhead's maker."*

The older vampire was just as Lily remembered from her visions, though she smelled even worse, almost as if she was decaying from the inside out.

One look at the dying vampire on the ground and the older vampire backed-handed the redhead, sending her crashing against the children's slide.

The vampire sniffed the air, whirling toward Lily and Jack, a guttural snarl coming from the back of her throat. Her eyes locked on Jack. Slowly the vampire advanced, her head tilted to the side as if curious or puzzled. She inhaled through her nose, her nostrils flaring slightly and her eyes narrowing.

"I'm guessing your scent is somehow familiar, but it's as if she can't place the smell."

"Great. You can stick around and be a midnight snack. Me? I vote 'no thank you'. She takes another step, and I'm phasing. Let's see how she likes playing with the big dogs."

Lily tried to touch the vampire's thoughts, but the minute she slipped into her head, it roared, ripping its gaze from Jack and settling instead on Lily. Fragmented thoughts raced through Lily's mind, but each laced with pain, both physical and emotional. This vampire had been tortured, and then left for dead.

The vampire's eyes met Lily's, as a flood of remembered pain washed through them both. Lily's knees buckled, and the vampire tore at its hair, wordless screams echoing through the quiet dark. Behind them the redheaded vampire screeched and took off into the park. The older vampire not caring, as it sobbed into itself. Their eyes met again, and a single blood tear fell, leaving a trail of crimson as it dripped down the skull-like face. Lily heard two words murmur back through her mind. They were lucid. They were scared, and they were female. *"Help me".*

In that one second, Lily's mind locked on the vampire's essence, and she saw her for what she was, and what she used to be. In a flash, the image was gone. The crazed creature was back, and with a feral snarl, she leaped over her and Jack and took off into the shadows.

Stake in hand, Lily scrambled to her feet and rushed to the injured vampire. Jack flanked her on the opposite site, standing with his body tensed for action and his feet in a defensive stance. He kept himself half turned toward the darkened park, stake out, ready for anything from any direction.

The vampire on the ground was a young male. With his baby face and hip-hop styled clothing, he looked to be no more than eighteen. Nevertheless, knowing the nature of vampires, he could have been any age. Somehow, though, Lily sensed he was just a kid —by any definition, vamp or human.

The boy-vamp's heart was intact, and though the redhead had ripped his throat from end to end, his head was still attached. He was healing, but much too slowly for such a young vampire.

His gaze flicked back and forth, and though fear expanded its hold from her chest to her throat, Lily approached with caution, her fingers itching for her crossbow. Injured or not, a vampire was still a predator, and there was nothing that got in the way of their blood-lust except death.

Looking at him now, that's exactly what Lily read in his eyes. He wanted to die. But why? None of this made any sense. Vampires rebounded from injury, even near fatal injury, faster than any other supernatural being. At least that was what she'd been told.

"Will you just stake him already before the queen vamp and her court decide to come back?" Jack's voice rushed from his mouth in a harsh whisper.

"Not a chance, Jack. He's been attacked, and if we help him, maybe he'll help us find out who's behind all this. If it's the female vamp, or if she's just a puppet." Lily answered, shrugging out of her coat and rolling it into a ball.

Jack's jaw dropped when he realized what she intended. "Have you lost your fucking mind? You're not seriously going to stick that under the vamp's head, are you? Why not read it a bedtime story?" he asked, throwing his arm up. "We are not nursemaids to the undead! You get too close to that creature, and I promise it will use your blood for a booster shot. Do you hear me?"

Not waiting for a reply, Jack scowled, sticking the stake between his teeth, he dropped to his hands and knees. His body contorted, muscle and bone reshaping in seconds under his clothes, shredding his shirt and pants. A majestic grey wolf stood in Jack's place amid pieces of torn fabric. Baring his teeth, a low, guttural growl rumbled from the back of his throat, directed at both Lily and the vampire, as well.

Lily stood with the rolled up duster in her hands, waiting for Jack to make a move. He chuffed, dipping his big head, and Lily answered with a nod of her own, acknowledging the big wolf and the message she hoped he meant to convey. She glanced down at the vampire. "Do you understand what we've been talking about?" she asked, watching its face and eyes, bracing for any quick movements. She doubted it had enough strength to draw breath, but she stayed in a defensive stance, nonetheless.

The vampire nodded.

"You understand something's wrong, don't you? You're not healing, and you haven't stopped bleeding. I know you can't speak, but I want to prop this under your head to help ease your breathing."

Jack growled, this time chuffing out his warning while he scored the grass next to the vampire with his front paw.

"My wolf friend would like nothing better than to finish what the redhead started and rip that head of yours the rest of the way off," she said, gesturing toward Jack. "The only thing stopping him is me. Understand?"

The vampire nodded again, his eyes moving from Lily to the

wolf and back again. They were full of fear, and Lily's heart squeezed. He was so young, and he was facing death all over again, but this time there was no deposit, no return. A twice cursed vampire.

"We need information, and I think you just might be the one to give it to us. There have been a number of serious attacks..." The vampire's eyes widened, and Lily stopped midsentence. She glanced over at Jack who chuffed again.

She shifted her gaze back to the vampire and crossed her arms loosely in front of her chest. They needed the information, but he was terrorized enough already. The last thing they needed was for the knowledge to die with him because of fear. The incongruity of the situation hit her, as she looked at the poor kid. Vampires, as a rule, were the ones doing the terrorizing, but any idea of payback being a real bitch was lost, as she watched the spectrum of emotion shadow the young vampire's face.

"I guess by that look, you know what I'm talking about. Here's the deal... I have this gift. I can sometimes see things that have happened in the past, and that helps me piece things together to find the cause. I have a strong suspicion your lady friends are involved somehow. Something's wrong with them, but I think you already know that, too."

Jack whined, covering his nose with one paw and then chuffing harder out his nose and mouth.

Lily smelled it too. The vampire's body was giving off a nasty odor, the same rancid smell as the redhead, only to a lesser degree. The older vampire smelled the worst, like true rot, and Lily wondered if it meant whatever this was, was occurring in stages.

She looked back at the vampire. "You strike me as reasonable, even though you don't have much choice. I'm willing to bet that you've made the connection between what's wrong with them and why you're not healing. It's why you want to die."

The vampire's eyes were like saucers now, and he nodded

slowly, blood tears misting his eyes like a red film and spilling over onto his already streaked face.

"I told you, I see things that have happened in the past, but when it comes to supernatural beings, I can sometimes read their thoughts. That's what I want you to help me with. I want to see what you've seen. Hear what you've heard. That way maybe you can help us stop this from happening again—to anyone."

Lily squatted down slowly, her eyes never leaving the vampire. "You try anything, and my wolf friend will gladly give you your death wish, and I guarantee it won't be pretty. Got it?"

The vampire nodded, trying to exhale, but a gurgle of bloody bubbles was all he could manage.

From the side, Lily lifted the vampire's head and fit her coat under its head. Blood pooled, seeping into the soft leather, but at this point, she didn't care. She moved to sit back, except the vampire's hand shot out from the side, grabbing her forearm. He squeezed, not enough to crush bone, but enough to let her know the urgency of time. He was dying, and his eyes searched hers in fear, searching for answers and a way to absolution.

Jack leaped forward, foam dripping from his mouth as he growled and snapped. Lily held up her other hand. "It's okay, Jack. He's just afraid. He knows he doesn't have much time, and he's telling me to hurry before it's too late."

Jack growled an acknowledgement but stayed close, nevertheless.

Lily covered the vampire's hand with hers, and closed her eyes, knowing Jack was primed and ready for the kill should anything happen.

She focused on the image of the vampire in her head, following the thread to the opening he had left for her in his own mind. The vampire met her there at the aperture and invited her in. The irony of the gesture registered in the back of her mind. Vampire's needed an invitation before crossing a threshold, and here she was, invited to enter his mind.

The vampire's image changed the minute Lily's mind merged with his. Suddenly he was young, as handsome as any one of the teenage heartthrobs gracing the cover of pop magazines. He greeted her with a smile, his fangs peeking out, just grazing the top of his lower lip.

"What's your name?" Lily asked, watching her words flutter like feathers in the air.

"Michael."

She nodded, more in acknowledgement than greeting. This wasn't a social call.

Without a word, he raised his arm, and they were surrounded at once by images on all sides, the vampiric version of Disney's circle-vision 360. Lily's mind reeled with the onslaught of his memories in full color, sound, motion, and smell. Her stomach flip-flopped, churning much in the same way it had at the crime scene. It had to be the way the vampire mind worked, how it processed information at the speed of light and sound that caused such vertigo.

Michael showed her glimpses of his human life, the ordinary day to day of school and friends. Then the scene shifted to the night he met the redheaded vampire. How she lured him from the club's dance floor into the bathroom with the promise of quick sex, only to leave him on the tiled floor covered in blood and writhing in pain, as the conversion began.

Lily's heart clenched, realizing Michael's own naiveté had been the means to his lost innocence and stolen life. How many other youths had fallen victims to their own stupid belief of, 'that will never happen to me'? With this creature on the loose, odds were, the stats would increase substantially if they didn't get to the source fast enough.

The scene shifted again, and this time Lily was no longer a spectator. She was there in a dark tunnel with the young vampire, the only sound, the echo of water dripping from the vaulted ceiling as they pressed themselves further into the stone. Following some sort of trail, they moved silently through the passage and out onto the great lawn of New York's Central Park.

Even through the scent of dank water, Michael's newly heightened vampiric sense of smell told them the creature was close. He had found the redhead who had changed him and left him for dead.

From the upper most part of the Bethesda Terrace, they spotted the creature. But she wasn't alone. The older one was with her, and they moved quickly, making their way past the pond toward the trees, but morning was still too far off for them to be heading for cover. What was making them move like that at this hour?

For Lily, it was obvious. These predators were also prey. Tracked and hunted, but by whom?

Her eyes snapped open as she slid out of the vampire's mind. He let go of her arm and slumped back onto the soft leather of her coat.

"You did well, Michael, thank you," Lily whispered, patting his hand. As she moved to push herself to standing, the vampire's hand shot out once more, but this time it was to grab the stake from Lily's hand.

She fell backward with a soft *whoomph*, throwing her arms up to protect herself from his strike.

Michael raised the stake in both hands, but instead, turned the pointed edge toward his own chest. Jack lunged as Lily scrambled to her knees, the realization of what he was about to do dawning on them both.

"No!" she shouted, but it was too late. The young vampire plunged the sharpened tip straight into his heart.

A rough gasp gurgled up from his ruined throat, but a ghost of a smile touched his lips as he slumped down, his body crumpling to ash.

"Michael!" Lily cried, hunched over the molded cinders, but afraid to touch what was left. His silhouetted shape mimicked the bodies found in Pompeii, frozen in volcanic soot at the foot of Mt. Vesuvius.

Her chin dropped to her chest, and her throat tightened as she whispered a quick prayer, Jack whining beside her in reply. The wind surged, encircling Michael's form and whirling the ashes into a mini vortex, before blowing them away like so much New York soot. The words *"Thank you,"* feathered across Lily's mind, and then all was silent.

Jack padded closer, nudging her shoulder with his muzzle. She ran her fingers through his silvery fur, the residual breeze drying her cold tears. "Did you see?"

"Yeah. Thanks for leaving the channel open. Poor guy. Almost makes me sorry for him," he sighed across her mind.

"I know what you mean."

"Your coat's ruined."

"Jack chuffed at the torn pieces of fabric blown all over the sidewalk and the street. *"Yeah, well. All in a day's work, but at least I saved the Jacket and tie."*

"That you did," she said, wiping the wet soot from her face with the back of her hand.

"Come on, I'll let you walk me home."

"No leash?"

"Hey...don't push it," he lifted his muzzle and looked at her with his dark, silver-rimmed eyes. *"You do realize all bets are off. You need to call Sean when we get home."*

"I know," she answered softly, picking up the bloodied jacket and giving it a good shake, biting the inside of her cheek trying not to cry.

"Jesus, Lil', if you're going to continue in this kind of work, you need to stop wearing your heart on your sleeve. What happened to that boy had nothing to do with you, but because of you, hopefully something good will come of it."

"One can only hope," she said with a sigh, refolding her coat before squatting to reach for her purse.

"I'm serious, and you'd better think about it before you call Sean. He hears that tone in your voice and he's going to go ape shit. A shot of Jamison's and a hot shower will help put things in perspective. I'll even pour."

She smiled, pulling at his fur. "Hair of the dog, huh?"

"Ayuh."

Chuckling, she put her hands on her knees, and pushed herself to standing. "Okay then, Fido, let's go home."

CHAPTER

TWELVE

Shifter Compound, Maine

From dense cover, Rafe Miller studied the big wolf as he paced frantically just outside the forest. The wolf's body language spoke volumes, or at least it did to the tracker's trained eye. The animal was tense, distracted, and the tracker chuckled, watching and waiting.

"Like a caged beast," he mused. But it didn't take much skill to guess why. The wolf's obvious distress had everything to do with the full moon riding high in the night sky, but Miller's calculated guess was that it had more to do with the human girl highlighted in the dossier Edward Parr had given him. This particular wolf was the Alpha of the much-scrutinized experimental Compound of Shifters, and Parr wanted him watched.

Miller had earned the nickname *cat's eye* for his expertise in surveillance. He was a rare breed, even as a half-blood. As unusual as it was for a Were Cougar to breed outside its kind, it was even more unusual for half-blood offspring to inherit full-blooded traits.

The tracker took full advantage of the anomaly, using it to add to his mystique.

In the Pacific Northwest, cougars were the ghost walkers of American folklore, secretive and rarely seen. Miller was the best in the country when it came to keeping secrets and keeping tabs, and for some reason, Parr wanted him to keep a close eye on Leighton.

Camouflaged, the cat's sandy brown fur blended perfectly against the weather worn bark of the fallen trees surrounding him. In cougar form, Miller took full advantage of his feline nature, its sharp nocturnal vision and acute hearing.

Surprisingly, he'd been able to track the large wolf without detection, and though he would love to claim his expertise, the fact was, a wolf's sense of smell was just as keen as a cat, a detail that made this situation remarkably telling.

Slinking through the scrub, he followed his gut instinct as well as the Alpha wolf. The night was freezing. But, orders were orders, and Parr was willing to pay extra for this kind of surveillance. He also promised a huge bonus if Miller seized the opportunity to dispose of Leighton, should the chance present itself. No questions asked.

There could be no dirt on the politician's lily-white hands. The big cat hissed quietly. *Lily.* That was the name of the human causing all the problems. Not that he cared one way or the other. A job was a job, and from the look of things, she had the Alpha so torqued it was going to make this an easy kill. *I'll have his throat ripped out before he even knows I'm here.*

Nose up, the cougar sniffed the bitter cold air and took off. Keeping low to the ground, he kept his distance from the wolf and his mind on the payoff. He couldn't care less about the reasons behind the job. Parr would pay through the nose for his services, of that he'd make sure. The politician was a fraud, despite his polished appearance, and the cat saw through his carefully cultivated pretense. He wasn't to be trusted. Lifting his face to the full moon, the sandy gray feline smiled like a Cheshire cat. *Fuck with me, expect to get clawed.*

The cougar stayed downwind of the wolf. Over the years, he'd learned to neither anticipate nor underestimate his prey. As a tracker, he'd been lucky. Of course, size and his natural feline abilities added to his success, but in all his years as a mercenary, Miller had never tracked anything like the wolf he hunted now. The animal was completely absorbed. It was obvious the wolf was in hunting mode, but his scent told the tracker it was rage, not hunger that drove him.

The wolf stopped, sniffing the air and circling. The large canine had caught the scent of something close. Something that didn't belong in these woods. Something big.

Instinct and hundreds of kills told the tracker to hang back. This wasn't going to be a pretty kill. Scenting an abandoned fox den, the cougar hunkered down in the brambles. The fox's scent would mask his for the time being, giving him time to maneuver.

The wolf's hackles rose, the dark, course hair bristling along its spine. A low growl had left his throat before he took off, launching himself through the trees. This was no play for power the wolf was purposeful, and he was looking for a fight.

Miller followed. Picking up speed, he circled around, using his keen sight to gain ground. This was it. Climbing to the low hanging branches of a bare oak, he crouched, waiting for the wolf to pass. The cougar's nose twitched. He was close enough to smell the musk from the wolf's fur, sense the heat from the canine's body and the vibration of his rage and bloodlust coursing through the air. This was going to be one hell of a fight, and the big cat's mouth watered in anticipation.

THE MOON WAS FULL. One more day and his craving for her would be unbearable. Lily had been gone a little less than a week. Sean raised his muzzle to the air and whined. He'd been so concerned about protecting her from the frenzy inherent in a shifter's need to race the moon, he never considered what marking her held in store for him.

Sean knew Parr was biding his time, hedging bets the alpha would abdicate. The wolf growled. Marking Lily was a double-edged sword, and a decision that played right into Parr's hand.

How could he have been so thoughtless? Every shifter under-stood what marking a mate demanded. Sean's inner wolf would never yield to the constraints, and the more time that passed, the more insistent his frustration would grow. The wolf's physical need to mate with his chosen partner would drive him crazy.

He and Lily had barely kept in touch through their shared mind link, choosing instead to communicate through neutral territory, namely, Jack. Deep down, they both knew how exhausting it would be, but for Sean, the torment was exquisite, knowing his need would only intensify as their separation moved from days into weeks. It was like living in a long distance relationship with someone close enough to touch.

Hunting was the only thing that kept the relentless longing at bay. He spent most of his time as a wolf, except for those duties that required him to be present in his human form. Sean reveled in the sheer animalistic pleasure of it—the feel of the earth beneath his paws, the natural scents and sounds of the forest—and what better way to patrol the Compound's perimeter?

The wind was high tonight, and he reached out to Lily, hoping the feel would be as exhilarating for her, but he found her mind jammed up, almost on overload.

Sean sensed it the minute he touched their link, mental alarms buzzing in his head like a swarm of bees. A quick link to Jack told him it was nothing more than just Lily being Lily, and a rush of edgy relief exhaled past his lips. He should have known she would plunge herself into work the minute she got back meanwhile, intense need coursed through his aching body, the current burning a path across every nerve ending with each passing hour. The wolf chuffed, scraping the frozen ground with its paws. The full moon couldn't wane fast enough.

He sent a howl full of frustration roaring over the wind, piercing the night like a dagger. Animals, large and small, took off in all directions at the sound, and Sean raced toward the deep woods in a frenzy of violence and unspent passion.

The wolf was pure alpha, his thoughts frenetic. The words, Hunt... Blood...Kill, rose in a wild frenzy from within. The diverse scents from the forest—fox, deer, even otter, mingled together making his mouth water, but none of them would suffice. He wanted something big. A black bear or even a stray grizzly. Something that would fight back.

He caught the scent of bear as he raced, but another scent lingered on the air, overpowering it. It was subtle, as if purposefully camouflaged, but still strong enough to catch the wolf's attention. With his muzzle to the sky, he inhaled again, but couldn't place the smell.

Unsure, the wolf postured, readying himself. Whatever was skulking in the shadows was his for the taking. Hackles up, the wolf's black lips curled back, exposing his fangs in full attack arousal.

Without warning, the air stilled. The wolf turned, his nostrils flaring as the largest cat he'd ever seen climbed silently down from the branches adjacent to where he stood. *Cougar.* But what the hell was it doing this far east? Mountain lions did not make their homes in New York. In fact, they were considered an extirpated species.

The wolf's eyes followed the animal, and it jumped from the tree trunk to the ground. Hissing, it paced back and forth, its expression calculating and intelligent. So close, the wolf breathed in, tasting the big cat's scent. This was no stray venturing too far from its environs. Nor was it some random happenstance. This cat was a shifter, and someone had sent for it.

Legs splayed, the wolf lowered his head, snapping and growling in a teeth-baring grimace. *"Who sent you? Why are you here?"* Sean tried the common telepathic path shared by most Shifters. One warning—that was all he'd give. He was in no mood to be civil.

The large cat snarled and hissed but didn't answer. Its curved, razor sharp claws scored the frozen earth like butter as it moved fluidly from side to side, advancing slowly.

In its animal state, the cat couldn't bar Sean from breaching the mental walls surrounding its most recent human interaction. Images, clipped and disordered, answered the Alpha's question, and the cat snarled a feline *"fuck you"* in reply.

The wolf's mammoth black shape flew through the air as he launched himself at the mountain lion. Driving it back toward the tree, the huge wolf ripped and tore at the sandy brown cat, locking his jaws around its hind leg. Bones crunched. The cat screamed, the shrill sound penetrating the silent forest. It twisted around, its movements fluid and graceful even through the pain, and with a high-pitched screech, it landed a vicious swipe across the wolf's muzzle. Sean coughed out a yelp, releasing his hold.

Breathing hard, they jerked apart, separate but still circling, shadowing each other's stances. The cougar coiled and lunged, its front paws hitting the wolf in the chest, knocking him backward. With a terrifying growl, it bit down on the wolf's shoulder, ripping through bone and muscle. But the wolf countered, twisting its body out from under the cat's heavy paws.

Panting, the wolf shook itself, splattering blood across the cold ground, causing tiny tendrils of steam to rise from the frost-covered earth. Growling and snapping, the wolf charged again, grabbing the cat by the throat. Ignoring the deep slashes, the cat's claws sliced across his flesh, the two locked together in a deadly dance. Blood stained the earth, mixing with dirt and leaves as it dripped from both animals.

Yanking himself free, the wolf raised his head and howled. The cat's head jerked to the north at the long, low-pitched sound. The pack was coming. With one final lunge, the wolf sank its teeth into the distracted animal's throat. The large cat spasmed once, its body falling silent. The wolf released the cat's throat. The sleek body, silver in the moonlight, slowly transformed back to its human state. The wolf howled once more, the urgent modulation letting the pack know it was over.

He backed up and sat on his haunches to wait. The answering chorus followed by the sound of paws hitting the earth echoed louder as they neared. Steam rose from the blood cooling on the snow and the lifeless body at the center of it all. One by one, the wolves passed through the trees to the clearing. The black wolf yipped, and in a snap of bone and electricity, phased back to human form.

The others followed suit, and within moments, four men stood naked and pumped in the cold wind alongside their Alpha.

"What the hell?" Mitch said circling the pale body lying in the snow. "He smells like a cat, but it's hard to tell what kind with all the blood and musk from the fight. Probably bobcat."

"Cougar," Sean said.

"Cougar? As in Mountain Lion?"

Sean raised an eyebrow. "I just fought the animal, Mitch, what do you think?"

Mitch whistled low. "Big cats like those don't usually venture this far east. What the hell was he doing in our backyard?"

"It was a hit."

Four sets of eyes turned toward Sean. "A hit? As in assassination attempt?"

"Are you planning to question everything I say tonight?" Sean eyed his second.

Mitch grinned. "Sorry. I just don't get it. Who's got a beef with you so big they'd risk hiring an assassin?"

Sean's eyes met his. "I'll give you one guess."

His second in command's eyes hardened. "Just say the word and he's a dead man."

"No. I want blood as much as you do, but this requires finesse or it'll end up spin-doctored, and we won't be able to touch him. Just take the body back to the manor. Don't let anyone see you. I know what I need to do, so just be ready."

SEAN KICKED in the door to the war room, flanked by Mitch and another of his hunters, the tracker's lifeless body wrapped in a blanket and slung over his shoulder. "Good evening, gentlemen. How apropos I find so many of you here, and in such good company," he said, letting the venom drip from his voice.

Almost half the council sat around the fire blazing in the large stone hearth, Edward Parr center stage as usual.

"What's the meaning of this, Leighton?" Ross Stanton asked, pushing himself up from his seat. The colorfully embroidered crest of the Avian Shifters was visible on his shirt pocket.

"Do you want to tell them, or should I?" Sean asked, directing the question openly to Parr.

"I haven't the faintest idea what you're talking about," the older man answered, his face a mask of nonchalance.

"Hmmm. How about assassination? How's that grab you?"

A collective gasp reverberated off the surrounding walls, all eyes turning toward Edward Parr. "This is ridiculous. How dare you barge in here and hurl accusations at me? Where's your proof?" Parr shot back with a dismissive wave.

Sean dropped the dead body at Parr's feet. "There's all the proof I need."

Except for the crackling of the fire, the room was silent. Mitch took a step forward and rolled the body over with a muffled thud. Uncertainty buzzed around the room, but Sean's gaze never wavered as he watched Edward's face.

The man was unperturbed, his expression a mask of complete indifference. "Rubbish. He could be anyone," Parr stated, his Cheshire cat smile cemented in place and his tone as smooth as silk.

However, after spending so much time in wolf form, Sean didn't miss the underlying tang of unease coming from the man, despite his apparent lack of concern.

As if he sensed it, Parr lifted his eyes to Sean, his gaze calculating. "And how convenient for you that he's dead. Now no one can question him."

Sean crossed his arms in front of his chest, his gaze still locked on Parr. "He was a tracker. An assassin, known in certain circles by the name of Cat's Eye. Perhaps you've heard of him, considering he hails from the Pacific Northwest, not far from where you originally came from, Edward."

"Sean, surely you're not accusing Edward of such a heinous crime? It's unthinkable..."

Sean put up his hand. "Don't waste your breath, Stanton. I was in the tracker's head as we fought. I saw everything. But as Edward has so opportunely pointed out, it's too late to question him, although you're all welcome to see for yourselves," he said tapping the side of his head. "Those of you gifted with telepathic ability are more than welcome to the instant replay."

No one moved, but furtive glances rounded the circle, making it clear to Sean and his hunters that Parr hadn't acted alone.

Sean frowned. He reached into his jacket and pulled out a set of falconer's gloves, the same set given to him when he had accepted the call to be Alpha. Smacking them across his palm, he then threw one of the wide leather gauntlets to the floor between Parr and the dead tracker—the Alpha's crest emblazoned clearly on the cuff for all to see.

"All bets are off. As the Alpha of the Brethren, I hereby dissolve this council and retain complete rule by right of blood. I also claim Lily Saburi as my chosen mate. She is, by my decree, the Alpha Female. By clan law, anyone who brings harm to her, dies."

"Leighton! You have no right!" Ross Stanton shouted over the din of the other council members.

Sean turned toward him. "Oh, yes I do, Stanton. I have every right, given to me by each of the clans when they gave me their blood and their oath. The diplomacy we shared was by choice—my choice. You and the rest of your cronies abused my trust and my loyalty. It is, therefore, now my choice to rescind that diplomacy, and reassert my sovereign right as Alpha."

Edward's face was a still a mask of calm, but Sean knew the wheels were already turning behind his composed facade. The tracker was only round one.

Sean turned his full attention to Parr. "You wanted the return of the old ways, Edward? You got it. You want to challenge me? You got that too. By decree, fights are held in a blood arena and are to the death, where there are no words for you to spin and nowhere for you to hide. Think you could handle that?" Without waiting for an answer, Sean turned on his heel and stormed out.

THE POWER WINDOW whined as it rolled a quarter of the way down between the front and back seats of the posh black Lincoln. "Just pull the car around to the back of the house." Edward Parr said, his eyes the only thing visible from behind the smoky glass.

The driver glanced into his rear view mirror. "Yes, sir. Would you like me to park and wait?"

"That won't be necessary." Parr pressed his finger to the console on the side of the door and closed the window between them. The last thing he was in the mood for was a chatty, inquisitive driver.

He pinched the bridge of his nose and closed his eyes, squeezing against the pressure pounding his head from the inside out. Things were not going according to plan, but then again, when did they ever? Miller had failed, unfortunately, him ending up dead instead of Sean. To make matters worse, the tracker hadn't been astute enough to keep Leighton out of his head, thus implicating Parr in the assassination attempt. Exhaling, he ran his hand though his hair and opened his eyes.

His eyes narrowed, despite the dim light. He'd have to keep a low profile for a while, until some other opportunity presented itself to take the spotlight from him.

Parr was used to relying on his wits to succeed, and over the years had mastered the art of contrivance, of exploitation and subterfuge. An outcast without a pack, he never knew what it was to have strength in numbers. He was a loner, a throwback, a genetic anomaly forced to rely on his own instincts for survival.

His kind was believed extinct for millennia. Yet, latent recessive genes, from years of prehistoric crossbreeding had somehow become manifest in his bloodline. Combine that with the preternatural nature of shifters, and voilà, the last American Lion, once the most feared predator in both North and South America, was reborn.

If it could happen once, then it could happen again. Parr had experimented with cross breeding and mutation and eventually found a way to bring the big cats back from the brink. Of course, they weren't exactly the same as their ancient ancestors, but they were close, with a few added talents thrown in just for kicks. The American Lion would once again rule all Shifters, and humanity would fear them the way they had once upon a time. Now he just needed the right host. A woman.

His dream was within reach, and to make sure it came to

fruition he'd have to sharpen his claws even more. Across Leighton's throat... he thought with a smirk.

The car swung wide onto the long drive, the tires crunching through unplowed snow. The house up ahead appeared to be deserted, just as he'd requested. Marcus had done well in choosing this latest venue. One of Leighton's 'hunter's in training', the Alpha had misapplied the boy's talents, keeping him pigeonholed at a computer with mundane internet searches. Of course, it didn't take much to coax Marcus into switching sides, and with the promise of doing real Intel dangled in front of him for good measure, he gave up the goods on Lily without question.

The sleek, black sedan came to a stop just to the right of the snow-covered porch. Its railings and supports had seen better days, with the weight of the snow adding to its imminent collapse at any moment. Two icicles hung from either side of the pitched roof like a set of jagged, crystal fangs. Parr's lip curled, and his crotch tightened.

Vampires were a taboo in their world, but his proclivities had always leaned toward the forbidden. The remembered feel of icy cold incisors against his skin had set his mouth to water. His gaze flicked to the small rectangular windows dotting the foundations edge, and his cock thickened even more.

"Are you sure this is the right address? By the look of things, I don't think anyone's been here for a while."

"This is the correct address, so if you would just get the bags..." Parr's voice trailed off, letting the distain in his voice finish the sentence for him.

"Been driving people around these parts for years, but I never even knew this place existed. Who'd a thought, right off the main road like that...bam, a farm? Would you like me to clear a path to the door?"

"No, that won't be necessary. Just get my bags."

The driver got out, making his way around to the back of the car, opening the rear passenger door as he passed. Stepping out into the ankle deep snow, Parr followed him around to the trunk.

"Here you go," the driver said, placing the bags on the ground.

He never heard the shot.

The bulkhead door to the storm cellar opened, and a stocky young man in a fur-lined parka poked his unkempt head up through the partitioned steel.

"Get the bags, and then have someone clean up this mess," Parr said, as he walked toward the enclosure, gesturing toward the steaming circle of crimson spreading under the rear tire. "Good job on the location, Marcus."

With a raised eyebrow, he looked at the young man's coat. "Planning a trip to the tundra or are you telling me there's no heat inside?"

"No heat in the concrete corridors leading down to the bunker, sir. Been patrolling non-stop, ever since...well, you know..." Marcus answered quickly, flinching somewhat. Parr's temper and lack of tolerance was something no one in his command wanted to incite.

"Yes, that was an unfortunate, if not entirely unexpected complication," he said, pulling his gloves tighter onto his hands. His gaze lifted. "I was under the impression you had taken care of that situation weeks ago, so why the need for patrols at this point? What haven't you told me, Marcus? You know how I hate surprises."

"We did take care of it, just as you instructed. But it appears things didn't go as expected, again."

"...and?"

"According to tracking and intelligence, the situation has resolved itself..."

"Where?" Parr asked, cutting the young man off midsentence.

New York. Manhattan, specifically." Marcus held his breath waiting for the explosion.

Parr's mouth spread into a wide grin. "New York City. You're positive?"

Stunned at his reaction, Marcus nodded. "Yes sir. Also, the latest report from our mole says the girl is headed that way, as well. Cochran is being sent as escort."

Parr threw his head back and laughed. "Cochran? He's a fool. I couldn't have asked for better news."

"Sir?"

"Do what I said and get the bags. When you have the mess out by the car taken care of, grab Leon and Tony and meet me in my office. We have a lot to discuss before I head back to the Compound."

CHAPTER
THIRTEEN

I t was close to two a.m. when they finally got back to the apartment. Jack had phased to human the minute they hit the lobby, scaring the hell out of Mrs. Kwon as she poked her nose out of her apartment door. The poor old woman screamed so loud, Jack phased back, probably figuring a big, grey dog in the lobby was a hell of a lot easier to explain, than some random naked man. Lily shook her head. Jack still didn't get that this was New York.

Too tired to sleep and too wound up to call Sean, Lily finished washing and drying what was left in the sink from breakfast. There was nothing like mindless work to settle your brain and help you think clearly—that and a quick shot of Jameson's eighteen year old, limited reserve.

"Can you take this downstairs to the curb?" she asked, handing Jack the garbage.

"Now?"

"Yes, now. If we don't do it now, we'll miss the morning pick-up," she said, hanging the damp dishtowel over the drying rack.

Grumbling, he took the bag and headed down the stairs,

smirking as she called after him to keep his paws off her neighbor's cat, and his clothes on if he ran into Mrs. Kwon.

For the most part, Jack had listened while she reiterated what she saw in Michael's mind, even though he had seen for himself via the channel she supplied.

He let her talk as she washed the dishes, not really saying much, almost as if he knew she needed to go over it in her own mind just to be sure. Both agreed Sean needed to be told, but Jack wasn't too keen on telling the police. Telling him Martinez already knew, went over like a lead balloon.

Lily should have known better. No supe liked to have their existence outed, but her gut told her the detective was smart enough not to dismiss something outright just because it was outside the box. Martinez had his own brand of sixth sense, and that had to count for something.

Rubbing her lower back, she headed down the hall to her room. All she wanted was a hot shower and her pillow, but somewhere in between the two, she needed to call Sean. She gathered up her toiletries and plugged her cell phone into the charger. Plain and simple tonight, that's all she had strength for, so if that meant using human means of communication, then so be it. Just the idea of a telepathic battle with Sean exhausted her more than she already was.

He wasn't happy with her being in New York to begin with. Add her involvement with hunting a rogue vamp to the equation, and it wasn't hard to guess what he'd say. But she was prepared. If he went all Alpha Male on her, well then...sorry...click. Sean wasn't stupid, though. He understood her well enough to know she would never just sit back and let humans handle things by themselves. It would be tantamount to signing their death warrants.

Her apartment had only one bathroom, and it was in the hallway. Armed with her fleece bathrobe and pajamas, Lily closed the door behind her and turned the lock. If Jack had to use the facilities, he'd just have to hold it until she was through. Then again, he could always head back downstairs and lift a leg against the nearest tree.

She turned on the tap and brushed her teeth. Running a hand through her tangled hair, she grimaced at the dark smudges beneath her eyes and the hollows in her cheeks. Sean would hate how tired she looked. Not that he would say anything, though. To him, she always looked beautiful. God, she missed him.

The bathroom was small, and like most apartments in the city, it took forever for the shower water to warm up. The complete opposite of the luxury she shared with Sean up at the Compound.

With a sigh, she pulled the ivy patterned lace curtain back and stepped into the tub, making sure to spread the clear plastic liner evenly across the inside of the porcelain. The water was finally hot, and she turned, allowing it to cascade across her chest and back. She drenched her head, closing her eyes and sighing as the warmth and steam went to work loosening the knots in her neck and shoulders.

Humming the theme song to *Charmed,* she wiped the water from her eyes, and then reached for her shampoo to lather, rinse and repeat, as the familiar words and tune numbed her thoughts. She finished up, rinsing the soap from her body, but stayed in the warmth and the heat, enjoying the peace and the mindless roar of the water pouring from the showerhead.

As she stood in the spray, a sudden chill crept over her skin, giving her goosebumps despite the moist heat. The sensation of wind, bitter cold and howling, caressed her skin and her mind.

Sean.

He was in wolf form. She'd know the wild animalistic feel of him anywhere. His need hit her full force, as did his growing frustration waxing full right along with the moon. Sean did his best to hide it from her, but they were so connected, she knew his discomfort the minute their minds touched.

She sighed, but the sound was full of regret. Her body craved his too, but unlike hers, his need was primal, driven by a desire more lunar than love starved.

His mind was a barrage of want, buffeting at hers at every turn since she left Maine. It was exhausting, and after the day she'd had, the last thing she wanted was to deal with Sean and his amped up sex drive. Moreover, she hadn't had the chance to talk to him, to tell him what she had found out.

He had warned that things would get wilder the closer they got to the full moon, but he'd never said a thing about how their separation would worsen the effect on him. Sean was in agony, and her heart broke. But as things stood at this moment, he would have to wait. Guilt washed over her like a cold rain despite the heat from the shower. But what else could she do? She needed Sean rational so they could figure out what to do, and if that meant putting a lid on his libido for the time being, then so be it.

She pulled the shower curtain back and stepped out of the tub, wrapping a long, thirsty bath sheet around her body, humming even louder. Sean was in the back of her mind, and she sighed. *Lily...* he called, and she sighed, again. *Ding, ding...round one.*

It was dark, but the full moon hung high in the blackness, illuminating the trees in silver light. *"Lily..."* His voice held a desperate edge even as it brushed gently across her mind.

He heard her humming, as she tried to drown out the feel of his voice in her mind. The sensation of warm water and the gentle rasp of a sea sponge feathered back along their shared path. She was in the shower, and his groin tightened, even as his paws scored the earth.

The wind picked up, and he howled, the sound like a lover's lament reverberating through the trees. He let the sound carry a caress, soft but insistent against her lame attempt at ignoring him.

He sent an image of her, wonton and wet, from the last time the two shared the shower together. Her hair wild and hanging in wet strands clinging to her breasts, her chest heaving as she straddled him on the marble shower bench. He sent the memory of how she'd looked to him as she climaxed, with her eyes dark and dilated with need.

Lily moaned, and the sound echoed through his mind. Her body tingled, the feel echoing through him as the ghost of his hand skimmed across her belly to stroke the juncture between her legs. *"Lily...I need you."* His voice was a pure growl, rough with desire.

The pull of the moon stirred his body as it rose to its zenith in the sky. Her body reacted intuitively to his, and his craving for her filled her mind, overwhelming her. With a shove, she forced him to the back of her mind, his ache and her guilt flooding them both completely.

He was as relentless as the animal living inside him. More images flowed, filling her with his desperation. He showed her his body, tense and aching as he tried to give himself release, his hand working his cock, but the wolf inside him refusing to be satisfied. *"Lily, I am on the edge of insanity. I need you."*

Lily turned the water off, twisting the knob with a jerk of her hand. Through their mind link, Sean saw everything, felt everything and she let the full force of her own frustration flow through. He was not the only one who was torn. There was more involved here than just the need to satisfy pheromones.

Barefoot, she grabbed a towel and wrapped it around her, humming loudly as she charged out of the bathroom, dripping across the cold, hardwood floor. Through her window, she gazed up at the same moon that had him pacing like a caged animal, the wind whipping at him. *"Sean...I want you too, but I want you here... there's too much going on."* The words drifted past, along with her silent plea for the full moon to be done with, soon.

Lily rested her palms on the ice-frosted glass, her mind and body at odds. Sean felt so close, but the glass beneath her fingers might as well have been a chasm between them.

He howled, the sound mournful and heart wrenching, but Lily felt the underlying violence beneath the surface. Sean was walking a razor's edge, and she prayed she hadn't pushed him over the precipice.

"Please Sean, Stop this. I need you...I think I'm in trouble."

Lily froze. Sean was all of a sudden lucid. The hardwired need to protect and defend had completely overruled his cock.

"Does this have anything to do with why I couldn't reach you this afternoon?"

"Yes."

"Where's Jack? Does he know? He told me everything was fine..."

"He knows. But only just..." she hesitated. *"I was going to call you after I got out of the shower. We have a huge problem, Sean. There's a vampire wreaking havoc in the city. We saw it tonight. I was in its mind, but I'm telling you, something's wrong with it. Whatever it is, I swear it's familiar, but not."*

"A vampire? Are you sure?"

Lily pressed her lips together. Didn't anybody trust her assessment these days? *"Yes,"* she shot back, allowing visual and olfactory images from the scene at the park to filter through their link.

Sean's growl was as menacing as it was worried. *"Tell Jack, I'm on my way."*

Sean coasted down the highway heading toward the Henry Hudson toll bridge, just north of Manhattan. He was making good time, considering GPS set his arrival at just over five hours before reaching Lily's apartment. The roads were clear, and if luck held, he'd be at her front door in about a half hour.

It felt like days since he'd briefed Mitch and his hunters about the situation in New York. While they were privy to what was going on and where he headed, Sean had instructed them to say nothing. As far as the disbanded council was concerned, the Alpha was otherwise occupied with a full investigation into the recent assassination attempt.

Mitch had full authority by proxy while Sean was in New York, with the complete understanding he would supply the alpha with a daily dossier of all Edward Parr's comings and goings. Not one of his hunters balked at the idea of Sean going to New York, not when they learned it was to investigate a rogue vampire. Shifters and vampires were notorious enemies, yet their differences were set aside when it came to protecting their mutual anonymity. An unwritten truce existed for the greater good of keeping both their worlds hidden.

As to keeping things at home status quo, Mitch and the boys would keep Parr in check. Sean doubted anything overt or premeditated would happen, not in the time he planned to be away, and certainly not after the way he'd dealt with the tracker. Parr might be many things, but he wasn't stupid, and he had to know Sean's hunters would be on high alert.

With accusations fresh on his heels, Parr would lay low, but not for long. The ruse of gathering intelligence was the one cover Parr would buy, and if he proved himself more foolish than Sean or Mitch anticipated, perhaps this trip would then rid the supe community of two evils, one as cunning as the other, and both just as parasitical.

It had taken the better part of the day to tie up loose ends at the Compound, with Sean's inner wolf gnawing at his gut every moment he was delayed. However much he wanted to just dump everything and run, his conscience would never allow it. Being the Alpha came with price tags and putting the concerns of the pack before his own wants was one of them.

Clouds covered the night sky, obscuring the moon. The air was both cold and heavy a sure sign snow was on the way. However, a winter squall wasn't the only storm brewing. Sean's entire body reacted when Lily's visions filtered through their mind link, and the violence of the attack wasn't the only thing to cause his hackles to rise.

Lily had said that something wasn't right, and as usual, the woman's intuition was dead on. He sensed it too, but the images and emotion he'd read were not firsthand. They had been compromised, slanted through no fault of her own, by Lily's knee-jerk reaction to what she had witnessed. Understandable, of course, considering how horrific the images, but he needed to make his own evaluations.

Based on the severity of the situation, and the violent, not to mention, overly conspicuous nature of the attacks, it was curious that vampire adjudicators hadn't yet moved to have the rogue destroyed. When it came to policing their own, vampires were the Nazis of the supernatural world. In the grand scheme of things, they had the most to lose. Aversion to daylight and subsisting on human blood limited their ability to coexist with humanity. But for thousands of years they had managed to do just that, with only a few rogue instances giving birth to folklore and legend, and eventually Hollywood's fascination with their kind.

It had taken vampires years to recover from Vlad Țepeș and his little hiccup in history, not to mention Elizabeth Báthory and her penchant for bathing in virgin blood. The advent of modern science and the industrial revolution almost won them back their anonymity—that is until Irish novelist, Bram Stoker, rekindled the fervor. His gothic melodrama, *Dracula*, had paved the way for countless stories of romanticized vampires, forever fighting against their base nature in search of love and redemption.

This new depiction presented a double-edged sword for the vampire council. Newly created vampires bought into the idealized hype, finding the dangerously romantic role intoxicating enough to try to live it outside the boundaries of their kind. Sean had heard stories of how tribunals had tripled in the last few decades alone, as adjudicators tried to keep rein on the havoc triggered by the new guise. The situation forced the council to reevaluate some of its ancient laws. He chuckled, shaking his head.

Tell me about it.

Truth be told, Supes were no different from any other society of beings on this planet. Either you adapted, or you died. Period. He just wished Parr and his flock of sheep would see it that way. Sean exhaled. No, Parr knew it all right he just twisted it for his own gain. Perhaps the Vamps had it right. No questions. No quarter. No second chances.

The Westside Highway was a deserted straightaway, tempting Sean to blow through the traffic lights once he reached 57th street, and speed south toward Jane Street. He could almost smell her, and the thought of how close they were shot jolts of anticipation into his groin. The idea of waking her with telepathic foreplay, and having her wet and waiting for him when he got there made his cock jerk, but he'd had enough of the Werewolf version of phone sex. He wanted Lily in the flesh, warm and willing and in his arms. Just ten more minutes...

The small-intertwined streets of lower Manhattan were a night-mare to navigate, but he managed to keep his focus on driving instead of on the promise of Lily's warmth. He wound his way around Abingdon Square, craning his neck at the postage-stamp sized area the city deemed a park.

GPS had him bear left off 8th Avenue. "Finally," he thought, and turned the car onto Lily's street. Searching for a parking space, he raised an eyebrow at the tree-lined sidewalks and quaint cobble-stoned street, surprised to see neighborhood shops nestled between the buildings, and a charming corner bistro with its colorful awning and café seats. He smiled to himself. New York might be a concrete jungle but leave it to Lily to find a place of beauty nestled within its madness.

Forewarned, he wasn't surprised that parking was practically non-existent, so he rounded the corner again pulling instead into one of the city's many 24hr parking garages. Talk about a racket.

"How long you gonna be, Mac?" the attendant asked, handing Sean his claim ticket.

"A few days, and I'll probably be in and out a lot," he answered, handing the man his keys and a fifty-dollar bill. "Park it short if you can. Traffic here is bad enough, and I don't like to wait if I can help it."

The attendant took the money, stashing it in his pocket. "You got it, chief."

Like everywhere else, money talked, and with a nod, Sean walked out of the garage, turning left to head the two blocks over toward Lily's place. The street was deserted, not a sound except for a few stray cats, at least he hoped they were cats, but considering the fabled size and prevalence of New York City rats, he wasn't so sure.

The sky was almost completely devoid of stars, and the glare from the streetlights cast a garish sheen across the dirt-splotched sidewalk. His footsteps echoed in the dark quiet, and combined with sound of sirens in the distance, gave the night a certain film noir quality.

He crossed the street and stepped up onto the curb in front of Lily's red brick walk-up. Glancing up, he watched a female silhouette pass behind lace curtains on the top floor, and his body hardened.

It was her.

Squelching an overwhelming urge to scale the fire escape, he pushed his way through the building's street entrance only to find the inside door locked.

Peering through the glass, his fingers closed around the doorknob, leaving dents the dull brass. With a low growl, he considered crushing the lock, but didn't. He pulled his hand back, digging his fingers into his palm, instead. She was so close.

His eyes scanned the tenant list for her name, but the door clicked open before he even unclenched his fist. She knew he was here. Anticipation flooded his body with adrenaline, and he took the stairs three at a time, his blood pulsing through his veins.

Lily's scent thickened in the air with each step, sending his inner wolf to near madness, shredding his tenuous grip. He rounded the top landing, and there she stood, waiting for him in the doorway with a ready smile.

"Sean..."

Her words cut off along with her breath, as he threw her over his shoulder. Without missing a step, he slammed the door with his foot, ignoring her protests as he headed down the hall in search of a bedroom.

"Sean..." she tried again, only to be silenced with a savage kiss. With another low growl, he pushed the bedroom door open and deposited her on the mattress, sliding himself along her full length.

He kissed her more, his fingers slipping beneath the front of her robe, her bare skin silky and warm beneath the flat of his palm. Lily shivered as his hand traveled across her belly, searching out her full breasts. He teased her, cupping the full weight of one in his hand, his thumb grazing the ridge of her taut nipple. Her breath hitched in her throat, and the sound jolted straight through his groin.

"Open for me Lily," he said, his voice deep and rough with need. He squeezed her breast, rolling her nipple between his thumb and forefinger while devouring her mouth with another kiss.

Her fingers fumbled with the knot on her belt, but the soft cotton refused to budge. Her moan of frustration was answered by a smooth, seductive half grin as Sean tore the fabric in two and with a single twist.

He pushed the front edges of her robe apart, exposing her naked flesh. A warm flush crept its way across her creamy skin, from her bare thighs to her throat, staining her cheeks with desire.

Sean's nostrils flared at the scent of her wet arousal, and he half moaned, half growled, rolling her onto her stomach and ripping the rest of her robe from her body. He could wait no more.

Lily read his urgency and came up on all fours, her hair splayed across her back, arching, and pushing her swollen sex toward him, hearing his sharp intake at the wetness glistening between her legs.

Sean grabbed her hips, grinding himself against her, his cock throbbing as he rubbed himself across her slick entrance. Leaning across her back, he cupped her breasts, rolling her nipples again, before trailing one hand down over her chest and belly and delving his fingers into her moist cleft. His thumb circled her taut, swollen nub, her juices dripping.

Lily gasped, moaning and grinding herself further into his hand. Sean's inner wolf snarled, its need to dominate, to take its chosen mate overwhelmed him. Gripping both her hips, he dragged Lily up and back, driving his thick, corded cock into her wetness. Her cries turned to moans of pleasure as he thrust, pushing his engorged member deeper and harder.

His body shivered, every muscle taut and hard, pulsing along with his cock. He pulled back, and ignoring her protests flipped her onto her back, impaling her with a single stroke. He rode her hard, lifting her legs to delve even deeper. Lily's body trembled, slick against the rock hardness of him, her thigh muscles burning and straining to hold on as he thrust harder and faster.

Sean's upper and lower canines descended, hurtling him toward the edge of sanity. He needed her in submission, his alpha female, his wolf-bitch. With a feral growl, he flipped her onto her stomach and pulled her hips back, driving himself into her again and again, his cockhead swelling to near bursting. He bit down on Lily's shoulder just as he had before she'd left, his body shuddering in climax and his inner wolf snarling in unleashed conquest. Lily threw her head back in a swirl of pain and pleasure, her inner walls convulsing in time with Sean's release.

Time stood still for a moment, neither daring to move until the last waves receded and they slumped forward on the bed, panting and sweaty.

Lily pushed her hair back from her face and peered up at Sean from behind her shoulder. "I guess this means you can't live without me, huh?" she said, kissing his fingers as they came up to stroke her cheek.

"You could say that," he answered, his voice still rough and growly. He pulled back, trailing his fingers down her damp back and smacking her butt as he withdrew.

"Hey!"

"You didn't seem to mind my smacking that part of you a minute ago," he said with a grin.

"That's completely different."

"Hmmm...and here I thought you liked it rough."

"Me? You're the one doing the caveman impersonation, throwing me over your shoulder like a sack of grain. What's up with that, anyway? Did you really think I was going to turn you down?"

He smirked, tucking a piece of stray hair behind her ear. "I told you I was on the brink."

"Brink? That's the understatement of the decade. Is this what I have to look forward to every month?" she asked, tilting her head a bit.

Sean looked down at Lily's fingers as she absently traced the pattern on her duvet cover, a sexy smile spreading toward the corner of his mouth. His gaze flicked back to hers. "Only if you want it to be."

Lily laughed, giving his shoulder a gentle shove. "Ha! Typical male answer."

"So, you're saying you didn't enjoy yourself?"

Lily's face pinked, and the color was glorious against her creamy complexion. She was tough as nails, but he loved that he could still make her blush.

"No, but..."

Sean's lips silenced any further reply. He broke their kiss, resting his index finger over her lips. "Ssh. I missed you. Let's just leave it at that, okay?"

His initial urgency for her had ebbed, however, as Lily looked at him, one glance told him her antennae were up and pointed his way.

"What's going on, Sean? There's something you're not telling me."

He blinked but didn't answer. Damn that mind of hers.

"Sean..."

If he told her there had been an attempt on his life, she'd be gunning for Parr before he even finished speaking. Not that he could blame her though, not when he'd do the same. Like it or not, the attack had actually bought them some time. Time for him to be here, with her.

"Lily, it's nothing, just Parr grasping at straws. He tried, he gambled, and he lost. Nevertheless, I took care of it, and now he's off somewhere licking his wounds. Trust me, his miscalculation cost him, and he won't be trying anything else for a while. I'm here now, and Mitch has everything under control, so there's nothing to worry about."

"If you say there's nothing to worry about, then how can I argue? Parr tried a different approach...okay. What kind of approach? Is that why you were in wolf form for days, or can't you tell me?"

"Lily, I'm tired, that's all. Having to deal with Parr, while at the same time trying to keep a lid on my libido, is just exhausting. Of course, I feel a whole lot better, now," he said, rubbing his knuckles over the swell of her breast.

Lily chewed her bottom lip. He could see the wheels turning in that head of hers, but at least there was no steam coming out of her ears. Not yet, anyway. The only steam he wanted tonight was the kind generated between the sheets.

She lifted her hand, resting her palm against his cheek, and a familiar prickle danced along their shared mind path.

Lifting one eyebrow, he gently took her hand from his cheek and held it in his. "Don't you trust me?" he asked, sending her a mental kiss, while at the same time redirecting her out of his head.

"Of course, I do, but..." she said, hesitating.

"Then leave it, Lily," he told her, linking his fingers with hers. "We'll both be back in Maine soon enough, and you can have full access to the files, both in my desk and in my head. Right now, we need to focus on what you sense here. If it seems familiar, like you say, then perhaps there's a connection to the Compound. Vampires are no joke under the best of circumstances, and I want you sharp. No distractions, not even me. Even a Shifters accelerated healing is no match for a full on vamp attack. You're still human, Lily, and that makes you completely vulnerable."

She considered him for a moment. "Jack said the vampire council would consider me a shifter, regardless of the trace amount of Jerard's blood in my system. He thinks I've put us in a precarious position, working with the police on this case and all. Is he right?"

Sean let go of her hand and sat up, running his fingers through his hair. "Technically, yes. However, you are also the alpha female. I took care of that before I left the Compound."

"Took care of it? How?"

He flashed a sheepish grin her way. "Since we're talking in technicalities, I basically took back what was mine. I disbanded the council and took back the traditional role of alpha, naming you as my mate. That should give you enough status to circumvent any trumped up legalities the vamps might throw at us."

Lily sat up as well, hooking one leg under the other. "Wait a minute, disbanded the council? Why? Is this because of me? Does this mean the debate over my acceptance by the pack is over?"

"Technically yes, but in reality, no. I threw down a gauntlet, literally, telling Edward if he wants to challenge me as Alpha, it will have to be done old school."

Technicalities. The word was starting to get on her nerves. Lily exhaled, her eyes narrow and questioning. "What does that mean?"

Sean shifted on the bed, lifting Lily's hand to his mouth and kissing the tips of her fingers. "It means simply, if Edward wants to be Alpha he has to fight me for it."

Lily burst out laughing. "Fight you? Oh brother, how quickly did he turn tail and run?"

Sean smirked, shaking his head. "He's got a good poker face, but I think my dictate made everyone think twice about the prospect, Edward included. He'll never agree to a blood arena, especially not when the rules state it's a fight to the death."

Lily's eyes widened, and she swallowed hard. "You didn't mention the fight was to the death. That son-of-a-bitch is sneaky, and he'll cheat anyway he can. I don't like it, Sean. Not one bit," she said, shaking her head.

Now it was his turn to laugh. "What's the matter, do you doubt my abilities? Where's your faith, alpha girl?"

Lily shot him a dirty look. "I don't doubt you. What I doubt is your hunter's intel, and their ability to flush out Parr's con before you end up dead."

Slipping his arm around her waist, he pulled her to standing. Leaning down, he kissed the tip of her nose. "That's what I have you for, my beautiful stealth weapon," he said with a grin. "No one can get in and out of people's heads like you. They won't even know what hit them."

Lily leaned back, searching his eyes. "My abilities aren't exactly state secrets. They all know what I can do, and I doubt they've forgotten my little display in the war room. Don't you think they'll expect some kind of telepathic surveillance? I wouldn't put it past them to plant false information just to throw me off the scent."

He shook his head. "Edward is cavalier, and overly confident. If he thinks you're still exiling yourself in New York, he'll believe he has us at a disadvantage. They know what you can do when you're close by, but none of them know about your long-range capabilities." He waggled his eyebrows and kissed her mouth hard. "But enough about that. I'm hungry, woman! Then after you feed me, I'll throw you over my shoulder again and show you just how caveman I can get."

Lily laughed, but her eyes never left his muscled thighs as he pulled on his jeans. He left his fly undone and standing there with his bare chest and the subtle invitation of what waited for her south of his belly button left her mouth watering. "Whatever you say, baby...you Tarzan, me Jane."

CHAPTER
FOURTEEN

A delicious soreness greeted Lily as she stretched, her feet searching out Sean's under the downy comforter. She shifted, wincing at the familiar yet satisfying twinge in her thighs, twisting to mold herself to Sean's broad back, softly rising and falling with each breath. He was still asleep, but as far as she was concerned, he'd more than earned his rest. "You're amazing," she murmured, snuggling in closer.

"You're not so bad, yourself," Sean's deep voice answered, still rough with sleep.

His voice and the memory of how he'd filled her, sent jolts through her lower abdomen and a fresh dampness slicked between her legs. Her eyes closed, and a secret smile spread into a full on grin against the warmth of his back. With a sigh, she slipped her arm under his elbow, curving it around his waist. "Good morning," she said, kissing his shoulder.

She breathed in the clean, masculine scent of his skin and sighed, resting her cheek against his shoulder blade. At the contented sound, he twisted to face her, his gaze taking her in as if memorizing the contours of her face. "That it is," he murmured back, brushing her lips with a soft kiss.

Scrunching up her nose, she rubbed her chin and lips with the side of her hand. "You're tickly and scratchy this morning. What's with all the scruff?"

With his chin up, Sean stroked his heavy stubble. "Beats me. Maybe it's you."

"Me?"

A low, seductive growl rumbled deep in his chest. "What can I say, you bring out the animal in me," he said, running his hand over the curve of her hip and waist.

"Cut it out, Sean! Anymore and I won't be able to walk," but her own body betrayed her with a dull, wet ache between her thighs.

He nuzzled her neck, rubbing his chin against the hollow at the base of her throat. "You won't need your legs once I get you on all fours." His voice was low, with an edge of sex and sin that made her gasp in spite of her protests.

"Sean..."

She didn't stand a chance. He rolled her over onto her stomach, entering her with one quick thrust. With a swift, sharp breath, Lily brought her knees up, grinding her hips back. She met him thrust for thrust, and when he drew back to enter hard and deep, she winced as his thick member slid between tender folds.

Tension gathered as the electricity of pleasure and pain sent her to the edge faster than ever before. Reaching down between her legs, she wrapped her fingers around the base of his corded shaft and squeezed. His cock already rock hard, spasmed in her hand, and his balls rose high. Sean growled, plunging himself deep as Lily's walls convulsed around him. Good morning, wolf-style!

He sighed heavily, the sound both satisfied and exhausted, before kissing the hollow between her shoulder and throat. Rolling over onto his back, he smirked. "Now that's how you say good morning. Care to try for good afternoon?" He turned his head on the pillow to face her, waggling his eyebrows.

Lily snorted. "Uh, no. A quickie good morning is one thing, but unless you want to see me wearing icepack underwear all day, we need to give it a rest. And by it, I mean me! I'm not a full shifter, yet. More to the point, we have a lot to do today, or did you forget about the little problem we have with an unwelcome member of the undead? Besides, you haven't even checked in with Jack, yet."

"Oh, I think he knows I'm here."

Lily's cheeks grew warm, and from the look on Sean's face, she knew she had pinked to the tips of her ears. "Don't remind me."

He chuckled, deep and resonant "Lily, Jack's a wolf. If anyone understands mating and the moon, it's him," he said, sitting up and swinging his legs off the edge of the bed. "Trust me. He's not going to say a word."

Lily frowned, despite watching Sean pull up his jeans commando style. "Maybe not while you're around, but I know he'll find a way to break my chops about the noise last night—not to mention this morning's little interlude."

Sean pulled her to her knees and wrapped his arms around her naked waist. "To use your word earlier, it was amazing—noise, and all— both last night and this morning," he said, smacking her bare bottom. Kissing her quick, he released her. "I smell coffee. Jack must be up, so get that shapely butt of yours out of bed, and let's put together a plan of undead attack."

Grumbling, she pulled on sweats and a long-sleeved tee shirt, and followed him out into the hallway.

"Something smells great," Sean said, taking the lead and heading into the kitchen first. "Your first rate coffee-making skills were one of the reasons we let you into the hunters so young, Jack."

He clapped the younger wolf on the back, pulling him into a hug, but Lily didn't miss the faint scowl that passed across Jack's face.

"Leave him alone, Sean. Jack probably hasn't had his coffee yet, either." Lily said, giving the younger wolf an apologetic shrug.

Sean let go, lifting his arms in surrender, but shot Lily a questioning glance. *What's going on?* The words filtered through their shared mind link, but Lily gave her head a quick, almost imperceptible shake. *Not sure, but he's been a little touchy since yesterday.*

As if Jack knew they were talking about him, the tension in the kitchen seemed to ratchet up a notch. He rattled the frying pan on the stove, plopping a couple of pats of butter in the center before turning the burner to low.

"Anyone else up for eggs?" he asked, taking the pink and white carton from the clear Plexiglas shelf in the fridge, and closing the door with his hip.

Lily leaned against the dark green counter next to the sink, watching Jack's short, terse motions as he went about making his breakfast. A slow drip from the faucet behind her sounded metronomic, adding to the tension floating through the room.

"Don't everybody answer at once," he added, swirling the butter around in the pan. He looked over his shoulder at Lily and flashed a quick smile, but the ghost of a frown still lingered puckering the area between his eyebrows.

"None for me, Jack, thanks. You know how I need my coffee first," she answered, lifting her hand mutely when Sean looked at her for an answer.

Something was bothering Jack. It was there, just beneath the surface, even at dinner, though he waved it off with some lame excuse about bedpan duty. Lily was certain Jack knew Sean didn't mean anything by his remark. He trusted Jack, or he wouldn't have sent him to New York. The hunters were a brotherhood. They laughed hard and fought hard, but each was willing to spill blood for the other. Little digs were just part of the sibling rivalry. Perhaps Jack just needed to be reminded of that.

Jack grabbed a mug and poured himself a cup of coffee, while three eggs sizzled and popped in the frying pan. "Don't mind me I'm just grouchy because I didn't get much sleep. If I didn't know better, I'd swear a pair of feral cats was getting it on right outside my door." He glanced down at his mug, but a wicked half-smile teased the corner of his mouth.

Lily just stood there for a moment. And men complain about women and their monthly mood swings. Can we say moon-mad wolf? She shot both men a dirty look and picked up the pot to pour herself some coffee. "See? What'd I tell you?" She gestured toward Sean with her mug. "You're both nuts...mad as hatters with hard-ons!"

Both Shifters just looked at each other before they both burst out laughing.

"Oh, come on!" Lily hmphed, banging her mug down on the counter. She turned her back, but only so neither would see her satisfied smirk. At least the tension had ebbed, even if it was at her expense. Now they could get down to business.

THE MORNING WAS BRIGHT, with a clear, crisp blue sky. Snow had fallen overnight, and light Sunday traffic allowed the delicate white drifts a little more time before eventually turning them to puddles of grey slush.

The cobblestone street held a turn of the century appeal, despite the cars parked alongside lengths of concrete curb. In Manhattan, no one voluntarily gives up a parking space, especially on the week-end, so both Lily and Sean decided to leave their cars where they were and walked to the corner to flag down a cab.

Shopkeepers had cleared the sidewalks, though Lily's biker boots gathered slush along their bottom edges as she walked beside Sean. Jack was directly to her left, and the three made quite a picture—two hulking Shifters flanking a petite, leather-clad porcelain doll. At least that's what Sean always said she resembled.

Sean glanced sideways, watching Lily from the corner of his eye. "What's the matter? You haven't said more than twelve words since that detective called earlier."

Lily looked across her shoulder at him and shrugged. "Nothing's the matter. He just sounded different on the phone, almost urgent. There's been another attack, but there is no way it's the same one Jack and I witnessed in Washington Square."

"Not unless the NYPD has bloodhounds that are part shifter," Jack snorted.

With a cheerless sigh, she nodded. "He's right. There was nothing left in the park for anyone to find. No body, no witnesses, no crime. That's how it works in the human world, usually," she added.

Martinez wanted her down at the morgue, insisted, in fact, but this time, she was bringing reinforcements. The detective's voice had held an edge that went beyond the clipped tone of a professional phone call. Maybe he was good to his word and had actually thought about everything she said the other night.

Sean stuck two fingers in his mouth and whistled for one of the gypsy cabs waiting for the light at the corner. One pulled over, and the three of them slid in across the scuffed and taped blue leather seat.

"Bellevue Hospital Center, 462 1st Avenue," Lily announced into the dirty speaker at the center of the scratched Plexiglas divider. The driver mumbled something unintelligible back, starting the taxi's meter before pulling away from the curb.

The inside of the cab smelled like the subway in summer, and both Sean and Jack looked sick. Neither said a word, but both rested a hand above their upper lip. The main roads were wet, with most of the snow now a sooty, black sludge, as opposed to the white fluff still decorating her tiny side street. Lily bit the side of her cheek watching the two big Shifters take each pothole and traffic swerve in stride.

The taxi's windshield wipers went back and forth, keeping pace with the dirty spray kicked up from the street and the cars ahead of them. She looked out the window at the rainbows spreading across the road, where water mixed with residual gas and oil, giving the blacktop a hazy, broken dream-like appearance.

Traffic was still light and moved at a steady pace, despite Sean and Jack's discomfort, and before long the cab pulled across from the hospital's main entrance.

"Well, that's a first," Jack hmphed as he climbed out from the back of the taxi.

"What's a first?" Lily asked.

"That I'd pay to ride in a moving sewer," he said, after dragging in a lungful of air.

Lily rolled her eyes. Jack was uncharacteristically moody, and if she hadn't uttered more than twelve words this morning, then he had said even less. "Oh, please. Are you sure you don't have the wolf equivalent of PMS? You're bitching about everything, and your mood swings are giving me whiplash, Jack. The cab was just old, that's all. So it had a funky smell, so do half the cabs and cabdrivers in the city. Get over it."

Jack grimaced. "What did I tell you about trusting that bulb in the middle of your face? It smelled like something died in there."

"Okay, you two, enough. First off, Lily's nose is not a bulb. And Lily, Jack is right. The cab stank. *Done.* Can we do what we came here to do, please?" Sean said, in an attempt to stop whatever was starting to brew. "You two are acting like siblings stuck in the back of a station wagon road trip. It's National Lampoon's, *Vacation*, without the benefit of it being funny."

"Exactly. So quit it, why don'tcha?" Jack added, glancing at Lily over the top of his sunglasses, a cheeky smirk plastered on his face.

Lily opened her mouth but closed it again. Jack was egging her on simply because he could. For some reason, he thought if he pissed her off, she'd keep better focus. That was bullshit, of course. She was a professional, but it struck her as ironic how Terri used to do the same thing when the stakes were high. *Am I that easily side-tracked, that I'm better pissed off?*

"So, Miss Leather and Lace, where are we supposed to meet this dude?" Jack asked, pulling her away from her thoughts.

"Detective Martinez,' she replied, stressing Ryan's formal title before continuing, "...said he'd be waiting downstairs, outside the morgue's main doors. I didn't exactly tell him you were accompanying me, so maybe I should just go in alone."

"Not a chance," Sean replied, with Jack shaking his head in silent accord.

Lily considered them both for a moment. Neither was going to budge, not even to let her through to reception. There was no arguing the point, so why waste more time and energy? *Pick your battles*—at least that's what Beverly always said.

She pursed her lips. "Okay but let me do the talking first. I already prefaced to Ryan this case might require extra help. He wasn't too thrilled about it then, but since letting him in on what I saw at the crime scene, he might be a little more obliging."

"Ryan?" Sean asked, lifting one eyebrow.

Lily nodded. "Detective Martinez. He suggested we use first names, since I'm working with him on the Q.T. I may be a NYPD profiler, but I haven't officially been assigned to this case, for obvious reasons."

Sean frowned. "He suggested?" His tone was not a happy one.

Lily just looked at him. The last thing she needed was Sean's alpha nature making him go all proprietary on her. Between that and Jack's moods bouncing around like a pinball machine, it didn't bode well. She'd come this far in establishing herself as independent and professional, she didn't need two macho overbearing Shifters to blow it for her now.

Standing on the sidewalk this long, they were starting to attract attention. From her peripheral vision, she caught the girls at reception glancing their way with more than just a passing interest. Not that she blamed them. Both men were model gorgeous, each looking like they belonged on the cover of a romance novel, bare-chested and smoldering.

Visiting hours on Sunday began at eleven a.m., and it was already near lunchtime. People milled around hospital grounds, and kids played in what was left of the snow in Bellevue South Park. First Avenue was abuzz with shoppers, despite the cold, and the day was wasting as they stood there debating.

"This is silly, and I've got an appointment to keep," she huffed out, and stalked toward the main doors, leaving both Shifters to follow her in from the sidewalk.

A young woman dressed in pink scrubs smiled up from behind the reception desk. Flowers waiting for delivery to in-patient floors covered the flat polished surface, but the woman's eyes did a double take, glancing past Lily to stare at Sean and Jack as they came in the door.

The woman actually stood, unconsciously licking her lips. "May I help you?" she asked, her voice breathy.

"Yes...you certainly can," Lily said, her over-solicitous tone dragging the woman's gaze back toward her. Flashing a guiltless smile, Lily casually slid one of the vases to the side, essentially blocking the guys from the young women's line of sight. *Oops. Sorry...not!*

Flashing her NYPD identification, Lily explained why she was here and what she needed. Not surprisingly, her name was the only one on the visitors list, but she didn't capitulate until she had priority passes for each of them. A single word from Jack in his silky rumble would have saved her time and aggravation, but Lily would rather gag. As for Sean...*ah no!* Alpha-female indeed, and green-eyed monster nothing.

Smiling sweetly, she thanked the girl and then pointed herself and the guys toward the elevators at the far end of the hall.

"Not nice, Lily," Sean murmured, as they walked away from the desk. Nevertheless, he slipped his arm around her waist and kissed the side of her temple.

"I thought the pink scrubs were sexy," Jack said, glancing back over his shoulder to wave at the young woman still watching them with her mouth open.

"Nice, Jack. Why don't you go back and see if you can get her digits. I'm sure she'd give you anything you asked for," Lily teased.

"Nah, humans always end up trailing after me like a puppy. You know what they say, once you go shifter, no one else comes near," he chuckled, lifting his hand to scratch just beneath his jaw line.

"So says the poet laureate of York County, Maine," Sean noted dryly, as the elevator doors slid open. "Last I checked, you were still the pup around here. Keep scratching like that and your leg's going to start to twitch."

"Ha, ha, very cute. Nevertheless, as our resident human, Lily could tell you I'm right. That's if she'd fess up," he shot back, stepping into the elevator car. He did a military about face, and wearing the same stupid smirk added, "Especially after the stereophonic symphony of heavy breathing I overheard last night."

Was the boy crazy, or just stupid? Not taking his bait, Lily ignored the hot flash of temper reddening her cheeks. If they wanted to accomplish anything this morning, confrontation was not a good idea. Today required a slow burn, so she pressed her lips together and smiled. "Okay, fine. Yes, you are correct. Shifters rock the bedroom. Now can you please just press the button for the lower lobby and shut up?"

Sean laughed, gathering her in his arms. "Glad you think so," he whispered against her hair.

Lily raised herself to her tiptoes and brushed a kiss onto his lips. She caught a glimpse of herself and Sean in the mirrored wall across from where they stood. Their reflection and what it meant overwhelmed her, that he loved her, that all this was real.

She stepped back from him and cleared her throat, her eyes trained on the blue-dotted wall-to-wall carpeting lining the floor of the elevator. Get your head in the game, Saburi, you're a professional. Focus. No distractions...regardless of how tempting.

The elevator bumped to a stop, and she cleared her throat again. A chiming ding announced the lower level, and the doors slid open to the same industrial tiled flooring she remembered from the last time she was here. A broken fluorescent bulb in the ceiling panel outside the elevator buzzed, adding to the friendless feel of the place. With a deep breath, she stepped out first into the long sterile hallway.

"Wow. This place definitely has the 'dead man walking' vibe down to a tee," Jack said with a low whistle.

Lily shot him a look that said, 'Shut it now or I'll shoot you,' earning her an ear-to-ear grin from the young hunter, but Sean intervened.

"Cork it, Jack," he whispered. "Let Lily handle this. At this point, we're only here to observe, so save the commentary, okay?"

Jack shrugged but didn't say another word. The double doors at the opposite end of the hall swung open, and an intern in green scrubs, complete with surgical booties and hair cap, wheeled a gurney toward the morgue's entrance. With the swipe of an I.D. card, the automatic doors swung open in tandem, and he disappeared behind them, stretcher and all.

"Guess somebody didn't make it," Lily said softly, swallowing hard against the atmosphere of death that was all of a sudden abundantly obvious.

The morgue doors opened again, and Ryan stepped out into the hall. Sean's head snapped up, his nostril flaring slightly. Whatever was left of Jack's earlier grin melted, and both men turned in the direction of the morgue.

"That's Martinez?" Sean asked, his head cocked toward Lily, the question a harsh whisper.

The alpha's eyes flashed yellow, and the menacing warning sent alarm bells peeling through her head. "Yes, that's Ryan," she answered haltingly, her eyebrows puckering at his sudden hostility. "Did I miss something?"

Sean stepped forward, pushing Lily behind him as Martinez walked toward them. She stiffened, not knowing what Sean sensed, but she trusted his instincts enough not to question him...yet.

The air around them crackled with anticipated violence, and she bit her tongue watching Sean's back and shoulder muscles tighten.

"You're late," Martinez said, as he came up to where they stood. "And I see you brought company." His expression wasn't a pleased one, but to his credit, he extended his hand, "I'm Detective Martinez, Lily's partner in all this craziness."

Sean's eyes flashed, and he grabbed the detective by the throat to shove him up against the wall. "Who sent you? Who do you work for?" he growled, compressing his hand until the man's eyes bulged.

"Holy Christ!" Sean's arm moved lightning fast, and Lily bolted to where he stood like stone, staring into Ryan's red and purple face. She pulled on his arm, but it was rock solid and wouldn't budge. "Have you lost your fucking mind? Let him go! He's a New York City Homicide Detective! He's no threat to us, you giant hairball!" she said, only to have Sean snarl for her to get away.

Jack shot to his other side, knowing better than to touch the wolf at this point. "Calm down man! You're going kill him before he can even answer you."

"I asked you once, Cougar... who sent you?" Sean's voice was low, but there was no question as to his intention. He would kill the cop if he didn't answer. With a frustrated growl, he pulled Ryan away from the wall and shoved him back again, hard. "Answer me, Cat!"

Ryan rasped out, "N.Y.P.D," while his hands scrambled for his gun, but he couldn't reach it.

"He's serious, man, so unless you want to eat that steel of yours, I suggest you keep your hands at your sides." Jack added, gesturing with his head for Lily to move away.

Back away? Yeah, right. She was having none of it. Gritting her teeth, she pulled on Sean's arm even harder. "Answer you? You need to answer me! What Cougar? What is going on, here?" Her eyes flashed between both men.

They were between the elevator bank and the main doors to the morgue. Thank God no one came down here unless they had to, but that didn't prevent the concrete walls from acting like an echo chamber. How no one came in or out during all the commotion, was a miracle. Nonetheless, Lily kept both sets of doors on the other end of the hall in her peripheral vision.

On their way over the last time, Martinez had mentioned that a few morgue techs had rigged music to play through the intercom whenever their boss was otherwise occupied. According to the reception desk, the deputy medical examiner was in a meeting for most of the afternoon, leaving instructions for whoever was on duty to help her and Martinez should they need it.

Faint lyrics from Coldplay's *Paradise* filtered through the hallway, and Lily thanked God for small favors. She didn't care why or how, but knew their luck wasn't going to hold much longer. Someone was bound to show up sooner or later.

"He's bleeding, and he's turning blue. Let him go, Sean. This is not the way the Alpha of the Brethren handles things...," she trailed off.

It was a low blow, and she knew it, but she also knew she needed to snap Sean back to his senses. He was her mate, and for some inexplicable reason, he was in extreme protective mode.

Sean's head snapped around. Ire flared deep in his eyes at the accusation, and his shoulders stiffened, but after a moment, his natural blue streaked the yellow depths of his irises and Lily knew she had reached him. The alpha had regained control of the wolf.

Ryan slumped against the white painted concrete, stretching his neck upward as he gulped in air. Still growling, Sean paced in front of the man, clenching and unclenching his fists.

Lily scowled at Sean. Her eyes narrowed to the point of daggers. "First Jack goes all off-the-wall moody on me, and now this. All I know is someone better explain, and I mean now!"

Sean ignored her, his eyes trained on Jack. "You let her traipse around all week with a Cougar? What the hell were you thinking, Jack? I was there when Mitch briefed you on the attack up at the Compound, or didn't you think the assassination attempt would extend as far as to include Lily?"

"Assassination? Cougars? Sean, what the hell is going on?" Lily stood glaring at the big wolf with her hand on her hips.

Both wolves ignored her. Jack pressed his lips together, but his gaze sparked with anger. He inhaled deeply, the muscles in his shoulders and biceps bunching, in restrained resentment. "You need to calm down! I've never laid eyes on the man before, so how could I know he was a Cougar, or any kind of shifter?"

"Sean!" Lily prompted again.

This time he answered her, but his eyes stayed locked on Jack. "Parr hired a tracker, a WereCougar. Very skilled and very stealth. He made his move out in the woods a few days ago, but I killed him before he could kill me. Edward's denying it, but everyone knows he was at the center of the plot. He's laying low—for now."

Lily threw her hands in the air. "I don't give a shit if Parr is so far underground he's eating Chinese food in Shanghai. Assassination? That's what we're dealing with on top of everything else? And how do you know Ryan's a Werewhatever?"

"Cougar," Jack interjected angry and impatient before she could finish. "And how do you think we know? Duh?"

Lily clenched her fists, and squeezed her eyes closed for a

moment. "Cougar, whatever. I haven't sensed one thing, not one shifter attribute in all the time I've spent with him. No scent, no inkling."

Jack huffed. "...and that bulb on your face strikes again."

"Really? And who was it that didn't recognize Ryan's scent in my apartment? Who was it that sniffed around asking if I had a cat, but when he learned the detective had been there, accused him of leaving a funky odor behind? Looks like I'm not the only one whose bulb doesn't work, Jack."

Sean glared at him, and then shifted his gaze to Lily, watching as she glanced between him and the detective. "Stop worrying, he's fine. I can smell him healing already."

Ryan coughed, trying to stand up straight. "Smell me?" His voice scraped out of his bruised throat. "What the hell does that mean?"

"You are so lucky," she said, crossing her arms in front of her. Looking between Ryan and Sean, she exhaled. "Well, we can't stay here like this, and I still need you to go inside and take a look at those bodies."

Ryan's eyes widened, and he took a step toward them. "Am I in the fucking Twilight Zone?" he blurted out, grimacing with the effort. "I'm giving you people to the count of three to start talking. I don't have to remind you, Lily, assaulting an officer is a criminal offense. Don't make me have to arrest you and your friends."

Lily gave Ryan a quick glance but turned her attention back to Sean. She wasn't letting him off the hook that easily. "Ryan's human, Sean...regardless of what you smell or sense. Do you honestly think he's a plant? That I wouldn't know by this point?"

Sean was still staring at Jack. "So you didn't know he was a shifter, huh?" he said, ignoring Lily's questions. He moved across from where she stood, positioning himself directly in front of the young hunter. "Granted, you never saw him before, but you did sense him." Raising one hand, he gestured toward Martinez then let his hand drop. "...and yet you still chose to ignore the signs, didn't even bother to check things out."

"Sean!" Lily yelled, annoyed at being ignored.

"Lily!" Ryan shot back at her for the same reason.

Jack broke eye contact with Sean, sliding his gaze over to the wall where Lily stood next to Ryan. He raised his finger, pointing it in her direction. "She's the one who told me to go play tourist, that there was no threat, and no reason for me to accompany her to the meeting—that Parr wouldn't have had time to infiltrate the NYPD." He paused, his eyes hardening even as his shoulders dropped. "It made sense at the time..." His voice trailed off. His words as inept as his excuses.

"You're on thin ice already, Jack, so shut up and stop blaming this on Lily. She's still human and doesn't have the ability to make that kind of an assessment. It's true she has her own set of skills, but she doesn't know everything Shifters are capable of in terms of supernatural abilities and cunning. Especially Parr."

Ryan's head swiveled left and right, his face a cross between incredulous and manic. "Human? Somebody better start talking or I'm going to start shooting!"

Jack snorted. "Yeah, right. Lily's so guileless and forthright, that's why she had hunted supes before she got her ass handed to her by your brother. Ever since she came into your life, Sean, you've reduced the hunters to nothing more than glorified boy scouts. I'm sick of it! But then again, what does my opinion matter? I'm only good enough for bedpan duty, right?"

"That's bullshit, and you know it!" Sean shot back. "I sent you here to protect Lily. I trusted you and only you with the one thing that means more to me than anything, but I guess I chose wrong."

Jack's upper lip rose at one corner in a sneer. "You're right, I'm the hunter, and I should have taken care of this situation then." Without warning, Jack's body shook. Sinew and muscle trembled, and bones snapped, reshaping themselves into a four-legged stance. Phasing on the fly, his clothes shredded around him, and Jack stood in wolf form with his head lowered and his teeth bared.

"What the fucking holy hell?" Ryan muttered in disbelief. His eyes wide as he stared at the wolf standing where Jack had just been. Hands shaking, he pulled his gun, but Lily grabbed his arm.

"Ryan NO!"

In an instant, Sean lifted his head and sprang forward from a standstill. His body contorted in midair, and the distinct scent of ozone was sharp in the hallway as his body reshaped into a large black wolf before he hit the ground again, this time on all fours.

The two wolves circled each other, Jack's silver grey was much smaller than the alpha's sleek black, but just as menacing. The grey wolf snarled with its head low, snapping and growling, its thin lips pulled back over sharp canines as he postured, its tone frustrated and angry. The black wolf was quiet, its teeth bared but otherwise calm as he matched the grey step for step, its keen yellow eyes following its every move, every nuance as it waited for the inevitable assault.

With a violent jerk, Ryan shoved Lily off of him and raised his gun toward the wolves.

"Ryan don't!" she said, jumping in front of his line of sight. "You don't understand!"

"What don't I understand, Lily? Tell me..."

Lily's eyes glared. "I think you already know the answer to that question, Ryan. They're just as much human as they are animal. Just like you..." she trailed off, watching his eyes register everything he saw with what she just said.

The detective lowered his gun, his handsome face ugly with anger and disbelief. "First vampires and now werewolves? What kind of fool do you take me for, Lily? What's next? You telling me you fly around on a broomstick by the light of the full moon?"

"Ryan, please..."

He raised his gun again as he backed away, two hands on the

grip as if to steady himself from shaking, his eyes never leaving the wolves. "No, you please. I've had enough. I'm not buying any of this —especially not when you're telling me I'm some kind of being, a 'Were-something-or-other'! In fact, the only thing I'm 'awere' of, is that you and your friends are consummate illusionists. Ever think of taking your act to Vegas? You'd give Criss Angel a real run for his money."

When he was far enough away, he holstered his gun and adjusted his suit jacket, as if the routine motions would make this anything else but what it was. "I'm outta here. Tell your boyfriend to steer clear, payback is a bitch."

"Ryan, wait. You need to hear this. Just let me explain."

He shook his head, this time his eyes meeting hers, his gaze painful in its intensity. "Not a chance, sweetheart. I am so done with you and your freak show."

Sean whined, his head swiveling toward where she stood, but Lily knew there was nothing he could do to help. At that moment, Jack lunged, mouth open and teeth dripping saliva as he aimed for the alpha's throat. It was a blatant challenge, but the grey wolf's posturing was raw with blind anger and that made it an empty threat.

The two collided in a hailstorm of snarls and teeth, with Jack's front claws scoring bloody gashes along Sean's flank. The wolves twisted in a vicious dance, crashing into the concrete wall, the hit splintering the painted cinderblock, and leaving a gory smear of fur and blood.

Lily pulled Ryan out of the way, chipped paint and concrete dust covering their hair and shoulders as they cleared the impact zone.

The grey wolf yelped as the alpha gained the advantage, pinning him to his side before he had the chance to strike again. Front and hind legs extended, the grey pushed at the alpha, keeping the larger wolf's teeth at bay and tucking his neck against its razor sharp incisors.

With a low pitched growl, Sean bared his teeth once more, biting down on the side of the grey wolf's throat in a show of clear dominance. Jack whined, its tenor a sign of submission and acceptance, and as quick as the fight began, was as quick as it was over.

Ryan coughed, his mouth a grim line as he shook out his hair and wiped his hands over his sleeves. His movements were stiff, as if he had to compel himself to stay calm, yet his face had paled and his pupils had dilated to the size of saucers. "Yup. I'm done. And I have news for you too you're done with this case." Without as much as a backward glance, he turned and walked toward the exit. His stride moderated with restraint like he refused to let them see him run.

"Ryan!" Lily called after him.

"*Let him go, Lily. There's no place he can run. When he wants answers, he'll be back,*" Sean's voice feathered across their shared mind link.

She looked at him, her body and mind weary with the weight of everything. "I hope sooner than later," she murmured. She didn't need to verbalize it. Each understood the situation would only get worse before it got better if Ryan didn't get a grip.

Sean nudged her arm with his muzzle. "*Stop worrying. You can always find him later and try to talk some sense into him. In the meantime, why don't you find hothead and me something to wear so we can do what we came here to do?*"

Lily nodded. "Okay, but are you two going to behave while I'm gone?"

Sean rumbled a low wolfish chuckle low in his throat and bumped her hand with the top of his head. "*Junior and I need a little heart to heart, but I promise there'll be no more trouble*".

She looked down at Jack's shaggy head and twined her fingers into the fur at the scruff of his neck, giving it a short tug. "Be the hunter I know you to be, and pull yourself together, okay Jack? We have work to do, and not a lot of time to do it. If what you both suspect is true, then Ryan is a half-breed who has no idea who or what he is. It's our duty to help him acclimate, not scare the piss out of him or make him think he's crazy. You're not the only one at fault, though," she said, sliding a critical glance toward Sean. "We'll all handle it better once I bring him around."

Jack whined, the sound mournful, and full of doubt and regret.

Lily slid her fingers around, giving Jack a quick scratch beneath his chin before turning toward the double doors and the main hospital corridor. "I'll be back as soon as I can. Try not to be any more conspicuous than you already are."

FIFTEEN

"This is the best I could do without calling too much attention to myself," Lily said, handing Sean the bundle. Her adrenaline level was still in overdrive nonetheless she nearly went into full panic mode when neither wolf was in the hall where she'd left them. She crossed her arms in front of her chest, a plastic supermarket bag with other essentials dangling from her wrist. "Clever. I didn't even notice a utility closet on this floor." She ran a hand through her hair, taking in the small, confined space. Leave it to Sean to stay quick-witted in an unexpected crisis.

His face and body language made it clear he'd done this before. "Like they say, any port in a storm," he replied, stepping into the navy blue scrubs he unwrapped from the bundle. "You've got to be resourceful otherwise you end up in jail for public nudity."

Jack whined from the corner towards the back, still in wolf form and lying on a stack of standard issue hospital towels, as if to say, 'been there, done that.'

She snickered, a sound somewhere between a chortle and a snort. "Public nudity, huh? I can see it now, WeTV's newest reality series, Shifters gone Wild...drama, hot guys and lots of infighting.

Right up Edward's alley, dontcha think? It has everything he wants...fame, devoted fans...throw in a little network control and you've got a real ace up your sleeve. A real dealmaker."

Sean glanced up from knotting the drawstring on his pants. "Not funny."

Lily slid in behind him, slipping her hands onto his shoulders and skimming her palms across their broad expanse. "It would be worth it just to see the look on his face at the proposition," she said, resting her chin on the back of his shoulder blade.

He turned, glancing at her crosswise. "How about we stick to removing him from the equation, altogether?" Taking her hand, he planted a quick kiss on the flat of her palm and then moved to look at where the pants met his bare feet. "Not a bad fit," he said, turning around to face her. "Looks like you can be pretty resourceful yourself."

"A perfect fit, if I do say so myself," she said, helping him slip the boxy shaped top over his head and wrapping her arms around his waist in the process.

"*Hmmm*," he murmured, leaning in for a little more than a quick peck. "A perfect fit, indeed."

With her hands on his chest she took a step back and scooted under his arm. "Bad timing, bad place," she said, wrinkling her nose. "*Not that the idea of wild monkey sex in a utility room isn't appealing, but we have work to do,*" she murmured through their shared mind path.

Sean's lips curved up, and his eyes darkened. Even without the telltale bulge in his pants, Lily knew exactly where his thoughts were headed. Psychic sense not required.

"*Maybe later we could play the night nurse and the custodian,*" he grinned, eyeing a utility belt on one of the shelves," he replied with a mental smirk.

Ignoring him, she looked at Jack sitting patiently in the corner. "Is there a reason why he's still a canine?"

Considering the two of them and the size of the grey wolf, the closet seemed even smaller, with every type of cleaning supply known to man crammed into the six-by-six room. PCV shelving, brooms, mops and an industrial shop vac took up most of the space.

Sean shrugged, tucking the top of his scrubs into his pants. "Just easier that way."

Lily didn't even pretend to know what that meant, nor at this point did she care. With a soft breath, she rubbed her hands together. "Okay Fido, your turn." He whined in response, and Lily felt horrible. The poor guy had been through enough, even if it was his own doing.

The grey wolf chuffed, and with a snap of bone and muscle, and a quick whiff of ozone, Jack was in human form, utterly naked and standing adjacent to the bucket mop.

Woof! Down boy! Self-conscious, Lily did an about face, looking for somewhere else to direct her gaze. Bingo! She grabbed the second set of scrubs from the shelf next to the floor polish and reached behind to hand them to Jack backwards.

The third bundle on the shelf was the lumpy plastic bag she had carried in with the clothes. "There are two pairs of sneakers inside, and a box of wet naps. I swiped them from an open locker in the nurses' station," she said with an apologetic shrug, and handed the bag to Sean. "I can't vouch for the sizes."

Sean took it and tore open the plastic, reaching in for the first pair. "I'm sure they're fine," he offered, tossing the bag to Jack. "A little snug, but nothing a strategically placed rip can't fix."

"I grabbed some of these, too. Just in case," she said, handing them each a pair of blue surgical booties.

"Good thinking," Jack nodded, tying the drawstring on his pants. "...and you can turn around, now."

He struggled into the shirt, which would have been roomy on anyone else, except a broad-shouldered wolf. Lily did an unconscious double take. Sean was her mate, without a doubt, but a woman would have to be blind not to notice the hunter's muscular good looks. If the girl in pink scrubs could see Jack now, she'd faint.

McDreamy? Ha! Eat your heart out Grey's Anatomy... you've got nothing on my wolves!

Lily's appreciative smile disappeared almost as fast as it came. "What?" It was all she could say in response to Sean's amused smirk, and the words, *"You are so busted,"* feathering across her mind.

The big alpha grinned, shaking his head, and bending to slip the booties over his too small sneakers.

"Okay, then...," Lily breathed out. "Just so you know, I checked with the front desk, and the deputy medical examiner is still in a meeting. There's only one person inside right now, and he shouldn't give us any grief about Ryan being M.I.A. Plus we have a little time before our resident detective regroups enough to do something stupid."

Sean looked up, raising an eyebrow.

"I tapped into his head just to check he's okay," she clarified, with another shrug, handing them each their passes. "He's having a drink at some random bar by the river. I didn't want to poke around too much or for too long. We don't need him freaked out any more than he already is."

"All things considered he didn't seem to be that freaked out. He actually seemed pretty calm," Jack replied, clipping his pass to the top of his pants.

"He's a good cop. He keeps his emotions in check and out of the equation," she said, regretting her words immediately.

Jack's lips compressed. "Maybe Sean should send his hunters down to the N.Y.P.D. for training. That way he can limit the collateral damage."

"Jack, I didn't mean anything by that. Ryan just handles things bet..." She hesitated, pulling her foot from her mouth before it was too late. Exhaling, she recovered tactfully. "I mean, differently," she added with a quick smile.

Sean clipped his pass to the front pocket of the scrubs and cracked open the utility closet door. "All right, it's been a rough day all the way around, and my hunch is it's going to get worse once we see what's waiting for us inside. Let's go. I've had enough of this place."

LILY RAPPED on the double doors, pushing one side open the same way Martinez had done previously.

With Jack and Sean close behind, she stepped through the threshold. Except for the music playing in the background, the place seemed deserted. A single tech worked alone, occupied at one of the aluminum examination tables lining the side of the room. It had been raised and was slanted toward one of the sinks where he busied himself with the business end of a long hose, rinsing instruments and any collected blood from a previous procedure.

Harsh smelling disinfectant bubbled along the curved edges of the examination table, and even from their vantage point, it wasn't hard to guess what tinged the foam red as it funneled toward the drain. Jack coughed, wrinkling his nose at the noxious cloud of bleach and blood in the air, and even Sean's eyes watered despite his stoic expression.

The room was exactly as Lily remembered, except this time there was no lifeless body in plain view prepped for autopsy. The fluorescent lights cast a sterile gleam across the industrial polished concrete floor, and despite its careworn feel and the barbaric subtext attached to the equipment, a sense of purpose encompassed the room.

"Don't only doctors perform autopsies? I thought you said the deputy M.E. was in a meeting?" Sean whispered from the corner of his mouth. Based on the routine cleanup that was front and center, they must have just missed the main event.

Lily gave him a wide eyed shrug. "That's what I was told. Maybe this guy is higher up on the food chain than I thought."

The tech spotted them and released the trigger on the hose, turning the sprayer off. "Can I help you?"

Lily stepped forward. "Yes. I'm Lily Saburi. I believe I'm expected."

The man put the nozzle down and wiped his gloved hands on a paper towel. "Yeah, I remember seeing your name on the list. What happened to the detective? He was here earlier."

Without so much as a blink, Lily met the man's gaze. "He was called away on another matter. I've just arrived with my associates to view the latest victim and any evidence you may have collected. If you need to check our credentials..." she trailed off, hoping her face didn't give away their bluff.

He lifted his clear plastic face shield and looked her over, sparing a glance for Jack and Sean standing off to her side, his eyes resting for a moment on their hospital passes. "That won't be necessary. You wouldn't be allowed down here without the proper paperwork. I'm Jeff Holton, Bellevue Morgue Diener."

Jack jerked his eyes away from the deli-style slicing machines and dissection equipment, his gaze speculating as he looked at the tech. "You work in the morgue, and you're called 'the diner'?

The man gave a snuffling sort of laugh. "Kind of creepy when you put it that way, but it's actually pronounced, 'deener'. It's from the German word, *leichendiener*, which literally means morgue servant. Basically, I get to do all the grunt work. You know, clean up after the big boys finish with their slicing and dicing. It ain't pretty, but it's a living."

Jack swallowed hard, still considering him.

"You okay, buddy?" the tech asked, raising a gloved hand to wave in front of Jack's distracted face.

The young hunter nodded. "Yeah, I'm good. I'm just trying to imagine what a regular workday must be like around here."

The diener shrugged, picking up the nozzle and turning on the spray to continue his wash down. "It isn't pretty, that's for sure. And speaking of which, the guy you want is down at the back end of the freezer section. The doc already marked the drawer. He also asked me to let you know that most of the bodies in this case have been released back to their families. That is, except for that teenage girl. She's a Jane Doe. Do you want her drawer number, too?"

Lily shook her head. "That won't be necessary. I have all the information I need on that. It's the newest addition to the list of victims we need to see."

"Help yourselves," he said, gesturing toward the back of the room. "Mind if I turn up the music? Dr. Weaver won't be back for about an hour or so, and Dr. Rush left a little while ago. Trust me, that one's name says it all."

Lily and Sean exchanged glances. "Thanks, we'll take it from here."

He nodded. "Hey, if you don't mind my asking, what's with the scrubs? They're not exactly police issue, if you know what I mean."

"Slush puddle and an uptown bus," Sean answered before Lily could open her mouth.

The diener made a face. "I feel for you, buddy. Ouch."

Sean rubbed his side where Jack's claws had slashed him. "Ouch, indeed."

SEAN GRIPPED the stainless steel lever, the metal in his hand as cold as the air that rushed out from the compact refrigerated compartment. Jack faced the three foot square box, his hands on the end of the cadaver tray. One pull and the gurney slid out with relative ease.

"Whew! The stench coming off of him is almost worse than the bleach," Jack frowned, lifting his hand to his nose.

Unlike the last time, the body wasn't covered with an evidence sheet. The victim was another young male, stiff but not yet completely rigor mortised. His skin was a bluish hue, with tiny ice crystals dotting his body hair.

"Another kid," Lily murmured, her jaw set and her stomach dropping at the slashes crisscrossing the young man's throat and chest. The marks were almost identical to the ones on the young vampire in the park, and there was no question as to the creature responsible for his death.

"Jack, do you see the similarities to the wounds? Any patterning?" Lily asked, turning the man's head to offer him a better look at the gash marks. "The smell coming off this guy is also comparable to that on the other victims I inspected, but why is it so strong? The vamp in the park had the same putrid scent, but it was subtle."

"It's because this one's a shifter," Sean announced, his face as somber as his tone.

Both Lily and Jack turned. "Are you sure? How can you tell with that rancid odor masking every other clue?" she asked.

Sean took a deep breath, despite the smell. "The symbol on his chest."

There above the victim's right pectoral muscle was a tiny fleur-di-lis. The symbol was ornate, despite its small size, only this was no tattoo. The mark had been burned directly into the skin, a brand, and as it was the only mark on his body that wasn't raw, it was easy to assume it had been there for a while, despite the owner's youth.

"It's a mark from one of the badland wolf packs," Sean surmised. "They're the only ones I know of that still use branding. They live out on the edges of the great plains near the mountains of South Dakota."

"What's he doing this far east?" Jack reached out to run his fingers over the blackened mark, but Lily caught his wrist. The admonishment subtle, but clear: Don't touch till I'm done.

"People come to New York from all over the world. Maybe he was here on business, or just curious to see how we east-coasters roll."

"Well, whatever the reason, it's now up to me to let his pack leader know what happened. It's protocol, alpha to alpha." Sean looked down at the dead wolf, and then formed a symbol in the air over his chest, almost like a benediction.

Sean's fingers curled into his palm as he pulled it back to his side as if he held something of value from the dead boy, the simple gesture reminding her of how much she still needed to learn.

With what sounded like a sad, tired breath, Sean looked at her. "Lily, I need for you to find out what happened to this boy. I'll need all the particulars when I call his pack..." he hesitated, then added, "...and for when I demand a meeting with the vampire council and their adjudicators."

Jack opened his mouth to object, but the alpha raised his hand, stopping him.

"Don't. Neither you nor I need Lily to validate what we already know. A vampire murdered this kid. As to why..." Sean trailed off, letting his hand fall mutely. His gaze moved to Lily again. "That's where you come in. Whatever images you gather will tell us what we need to know, or at the very least, point us in the right direction. It may be this kid brought it upon himself through his own stupidity, but in light of the stench coming off his body, I doubt that was the case."

He pressed his lips together, tracking his fingers through his hair. "Either way, it doesn't matter. A vampire killed a shifter and that's enough for an Alpha of the Brethren to demand parley. Vampires are at the root of what is happening in this city, you know it, and I know it. What I don't know is why their death squads have done nothing about it, but I'm damn well going to find out, and this kid's death certificate is my engraved invitation to do just that."

The East River was just ahead, across from the promenade, where evening joggers moved swiftly along the concrete path following the water's edge. Seagulls keened sharply, flying in frenetic circles as the sun set on the horizon, their obnoxious cries muted somewhat by the dull roar of the wind coming off the water.

Ryan sat alone on a park bench about fifty feet ahead as Lily approached. Decorative flags flapped overhead in the gusty breeze, their snap keeping time with the noise from the gulls. From her vantage point, Lily watched the detective's absorbed gaze as he stared unblinkingly at the rough brown water and its wind-churned peaks, oblivious to the cacophony surrounding him. She flinched inwardly, ignoring the urge to stack the odds in her favor by taking a quick look at his thoughts.

"Ryan..." Lily said, as she came up to the bench.

"What do you want?" His voice was flat and his tone hostile, but Lily slid her bag from her shoulder and dropped it next to him. This wasn't going to be easy, but then, nothing ever was when it came to the supernatural.

She sat down, careful to leave enough space between them. "I know I'm the last person you want to speak with right now, but like it or not, we need to talk."

He turned his head to look at her. His eyes weren't angry anymore, they were just tired. "I don't have anything to say to you."

"That's bullshit, and you know it," she shot back, but watched as his jaw tightened at her tone. She raked a hand through her hair, pushing it away from her face only to have the wind blow it right back. They would get nowhere fast if she didn't force herself to relax and dull the edge in her voice. "But that's okay, because all you have to do is listen," she added evenly.

His answering grunt was almost lost to the wind, but at least he didn't get up and walk away. Either he wanted answers, or he was waiting to dump her in the river as soon as it was dark.

Lily turned her back to the wind, twisting her hair into a knot and tucking it inside her collar. "Hey, it's really cold, and the wind is annoying the crap out of me. Can't we go somewhere warmer and talk? I'll even spring for coffee and donuts."

He blinked, giving her a look that said don't push it. "I'm fine right where I am. If you have something you want to say, then say it. I'm not going anywhere with you, nor am I guaranteeing that I'll stay to listen once you start talking."

He turned his gaze back to the water, and Lily watched his frown relax into a practiced expression of noninterest. She took in the curve of his strong jaw, his high cheekbones, and the shape of his nose, even the tiny beauty mark above his lip. His profile was perfect.

"My best friend had a beauty mark like yours, almost in the same exact place," she said, trying to disarm the conversation before it even started. "I used to tease her, call her Cynthia...you know, for Cindy Crawford."

He hmphed, slouching further into his coat. "Some friend."

Lily slid her knee onto the bench, shifting her body even more to face his. "Hey, equating a friend's looks with that of a supermodel doesn't exactly make it an insult. Terri had that sultry Spanish look going for her, and I personally know plenty of women who'd gladly have surgery to look like that."

"So?"

"So nothing. Little things sometimes remind me of her, that's all," she said with a shrug. What she didn't tell him was that right now, he reminded her so much of Terri it hurt. Coincidence.

For a long moment Lily looked at him, squelching the urge to turn his chin so she could see his eyes. Despite the scowl, he looked good. Really good, and he smelled incredible.

Unsettled, she shifted around to sit straight, forcing herself to look at the ground. Ryan was virtually a stranger, but an undeniable connection had managed to tingle its way into her lower belly. Whether it was the moon, or their collective shifter blood, or some strange combination of both, she didn't like it. Sean had warned her about lunar-driven desires and the provocative lure the full moon inflicts, but as usual she dismissed it.

Her pulse quickened, and she sucked in a deep breath, but the richness of his scent in the air only made her mouth water. Holy crap! She repeated the words like a mantra, reminding herself that nothing and no one controlled her—not Sean, not the moon, nothing—only now she wasn't so sure. If this was what Sean meant, then instinct sucked the big one. Instinct? Really? You'd rip Sean a new one without batting an eye for even thinking about using that excuse, and here you are being a scent slut. Get a grip.

"Damn," she cursed, crossing her legs tightly against the itch between her legs. She pictured Sean's face, his smile and his eyes, and a sudden coolness flooded her veins, soothing taut nerve endings as it discharged unwanted tension.

Lily held her breath. If Ryan's innate shifter senses noticed the unusual spike in pheromones, he gave no clue, and she exhaled the last of her unease, clamping an iron fist around her lunar libido.

Annoyed at herself, she glanced at the sky to gauge the time. Darkness fell too quickly this time of year to be out in the open with a deranged vampire roaming free. Sean had gone back to the apartment to plan their next move, and she needed to be there, with or without Ryan. Back to business, she took another breath, thankful it tasted of nothing but snow.

Ryan hadn't moved. He slouched back against the curved wooden slats, but however relaxed he wanted to seem, his underlying physical response screamed otherwise.

"Do you remember in the morgue, when I said one day I'd tell you how I learned about all this, about all the weird shit around us?"

He stared straight ahead, his gaze locked on the water. "I don't want to know, and I really don't care."

Lily followed his gaze. She didn't say a word, just watched the gulls circle the dirty water, biding her time. Patience wasn't exactly her strong suit, and after her lunar-induced sex tangent, she wasn't going to force the issue. Not yet, anyway. "Your body language tells me otherwise," she prompted.

"Really? Is that your professional opinion, or are you doing a tap dance all over my head?"

Lily stiffened at the accusation.

He slid his glance sideways, his eyes sharp. "Hey, don't give me the hairy eyeball, sweetheart, those are your words not mine."

Sweetheart? If he wanted a mind tap she could certainly accommodate him with one he'd never forget. She shot him a warning look but otherwise bit her tongue. Ryan was just being a prick—unless he had sensed her earlier attraction and was deliberately baiting her. A bad feeling crawled across her chest.

Sucking in a quick breath, she ignored his glare and tried not to sound too indignant. "I don't do that unless I'm forced to," she said, putting stress on the last two words. "Look, you said if I had something to say, I should just say it, so here it goes. My best friend—the one with the beauty mark—she was killed a few months ago. She was murdered."

Pokerfaced, Ryan didn't flinch. However, Lily was astute enough a profiler to register his slight shock, and she knew her matter-of-fact statement was the last thing he'd expected her to say.

"How? Where?" His voice was clipped and professional, despite the unease in his eyes.

Once a cop always a cop, she thought, ignoring the ping of guilt pricking at her heart for using Terri's death to get him to listen. She uttered a silent prayer for forgiveness, keeping her face impassive as she drew his attention further. "The police report said animal attack. We were up in Maine taking EMF readings on a case."

Ryan's brow furrowed. "EMF readings? What kind of case are you talking about?"

"Paranormal investigation."

He didn't comment, but his expression had him mentally jotting down notes, processing the information the way he would after canvasing a witness. "You said animal attack. Now I suppose you're going to tell me it wasn't an animal that killed your friend, but some kind of shape shifter, right?"

Lily's chest squeezed, but she was careful to keep the emotion out of her voice. "No. It was a werewolf. A rabid one, which I subsequently hunted and almost died trying to kill. My friends you met this afternoon, they're from the same pack. In fact, Sean is the alpha." She purposefully left out the fact that he was also her mate. Not the place, and after her body's pheromone mutiny, definitely not the time.

"Okay. Next, you'll be telling me the attack was on a full moon, like something out of *An American Werewolf in London*," he shot back tightly.

The wind kicked up even more, and Lily pulled her coat closer around her body. "No, but it could have been. Unfortunately, the situation turned out to be more hospital drama than Hollywood horror. There's a virus at the root of what's causing the Shifters to degenerate. The wolf that killed Terri also infected me, but, for some reason, I'm immune. In fact, my antibodies are what their doctors are using to develop a vaccine."

"Their doctors? Their vaccine? Didn't the police investigate the nonsense you're trying to get me to buy?"

Lily stiffened, struggling against the flare of temper sending heat into her cheeks. She pulled her hand out of her pocket and banged her fist down on the green-painted wood between them. "If you would stop being such a pigheaded asshole for one minute, you could use that trained mind of yours to connect the dots. Not everything is by the book, nor does everything fit neatly into definitions of plausibility. Sometimes things happen outside the box, without explanation. You know this, and if you were truly honest with yourself and me, you'd admit it."

She paused, dragging in a cold breath. "You called this morning for a reason. What was it that made you pick up the phone? And don't say it was to give me my walking papers."

He wouldn't look at her, but the weight of her gaze was not letting him off the hook. Ryan pushed his feet out, shoving his hands deeper into his pockets. "I don't know why I called."

"That's a cop-out, and you're not that kind of a cop."

His head jerked around, and from the set of his mouth, Lily knew she'd hit a nerve. It was a cheap shot, but time was running out and she'd never get another chance if she backed off now. "Your instincts aren't wrong, Ryan. They've been telling you what you are for years. Don't you think it's about time you listened?"

Ryan pulled his hands from his pockets and slid forward gripping the edge of the bench. His posture was so tense, he looked as though he'd shatter in the wind.

"I know this is a lot to take in, and I'm not helping by shoving it down your throat, but we need to work together on this case, or things are going to get much worse. That, and I care about what happens to you."

In one swift motion he slid in close, and without warning palmed the back of Lily's head, crushing his lips to hers.

Lily's eyes flew open, and her heart rate jumped in unfamiliar alarm. Think, Lily... think. She needed to act rationally. If Ryan was anyone else, he'd be clutching at the hole in his crotch where she shot him.

There was no doubt he had caught the scent of her unintended arousal. Shifters and their fucking instincts. Her palms were moist with sweat against his chest as her thoughts raced. She needed to get him off of her, but not piss him off, or insult him to the point where he stormed off.

He leaned in and inhaled the scent from her hair, snaking his other arm around her waist. Lily's body screamed in confusion, nerve endings warring between instinct and Sean's claim. The four puncture marks on the back of her shoulder throbbed in warning against the errant feelings coursing through her body, and she squeezed her eyes shut ignoring the heat and electricity slashing her lower belly.

Gritting her teeth, she slid her fingers up and through his hair, feeling his lips slant in an eager smile against hers until she jammed her thumb into the soft tissue behind his ear.

Ryan jerked back, his hand scrubbing at the spot like he'd been hit with a cattle prod. "Jesus, Lily. What's with the Vulcan death grip?"

"Because, it's the only way I knew I could get you to stop and listen to me."

His gaze flew to hers, accusing and angry. "You want this, too. I can feel it."

Face burning, she shoved the reality of his words away and dragged a hand across her mouth, drawing a deep breath in through her nose. "You think so? Is this why you called me this morning? To see if I was willing to play house?"

He didn't answer, just huffed and puffed, scowling as he rubbed at the spot behind his ear.

"For Christ sake, stop being such a big baby, pressure points are self-defense 101. Half your problem, detective, is you only hear what you want to. I said *listen* to your instincts, not *act* on them— for the record, cats don't huff and puff. Shifters leave that to the big bad wolves. You think you know what I feel? What you feel? Chances are you do, but did you ever stop to think why?"

Ryan shifted away from her, his scowl back in place and deepening by the moment. Fingers still massaging the tender spot behind his ear, he mumbled something under his breath before looking across his bent arm at her, his eyes uncertain. "I'm sorry, Lily. I have no idea where that came from."

Lily frowned. Despite everything, he was still ignoring what was right in front of his face. "I don't understand you, Ryan. You're a detective. Your whole world is digging up answers to hard questions. You can't tell me trying to kiss me is the only unexplained, instinct driven thing that's happened to you. I'd bet my lungs you've had plenty of practice with things you can't explain or rationalize away. Things that raised an eyebrow or two from people around you. Or have you gotten so used to it that you don't even notice anymore?"

He looked out at the water again and sighed softly. "I don't know," he answered, as if to himself.

She reached across the bench and placed a tentative hand on his. "Yes, you do."

At the simple touch, his defensive posture relaxed a notch. His back was still up, but his slow exhale told her unequivocally he'd let go enough to at least listen to what she had to say and really hear her. She leaned forward, craning her neck to tilt her head in his direction. "For someone who carries the weight of the world and a loaded gun to prove they've got it all figured out that exhale sounded a lot like cease-fire."

She wanted him to smirk or pass a snide comment, but he just stared out at the water. "And for what it's worth, you may not be a big bad wolf, but that kiss would have blown the house down for any other girl.

From the side, he lifted one shoulder and let it drop, and his mouth lost its hard slant, but he still didn't turn to look at her. "Girls don't usually taser me like that when I kiss them."

"I'll bet. It's a Were thing, you know. Just one of the many perks.

Something to do with animal magnetism and the proximity of the moon."

He exhaled again, but this time in one quick stream, his expression a tangle of confused unease when he finally looked at her. "Well, that explains a lot of what I've been feeling lately." He hesitated, his voice barely above a hush, but his eyes searched hers, making it clear exactly who was at the heart of his internal wrestling match.

Lily paused, glancing down at her hand still resting on his, and tactfully pulled it back into her lap. shifter relations, lunar influenced or not, was not a topic she wanted to discuss right now. They had a vampire to kill and a council to placate.

"I know you've wondered about your abilities, but didn't you ever question why you can do what you do? I know I did. I hated being psychic, and I tried to hide it for the longest time. I didn't want to be labeled a freak," she said, carefully deflecting the topic. Sean could explain the ins and outs of shifter mating when he gave Ryan his 'welcome to the club' speech.

Ryan exhaled, sliding back to sit up straight. "I know exactly what you mean." He leaned his head back to look at the eggplant colored sky. "Sucks sometimes."

Grateful he took the hint and dropped the "why am I so obsessed with you?" question, Lily just nodded in agreement. "Sucks is right."

"I grew up in an orphanage with almost no information about my mother except that she died when I was born. I was labeled unadoptable, because of some rare blood disorder the doctors couldn't identify. It never limited what I could or couldn't do, but it was in my file, and no one wants to adopt a baby with medical issues." A practiced mask fell into place on Ryan's face, letting her know the rest of the topic was clearly off limits.

"Hmmm," she muttered noncommittally. "Terri, the friend I

mentioned, she was adopted as an infant, but then again she didn't have any medical issues."

He pushed his foot out, scrapping his heel on the pavement. "She was one of the lucky ones."

"I suppose, but then again what's lucky? She was killed by a werewolf."

A wet cloud of breath fogged out in front of him at her words, like he still didn't want to think about it, but was unable to ignore the reality any longer. "I guess I know now what it was that made my blood different made me different."

She tugged on his sleeve, and he turned to look at her. "For a detective, you certainly have a lot of unasked questions. My question to you is, are you ready for the answers?"

"Do I have a choice?"

Draping her arm across the back of the bench, she tilted her head in his direction, a grin spreading across her lips. "Nope, and I'm glad you finally realize that. Now I won't have to drag you in at gunpoint."

Ryan hoisted himself up from the bench and shivered. "I've probably got frostbite from sitting here so long, and it's entirely your fault. Tell me, can I snap my fingers and turn into a Saint Bernard, complete with keg collar?"

Chuckling, she shook her head. "Sorry, but for the record, shifters don't get frostbite." Still grinning at the image the idea conjured, she pushed herself to standing. "And besides, you're probably going to need something stronger than rescue brandy after you hear what Sean has to tell you."

"That bad, huh?"

"No. Just a lot to take in at once."

It was dark, the sun had set, allowing the ambient light from office buildings and streetlights to filter across the river, highlighting the water in hues of iridescent black. Park lamps popped on, casting yellow spheres in rows along the pavement, illuminating the ramp that led to the overpass crossing from the promenade over the FDR Drive.

Lily linked her arm with Ryan's, her need to make sure he didn't bolt overriding her better judgment at prolonged contact. "So, are you ever going to tell me why you called this morning, or do I just assume it was a case of animal magnetism?"

Now it was his turn to chuckle. "Oh man, I can hear the puns now. Actually, I went back to the crime scene. I saw what you saw, smelled what you smelled. It was then I realized you were right about what happened...about everything."

She stopped, pulling him to a standstill. "Then why the hell did you put me through all this today? Why the theatrics and the prick attitude, if you were already willing to accept what I had to tell you?"

He shrugged. "Because it wasn't me. Accepting that supernatural beings exist and tracking one as a possible perpetrator is one thing. Finding out I'm an unwitting member of the club is quite another. I didn't want to admit I was part of it. I'm still not sure I want to know."

They started walking again and headed away from the water and wind. Lily chewed on her bottom lip. "I get it, believe me. Cooperation isn't exactly my strong suit, either."

He lowered his chin, fixing her with a 'no shit, Sherlock' stare.

"Don't be such a jerk, all I'm saying is no harm, no foul. Still, if it's true and you are part cougar, just remember what they say about curiosity and cats. Cop or not, there are forces out on the street right now that you're unqualified to fight, and there's no such thing as nine lives."

He shoved his hands into his coat pocket. "No such thing, huh?" he repeated, his gaze taking on the feel of a thousand mile stare. "Too bad those words are no longer part of my vocabulary."

Lily put the key in the lock and opened the door, the tangy scent of pizza greeting her in the hall along with Jack. Coat in hand, he gave her a quick once over.

"Damn girl, you look like a hot mess," he noted with a chuckle.

Her hand immediately went to her hair, pushing the heavy curls and windblown volume back off her face. From the corner of her eye, she caught what he meant in the hall mirror, and frowned. She looked like a Barbie doll or a big-haired refugee from a 1980s catwalk.

"You're such a charmer, Jack. I'll have to remember to return the compliment."

Grinning, he tossed his jacket over the high back chair just inside the living room. "Anytime, cupcake."

She dropped her bag and her keys on the credenza, intentionally ignoring the playful jibe. She hated chauvinistic tags of any kind, so of course Jack slid one in every chance he got, but she was in too good a mood to give him the satisfaction of even rolling her eyes. She glanced from his face to his jacket and back again. "Where's Sean? Were you guys heading out somewhere?"

217

Without waiting for an answer, she turned her attention back to the mirror and smoothing out her errant curls. A disgusted sigh escaped her lips after a minute or so and she gave up, tucking what she could behind her ears.

"Don't worry," Jack said with a chuckle, gesturing toward her tangled mess. "That's nothing a hot shower and a little axle grease won't fix." At her dirty look, he grinned even wider. "Take your time. Sean's in the kitchen, and no, we're not headed anywhere, yet. We've been waiting for you."

As if on cue, Sean stepped through the kitchen doorway. Still looking in the mirror, Lily's eyes met his in the silvered glass, and she flashed him an awkward smile.

He leaned against the door jamb with his arms crossed casually in front of his chest, a sexy grin spreading across his lips. "This is a new look for you. Kind of untamed. I like it," he said, with his eyes sweeping her face and wild hair.

Sean's voice held a hint of a growl, and the familiar bedroom pitch left Lily's knees a little weak. He pushed himself away from the wall and walked across the parquet floor to where she stood. Reaching for her, he dipped his head in for a quick kiss, but straightened, wrinkling his nose. "Why do you smell...?" He let his words drift. His face suddenly leery. "Did your pet detective pull something I should know about?"

Lily shook her head. "Not really, but let's just say I owe you a huge apology for giving you such a hard time when you marked me."

Sean's face went dark. "Are you okay?"

Lily grinned. "I can take care of myself, wolf man, but, at the same time, I'm glad I had a supernatural firewall punctured into my shoulder to prevent things from getting too hairy." She lifted her fingers to his urban chic stubble, the rough feel sending a familiar shiver through her belly. "Those canines of yours pack quite a punch."

218

Sean shot her a questioning look, then dipped his head again close to her hair and inhaled. His posture eased, and he burst out laughing at the mental synopsis of how she handled the situation. "That half-breed cat and I need to have a nice long talk, or the fur is definitely going to fly."

She let her hand drop, breaking the flow of her recap. "Sean..."

He tweaked her nose. "Don't worry, I get it. He doesn't know which end is up when it comes to being a shifter, but he's going to get one hell of a crash course soon enough."

"Sooner than you think. He's due here in about an hour and half." She peeled off her jacket and walked toward the aroma of tomato sauce and Italian spices coming from the kitchen, her gurgling stomach leading the way.

"Smells great. Nino's?" she asked, tossing her coat onto the chair beside Jack's.

Jack nodded. "Yeah...I can't seem to get enough of the stuff. They were just taking the pizza out of the oven when I got there, so it's really hot and stringy. I had them go easy on the garlic, though, considering tonight's agenda."

"And?" she prompted, following them both into the kitchen. She didn't really need to ask. The sun had set long before she and Ryan said goodbye at the Starbucks on First Avenue across from the promenade, which meant the vampire race was awake and ready to be reckoned with.

"And nothing," Sean replied, reaching above the refrigerator for a stack of paper plates. "You know exactly what's on the agenda for tonight." Putting the dishes on the counter next to the open pizza box, he glanced over his shoulder at Lily. "Don't get crazy..." he paused, sliding an extra cheesy slice onto one of the plates and handed it to her. "...but I've decided it's for the best if you don't come with us tonight."

The welcoming feel of coming home after a hard day seemed to dissipate along with her hunger. She stood speechless, chiding herself that she should have seen this coming a mile away. Sean wasn't exactly happy with her involvement in this case on any level, and now that the stakes were high, he voiced his disapproval at every turn—but for him to exclude her altogether? She took the plate from his hand and put it down on the table without as much as a sniff.

His back was still to her as she stood waiting for an explanation, but as neither wolf elaborated, she crossed her arms in front of her chest and issued a loud, rough sigh. "When did I get vetoed out of this investigation? I thought we were handling this as a team, and the plan was to leave around midnight when the council would be in full swing."

Sean turned around, the resolute set of his jaw evidence that he was primed and ready for a litany of questions. "You haven't been vetoed out of anything. It's just better this way."

The phone rang, but Lily barely gave the handset on the kitchen desk a cursory glance, letting the answering machine grab it while she tried to keep a handle on her rising frustration. A telltale click followed by an empty dial tone told her whoever it was had hung up.

"Why? I don't understand. What happened? What's changed?"

Sean didn't answer. Not knowing what to say and not wanting to overreact, she sat at the table and absently watched Jack busy himself with his own plate. The boy's appetite hadn't let up at all, and she stared as he stacked three slices one on top of the other and took a bite. The clock above the sink read seven-thirty. It had been only a matter of hours since she had left Sean and Jack outside Bellevue to go and look for Ryan. One by one, she replayed the day's events, looking for anything that might have led to this change in plan. Nothing.

She had done everything Sean asked—from sifting through the residual psychic images retained by the badlands shifter, to requesting the latest case pathology. According to the coroner's report, bite marks on the victim's hands and forearms, as well as tissue scrapings from under his fingernails, pointed to the attack being a random hit. The unfortunate shifter had obviously fought for his life.

Inconclusive lab results couldn't provide a positive DNA identification on the attacker—no surprise there, since the perpetrator was a vampire, and what little blood remained in the victim had degraded to such an extent, it didn't lend itself to anything decisive, either. In fact, the only definite thing the human lab had provided was the time of death.

A dozen reasons played through her mind why Sean would intentionally discount her, but she dismissed each one.

Sean took his own plate and sat down across from her. "You're not eating," he said, folding his own slice in half and talking a bite.

"I'm not hungry."

As he chewed, the weight of his eyes watched her tear little bits from her paper napkin and curl them between her fingers. Lily still didn't say a word, instead collected her shreds and piled them in front of her on the table, even as she collected her thoughts.

"Sausage pizza is one of your favorites. Are you really not hungry, or just boycotting to try and punish me?" he asked, taking another napkin from the decorative holder at the center of the table and wiping his mouth.

Childish as it was, she pushed her dish even further aside. "Like I said, I'm not hungry, and if I wanted to punish you, I'm sure I could think of a better way to do it than starving myself."

Jack hoisted himself onto the counter, munching away with an open bottle of beer between him and the pizza box. "Ha! I'd take a piece of that bet," he said between chews.

Sean crumpled his napkin and threw it down next to his plate. "This is ridiculous. I heard your stomach growling when you came in. You're not the sulking type, Lily, so why now? No one is questioning how valuable you are in a tense situation, but this is different, and Jack and I already discussed it."

Shoving the tiny pieces of paper away, Lily leaned forward, her forearms pressed into the edge of the table. "Oh, you discussed it? Didn't anyone think it necessary to *discuss* it with me? Like I said, Ryan is coming here in an hour or so to talk. What am I supposed to do with him while we wait for you two to get back from playing summit meeting with the vampires?"

She cringed inwardly at the possibilities. Close proximity with Ryan at this point was not a good idea but letting Sean in on why she didn't want to be left alone with him was even worse.

After all her sermonizing, Ryan was finally willing to talk with Sean, and now they were leaving it to her to explain why neither shifter was around to meet with him.

Gee, thanks guys.

It's not that Ryan wouldn't understand, at the end of the day he was still a homicide detective, and this was still his case. Hell, if he knew where Sean and Jack were headed, he might even insist on going with them. Just the same, there was no way she was sitting home alone minding the castle.

"I know it's an inconvenience, but you'll have to call him and reschedule." Sean shrugged apologetically. "If you want, tell the detective I'll meet with him after I meet with the vampire council." Clearly trying to soothe whatever feathers he'd ruffled, he reached across the table and brushed her forearm with his knuckles. "I am sorry, Lily."

She squashed the urge to shove his hand away. "No, you're not... but I am. Sorry for a lot of reasons."

"Uh oh..." Jack uttered, scooting further down the counter away from them.

Sean pushed himself up from the table and stood with his hands on his hips as if weighing his next move. With a rough breath, he walked to the fridge and grabbed a beer from the open six-pack on the top shelf. "You're being ridiculous, even for you. For once can't you just do what I ask, without turning the request into a grand inquisition? You're not coming. I won't allow it."

He leaned against the counter and twisted the cap off the bottle, tossing it into the sink. The metallic plink as it hit the stainless steel like an audible exclamation point.

Since when did they use words with that connotation between them? "Allow?" she questioned.

Silent, Sean tilted the bottle to his lips and swallowed a good mouthful before dragging the side of his hand across his mouth and chin. "I don't have time to debate this, so you can save your daggers for later. This is shifter business. Bringing you along will only arouse things best left in peace."

Lily's eyebrows creased. "You're just chock-full of surprising semantics tonight, aren't you? Arouse? That's an odd choice of words, even for this situation. What could I possibly do, or possibly have, that would provoke the vampire council?"

Sean looked at her, not an ounce of humor in his face. "Not everyone appreciates a passionate disposition the way I do, and it's no secret that mouth of yours could provoke a saint to profanity, but that's not what I mean. You're a smart girl, think about it for a minute."

Lily beat back on her rising impatience and considered him. Sean wasn't usually cryptic, especially not with her. Although sanctioned, this meeting certainly wasn't classified, so why was he being so bullheaded about her going? What was so worrying, he couldn't come right out and say?

She blinked a couple of times, and then lifted her eyes to his, her body frozen in place. No wonder he thought she was slow on the uptake tonight. This wasn't just a meeting. It was a possible death sentence. Jack and Sean were walking into the belly of the beast, and the vampires would tear them to pieces if they so much as blinked the wrong way.

Or just because they felt like it...

Shivering mentally, her eyes moved from one man to the other. How could she be so stupid? So wrapped up that she couldn't read between the lines? They were both prepared to die, and she would be left to carry the news back to the Compound. A cold reality crept over her shoulder and wrapped its icy fingers around her heart, and she swallowed hard against the unfamiliar nudge of fear tightening her throat.

Hands shaking, she curled her fingers into her palms and got up from the table, moving around to where Sean stood. Facing him, she tried to conceal the depth of her realizations.

"I understand what you're trying to say. I'm human, which in itself is enough of a distraction, not to mention I have shifter blood and carry your mark. The combination probably makes me some sort of delicacy." She paused, watching Sean nod in agreement while surprise drifted across his face that she didn't press the issue and took the obvious hook.

He put the beer bottle down on the counter, his eyes still serious, but relieved. "I'm glad you realize that. You would be in tremendous danger, not to mention an unwitting liability. Jack and I alone would be no match for the conclave of vampires we expect to face in the council's lair, should anything untoward happen."

Leave it to Sean to make her safety a priority and downplay the risk to himself and Jack. He was right, of course. When it came to things like this, he was always right.

Suddenly, the last of the internal walls she'd built against fear and loss crumbled, and a surge of bottled up panic and dread rushed passed. She steeled herself, closing her eyes against the horrible probabilities floating across her mind. Terri 's voice echoed in the midst of it all, reminding her, this is what life was all about— to feel love as well as pain, or run the risk of feeling nothing at all.

If that was the case, then it was party time.

Now more than ever, she refused to be left waiting. Better to face real demons up front, then face the ones she conjured in her head. Whether she wanted the title or not, she was Sean's alpha female, and better to fight beside him, then be left behind to be his widow before she ever got the chance to be his bride.

Determined, she opened her eyes. "You're right," she said, knowing she had to meet them halfway, or Sean would never agree to listen. "I get it."

Sean didn't say a word, just raised an eyebrow as if waiting for the other shoe to drop.

"Can you repeat that, please? I don't think I quite caught what you said," Jack added, his snort unconvinced.

Lily bit her tongue. "Okay, okay, I'll say it again. You're right, and yes, the words taste like vinegar in my mouth."

"Halleluiah! Can I get an Amen?" Jack mocked, his hands high and spread wide. Sean lifted Lily's fingers to his lips, but she gently pulled her hand back.

"You're both forgetting one important thing," she said, pausing for effect, waiting for both men to focus on what she had to say. "I'm the one who can prove a vampire is responsible for all the lime-lighted bloodshed, and I'm not just talking about the shifter in the morgue this afternoon. I'm talking about all the attacks."

"Oh, God," Jack moaned, his sixth slice of pizza halfway to his mouth. "Just when you think you're out, they suck you back in— listen, you two can ping-pong this back and forth all you want, but I'm done." He tossed what was left of his half-eaten slice into the open pizza box and slid off the counter. "Call me when you're ready to roll. I'll be in my room." He spoke directly to Sean, purposely ignoring Lily, before pitching his crumpled napkin into the trash and then walking out.

Even with Jack's impatience weighing on him, Lily knew Sean couldn't ignore the truth of what she said, but that didn't mean he had to like it. The big wolf folded his arms in front of his chest.

"You've got it all wrong, Lily. You think you have proof, but you honestly don't. At least nothing concrete, and you don't seem to grasp the ramifications. I have demanded a meeting with the Vampire Council of New York City, one of the largest in the country I might add, with nothing more than a post-mortem psychic assessment and an allegation of guilt. Nothing in this bodes well for anyone, no matter how you look at it."

Lily opened her mouth to speak, but Sean unfolded his arms and raised a hand for her to just listen. "I know what you're going to say, and Jack is as much a witness to what happened in Washington Square Park, as you. He's a full shifter and a skilled hunter. He can phase on the fly if necessary.

"Vampires are cruel and devoid of emotional attachments by nature, instead they create a semblance of courtesy and decorum through their laws and the treaties made with the supes they refer to as *daylighters*. They do not take kindly to unfounded accusations, so unless you want to break into the morgue and throw what's left of that badlands shifter at their feet, it's best you let us handle it."

He let his arm fall to his side, and he drew in a breath. "Whatever the collateral damage, we stand a better chance of walking out of there alive without you to worry about."

Lily's eyes were on the floor. How could she argue with him? Did she want to go with them simply because she was afraid of being left alone, or did she have a death wish like Terri had accused? Or was it pride? Her case, her deal.

Sean lifted his hand again and drew his fingers along the curve of her cheek, gently raising her chin until their eyes met. "Lily, you and I have always told each other the truth, and this situation is no exception. It's a gamble, but my gut tells me this goes beyond the attacks in the city, and I'm willing to bet the vampires are just as stumped as everyone else involved. I'm hoping they'll be receptive, because odds are, they need all the supernatural help they can get."

Letting go of her chin, he picked up his bottle and placed it upside-down in the drain. He'd had enough of beer and talk. *"It's for the best, love. I couldn't live with myself if something happened to you because of a decision I made. You're my life, my heart."*

Sean's voice feathered across her mind, the intimacy of it robbing the breath from her throat. He leaned in to kiss her gently, then raised his fingers to brush the hair away from her eyes.

"I love you, too," she answered, sending as much trust and warmth as she could along their shared mind path.

"I'd better get Jack, the night's wasting," he said, and pushed away from the counter.

"Wait," she said, pulling on his hand.

He exhaled, his shoulders slumping as he turned.

"Don't be like that. I get that neither of you want my scent to add fuel to the fire and bait the vamps, but I had a thought. Unless Hollywood has it completely wrong, vampires have abilities just like Shifters, right?" She glanced up at him hopefully, but the man just crossed his arms again, not giving an inch.

She exhaled, blowing stray strands from her forehead. "Are all Shifters so pigheaded or just the ones in my life? Admit it what I'm saying makes sense. If vamps have talents similar to other supes, wouldn't they stack the odds in their favor and have a telepath on the council? Or at least in their guard? They would probably pick through my brain as a matter of protocol before we even got through the introductions, and there you'd have it, proof positive."

Sean didn't say a word, but the muscle in his jaw worked overtime. Considering he walked the fine line between overprotective mate and Alpha of the Brethren, it was no mystery as to which arguments he was biting back, and Lily knew it. In the end, her theories were valid, and she'd bet dollars to donuts that Sean already knew there was a telepath on the council. Perhaps that's what worried him.

"All right." He spit out the words like they were wrapped in barbed wire. "However, you need to stay close and listen to me. I mean it, Lily. I let you take the lead at the morgue, but this is my jurisdiction. None of your vigilante style antics, and for all our sakes, speak only when spoken to, and think before you answer."

Lily pursed her lips slightly, raising her chin a notch. She lifted onto her toes to press a kiss to his lips. He may have acquiesced, but she was smart enough to know at what possible cost. She slipped her arms around his waist and looked up at him, resting her chin on his chest. "I may be hot-headed, but I'm not stupid. You'll get no argument from me."

Jack walked back into the kitchen, a smirk on his face. "Ha! I'll believe that when I see it!"

"Eavesdropping, Jack?" Lily asked.

"Nah. More like reconnaissance," he said with a chuckle. "You two are about as obvious as water is wet, so can we go, please? I'm getting gray from all the time we waste talking."

Sean's shoulders shook, and Lily glanced at the young hunter across the hard muscled expanse of the alpha's chest. "You're a gray wolf, Jack you couldn't get any grayer if you tried."

"Ha, ha. Since you wheedled your way onto this pleasure trip, why don't you stick a couple of those homemade stakes of yours in your boot?"

Sean shook his head. "No weapons. If we go in armed, it sends a bad message. Besides, my guess is, they'll search us beforehand."

Jack raised an eyebrow but didn't say a word. Lily stepped back from Sean and pulled open the thin utility drawer at the end of the counter. Reaching in, she grabbed a handful of pencil sized pieces of wood, all with razor sharp tips and notched for a small, concealed crossbow.

"Would you look at that?" Jack said in surprise, stepping up beside her. He picked up one of the stakes and turned it over in his hand. Each stake had perfectly flared wings and a weighted silver tip. "You've been holding out on us, huh? You make all these yourself?"

She nodded.

"Where's the bow?"

"Second drawer on the left."

Jack reached in and took the mini bow out. The weapon was barely half the length of his arm, but its precision was unquestionably deadly. "You are one scary bitch, aren't you? I think maybe we need to do something about that."

Lily chuckled, but at the same time, took the bow out of Jack's hand and put it back in the drawer along with the stakes "Another time, maybe. Sean's right. No weapons tonight."

"If we're going to go, then you need to clean up. You still stink like cat."

She glanced down at her clothes. "I'll only be a minute, and I need to let Ryan know we'll meet up with him later."

THE VAMPIRE underground and its sanguinaria population thrived in New York City. The place was a veritable playground, where every fetish imaginable was indulged. Shadow houses dotted Manhattan's grid, sanctuaries for vampires sampling the city's pleasures a little too close to dawn, and havens where donors could be accessed without the least threat of repercussion.

A veil had been drawn across vampiric life, with access forbidden to outsiders. Of course, Sean had legitimate justification in requesting a temporary stay in that ruling, and permission to approach their inner sanctum had been granted, surprisingly.

With Lily in tow, he and Jack crossed Jane Street, heading west toward the Hudson River Greenway. Their destination was a hip new hotspot on Vestry Street, a dozen or so blocks south in the heart of trendy Tribeca.

Despite the cold, Sean put the nix on taking a cab, not wanting anyone, not even a random cabbie, to be able to pinpoint their destination. He quickly scanned the street and the alleys ahead of them. The invitation of Warm shifter blood on a cold night was tempting for any vampire, and the last thing they needed was an ambush from the shadows. Odds were, they would need all their reserves for the main event.

"Well?" Jack prompted.

Sean frowned at the younger wolf's mounting impatience and shot him a warning look before he nodded the all-clear. "Take your enthusiasm down a peg, boy. As of now, this is a non-confrontational parley, nothing more than a good faith transfer of information in hopes of preventing further bloodshed."

Jack huffed. "Bullshit. One of theirs killed one of ours."

With a sigh bordering on aggravated, Sean ran a hand through his hair, stepping up to the corner to wait for the light to change. Traffic still flowed in a heavy northbound pace on the Westside Highway, passing in a blur of car horns less than a block from where they stood.

"We still don't know all the particulars about that, and I'm not starting an all-out war over a random wolf, hundreds of miles from where he belonged. It's no secret there are Shifters who partner with the undead, and even those whose tastes stray toward the unthinkable."

Jack snorted. "No shit. I haven't run into one yet, but as far as I'm concerned a silver bullet to the head is too good for them."

"What are you two talking about?" Lily asked, her face surprised by Jack's grunt of disgust.

The wind off the Hudson was high, and Sean slipped his arm around Lily's shivering frame. For someone so small, she carried the weight of everything she'd witnessed over the past months with such strength. Anyone else would be downing cocktails of Prozac and antipsychotics. She knew so much already, but it was times like this when he realized how much she had yet to learn. A protective knot twisted in his stomach, and again the feeling warred with his sense of duty. Perhaps Lily was right to be so averse to the idea of being turned. It truly was a whole new world for her.

He sucked in a cold breath and pointed for them to take West Street, following the quieter road southbound along the highway. Construction scaffolding lined buildings along the inside edge of the street for what seemed like miles, offering them shelter against the wind. They slipped easily under the metal frame and ducked inside the plastic sheeting. Lily's shoulder's visibly relaxed with the sudden drop in wind shear, but Sean kept her close regardless.

"I'm not sure I know how to answer that question without it reeking of bias. Right or wrong, every culture has unwritten codes of behavior. Opinions about what is acceptable and appropriate. In that respect, Shifters are no different from anyone else, and, like other groups, we change with the times, or at least try to," he said, fixing his eyes on her.

"Nevertheless, there is one taboo regarding the undead that will probably never change. Vampires, their narcissism and the atrocities they commit, have branded them a depraved race by most Shifters. They are considered so obscene, anyone who panders with them is an outcast in the eyes of the Shifters. Even basic friendship is frowned upon, but to have relations with a vampire is unconscionable."

"I assume by relations you mean sex, right?" Lily asked, unwinding her scarf from her neck.

They had all warmed up, and Sean slid his arm from around her shoulders, but kept her hand wrapped in his. He nodded, twining his bare fingers with her gloved ones. "It's unthinkable, regardless of existing treaties. Vampires are dead, and their bodies are reanimated in a way most supernaturals find abhorrent. After all, we have living blood running through our veins, too. To make matters worse, vampires lump all daylighters together, regardless of species or race. Shifters, Fae...it doesn't matter to them. In their eyes, we are no more than a step above human, and they consider themselves the master race."

"Jeez, and all those vampire romances portray them as so anguished and long suffering."

Jack laughed. "Yeah, what a shocker for all the teenage girls hoping for their own brooding vamp. Go team wolf!"

Sean shot him a look. "Quit it, Jack. There are enough of the angst-ridden varieties still pining for their humanity to make our treaties worthwhile. As for teenage vampire romances, the world has been spellbound ever since Bram Stoker published *Dracula*, so go figure. *Our* species will *never* comingle, but the vampires who retain shreds of their humanity give us hope for a peaceful coexistence. Now, I'm not saying the wolf in the morgue had anything to do with breaking the taboo, but it's a possibility we can't ignore until we gather more facts. Lily, you were able to see the attack, and that information gave us a rough estimate of the vampire responsible, but the events leading up to it, and whatever was said between the victim and his attacker were garbled, right?"

Lily nodded, lifting her hand to tuck a few windblown strands back into her *Laura Croft Tomb Raider* style braid. "The way it felt in my head was similar to a glamouring, but not. It felt as though the vamp picked through the shifter's memories and jumbled them beyond recognition after he was dead. I'm not even sure that's possible."

With a huff, she pulled her left glove off with her teeth and shoved it into her pocket, letting go of Sean's hand to do the same with the other. A faint smirk danced at the corner of his mouth, and he chuckled inwardly at the classic Lily move. She was fidgeting, something she always did to channel tension before the hammer came down on a situation.

As expected, she had changed into her leathers before they'd left the apartment. It was as if she donned a certain persona, like superman changing into his tights and cape in a phone booth. Lily was gutsy and bold, and for some reason, she needed the outward show. Not that Sean minded. His eyes swept her shapely legs, noting the tight fit of her pants and how the black leather showcased every curve not covered by her short jacket. She might be freezing, but for him, she was hot enough to melt the ice floes on the Hudson. Need, unexpected and intense, flashed through him, thickening his groin. Lily tilted her head in his direction raising one eyebrow, and he answered with what he hoped wasn't a leer, squelching the urge to have her loosen more than just her scarf.

He refocused on the street ahead, clearing both his mind and his throat. "The confusion you encountered while reading him is certainly something we can put to them as questionable, but remember, for all we know, the vampires are just as concerned about what's been going on in this armpit of a city as we are."

"Armpit?" Her eyebrow stayed up, but this time for a different reason.

They were walking at a fast clip and had reached the end of the construction tunnel. Lily shoved her hands back into her gloves and rewound her scarf around her neck as they stepped back into the wind. Jack spit on the street next to the curb. "Sweet Cheeks, if you smelled what we smelled, you wouldn't be questioning Sean's description. Armpit is certainly a politer metaphor than I would have given."

"First cupcake, now sweet cheeks? Well, aren't you the colorful one this evening? Just a couple of days ago you were all about the city and its diversions, Jack. What's the matter? Bored already?"

The wind kicked up refuse from the street, and a plastic bag flew at them, billowing out and leaking the dregs of something rank. "Yeah...well even pigs want a break from their sty now and again," Jack commented, sidestepping the foul-smelling projectile.

"Enough, you two. We're here." Sean's game face shut them both up, and they each glanced across the street to the large warehouse on the corner. The building was old, its brick frontage as much a throwback to a bygone era as the matching paving stones set into the street it occupied. Tall, lead-paned windows had been cut into the structure, lending to its turn-of-the-century appeal, as did the old hand-truck ramp demarcated in red velvet rope, leading to the front door. The establishment's name blazed in ornate lettering on the beveled glass doors.

"The Red Veil? *This* is the home of the vampire council? Sean, this place was just written up in New York Magazine. The restaurant is booked solid for six months—and the club—it's strictly A-listers only," Lily said, a little shocked. "When you said we were heading to the old meatpacking district, I expected the seedier side, not high-end, red-carpet."

Sean cracked a smile. "Nope. Like I said, vampires are narcissistic. Trendy and expensive is right up their alley. And their lair is right behind that alley."

Lily slipped her hand into Sean's pocket, her delicate fingers seemingly fragile beneath his own. Yet the warmth and pressure of their fingers entwined calmed him, kept his focus on the task at hand, as they stepped off the curb and into the unavoidable.

Through the windows, it was obvious New York's latest 'in' place to see and be seen was packed for the evening. The Red Veil would serve its patrons until the basement nightclub by the same name opened its doors at eleven pm—two hours from now. By New York standards, it was too early for clubbers to start lining up, but already there was a queue down and around the alley that led to the club's main entrance.

Adrenaline coursed through Sean's body, despite his outward appearance of calm, the only hint to his unease, the tight set of his jaw. The next few hours would determine more than just the course of events for the here and now. What transpired could lay a foundation of accord between vampires and Shifters everywhere.

Or not.

"Ladies first," Sean said, pulling his hand from his pocket and steering Lily across the street.

"Where are they, exactly? I mean the vampires— they know we're coming, right?" she asked, glancing crossways to the restaurant and then back at Sean.

"Oh, they know we're coming."

Flanking Lily on her other side, Jack gave his characteristic snort. "I bet they already know we're here. In fact, I bet they're watching us from tiny peep holes in the walls."

"Jack..."

The younger shifter just shrugged, but his face was wary, despite his humorous bravado. "Well, what do we do now? Do we just walk into the restaurant and tell the maître d' we have a reservation with the master? I don't want to get this wrong, Sean. You know how vampires are about protocol, and an angry, insulted fanger is never a good thing."

"I've got it covered, Jack, just relax," Sean said, taking his cell phone from his inside breast pocket. With one touch, the screen illuminated, and he scrolled through the choices until he found what he searched for. His phone beeped once, and immediately instructions were issued via the speaker in a foreign language."

"What the hell kind of dialect was that?" Jack barked, clearly unnerved.

Sean held a finger to his lips, then punched a four digit code into his phone and hit send. The screen went dark, and he stuffed the cell back in his pocket. "Done."

Agitated, Jack scuffed his heel against the curb. "Guess I was absent the day they taught Transylvanian secret code, huh?" Jack remarked, but before Sean could reply, an older gentleman stepped through the main doors of the eatery and beckoned them forward.

Lily squeezed Sean's hand. It was show time.

SEVENTEEN

S ean entered the building first, pausing for a fraction of a second before motioning for the others to follow. The three of them stood in a v-formation just inside the door, with Sean at the head. His eyes quickly scanned the lobby and the wide arc of the dining room, noting the emergency exits, before his gaze shifted to the mahogany reservation desk at the center of the reception area. It was manned by two pretty hostesses and flanked on either side by low curved couches where patrons waited for their tables to be readied. Drinks in hand, people also queued along the wide, red carpeted stairs that he assumed led down to the club. It was game on, and one look from Sean reminded both Lily and Jack each to keep their thoughts and their comments to themselves.

The gentlemen nodded for them to wait between the reservation desk and the coat check off to its left, while he had his ear pressed to the receiver of one of the house phones. It wasn't hard to guess the subject of his one-sided conversation.

Jack gestured toward the chic, open-view, kitchen centered at the back of the dining room. Tables hummed with conversation while patrons were treated to a full on view of white uniformed chefs working at a frenetic pace. The dining room was as sumptuous as the scent of the food they served, with its gorgeous trey ceiling and trompe l'oeil murals. It was Victoriana at its best, and the whole scene was a surreal counterpoint to the reality of whom and what controlled the place.

The man hung up the phone, firing off a string of orders to one of the women standing behind the reservation desk. The language he spoke sounded too similar to that of the instructions left on Sean's phone for it to be coincidence, and both Lily and Jack exchanged glances. The woman's eyes darted toward Sean before a guttural reprimand from the maître d' made her jump. She bobbed her head and scooted behind him through a concealed door in the wall.

With a clap of his hands, his demeanor softened, and he turned his attention to Sean. "Welcome to The Red Veil," he drawled, addressing Sean directly while his eyes swept the alpha's big frame as if accessing his worth. The man inclined his head in an almost courtly manner, picking up a stack of reservation cards, and tapping them lightly on the desk. "May we take your coats?"

His facial pallor and the map of chalky blue veins ribboning his hands, wrists and throat made it clear he was a vampire. He held out a stark white hand, patiently waiting while Sean gathered everyone's jackets. "I'm afraid you're quite early. We weren't expecting you until midnight."

Sean ignored Lily's mental *I told you so,* instead pasting a polite smile on his lips. "I'm aware of that... please convey my apologies. As we are unfamiliar with the ebb and flow of the city's traffic, we didn't want to risk being late."

The man didn't comment, but his smug expression spoke volumes, despite his outward courtesy. He made no pretext that Sean's excuse was a complete fabrication. The alpha had given the devil his due, as was expected, so it was all good.

The gentleman took the jackets from Sean and handed them off to the remaining hostess. "Natasha will have your coats ready for you here at the end of your visit. In the meantime, I have been instructed to give you the choice of either waiting at the bar..." he gestured to a sumptuous lounge visible through a set of double doors to the right, "...or you are invited to partake of the V.I.P. activities downstairs. Like Disney, The Red Veil offers our own version of extra magic hours for special guests." The man's tone made it clear 'special' was a relative term.

The maître d' stood waiting for an answer, and though he stood quietly, his nostrils flared, and his tongue darted from his mouth to lick his lips. Sean felt Lily's body stiffen in a wave of answering hostility through their shared mind path. He gave her a swift mental knuckle rap, warning her to relax. With a polite smile, he inclined his head toward the man mimicking his courtly style. "I think it's best if we wait in the bar until summoned."

The corner of the man's lips twitched in truculent approval, giving them a swift hint of fang in the process. Now it was Sean's turn to stiffen. Respect was a two way street. He was the Alpha of the Brethren, the shifter equivalent of the vampire's master, and he refused to be intimidated. It was way too early to play this game, and he certainly wasn't playing it with a vamp lackey.

"Please tell *your* masters, that while I understand having to wait, due to our early arrival, as Alpha of the Brethren, I do not expect to be kept waiting past our agreed upon time." Sean made sure his underlying censure was heard and understood, before turning on his heel and walking across the shiny marble floor toward the bar.

~

"DON'T JUST STAND THERE *like an idiot, Jack, follow him.*" Lily's voice was insistent as it floated across the common shifter thread. For some reason, the younger wolf was bolted to the floor, and it took everything she had not to whack him upside the head. *"Sean's halfway to the bar, what's the matter with you? Show of solidarity and governance, remember?"*

With a quiet exhale, she brushed past Jack giving him a subtle elbow, finally waking him up.

"What the hell was that? Did the maître d' glamor you or something?" she murmured under her breath, when they were far enough away from prying ears. Not that the vamp couldn't hear them from the other side of the street, let alone the other side of the room.

The corners of Jack's mouth pulled down, and he glanced back over his shoulder as they walked toward the bar. "No. Forget it."

"Jack, we just got here. If you're going to freeze up, maybe you'd better take off now before things get, well, however they may get."

He grabbed her arm pulling her to a standstill, the differences in their height and body size making the move nothing short of intimidating. "Don't forget whose bitch you are. You might be able to pull that crap with Sean, but not with me." His tone was clipped and ugly, but now was neither the time nor the place to make a big deal out of it, and Lily just shot him a warning look.

With a quiet sigh, he glanced up at the ceiling, and when his eyes met hers again, they were softer. "Look, joking around is one thing, but you forget I'm a full shifter, and I'm a hunter. If I pause because I sense something, don't interrupt me, and never assume I hesitate out of fear."

A wash of guilt sent heat flooding into her cheeks. He was right. She shouldn't have assumed. Lily put her hands on her hips, careful to keep her voice low. "Did you sense something?"

"Perhaps."

She exhaled, her eyes taking in his face and eyes. He was being evasive again, but she wasn't going to push the issue. "Something disturbed you back there, and it wasn't just my mouth. I can feel it. If you don't want to tell me, fine, but I think you'd better tell Sean."

His mouth puckered. "I plan to, when I have more to tell him. In the meantime, remember what I said." Jack pushed past her and walked into the bar.

She trailed in after, skimming the room for Sean. The place was photo-shoot worthy, with its intimate booths and polished pub tables. Club chairs were situated in groups of two beneath the tall windows, the paned glass draped in translucent veils of varying shades of crimson. Flocking damask in the same cerise hues covered the chairs, their patterns harkening back more than a century, like the heavy dark woods and rich accents throughout the place.

Lily slid into the booth at the farthest back corner beside Sean, while Jack chose to belly up to the bar.

"Everything okay?" Sean asked, cocking his head suspiciously.

She nodded her answer, not trusting herself to open her mouth. Jack said he would tell Sean when he had more to say, and she'd take him at his word.

"You sure?"

She nodded again, drawing in a quick breath through her nose. "Yeah, I'm good. You know how I get when I have to wait." She flashed him a quick smile, hoping it would be enough for him not to press the issue.

Sean picked up one of the menus from the table. "Hmmm," he murmured, glancing at the specialty drinks on the cover. "You do know this is all about finesse and diplomacy, right?" He eyed her over the top of the laminated cardboard.

She nodded.

"Good. Just because I put the vamp behind the desk in his place doesn't mean you have carte blanche to do the same." He eyed her knowingly. "If the maître d's elders learned of his blatant disrespect, he'd be..."

"...a very sorry vampire?" Lily interrupted.

Sean shook his head. "No. He'd be a very dead vampire. Jack was right when he said vamps are all about respect for hierarchy and protocol. The maître d' needed to be reminded of that, and just the same way an apology was expected over us being early, a wrist slap was necessary to let him know I mean business. If I hadn't done so, it would have been viewed as a weakness. In their eyes, anyway."

Jack came back from the bar with three coronas and dish of sliced limes. "I figured we'd stick with what we started with earlier."

Sean nodded. "One beer each acknowledges their hospitality, but any more compromises us in more than just the obvious way."

The three of them clinked bottles then settled in to wait. The bar itself was packed four people deep, but there were still a few tables left open. A young waitress approached, carrying a half liter wine bottle and two long stemmed glasses on her tray. "I'll be with you in a sec," she said, as she passed to place the wine on the table next to theirs. Pad in hand, she turned on her heel, placing a bowl of fancy vegetable chips on their table along with a few napkins. "Are you guys all set, or can I get you something else from the bar?"

"We're good for now, thanks," Sean replied with a smile.

She nodded once. "Great. Just give me a shout if you want anything." With a tip-worthy smile plastered on her face, she turned to head toward the bar.

A couple in their mid-twenties had just sat down at one of the high-top pub tables not far from their booth. The woman was a stunning brunette, with long silky hair swept back off her face and fastened with a glittering clip at the nape of her neck. Her black dress barely whispered across the top of her thighs and plunged to her navel at both the front and the back, leaving almost nothing to the imagination.

Her escort was what New York fashion magazines would call a metrosexual, a man with taste and chic style, who knows about fashion, art and culture. They were a typical A-list wannabe couple, as alien as two people could be, to the two Shifters sitting at the booth with Lily.

The woman struck a pose, crossing her long bare legs. Jack's eyes were glued to her, his beer poised halfway to his lips.

"Wipe your mouth, Jack." Lily said, tapping the corner of her own. "You've got a little doggie drool going on there."

Sean smirked, taking a sip from his corona, the little slice of lime bobbing up and down in the amber liquid as he tilted the bottle up to his mouth. "Can't say as I blame him."

"Ha. And I'll lay dollars to donut she knows it too," Lily added, taking a purple chip from the bowl at the center of the table.

Jack wiped his mouth on the back of his hand, glancing once more at the woman. "What can I say it's been a long, dry week." He tipped his bottle back, giving Lily a wink. All was forgiven between them, and she blew him a kiss.

Lily munched on what she could only guess was a taro chip. Not that she knew one vegetable from the next in this mix, but they had a salty crunch and were perfect with the beer. Condensation dripped down either side of her hand as she took a sip from her bottle, her thumb absently running up and down the blue and gold label.

Her hand was cold and wet, but an odd sensation crawled up her arm and settled in a weedy tingle at the back of her neck. She reached behind to rub at the spot, twisting her head back and forth, but it only worsened. Dull needles and pins pricked her skin, sending numb fingers stabbing across the base of her skull.

"What's the matter?" Sean asked, watching her oddly.

"I don't know. Just a weird feeling at the back of my neck."

"Weird how? Like a pinched nerve?" Sean slid in closer, but Lily dropped her head backwards and arched her back as the prickling turned into a stabbing sensation. In her mind she heard someone chuckle, and then the feeling stopped.

"The wolf can't protect you forever..."

Lily's head snapped up, and she froze.

"You sought your revenge, now I wait for mine."

243

A new wave of angry thought tore through her and she clenched her teeth, jamming her fingers into her temples. "Get out of my head!" she hissed, low and fierce.

Grabbing her shoulders, Sean turned her around to face him. Without warning or permission, he merged his mind with hers, and she whimpered at the assaultive sensation. *"Who are you and what do you want?"* His defensive presence snarled with menace along their breached mind path, but the voice just laughed.

"Be warned, wolf. Not all is as it seems, and I am waiting..."

At the oily feel of the voice in his own head, Sean's eyes turned from blue to yellow and a savage snarl escaped his throat, turning heads in the bar.

Jack slipped around the table to flank Lily's other side while he scanned the room, staring down the prying eyes.

Lily slumped forward, dropping her forehead into her hands. The voice and its evil chuckle faded, along with all trace of whoever it belonged to. Sean skimmed his hand across the center of her back, gently massaging the space between her shoulder blades.

"Can you tell me what the hell just happened? One minute she's eating a chip next she looks like the chick from the exorcist," Jack said out of the side of his mouth, while staring at people to mind their own business.

"Someone or something just invaded Lily's mind. It threatened her. And me," Sean answered, not taking his eyes or his hand from Lily.

Jack dropped back down into his seat across from them, and grabbed his beer, taking a long pull. "Jesus. Any idea who? What did they say, exactly?"

Lily took a ragged breath, leaning up on her elbows. "They said the wolves couldn't protect me, and that they wanted revenge."

"Revenge? For what?"

She pressed her fingers to her temples and rubbed in a gentle circular motion. "I don't know. All I do know is that it wasn't human. Terri warned me about my practice runs maybe whoever it was wanted retribution for someone I killed last fall." She sat up, her gaze and her hands dropping to her lap. "It's not like I've been keeping my presence here on the down low."

Sean shook his head. "No. Whoever it was knows about us," he said, gesturing to himself and Jack. "They know you're under my protection, and that means this could be another of Parr's tactics."

She looked up, her eyes rising to meet Sean's. "Could he be tracking us?"

"I wouldn't put it past him. He'd never soil his own hands doing the work himself, but he's certainly convinced enough Shifters to follow him that anything's possible. Plus, he's skilled enough to cloak himself telepathically."

"You said Parr was backing off. Why would he risk something so outright?" Jack asked, distractedly rolling the base of his bottle between his palms.

"Because it wasn't outright. Parr could deny it, claiming it could be anyone connected to the trail of bodies Lily left in her wake before she even got to the Compound."

Lily made a face. "I wouldn't exactly call it a trail, and each one was popped while attacking a human."

Sean slid his hand the rest of the way around her shoulders. "Unfortunately, that doesn't matter. Still, whoever this is, made a huge miscalculation and all we need to do is tighten the hold. He thinks his threats will panic us, but all he's done is put us on alert and ruined his chances at a surprise attack."

"Gee thanks, that's a comforting thought," she hmphed. "Like we don't have enough to worry about already."

Jack didn't interject. Instead, the younger wolf's nostrils flared, and he jerked his head to the side, his gaze tracking across to the man sitting at the high-top table with the brunette. She was practically in his lap, and he had one hand shoved up her skirt and the other curved around her waist.

"You're bordering on stalker, Jack. Leave them be." She was still shaken, and his adolescent attention span only served to irritate her more.

Jack waved her off, his eyes riveted as the man's tongue licked the brunette's throat from her cleavage straight up to the base of her ear. The woman moaned, and as she did, he sank a pair of small, razor sharp fangs into her jugular, his hand sliding up from her waist to unclip her hair. It fell forward in a curtain of brown silk, obscuring his activities from prying eyes.

"No fucking way!" Jack's words were no more than a breath, but their harsh undertone matched the look on his face. "This place is just about as fucked up as it can get."

"What?" Sean asked, his body language broadcasting his alert level at DEFCON 1.

"Them." Jack jerked his head toward the couple. "The Dapper Fanger and his happy meal."

Both Lily and Sean turned, but there was nothing to see, that is, until the vampire pushed the girl's hair back off her shoulder, giving them a close up view of his blood-stained teeth piercing her exposed flesh.

Sean's grip on Lily's shoulders tightened, and a low growl rumbled from the back of his throat.

With an arrogant sneer the vampire released the woman scraping his finger across his lips and licking it clean, before doing the same to her throat. The woman's eyes seemed almost drugged as she glanced across her shoulder at them. "Don't knock it till you try it." Her words and her body were no more than a languid murmur as she slid off the barstool into the vampire's waiting arms. The woman practically purred as the two walked past on their way to the door.

"Ugh. This whole evening... Don't vampires fear anything? I mean, *jeez*, this is a public place," Lily grimaced. "If they're supposed to be all about respect, then don't they have rules about indecent exposure or something? But I suppose consensual feeding doesn't count, huh?"

Sean's shoulders rose and fell. "Respect is a big deal to them, or at least it is to their elders. Perhaps the undead are going through their own version of a civil war regarding tradition and law."

"Okay, so rogue vamps and rule breakers aside, what about natural enemies? Don't all creatures have competitors?"

Jack huffed. "I can tell you what they fear. A sharp stake and high noon," he said, peeling bits of label from his bottle of corona. "Those little numbers you have hidden in your kitchen drawer would make any one of them shit their pants. That is, if they could take a shit."

"That's not what I'm talking about, Jack. Everything on this earth has a natural enemy. It doesn't make sense for them not to, as well. There has to be some other species that pits against them to maintain checks and balances. Or are they completely outside the natural order?"

Sean nodded but didn't elaborate.

Her brows knit together as she ran the possibilities, despite the hedgy look on Sean's face. It wasn't that he was hiding anything. She knew, without a doubt, whenever that was the case. This had to be something extraordinary for him to doubt her skills.

"Okay...give. Either you nodded because I'm right, or you don't have a clue either. I think I'm right, but nothing I can think of fits the bill, so it must be something I'm unaware of."

Both perplexed and annoyed, Lily let out a sharp breath, but Sean's gaze said he got no satisfaction in stumping her this time. The answer to her question was no laughing matter, and one he clearly didn't relish talking about.

"Don't be so hard on yourself. The answer isn't an obvious one. A vampire's only natural enemy is another vampire—and yes they are that outside the natural order. But that's not to say they don't fear."

"And?"

Sean rubbed his face with his free hand. "And nothing. This is a topic I don't care to discuss right now. It's the wrong time and definitely the wrong place. There are entities out there beyond comprehension, even for supernaturals, and they are what vampires fear."

Lily blinked, considering all he'd said. Every legend she'd ever heard of ran through her mind. She added up and tossed out likelihoods, running the scope from folklore and mythology to religion, until she looked up, giving each of them a quizzical look. "I think I figured out what you mean. You're referring to entities from another plane, ones with no explanation as to origin, even beyond mythology."

Sean just stared at her, giving nothing away.

"You mean angels and demons, right?" she asked, looking from one to the other.

Jack shook his head slowly. "How did you work that out so quickly, or is it a psychic thing?"

Sean didn't give her the chance to answer. "Did Terri say something to you about this before she moved on?"

The question took her by surprise, and her satisfaction at solving the riddle evaporated. "No, of course not. Why would you think that?" Her eyes searched his, trying to get a bead on where he was headed. "The reason Terri was here, had everything to do with helping me get over...well, me. You know that. It had nothing to do with supes and their interrelationships. If she earned angelic brownie points or was downgraded to demon for breaking some spiritual protocol, I haven't a clue. You were there, she didn't exactly say much once she went into the light."

Concern flooded her, and she shifted her body to the side, to eye Sean straight on. "Why are you asking this? Are you hoping to intimidate the vampires with the threat of a celestial sword?"

"Don't be that way, Lily. It was a legitimate question," Jack shot back in Sean's defense. "You're the only frame of reference we have, when it comes to contact with other planes of existence. It's not like we can walk and talk with the dead. You're the one that's tuned into that channel."

"I'm not tuned in! It's not like I can control it or anything. It just happens."

"Okay, enough. This is why I didn't want to get into this. Yes, vampires are afraid of both angels and demons, for much the same reason. Neither can be controlled, and they are untouchable. It's been that way since God said, 'Let there be light.'

"Angels aren't exactly the benevolent creatures history paints them to be. They are warlike, hence why they are referred to as legion. It has as much to do with their nature as their number.

"Demons, on the other hand, are exactly as they are depicted. The only difference between the two is that angels aim for the greater good, although they don't always see things the way we do. Demons love to play 'let's make a deal', but no matter how you slice it, you always end up owing them something, and they love nothing more than to take their pound of flesh. Literally."

"And I suppose they don't care if the flesh is living or dead, right?" Lily asked.

"Yup."

"Great. This evening just keeps getting better and better. Can we go home, yet?" She sighed, slumping against the soft damask of her seat.

Sean clasped her fingers in his, bringing them to his lips. "Nope."

"It's settled then." Jack folded his hands on the table. "Since we're forced to wait, let's get another round and shake this off. I know you said only one round, Sean, but this is medicinal." He snorted. "There isn't anything we can do at this point to trace the telepathic threat you both felt, and since Terri isn't likely to swoop down in a blaze of celestial kickass, who cares if harp music leaves the vamps shaking in their shoes? Dinner hour seems to be clearing out, so things must be coming to a close. At least up here, anyway."

"Jack..."

"You just love saying my name, don't you sweetheart?" he asked, sucking the beer soaked lime from his bottle, and holding it between his teeth. "Better keep an eye on this one, Sean. I think she likes me."

Laughing quietly, Sean raised one finger to signal for the waitress, then, slid his gaze toward Lily. "What is it you always say, babe?

A smirk slanted across her mouth. "In your dreams, wolfboy."

EIGHTEEN

"I think it's finally show time, people." Sean's gaze tracked past Jack's shoulder to an extremely thin, extremely pale beauty walking across the bar in their direction.

"About time. I can't make myself swallow any more of these wood chips," Jack replied, smacking his lips like he'd just eaten dirt.

Lily gave him a smile with her lips closed. She was usually the restless one, and though they had only been waiting an hour, Jack was right, however silly his comment. Waiting around like this sucked, especially considering what lay in the balance.

Her eyes darted past his shoulder as well, and her smile faded. After the maître d' thing, there was no doubt in her mind which side of the coffin this chick preferred. The woman fast approaching was undeniably a vampire, and from her carriage and demeanor, one of some age and importance.

Not sure what to expect, Lily uncrossed her legs beneath the table and set both feet on the floor, scooting herself back in her seat, muscles tensed for anything. "Something evil *definitely* this way comes," she murmured, catching Jack's eyes.

The vampire was sophisticated, to say the least. From the top of her coiffed head to the bottom of her 1940s-style sling back heels, she was an undead version of Jackie Kennedy. In this instance, claiming the 'Devil wears Prada' wasn't too far of a stretch, except this devil was dressed in a vintage Chanel. The pale woman carried herself with grace, but beneath the classic elegance was an underlying current of "don't fuck with me or I'll eat you."

She stopped just a foot short of their table, her eyes assessing them without as much as a blink. "Mr. Leighton?" she inquired, though her mien indicated she knew exactly who was who.

"Yes, and who might you be?" Sean replied, his answer polite but wary.

The woman raised a perfectly arched eyebrow, hesitating as if weighing whether or not to answer the question. "Abigail," she replied with a quick nod, her gaze clearly reassessing Sean's standing. "I've been asked to escort you downstairs."

Sean glanced quickly at both Jack and Lily, but the vampire raised a manicured hand before he could say a word. "My apologies." She smiled sparingly. "What I meant is you have *all* been summoned. If you will follow me, the counsel awaits you downstairs."

Her voice may have flowed like silk, but Lily's senses perked up at the tacit trace of resentment hidden beneath her courteous manner. Undoubtedly, she took exception to being told to go fetch.

Steady but still wary, Sean nodded, and the three of them pushed up from their seats to follow her toward the door. The vampire smelled honey sweet, and her tone as she made small talk was both dulcet and intoxicating.

Lily hung back, her attentions divided between watching the woman for any sudden moves and trying to keep up with Jack's erratic mood swings. The boy's temperament was still bordering on bipolar, and she made a mental note to talk to Sean about it later.

In the meantime, she waited, taking in as much as she could, fascinated by how much the vampire's presence held sway in the bar. Men nearby all but unseated themselves as she walked past. At the door, she excused herself for a moment to speak with the bartender, and every man in the bar gazed after her adoringly. Lily couldn't shake the feeling the woman's voice and scent were some sort of siren's song, a vampiric ploy used to lure her victims in. She glanced at both Sean and Jack to see if either was affected, but thank God, neither was. Maybe her mastery only worked on humans.

With a single nod, the bartender went back to his customers, and the woman glided toward the doorway, gesturing for them to follow. Lily half expected the men from the bar to trail after her, like rats following the pied piper, but thankfully they didn't. The vampire smiled, giving them a glimpse of her small but deadly fangs as she directed them toward a narrow corridor off to the right of the bar's double doors.

Their footsteps echoed, despite the dull noise from the restaurant, until they stopped in front of a doorway that looked like a cross between an elevator and the entrance to the bridge on *Star Trek's U.S.S. Enterprise*. The woman slid her long tapered fingers into the front pocket of her boutique jacket and pulled out a hotel style keycard. One quick swipe through a concealed electronic eye, and the silver gray door slid apart from its center seam.

"Victorian Era meets Sci-Fi," Jack commented under his breath. "Guess someone likes steampunk."

The woman's eyebrows lifted, and the younger wolf blushed. Was he more embarrassed that she'd heard him, or that he knew about steampunk?

The vampire stepped aside for them to pass. On the other side of the threshold was another reception area, only this one was meat locker cold and resembled a demonic version of the Oval Office.

Lily's breath fanned out ahead of her as she walked with the others toward the center of the anteroom. The curved walls were covered in a thin layer of black leather that ran from the ebony hardwood floor to the base of the white domed ceiling. A thick circular area rug offered the only softness to the décor. There were no windows and no doors, and dim recessed lighting gleamed, illuminating the dome, and the streamlined chrome and glass reception desk at the center of the room.

The vampire extended her arm, indicating they should wait by the mirrored elevator bank recessed into the wall to the right of reception.

Behind the desk sat a human girl. She couldn't have been more than twenty years old, and Lily gave her a quiet assessment while the vampire instructed the girl to announce their arrival.

Still curious about a human stationed at the threshold of the undead inner sanctum, Lily gave her and her secretarial surroundings a gentle probe.

"Lily…" Sean didn't even bother with telepathy.

Lily winced, pulling back immediately. Hot searing pain exploded behind her eyes forcing her to break contact.

The girl tsked, shaking her head. Her thoughts had been booby trapped against prying minds, and she issued an evil smile as Lily winced again against the fading pain.

She shot the girl a dirty look, squeezing the inner corners of her eyes between her thumb and forefinger. Lily hadn't caught much, but what she had seen bordered on unreal, as she tried to reconcile the girl's 'pearls around the neck' prep school appearance with the twisted beyond hope workings she'd touched upon inside her mind.

Smoothing her braid, she avoided Sean's 'I told you so' stare and redirected her attention to the wall and its unusual patterning. "I didn't know they made leather wallpaper," she said to no one in particular, ignoring Jack's mental chuckle at her expense.

The vampire brushed past, bumping Lily's shoulder as she ran her fingertips across the smooth black. The woman inserted her same keycard into an electronic eye to the side of the elevator's silver frame. "They don't," she answered, barely acknowledging that Lily had spoken. "But we do."

Lily jerked her hand back, staring at the woman's profile as her words and their implication hung in the air between them. We do? She swallowed hard, not wanting to think about where they got their raw materials.

At that moment, the elevator pinged. "Guests first," the vampire said, as the doors slid open.

Sean entered the elevator car first, followed by Lily, then Jack. The vampire stepped in, positioning herself with her back to the others. Sean shot Lily another warning as the doors slid closed, his meaning clear. Loose cannon, strike one.

"Identification," an automated voice necessitated over the elevator's intercom.

The vampire punched a numbered code into a keyboard panel next to the door.

"Voice Analysis."

The woman fixed her eyes on Lily. "2141767, Abigail Bigly."

Waves of hostility poured from the vampire as if her name should mean something. Lily stared back, refusing to blink, even though an unspoken challenge had been dropped at her feet for no apparent reason.

"Verification completed."

The woman broke eye contact and turned again to face forward.

Sean raised an eyebrow at her, but Lily shook her head innocently. *"Don't look at me, I have no idea what that one was all about,"* she defended across their shared mind path.

He exhaled quietly. *"I knew I should have left you home."*

The elevator lurched, then started its descent. It only took minutes for them to reach the bottom floor, but the claustrophobic atmosphere made it seem like hours. Either Abigail had a score to settle, or she liked to play head games. Big deal. Hadn't they anticipated as much from at least one bloodsucker? Lily just needed to keep it cool.

The elevator doors slid open, and Lily stepped out into the club behind Sean and Jack. Garage grunge and acid punk set the tone for the place, and she glanced around, unfazed by the raw feel that emanated in waves from all sides.

It was only ten p.m., and the club was empty for the most part, with only a few people scattered around on the vinyl couches surrounding the concrete dance floor and in the corner shadows past the main bar. They were too far away to tell if they were vampires, but after what had zapped her upstairs with Goody-Two-Shoes Gone Bad, she had no intention of going fishing again.

Abigail pointed for them to follow her toward the VIP section, platformed off to the side and guarded by a rather large, rather intense looking bouncer. A quick flash of fang from him in an over eager smile, and it wasn't hard to imagine what he'd do with one word from Abigail. She led them up a few quick stairs and past the roped off area toward the back. Underground clubs all over Manhattan were notorious for their backrooms, and most people equated them with gay clubs and fetish bars, but this went beyond anything Lily had ever heard about. This was the true anteroom to the undead inner sanctum, not the sleek leather clad reception area upstairs.

A crushing feeling hovered over her as they walked through the corridor toward a steel reinforced door at the end. Random doors lined their path on both sides, but heaviness thick with warning actually forced her not to see, not to look. Wards may have blocked the rooms from view, but she didn't need her eyes to see what went on behind closed doors. The images bombarded her almost of their own volition.

Her throat tightened and she stumbled, grabbing onto Sean's arm. His hand gripped her elbow, and he helped her up. She felt the warmth drain from her face, and one look from him told her, he felt it too. These rooms were where vampires did the unspeakable.

"I trust you can keep up, yes?" Abigail taunted with a sniff. She turned, and a scornful breath escaped her lips at Lily's strained expression. "Oh, please, where exactly did you think you were headed? These rooms are what they are, and even among my kind they are not for the faint of heart. This one here is a favorite. *La Chambre de L'allaitement.*"

Jack gave Sean a confused look. With Abigail's sophistication and flourish, her posh accent made the words sound mysterious and chic, but after four years of high school French, Lily knew exactly what it meant. The images that hit her when they entered the corridor left no doubt in her mind it was a fetish room for vampires who liked to feed on lactating women. She looked at Sean, who knowingly met her gaze with the same revulsion.

What in God's name had they gotten themselves into?

Abigail's grin grew to ugly proportions, her fangs elongating like an exclamation point on their debauched lifestyle. "When you live for centuries, it gets harder and harder to find diversions. It happens." She shrugged, unremorseful. "Some of us grow bored with modern notions of political correctness and become nostalgic. This room is called *La Oubliette.*" She looked right at Lily. "Just think of the King Charles VIII and his war on the Borgias and the treatment their enemies endured. You'll get the idea."

Lily swallowed hard. "I don't need imagination to give me a visual. I get it unsolicited, complete in 4-D high definition. So, if you don't mind, can we just get to where we're going? I'm sure the council is waiting on us."

She let go of Sean's arm and straightened, squaring her shoulders, not really caring if that counted as strike two. He didn't say a word, though. Not verbally or telepathically, just sent her a mental kiss.

"Thanks for that," she feathered back.

"Anytime."

"Do you actually know who we're meeting with, or are we completely winging it?"

"The master goes by the name Sébastien. I met him years ago, and from what I remember he's nearly a thousand years old. His right hand man is called Rémy. They were both made by the same sire in France during the middle ages. Hence all the Gallic references."

"Great. Two vamp brothers who came from chaos and war. This just keeps getting better and better..."

"I BID YOU EASE, Sean Leighton, Alpha of the Brethren," Sébastien said, rising to greet Sean from his seat near the fireplace. "Though, I sincerely regret the reason for this reunion. If only it was under happier circumstances." He glided forward across the same ebony hardwood displayed in the upstairs lobby. His hand extended in welcome.

Lily slid her eyes sideways to Jack, who had visibly blanched at the sight of the master vampire. The man was imposing. Not that he was physically large. In fact, his physique appeared more in line with the men of his time, diminutive as compared with men of the twenty-first century, and downright small compared with both Sean and Jack. His commanding presence and the unmistakable aura of vampiric power and formidable magic made him lethal.

Sébastien moved fluidly and seemed to float above the ground. His dark curling hair set off his pale skin, but it wasn't the stark white Lily expected. It seemed to have a translucent appearance, like a thin sheet of velum or onion skin. Through the veil of her lashes, she compared him with the other vampires, surprised to find as many varying shades of pale translucence as there were human skin tones.

As the man came upon Sean, Lily shivered, her skin crawling

with gooseflesh from the cold knowledge that this was the first of many tests this evening would bear. The manner in which the master vampire acknowledged the Alpha of the Brethren would set the tenor for the rest of the undead seated around the room.

Sean stood tall and grasped the man's proffered hand in an ancient symbol of brotherhood, each clasping the other's forearm, though Lily knew it was for protocol's sake alone and not because of any abiding alliance. The inherent promise smacked of equality and fidelity, yet it was a pie crust promise, easily made and easily broken.

The fire crackled in the oak and stone hearth, sending shadows dancing along the walls. The warm light added richness to the heavy furniture and the brocade tapestries that hung in long decorative panels on either side of the fireplace. More of a library than tribunal, the room's ambiance lent itself to knowledge and contemplation rather than argued pleas and convictions.

Four chairs graced the thick hearth. They were unmistakably seats of power. As Sébastien greeted their guests, the three remaining adjudicators stayed seated, each with a vampire guard standing directly behind them, their eyes alert and unblinking. Abigail took her place behind Sébastien's empty chair, her long white fingers curved possessively over its tufted top.

None of the vampires were dressed casually, making Lily wonder if this parley was considered a formal occasion. She glanced down at her own attire, questioning her choice to wear her leathers. Glancing across to Jack, the younger wolf shrugged as if he read her thoughts. He was right, there was nothing she could do about it now. The important thing was Sean had dressed appropriately, thank God—as Sébastien was dressed similarly in a dark pinstripe suit, his blood ruby shirt paired with a tie of the same.

Sean met the master vampire's smile. "Thank you for your gracious invitation, especially considering the short notice. I am gratified you deigned this matter essential enough to oversee personally." Sean answered, his manner and his speech taking on as formal a tone as the vampire's.

Lily studied Sean's body language, sending a mental note to Jack to do the same. If this meeting required old fashioned formalities to be successful, then they'd both better be onboard with it as well.

The skin on the back of her neck prickled. Not in the same way it did in the bar, but more like when someone was watching you. Abigail eyed her, but the vibe wasn't coming from her. Lily swiveled her head around toward the doorway on the opposite wall from where they stood.

The guard standing at attention next to the exit was staring at her, his eyes narrowed and suspicious.

Abigail followed Lily's gaze and chuckled quietly, earning a sharp look from Sébastien. "And what is so amusing, Abigail?"

She snapped to attention, immediately dropping her eyes. "Nothing, my liege. It's just Etienne seems to have homed in on their psychic."

Lips tight, Sébastien gave her a withering glance. "You'll have to accept my apologies, Sean. My aide-de-camp is yet a fledgling, less than 250 years old. She was one of the original settlers here in the New World. I saved her from starvation by assuaging my own thirst on her lovely neck," he chuckled. "1767, I believe, isn't that so, chéri?"

Lily's gaze jerked toward Abigail, and the look on the woman's face confirmed what she suspected. They not only identified the vamps by voice, but also by date sired. *2141767*. Aww...Abigail was a valentine vamp!

The woman's eyes narrowed, and another wave of hostility surged in Lily's direction along with a protracted hiss.

"That's enough, Abigail. Your behavior is not only beneath your station, it's tiresome. The alpha's seer is no threat to any of us. In fact, she is quite the interesting specimen." Sébastien shifted his regard toward Lily and inhaled, holding his breath for a moment as if sampling a fine wine. "Yes, indeed. I do love a trace of shifter blood. It makes for such an irresistible blend. But I digress."

He returned to his seat, his second-in-command chastised, but still scowling. Arranging himself, he crossed one leg over the other. "Don't look so thrown my dear. You are all quite safe...for the moment. As to how I gathered my information, did you honestly think a complete dossier on each of you wouldn't be there at my fingertips? There has never been anything left to chance when it comes to those granted right of entry to *Les Sanctuaire*. From the minute this meeting was arranged, I have known all there is to know about you, especially. The wolves are of no consequence," he added with a flourish. "Such instinct-driven beasts."

Sébastien rested his elbows on the damask arms of his chair. He templed his fingers, studying Lily. "You look as though I've said something offensive." A pregnant pause hung in the air between them. "I assure you it was not my intention. We are all slaves to our natures however it has been my long experience with the children of the moon...as we call the Shifters...that they lack the finesse granted to the vampire race." He turned his eyes toward Sean. "Present company excepted, of course," he added with a smile, inclining his head before returning his attention to Lily. "Nevertheless, on whole the Shifters are still very much...human." The last word left his mouth like it tasted of vinegar.

Lily forced a smile. "I understand."

"Do you?" This time it was Rémy who spoke.

All eyes moved to the seat half turned toward the fire. The vampire's face was obscured by the angle and the sloping wings of his Queen Anne chair. He stood, pivoting on his heel as if in slow motion. The urge to cringe reigned hard and fast, but Lily bit the inside of her cheek. The entire side of the vampire's face was deformed, melted into a cascade of flesh. The glow of the fire did nothing to soften the shock, instead making him appear even more garish.

Lily looked at the floor, focusing on the wide, thick hearth rug across from her feet.

"Look at me, mademoiselle," he demanded softly.

Lily raised her eyes slowly. He was dressed in black, tight-fitting slacks and a poet's style shirt with a black on black brocade waist-coat. He had narrow hips and broad shoulders, but it was his shoulder length dark blonde hair that she couldn't drag her eyes from. It caught the firelight and seemed to glow with shades of gold and copper. He must have been beautiful to behold. At the thought of what he must have endured, her heart clenched, forgetting, for a moment, the man in front of her was a bloodless, heartless killer.

The untouched side of Rémy's face showed surprise. "My brother is correct. You are a sweet smelling anomaly. It has been many years since I've felt the weight of a compassionate gaze," he said, with an upward wave of his hand. Tell me, what kind of witch are you?"

Lily shook her head, taken aback by the question. "I...I'm not a witch at all," she blurted out, heat rushing to her cheeks as she realized she sounded like *Dorothy* from *The Wizard of Oz.*

"*Au contraire, chéri.* Every seer possesses a witch's soul. Your century merely refuses to see what exists right under their noses. Humans fear what they don't understand, and they abhor what they fear."

Lily opened her mouth to respond, but Sean held up his hand. "Rémy, Lily is by far one of the most compassionate women I have ever encountered—her fiery temper notwithstanding. She is more warrior than witch and uses her gifts for strategy and the preservation of life."

"Ha! I've read her mind. She's been filled with as much hate as anger. And she is a hunter." Etienne interjected.

Sean nodded, sending Lily's eyebrows into her hairline. "Sean..."

He glanced at her and then directly at Sébastien. "Etienne is correct, but his assessment isn't *au fait.* The operative words are in the past tense, and Lily is no longer a hunter, at least not at the present. She loves deeply, so therefore her loyalty runs deep. And we've all experienced how devastating loss can be, and how it fosters the need for revenge, but Sébastien, as this is all in the past, I move that we get on with the business at hand. If Etienne has truly read Lily's mind, then he is well aware of what she has witnessed firsthand, both in live attack as well as in the residual emotional impressions left in the victims at the morgue, one of whom is a shifter and the reason for this parlay."

The other vampires nodded, leaving Sébastien to consider Sean's words, his templed fingers pressed to his quiet lips.

"Etienne?" he questioned, but his eyes never left Lily.

The vampire sighed. "Yes, my liege. It's true. The vampire we seek is the one responsible for the attacks. She and her progeny are still at large in the city. Our trackers have picked up her scent in central park, just as the witch's thoughts revealed."

"Is it as I feared?"

The room grew deathly quiet, even the fire seemed to stop crackling in the grate. Etienne bowed his head. "Yes. It is Améile."

"I see."

Etienne shifted his feet, drawing Sébastien's eye. "Is there more? Tell me."

Etienne glanced at Lily and then at Jack, his mouth twisted as if what he was about to say tasted foul. Lily felt Sean tense beside her, but knew he wouldn't move unless they did, and she silently prayed he'd beat them to the punch.

"The witch witnessed Améile's progeny create another vampire and then leave him to die. He was degenerating and verging on delusional, yet she refused to stake him. Instead, she asked his help, and he allowed her into his mind to garner all that he knew of Améile and the redheaded one. The young one then staked himself in his last moments of reason. He is at peace."

Sébastien turned toward Lily, fascinated. "You are a double

edged sword, my dear. Fire tempered with kindness." His eyes swept her, and then he glanced over to Sean and Jack. "Perhaps we *can* learn from each other," he offered, before tilting his head back toward Lily. "Are you certain you wish to go the way of the moon? You would make an extraordinary addition to *Les Sanctuaire*."

"Haven't you enough additions, Sébastien?"

All eyes turned toward the elegant dark-haired vampire sitting in one of the four chairs. Unlike Rémy, he chose to sit back and let Sébastien take the reins of the parlay. Until now. The unnamed adjudicator's tone carried obvious authority, yet time seemed to stop at the question posed, despite his polite and mellifluous Spanish accent. He was the only elder seated without a guard posted at his back, and Lily noted the uncharacteristic lapse in protocol register with Sean.

"Carlos, not now." Sébastien's wave was offhand, but it was clear the older vampire was not pleased.

Carlos stood, muscular and fluid as he rose from the heavy chair. "This is precisely my argument. The same argument that drove Dominic to divorce himself from us, from this council. I shouldn't be in his chair. I should be standing behind him as the others stand behind you. We are not the only beings walking this earth, Sébastien. Our powers are great, but so are our limitations. What could you possibly want from this young woman that you don't already possess? Leave her be."

Sébastien exhaled, but his eyes narrowed as he looked at the younger vampire. "Still championing humanity and seeking absolution for the profane existence thrust upon you, eh? A story as old as the sum total of all our centuries and just as boring. Each of us whose veins crave living blood to breathe life into the blackness that courses through them has pondered the same thing. However, unlike you we do not let it preoccupy us to the point of stagnation. You have been as absent from these chambers as Dominic, even when you are here. I relieve you of your duties hence forth."

The room gasped even as Carlos inclined his head toward Sébastien and Remy. He turned to leave yet paused for a moment considering Lily. "Sébastien is wrong, *querida*. To be a vampire one needs a core fired to a cruel intransigence." The young vampire inhaled, letting his regard travel the length of Lily's small frame. "You are special, of that there is no doubt. However, you possess too soft a heart despite your hard exterior. The offer has been made, choose carefully. There is no turning back."

Lily didn't know how to respond. Her first instinct was to cringe, but with the way the vampire's eyes burned she didn't dare show it. "Thank you for your kind offer, but I am content to stay as I am."

Carlos smiled, and the sadness that clouded his eyes the entire time lifted slightly. He left through the steel reinforced door, a single nod his last salutation before the doors closed behind him.

Sébastien sighed. "Such a pity. We always welcome new blood, no pun intended," he said, chuckling at his own joke. At a wave of his hand, Abigail pulled on a thick silken cord next to the fireplace.

"I trust you gave the correct instructions to the bartender?" he questioned her over his shoulder.

"Yes, my liege, before we descended."

"Good. Let's hope he sent to the correct shadow house. I am a bit peckish and in the mood for AB negative."

Jack cautioned a look at Lily. The poor guy hadn't said a word. It was as if he was shell-shocked, or perhaps he finally woke up and cemented that mood-o-meter of his to level calm.

"Please, Sean, do sit down. Take the chair across from my own and make yourself comfortable. I apologize for keeping you standing for so long. Abigail, send for extra chairs for the witch and Sean's second.

"Please, sir, call me Lily. As I said before, I'm not a witch. I am an ordinary woman with one extraordinary talent."

Four sets of red eyes turned to her, shocked, and Lily swallowed.

"Was that strike three?" She whispered to Sean, and the same four sets turned back to Sébastien, his own eyes shining with amusement.

"No, my dear. I find you a ray of sunshine in our dark world. As to being ordinary, I greatly doubt that. In fact, I'll prove it. You see, we have many who are skilled amongst our undead brothers and sisters. Not only does Etienne read thoughts, but Maggie, my brother Rémy's second, reads auras. She too was once a witch." He held up his hand. "My apologies...psychic." She was in truth a healer and a midwife, and one of the originals accused during that unfortunate time in Salem."

Two male servants entered carrying the requested chairs, placing them each on either side of Sean. Lily slid into one of the comfortable seats, curious about what the vampire had just claimed. "I'm sorry, did you say auras?" she asked.

Sébastien nodded. "*Oui, c'est la vérité.* Maggie, if you would be so kind as to indulge me." He gestured toward Lily's chair.

Maggie stepped around Rémy's chair and stood in front of Lily. She held out her hands and closed her eyes. The air around Lily started to vibrate, causing the little stray hairs from her braid to stand on end. A blue light formed between the female vampire's hands spreading until it encompassed Lily entirely. Squinting, Lily tried to catch Sean's eyes, but the light was so bright she couldn't really see. Then as quickly as it began, it was over.

"Well?" Sébastien asked, almost breathless with anticipation.

Lily smoothed her hair down, trying to squelch the feeling of being the center attraction at a freak show. "Talk about experiencing what it's like to be inside a light bulb!"

The master vampire clapped his hands once in amusement. "And what say you, Maggie?" The woman stood back, turning to face both Rémy and the master. "She is a spirit walker."

Both vampires blinked, then turned toward each other in

unison, all semblance of mirth gone before they turned to stare at Lily.

Neither said a word, but there was a definite exchange, and just as Lily's senses picked up on Abigail's tacit resentment, there was a sudden air of fear swirling in the room at whatever Maggie had announced.

Lily looked from Sean to Sébastien. "Excuse me, but what did she mean?"

No one said a word, but Sean palpably relaxed, his body no longer giving off the numbing sensation she sensed whenever he went into tension overdrive.

"Will someone please explain to me what just happened?" she tried again.

Sean glanced at Jack, and then took Lily's hand in his, turning it over to kiss her palm. "It means the channel Jack accused you of 'tuning into' while the two of you were arguing is the real deal. And not only can you pick up on frequency signals, you own the damn radio station."

"English please, Sean. What the hell does that mean?"

"A spirit walker is someone who is gifted with the ability to call upon entities from other planes. Celestial ones." He fixed her with a poignant stare.

Lily opened her mouth to protest, but then thought better of it. Either the vamps would kill her now, or they'd think twice and let them walk, not wanting to tempt fate. "I see. I guess I've always suspected as much."

Sébastien cleared his throat. "So, you've experienced communication with other entities?"

Lily shrugged. "I suppose. I can talk to the dead, and they seem to seek me out. And I'm no stranger to the white light."

Maggie gasped, immediately dropping her eyes as it earned her a sharp look from Rémy.

Lily knew the claim was a stretch, but she kept the image of

Terri and the white light vortex she experienced clear in her mind, just in case Etienne decided to get nosy—and surprise, surprise, she caught the faint nod he sent his master, and the ensuing frown Sébastien wore before he censored himself and was once again the epitome of charm and hospitality.

He smiled, brandishing his hand in a flippant gesture, dismissing the obvious hole in his intelligence gathering. Although, from the set of his shoulders and straight back, it was clear some-one's head was going to roll. "As I said before, it is truly a shameful state of affairs that brought us together. We have been tracking Améile for weeks now, but, for some reason, she is able to evade us."

He sighed. "Sadly, I'm still not sure how to proceed once we do find her. She is, after all, my own progeny."

"With all due respect, Sébastien, she must be destroyed. There is no other way." Sean interjected.

For the first time, the master vampire looked like the killer he was. His face became void of chivalrous pretense and his gaze grew hard. "That is not for you to say, wolf. I, and I alone, deem what her fate is to be, and least you forget, yours, as well. So tread lightly. I care not that your witch can summon from on high or control the devil's own hellfire. Heed me. You will not be given a second warning."

At that moment Lily knew what Carlos meant and she wondered what cost the centuries had exacted on his heart.

She coughed, not out of fear but to draw the vampire's eye. "Sir, if you please. I understand that human life is of no consequence to you, and the fate that befell the unfortunate shifter we found in the morgue registers only slightly higher in your estimation. But that is not the reason for Sean's outburst. Nor is it the argument that brings us to you tonight. Améile is rotting from the inside out."

"I'm aware of this."

Lily wet her lips, trying to stay calm, but Sean interrupted. "Then surely you must be concerned about how this affects not only you and yours, but everyone. The consequences are far more reaching than you imagine. At the morgue, we could smell the stench. Améile has not only infected her own progeny, but everyone she has fed from, so it's only a matter of time before this situation becomes rampant.

"We fought something similar at the shifter Compound in Maine, and yes we've discovered a cure, but it's DNA based, and since vampire's no longer have living DNA other than that which is residual in the blood they ingest, it's unlikely our cure will suffice—that is if it's even the same virus—but based on the evidence we've collected, there is a real possibility it could be linked, and that means the virus is mutating."

The council's valet and the bartender entered at that moment, carrying a tray with fluted champagne glasses and a crystal decanter filled with a crimson liquid.

Sébastien exhaled sharply. "This is all too distressing to digest on an empty stomach," he said, gesturing for the bartender to pour the drinks.

"As requested, it's still warm," the bartender crooned, handing one of flutes past Lily to the master's waiting hand.

Lily glanced at Sean, whose nostrils were flared in revulsion too.

"Stop!" she said, her hand shooting out to grab the stem of the glass as Sébastien' tilted it to his lips. "It's infected!"

The flute crashed to the floor, and the blood seeped across the broken shards like an act of murder. Incensed, the master vampire pushed himself up from his chair, his fangs fully descended.

"How dare you!'

Fear gripped Lily's stomach, and she squeezed her fingernails into her palms to keep her hands from shaking. "Please, Sébastien... it's true, sir, can't you sense it? Smell it?"

Sean and Jack both stood, flanking her sides. They were so close to death they could smell it along with the fetid blood spreading across the rug.

"I smell nothing but waste," he slurred through his fangs and his anger.

"You have to believe us." Lily pleaded.

Sean stepped forward, pushing Lily behind him. He kept his hands in plain sight but was poised to phase if things got any more out of hand. "Sébastien, we came here in good faith, not only to help stop the bloodbaths, but to help you save your race. Surely you realize this is no joking matter, nor is it a bargaining chip. At least question where the blood came from. See if there is a tie back to either Améile or her redheaded progeny."

Sébastien sucked in a deep breath, and with it, his fangs receded. "Yes. Rational. That is the vampire way. You'll have to forgive my lapse in manners, Sean. It's just I have been craving all day, and I am not used to having my delicacies snatched from under my nose. Literally." He turned toward the bartender. "Where did this come from? Who was the procurer?"

"Lupo."

"Fine. Send him in."

Dismissing the bartender, the master sat down, straightening his clothing, and once again crossing his legs one over the other. A nervous vampire followed the bartender back into the room.

"Ah...Lupo. Tell me, my boy. From where did you procure this AB negative? I trust it is AB negative, correct?" he asked, indicating the remaining liquid still in the decanter.

The vampire's head bobbed up and down. "Yes, master. It's AB neg alright, and it's as fresh as it gets. I put the human donor in the holding chamber in case you wanted more."

"Good. And did you procure the donor from one of the shadow houses on the preferred list, or is it someone from a random hunt?"

Lily's mouth went drier than it already was at the images the conversation prompted. Shadow houses and willing donors were bad enough, but her stomach clenched at the memory of watching vampires stalk their victims on a 'random hunt'.

272

"Oh no, sir. Clovis supplied the donor tonight. She's from the shadow house on east 67th street."

"Bring her in."

"Sir?"

The master vampire hissed, and the vamp procurer jumped, nearly pissing his pants. "Right away, master... right away!"

The grandfather clock in the corner chimed 11:00p.m., but before it reached its eleventh peal, the sound of hurried footsteps and rushed harsh words could be heard in the hallway behind Etienne.

Both Lupo, and whom Lily could only guess to be Clovis, came through the door, carrying a half conscious woman. She was in a state of semi-undress, as was Clovis, and from the disgusted looks on the council member's faces, it was obvious they didn't much approve of procuring vampire's extracurricular activities.

The woman was already foaming at the mouth when they laid her on the floor in front of Sébastien. "Here she is, boss," Clovis said, tucking his too shiny shirt into his unzipped pants. He was an unadulterated pig of a pimp, by any standards.

Sean got up and knelt by the woman's head. He took a deep breath and coughed. The stench was so bad. With his fingers beneath his nose, he squinted up at Sébastien. "I find it inconceivable that you can't smell this. It's absolutely foul."

He spoke as much to himself as to the master vampire but didn't wait for a response. Instead, he turned his attentions back to the girl. Careful not to get any of her spittle on his hands, he shifted her head to the side exposing a series of bite marks on her throat. "Looks to me like she's been the appetizer for more than just a few vampires," he commented, eyeing Clovis and the obvious proof of his duplicity.

Lily didn't think it was possible, but the procurer actually blanched.

Wiping his hands on his thighs, Sean sat back down next to Lily. "From the look of things, I'd say you have an epidemic starting."

"Nonsense, we still don't know how she was infected, or if she's the only one," Rémy interjected.

Sean shrugged. "There's only one sure way to find out."

Both men looked at Lily. Not wanting to gag, she was already breathing through her mouth. "Oh no! I can't go through that again, Sean. The dizziness and the nausea—forget it!"

"We don't have any other option, Lily. It's the only way we can prove to Sébastien and Rémy that this situation is rife." His eyes were sympathetic, but resolute. She didn't have a choice.

She exhaled and stood up. "Okay, but only if we form a mental chain. I'll touch her first to open a conduit and get a read." She pointed to the half dead woman lying on the floor. "Then Etienne will have to channel my thoughts so you can see what I see as well," she said, addressing Sébastien directly. "On our end, Sean and Jack can follow via the Hunter's shared mind path. Sean's right. If we want to eliminate all doubt, this is the way it has to play out."

Sébastien rose from his seat, motioning for Rémy and Etienne to do the same. The other vampires moved into position, flanking them, but with strict instructions not to interfere. They linked accordingly, with Jack and Sean each with a hand on Lily's shoulders.

She knelt on the floor next to the now unconscious woman, smoothing the girl's matted hair in an effort to inject some humanity into this inhumane scenario.

Lily inhaled through her mouth, but still gagged slightly. Sean squeezed her shoulder, and the cool feel of his confidence flooded through at his touch. She glanced up, giving him half a smile. "I love you, too," she whispered, their eyes locking in a private moment.

"You got this," he feathered across. *"Show them what my girl can do."* He winked, and she covered his hand with hers, giving it a squeeze.

Foregoing another breath, she stretched a shaking hand out toward the woman, but stopped, glancing up at Sébastien. "Promise me you'll show mercy and end this woman's suffering as painlessly as possible."

Sébastien nodded. "We may be a master race, chéri, but that does not mean we are utterly devoid of compassion."

Satisfied the vampire would be good to his word, she placed her hand on the girl's forehead, but this time it was Sébastien who interrupted. "You must promise me something as well," he said, eyeing both Sean and Lily.

Sean glanced at Jack before shifting his eyes back toward the vampire. "Of course, if it is in my power to grant," he answered carefully.

Time seemed to stand still as they waited for the other shoe to drop, but the master vampire exhaled as if relieved.

"Good. To use your witch's turn of phrase, if this 'plays out' the way we fear, I ask two courtesies: first, that you help us track and kill my sad progeny and her offspring, tonight. And second, that you lend us the olfactory services of your Hunters to help find and eradicate those infected within our shadow houses, both vampire and human donor alike. This is a sad business throughout, and killing one's progeny is never easy, but for the greater good, I am left with no other choice."

Sean put his hand on Sébastien's forearm. "I hunted my own brother for the very same reason, so I understand. We'll help you clean house."

The sky was cloudless, but the air was damp and frigid. Lily stamped her numb feet on the red brick esplanade circling the Bethesda Fountain at the heart of Central Park. Her shitkickers were great for throwdowns, but their steel reinforced toes weren't much when it came to keeping her feet warm.

"Come on, you fanged bitch. Show yourself," she muttered, her warm breath puffing out onto her cupped hands. At least the rest of her was warm, having traded in her thin leather jacket and gloves for ones that were shearling lined. It was nearly two a.m., and still there was no sign of either Améile or her redheaded brat. Sébastien had warned that it could be a long wait, and so far, he was right.

The park was quiet, and she didn't know if it was the cold and the wet, or the vampires scattered throughout, but either way she was glad the homeless had decided to move indoors. Maybe this way they stood a chance at keeping the human collateral damage to a minimum.

Funny how none of the vampires seemed to know the redhead's name. Even Clovis. If he did, he'd taken it with him into the vampire great unknown. Sean had mentioned that vamps tolerated little, but if tonight proved anything, it was they tolerated deceit least. Ironic, really, considering the trickery they used to lure their victims, but who was she to point out the pot calling the kettle black?

The time was well past midnight when they finally left the Red Veil, stopping home only to call Ryan as promised. To say he was more than a little put out at being rescheduled was an understatement. That is, until he found out why, and where they were headed.

Lily exhaled, blowing a cloud of steam into the icy, wet air. She had to hand it to Martinez. His membership in the world of the supernatural was less than twenty-four hours old, yet already he was as stubborn and crazy as the rest of them. Talk about an argument for nature versus nurture. Martinez was still thinking in human terms, though. This wasn't a stakeout. It was a search and destroy mission. Sean had even tried to dissuade him, but the stubborn cop claimed this was still his case.

Ha. Tell that to the vamps!

She could see him across from the fountain terrace, watching the water that spanned the area between them and Améile's suspected lair. He was all in black, like that made any difference. To the supes, the full moon might as well be high noon.

Lily paced the perimeter around the fountain, her eyes scanning the tree line and the footpaths for movement. "Anything yet?" Martinez asked, coming up behind her.

She hooked her hand on her hip, her fingers wrapping around the base of her concealed crossbow. "It's really not a great idea to sneak up on people, especially when more than half the team is undead. I could have shot you, you know."

He smiled, lifting his hand to show her the 9mm in his palm. "Yeah, I thought about that, but you're too smart a hunter to just react."

Silent, Lily just looked at him. "Why did you want to come tonight? And don't hand me that bullshit about it being your case. The fact that you brought a gun to fight vampires shows you have no clue how to fight what we're up against."

He snorted. "I think I've seen enough to figure it out as I go," he countered, pulling a sharpened stake from his inside jacket pocket.

By now he'd seen her skepticism plenty to read the look on her face. Maybe he'd take the hint and go home where it was safe. "Well, good luck with that. Try not to get yourself killed," she muttered, turning to scan the trees again.

Ryan moved beside her, hands on his hips as he followed her line of sight. "I'm surprised the big guy let you take this area alone. What, no bodyguard?"

Lily could feel the heat coming off his body, and as he stood watch, his intensity was equal to that of any of Sean's hunters. There was no doubt Ryan would be an asset to the Compound, despite how much he bothered the crap out of her.

"Look. Sean is the Alpha of the Brethren, and like it or not, I'm his alpha female...his mate. If you really want to be part of the supe world, you'd better learn that loyalty and trust are necessary evils. As to being on my own, Sean knows I'm a competent hunter, besides, Jack is around."

Ryan huffed. "I guess the fact he put me in such close proximity doesn't count, huh."

"Nope. Not one bit. Until you prove yourself, you might as well be bait."

He frowned. His expression just shy of offended. "You seem to forget I'm a seasoned cop," he replied quietly. "I came tonight because all you've talked about is my accepting who I really am. In order to do that, I need to reconcile the world in which I grew up, with the world in which I'm genetically linked. If this really is my world, then I need to test my own mettle. I need to see if there's a place for me— as me. Get it?"

Ryan's posture was stiff, but insulted or not, she didn't care. This was dangerous. "Listen, I didn't mean to dismiss your abilities, but this is a whole new game with lethal players. Any badass mutt you've encountered in the past will look like a cartoon villain after tonight. You want in? Then you've got to be prepared to step up and smell the blood on the vampire's breath as you stake her. Literally."

Lily's gaze jerked toward the water.

"Hey! We've got possible movement near the center of the park, somewhere close to Belvedere Castle by the turtle pond. Can you sense anything?" Jack's voice floated across through the common shifter path.

"With all the supes Sébastien brought with him tonight, not a chance. The place is flooded with supernatural signal."

"Ugh...what good are you woman! What if you got closer? Would your antennae work then?"

Ryan made a noise, grabbing Lily's attention. "What's going on?"

She waved him off, sticking her finger in her ear, silently telling him to shut up so she could hear.

"Jeez, Jack, could you make me feel any more like a bug? To answer your question though, yeah, getting closer would work. I've got a clear radius for two hundred feet as we speak, and if I know which guards Sébastien has lurking around, I can segregate their feel."

"Good. Then get to the castle. I'm at the Boathouse, so I won't be far behind."

Lily's hand went to her temple. There was an odd hum behind Jack's voice that made her head throb. *"Okay. Where's Sean? Does he know there's been a possible sighting?"*

"He knows. He's with Sébastien at the lake. They'll have to catch up."

"I'm on my way..."

Lily knelt to adjust the stakes in her boot. "That was Jack..." she hesitated, looking up from her laces as Rémy stepped out from behind the giant angel at the center of the fountain. He

280

launched himself in the air, turning a somersault before landing silently on the red bricks not three feet from where Lily and Ryan stood.

"How long have you been there?" she asked, pushing herself to standing, unfazed by the vampire's acrobatic entrance.

"Long enough," he said, sliding a critical eye over Ryan's defensive bearing. "Etienne has been keeping watch, and he informed me Améile is in the area, or so your wolf guard thinks. Unfortunately, the opportunity to verify that escapes us as we speak, so I have elected to fly you to the castle. Your wolf will meet you at the designated place. Sébastien has one of our guards posted there already. His name is Chen."

Lily raised an eyebrow. "Not exactly a French name, huh?"

Rémy gave her a lopsided smile that did more to soften his deformity than all the firelight in the world. His period coat was right out of *Interview with a Vampire,* and his long hair blew across the ruined side of his face, making him seem both sad and romantic. "Shall we?" he said, holding out his hand.

"Wait..." Martinez said, his hand reaching for Lily's elbow.

Rémy fixed Martinez with an unblinking stare, but to his credit, the detective met the vampire's gaze head on without flinching.

"I want to help you, Lily, and not by standing here with my thumb up my ass," Ryan whispered, cocking his head closer to her ear.

The vampire raised his one intact eyebrow. "Unlike my face, detective, my hearing is preternaturally perfect. Don't think to circumvent the little witch's directive. However, if you'd care to demonstrate the trick you described using your thumb, I'm sure we could spare a moment or two." Rémy spread his hands invitingly, his amusement undisguised.

Martinez clenched his jaw, his eyes torn between wanting to take a swing at the vamp, and not wanting to die for the effort.

"Enough," Lily cut in, shoving the detective's hand away. "We don't have time for this. Ryan, you're right. Get to the boathouse and look for Jack. I'll meet you both at the castle."

Barely waiting for Lily to hook her arms around his neck, the vampire launched them both effortlessly into the air, hovering thirty feet or so before lifting over the treetops. She was surprisingly warm, considering the wind temperature as they flew, and the fact that vampires were ice cold to the touch. Rémy must have recently fed, and she shivered, regardless of being warm. Nope. Not going there, thank you...and she stopped that train of thought in its tracks.

The park looked beautiful from their high vantage point, and she wondered why Sébastien didn't have his vampires do an aerial search. For that matter, why wasn't he the one who gave the directive to head to Turtle Pond, if he had someone stationed there? Wouldn't they have spotted Améile first? A weird feeling tapped her on the shoulder, and she couldn't shake the feeling she was missing something crucial.

"Sean...where are you? I'm headed over toward the castle. Jack said they had movement there."

"Jack said what? When?"

"Just now, and Etienne sent Rémy to give me a ride, vamp style. Jack said you knew about this..."

"Hmmm. Maybe he thought Sébastien told me. Strange, though, he hasn't said a word. Hang tight. Don't do anything until I get there."

Hang tight. Ha. Considering she was in transit via an airborne piggyback ride, she would have found the directive mildly funny, if it weren't for the nagging feeling at the back of her mind. Rémy slowed as they approached the pond. A night bird's whistle echoed from the top of the castle, and Rémy answered, setting Lily down on the floor of the main turret.

"Chen this is the wolf's seer. See that she isn't injured." With a single nod, he launched himself with one leap off the side of the battlement.

"Impressive," she said, staring off after Rémy. "Can all vampires do that?"

Chen shook his head. "Skills like flying come with extreme age. I've only been dead for fifty years, so, nope. Just your run-of-the-mill vampire," he said, adding a very 1950s Draculaesque hiss for effect, followed by a hearty chuckle.

From the top of his shiny black pompadour to the bottom of his blue suede shoes, the Asian vampire looked as if he'd walked off the set of an Elvis movie. Chen seemed a tad more likeable than the others of his kind, relaxed—except for the fact he would drink Lily dry in a heartbeat.

He jumped up to sit on the wide stone railing and leaned so far backward it looked like he'd either topple over or snap his back. With his arms over his head, he stretched. "Not exactly the way I thought I'd be spending my night," he said, taking a pack of Lucky Strikes out of his pocket. He stuck one in his mouth then held the pack out toward Lily. "Want one?"

She shook her head. "No thanks." Her fingers itched for a cigarette, but she needed to keep her hands and her mind on target.

Chen shrugged, cupping his hands to light his own. "Probably better you don't," he replied, blowing a cloud of smoke out the side of his mouth. "You've still gotta watch out for cancer and shit. Me, I'm already a walking corpse." He laughed, flashing a fangy grin.

Lily couldn't help but smile back, half expecting him to drawl 'thank you, thank you very much,' the first chance he got. "Were you the one that spotted Améile?"

He shook his head. "I haven't seen a thing all night. To tell you the truth, I was a little confused when Etienne instructed me to signal my position to Rémy so he could land with you."

That same creepy feeling now walked itself from her shoulder to latch its cold fingers around her throat. "This doesn't add up," she muttered, gaze moving toward the wall overlooking the pond and the footpaths that lead to the road. She walked to the edge and rested her hands on the stone. Where the hell were Jack and Ryan? And why was it taking so long for Sean to get here? She shook her head dismissing the nagging feeling as ridiculous. Jack had to have gotten his information from one of the other vampires, otherwise this made no sense.

The water looked black, despite the moonlight, and the ice floes gathered along the rocky slopes of the embankment were eerily in shadow. Lily wheeled around on her heel. "I'm going to head down toward the water's edge. Keep me covered, okay?"

Chen busied himself blowing smoke rings. "Later gator." With a smirk, he saluted, cigarette in hand.

Lily ducked down the winding staircase, the sound of her boots clattering like gunfire off the masonry walls. Perhaps something down by the water could give her a clue as to what was going on.

She stepped out of the main keep and scanned the rocks sloping down towards the water. They were slick with ice, but there was no other way to get to the water's edge short of scrambling down the side wall.

"Lily! Help! Up here! The vamp bitch is up here!" Jack shouted from the castle terrace above.

"Jack!" Lily raced back inside, her heart pounding in her chest. Why hadn't she sensed him? She unclipped her crossbow and deftly grabbed a stake from her boot as she took the stairs two at a time.

Inside the arched doorway, she paused to listen, pressing herself as close to the stone wall as possible. There was an agonized scream, and she pushed herself away from the wall, crouching as she ran through the entry, her crossbow cocked and ready.

Chen was sprawled across the wet stone floor, his limbs broken at odd angles. A puddle of blood spread beneath his torn throat, and there was a gaping hole in his chest where his heart should have been. She blinked as flakes billowed past. The cool Asian vamp was already turning to ash.

In the corner was another body Lily didn't recognize. She

couldn't tell if it was human or supe as the scents were too intermingled. All she knew was he was dead, as well.

"Jack!" Lily hissed. "Where are you?"

From the shadows, a gray wolf menaced forward with his head low, four large canines dripping red as he bared his teeth. Jaws snapping, he let out a snarl and leapt forward, his large paws hitting the stone with a thud a few feet from where Lily stood.

With slow measured movements, she shifted the crossbow to her left hand and reached behind her back for her 9mm. "Jack, it's me. I don't know what you did or why, but if you can understand me, you need to stop and phase back to human."

He didn't, though. He kept coming, his teeth snapping as he advanced.

"Sean...Jack just killed Sébastien's guard and swallowed his heart. He's still in wolf form, and it's like he's been drugged or spelled or something. He won't respond. I've got my gun drawn. I don't want to shoot him, but I will."

Two men approached from the shadows behind the gray wolf. One had a coil of rope in his hands, the other a bottle and a rag, and Lily could smell the chloroform. In a snap of bone and muscle, Jack phased back to human and stood between them, naked, his mouth and chest covered in blood.

"Jack! Have you gone crazy? What are you doing? Both Sébastien and Sean are on their way." She was confident Sean heard her call, however, the smug look that spread across Jack's face told her otherwise.

"I'm afraid it'll be too late by the time they figure things out. It's nothing personal, Lily. I like you and I'm sorry it has to be this way. It's just Sean's made some serious enemies, powerful ones who can give me what I deserve. Unfortunately, you're the bargaining chip."

"Sean! It's a trap! Jack..." she tried again, but pain, white hot and piercing spiked through Lily's ears. Her knees buckled, and her hand shot out to grab the lamp post next to the stone overlook.

"Sean! Help!" The words seared her mind, the pain exploding behind her eyes, blurring her vision. Panting, she tried to straighten, but her knees gave out and she collapsed, her gun clattering to the ground.

Jack kicked it to the corner and stood over her. "I'm sorry, Lily, but you're just too smart, and I can't have you blowing the whistle on me." He squatted down, peeling her white knuckled fingers from her crossbow and helping himself to a handful of sharp stakes.

She looked up at him, trying to see past the swirls and double vision. "Why, Jack?" she rasped, earning a scornful sigh from the wolf.

"I'm surprised at you Lily, smart as you are that you didn't figure things out. You were suspicious, I'll give you that. Your instincts were right on target up until the very end, but you ignored them, buying into that goody-goody garbage Sean's been feeding you." His expression hardened, and the once handsome hunter suddenly seemed ugly.

"Poor Jack," he mimicked in a soft girly voice. "You and Sean, you're both the same and both stupid. You were better as a vigilante, Lily, until you let emotions rob you of your edge. It's weak. If it had been Edward at dinner with us the other night, he would have politely listened to my complaint, patted my hand, and then shot me point blank in the head."

Lily stared at him in disbelief. "And that's what you want for the Shifters? A power junkie, unmerciful and ruthless?" she asked.

He shook his head, his lip curled in distain. "You still don't get it." For a moment he stared at her, his expression almost disappointed. "It doesn't matter, I guess. You're a pawn now, and I get to call the shots. Using you to lure Sean back to the Compound was only part of the deal. After that, you're mine."

Lily lifted her chin and spit in his face.

Jack stiffened. He wiped his cheek, then backhanded her across the face. "Like I said... mine."

Pain reverberated through her jaw and up into her ear. With a sharp intake she winced, but gritted her teeth, refusing to let him see her break.

"Enough of this chatter, we need to get moving before Sean realizes I've sent him and Sébastien on a wild goose chase. Stupid fool. In wolf form I told him Rémy and Etienne were behind this and were flying you toward Columbus Circle—that it was a vampire set up, and I killed the guard while trying to stop them." Shameless, he drew himself up fully. "After all, Sébastien did say you'd make a wonderful addition to his group, and everyone knows vamps don't take kindly to being told, 'No, thank you'."

Lily stared at him, the puzzle pieces that had eluded her for a week finally falling into place.

"Oh, and don't worry. The telepathic block I'm using on you may be painful but isn't permanent. Just a necessary evil, until Sean is dead, and Edward is in control. You see, I learned a few things working all those nights on bedpan duty. Hunters are trusted, no questions asked, and I took full advantage of that and the access it gave me to Volkmann's research. Too bad Sean thought I was all brawn and no brains. Guess the joke's on him now, huh?" He kicked at the pile of wet soot that used to be Chen.

Lily stealthily slid her fingers over the outside edge of her boot. The single telltale bump under her fingers said she had one stake left, one chance for escape that Jack had missed.

Jack's back was to her, but there was still no chance to strike or get away. He had her crossbow, and her gun was in the corner out of reach. Time, though, was her ally for the moment. He had ordered his men to drag the remains of the dead guy down to the pond for the police to find, and the longer it took, the more of a chance there was Sean would figure things out and come for her.

Lily didn't recognize any of the men with Jack, including the dead one. They had to be Parr's flunkies. The one he called Tony hooked his arms under the inert bulk of what was left of his pal.

"Marcus, grab Leon's ankles," he said to the other, straining to lift the slumped over body. "Jeez, he's heavy, no wonder they call it dead weight," he snickered.

Lily shot him a dirty look, catching his eye, and the man's gaze drifted over her appreciatively. "I can see why Jack's got a thing for you," he said, his eyes lingering on the swell of her breasts.

Disgust left her throat, and he chuckled. "Why don't you make it easy on yourself, baby, and cooperate? And don't do anything stupid like trying to reach lover boy again, not unless you want your brain to fry. Jack's blocking frequency can be a little temperamental."

A feral hiss screeched through the air, pulling his attention, and both he and Marcus dropped the body, running for cover under the arch. Jack swore under his breath. "You pussies! The vamp bitch could be anywhere in the park!"

The dead guy's feet landed adjacent to where Lily sat still on the ground, and she fixed Jack with a scowl when he glanced at her. "Améile's coming for you, Jack. You killed another vamp tonight and she knows your scent from the last time, remember?"

Ignoring her, Jack kicked at Leon's lifeless feet, hoisting him up to drag him toward the stairs, and yelling for his men as he struggled. "Come help me, you two, or I swear I'll feed you to the vamps myself."

Lily gritted her teeth, waiting for him to get a little closer. Taking advantage of his inattention, she shot her leg out, nailing Jack behind the knees, sending him crashing down on his back, smacking his head on the pavement. The minute he hit the ground, she was on her feet, diving for her gun in the corner.

He rolled to his side, quickly pushing himself up and yanking Lily by the shoulders, tossing her back against the stone structure like a ragdoll. "You bitch, I'm bleeding! And with all these vamps around... Arrgh!" Jack hissed, his hand moving to the back of his head.

Jack used her momentum against her, but she had some skills of her own. Exhaling hard, she kept her wits and prevented her wind from being knocked out. At the last second, she threw her arms over her head and pressed her chin to her chest, deflecting the impact to her rounded shoulders instead of her lungs. Jack shouted for the others again, raising his leg to sidekick her in the ribs, but Lily was ready.

She sucked in a breath and dropped her forearm in a downward shunt, blocking his kick and throwing him off balance. Turning the tables, she used his momentum against him now, and swept his supporting leg out from under him. He crashed to the pavement dropping her crossbow, and she scrambled to pick it up before he rolled to the side and beat her to the punch. All bets were off as she unlocked the safety and pointed the razor's edge of the loaded weapon at Jack's heart, but another screech sounded, this time directly from above.

"Cochran wake up! Vampire 12:00!" Marcus shouted.

Perched on the extreme edge of the stone turret above them, was Améile. She had completely degenerated. Even the stringy hair that clung to her scalp had rotted away, leaving her nothing more than a skeleton with fangs. A cooing sound echoed from behind her, and all eyes watched as her progeny slid up next to her, resting her head on her maker's bony shoulder, her fingers lovingly around Améile's exposed ribcage.

"Kill the bitches or we're all dead!" Jack shouted, pushing himself to his feet, one of Lily's stakes in his hand.

The redhead's chin lifted, and she sniffed the air, her nostrils flaring. Her eyes tracked Jack as he crouched, waiting for an attack.

"Fuck! She smells the blood from my scalp," he said, his eyes narrowing at Lily in a death look.

On the balls of her feet, Lily slid into a defensive stance, adjusting her grip on the crossbow. The feel of the string in her fingers gave her focus and strength as she pulled it back, relocking it into place. Where the hell was Sean? She didn't need telepathy to know he was going crazy trying to reach her. If she felt pain on her end, he probably did, as well. Or maybe he sensed nothing but dead air. Either way, she was on her own. If she tried to reach him again, the pain would disable her, and she couldn't afford to lose the small edge she'd just gained.

Lily glanced from Jack to his men, her mind running the averages. If she shot one of the Shifters, the blood would draw the vampires, and she'd have a chance at staking at least one, but that left the other for her to deal with, and even in a weakened state, the vampire was still too strong.

Shifting her gaze to the turret, she watched the vampires, taking in every nuance of their behavior. They were wrapped up like mother and child, with the redhead tucking herself under the other's arm, while she still tracked Jack's every move.

Lily focused on the redhead, as there wasn't enough of Améile's face left to give any semblance of expression. The younger vampire was completely ensconced by the other. If Lily took out the mother, there would be a split second of shock before the daughter attacked. In her rage, she would lose focus and Lily could nail her then. If she missed, it was anyone's game.

Lily took aim at Améile's exposed ribs. If she could just angle the trajectory, she could hit her dead in the heart. She lowered her chin and held her breath, her own pulse beating in the tips of her fingers on the trigger.

The stake soared through the air, hitting its mark, and Améile's body jerked back. Her arms flew wide, and a bloodcurdling shriek echoed through the night. If that didn't bring Sean and Sébastien, nothing would. Lily had just killed the master's progeny, and she had no doubt he'd felt it. The tainted vampire burst in a cloud of ash, the particles wafting in the breeze, almost peaceful in the way they floated along.

The redhead stood on the turret like a disheveled goddess, her hair billowing out and her eyes blazing crimson. Lily took cover, pressing her back against the stone, her black clothing giving her just enough camouflage for the vampire's scrutiny to pass her by.

Instead, the redhead settled on the largest of Jack's men, swooping down like the angel of death, snapping his neck as he turned to run. Her jaws opened, exposing lethal fangs dripping with yellow, fouled saliva, and she drained him in seconds, tossing his dried husk of a body to the side.

Her nostrils flared, and she turned in Jack's direction, her head jerky and puppet like. He was still bleeding, and her eyes opened wide with recognition and deadly thirst. "You!" she slurred. "You smell like my mother's tormentor!"

Wild-eyed, she launched herself at Jack, her fury overriding her instincts. She never saw the stake in his hand. The redhead crumbled to the floor, Améile's name on her lips as her body imploded.

Jack slumped against the stone battlement, panting. "Marcus let's go. Grab Lily and let's get the hell out of here. The master vampire will be here any minute. We just killed his daughter and granddaughter, and I guarantee he's not going to be happy about all this."

Lily dive rolled over Leon's corpse, and then got to her feet at the entrance to the stairs. Without looking back, she clamored down the steps, but Marcus was on her heels, tackling her at the bottom. Her head snapped back, slamming against the stone, and the last thing she registered was the scent of fresh blood and stale urine.

Jack ran down the stairs after them, stopping short at Lily's prone body. "Please tell me, you didn't kill her."

"She's not dead, just unconscious."

"Good. Now let's get her into the van. It's parked in the trees of the 79th Street Transverse Road."

"What about Leon and Tony?" Marcus said, gesturing up the stairs. "We can't just leave them. They have family back in Maine."

Jack snarled, pushing past Marcus to hook his arms under Lily's shoulders. "Are you insane? I may have said Sean was stupid and weak, but only when it comes to her," he said, jerking his chin toward Lily. "He didn't get elected alpha for nothing. Don't underestimate him. By now he knows Parr is behind this set up. What he doesn't know, is that I'm part of it too, and unless Edward has sold you out, Sean doesn't know about you either. Don't fuck this up. It ain't over till it's over."

CHAPTER
TWENTY

Sean paced back and forth on the castle terrace, Lily's gun and crossbow in his hand. Her scent and the scent of blood were everywhere, yet the only thing that stopped him from going crazy, was that it wasn't her blood.

"My enemy is behind this. I know it," he said to Rémy, putting Lily's weapons down to turn the two prone bodies over one by one. "These two were his lackeys." He gestured toward both with a frustrated wave.

Sébastien was above them, lingering over the pile of ash on the top of the turret. He had Lily's small stake in his hand. With a sigh, he floated down to land beside Sean.

"Ah, what a sad night for us all. My Améile is dead," he said with a sniff. "However, at least I know she didn't suffer in the end." He opened his hand to show Sean the petite silver tipped weapon.

Rémy took the tiny stake from Sébastien's hand, careful not to touch the silvered tip. "Clever workmanship. Almost scary in its practicality."

Sean nodded. "Lily made that, and I can assure you Améile did not suffer. My alpha female may be small, but she's strong and

295

smart, and her aim is flawless," he replied, placing his hand on Sébastien's arm.

"Yes. It is a precise weapon. It's easy to see it was intended to be both lethal as well as compassionate. Not unlike its designer, eh." He glanced at Sean's pained face.

"As to the redheaded one, I guess we're not meant to learn her identity, though I'm sure she died as quickly and as painlessly as my Améile," Sébastien said, bending to pick up another stake. "But whoever killed Chen doesn't deserve the same swift justice. Such a heinous thing, to take someone's heart."

Sean didn't comment, just stared out at the black water.

Sébastien followed his gaze and slid his arm around the wolf's shoulder. "You think me a hypocrite to say such a thing, considering a vampire's nature. Well, perhaps, but some of us still hold respect for other species, and respect for living as well as for the undead. I have learned much from you this past night, my lupine friend, and it will not be forgotten." The vampire turned to glance up at the turret head again. "Your lady has done us a great service, and soon your wolves will help us deal with the aftermath. I am indebted."

Sean inclined his head. "Thank you, Sébastien."

The vampire glanced out over the water towards the east. "The sun will be rising soon. I must get my people to shelter. I wish I could accompany you to Maine and help you avenge tonight's treachery. There is nothing more unsettling than to learn those you have trusted and loved are false. The crime deserves the most painful sort of death, in my opinion."

Sean sighed. "Unfortunately, in this instance, I have to agree. I've already briefed my second-in-command. My problem is, I can't reach Lily. I can't feel her mind. It's void, though I know in my heart she's not dead."

Rémy clapped him on the back. "She is a very clever woman and a talented little witch. Though I am loath for you to tell her I said as much." He chuckled. "She will find a way to reach you, I'm sure."

"Thank you Rémy. And I promise you both, if I find who is responsible for Chen, I will be happy to lay them at your feet."

The vampire laughed out loud, his ruined face like a perverse version of the theatrical comedy and tragedy mask. "I will hold you to that." He clasped Sean's arm the way Sébastien had when he'd first greeted them. "Go. You have a long way to travel, and wolves cannot fly!" With a mischievous wink, he launched himself into the air and circled around toward the western sky. "Goodbye, my friend, and Godspeed," his voiced whispered on the wind.

Sébastien clasped Sean's arm as well. "Godspeed indeed. And you are always welcome. No parlay necessary." With a chuckle, he launched himself into the air, his call to his people echoing like a lark's song in the air.

LILY'S CHIN was pressed into her chest, and her head throbbed. Half awake, she cracked one eye open, but closed it again, too tired to sustain the effort. Her shoulders ached and her arms were stiff. Unusual smells tickled her nose, and she sneezed, her arms jerking in the process from where she'd been bound. Completely awake, she opened both eyes, the realization dawning that she'd been strung up like a side of beef.

Why was Jack holding her in a barn? Didn't he say she was the bargaining chip he and Parr needed to lure Sean back to the Compound? Hell, she didn't even know if she was in Maine.

Her mouth was a dry crust, and her tongue had cemented itself to the roof of her mouth, but she forced herself to look around, peeling her tongue down from her inside palate. A dull ache throbbed at the back of her skull, and tiny pins and needles bit into her hands and arms where she was tied at the wrists above her head.

Her head hurt so much. She must have smacked it on something. Probably Jack's fist, the traitor, but truth was, her memory toward the end was sketchy. The last thing she recalled was Jack killing the redhead. It didn't matter, though. She was here because of Jack's betrayal, and that fact remained crystal clear.

She kicked at the dirt below her feet. She needed to concentrate and find a way out of here. There was nothing to the dilapidated building, and from the huge holes all around, she'd bet dollars to donuts the structure was abandoned. Blue tyvek paper covered the largest of the holes, but it was frayed at the edges and torn in places where the wind had forced its way through. Wood shingles dotted the ground from where they'd fallen from the ceiling, and gusts of wind from the gaps left in the roof stirred up dust and debris. The floor was nothing more than frozen earth, and stale hay hung in clusters from an upper loft that had definitely seen better days.

Half a dozen feet away, smoke curled from a hollow oil drum, the glowing embers inside the only thing keeping Lily from freezing to death. How considerate.

Her ears perked up at the distinct rumble of a tractor in the distance. With people around, it might mean a chance at rescue, though somehow, she doubted it.

A warm, sweet scent rode just below the smell of barn debris, and her mouth watered just enough for her to swallow. She inhaled again, trying to identify the scent, and her chin jerked up at the olfactory memory it stirred. Terri's grandparent's farm and the scent of fresh milk! That was the scent, and it meant Jack was holding her for Parr at a dairy farm. Were there many of those in Maine? Christ, she hoped not.

Excited, she opened her mind to call to Sean, but slammed it shut again, forgetting for a moment about Jack's telepathic road-block. There was no way she could risk being incapacitated again. Fruitless anger suffused her body with heat. How did she miss the signs that Jack was working both ends? How did Sean? Nausea rose at the back of her throat. Because they both loved him, that's why.

She balled her fists together, ignoring the pain in her wrists from the rope. Jack was a dead man. That is, if she could figure out a way to reach Sean.

Resting her chin on her chest, she concentrated on what she had to work with. *Not much with me half hogtied.* Her head came up again. *Half...*

Lily gripped the rope above the knots at her wrists and lifted her legs straight out and waist height. The rope held. *Thank God.* Gritting her teeth, she swung her legs up and over her head, and wrapped them around the braided nylon. *Ha! Sean doesn't call me the flexible flyer for no reason!*

The tension on the nylon was severe, and even with her in a jackknife position, her body weight just added to it, pulling the knots tighter. *God, she could use a bowie knife or a straight edge about now.*

Voices drifted past on the opposite side of the tyvek, and she froze. *If Jack or anyone of Parr's acolytes caught her now*—she held her breath and held still. Her eyes darted around, but with her wrists tied she was helpless. *Unless...*

Six feet away on the bottom sill of one of the small egress windows, she spotted a small, thin box, red and gold with one word written on the cover in old fashioned lettering. *Gillette.* Lily grinned. *Seek and ye shall find!*

Pushing and pulling on the rope, she swung herself sideways, straining to reach the tiny box and praying, first— to get close enough to catch the box between her palms without dropping it, and second— that it had blades inside.

Sweat broke out on her forehead, and she wiped it on the rope, grateful for the cold draft coming from the holes in the roof. One more pass should do it. Her luck held, and she palmed the little square box. Sticking it in her teeth, she let her feet drop back to the floor, dragging her heels in the dirt to slow the rope's momentum.

Once the rope was steady, she hoisted her legs once more and hooked them acrobat style, bringing her face to her fingers. She took the box from between her teeth and opened the top flap.

Two straight razors. Thank God.

She closed the box with the spare blade inside and slid it back between her teeth before concentrating on the blade in her hand. Completely focused, Lily held the razor between her thumb and two fingers, glad for the tension on the rope, despite the pain it caused in her wrists.

With small movements, she cut fiber by fiber, each muffled tick a metronome counting off the minutes. Two thirds of the way through, she froze. The weakened rope groaned, and then *pop, pop, pop,* fibers snapped under her weight. The rope gave, and she dropped to the floor, landing with a *whoompf* in a cloud of barn dust.

Her head snapped back, making the dull ache at the back of her head scream. Her eyes watered, and she squeezed her nose to stop from sneezing, almost blowing out her eyeballs instead. She scrambled behind some old hay bales and sat back on her heels. So far, so good.

"You can do this, Lily. You're almost there," she mumbled over the box still in her teeth. She turned the blade over in her fingers, and taking short, measured breaths through her nose, worked the largest knot closest to the top of her wrists. Her saliva had saturated the thin cardboard, and it tasted of dust and lord knows what else. Her throat spasmed and she leaned over to finally spit the wet box to the ground, swallowing back on her gag reflex.

Concentrating on the task at hand, she sliced methodically through the coils. They came apart and she slumped down, exhausted, dropping the blade to the dirt and rubbing the raw skin encircling her wrists. Closing her eyes, she let her head drop back, a murmured, "Thank you," on her lips.

She sat for a moment just listening, before reaching for the limp razor box. The wet cardboard came apart in her hand and she pocketed the spare blade, just in case.

"Okay girlfriend. Let's blow this pop stand," she murmured, as she pushed herself to standing.

Her eyes moved from wall to wall, and up to the loft. But nothing looked feasible, not unless she wanted to slash her way through the tyvek. The main barn doors were the only real way out. They stood thirty feet ahead, but for all she knew, Jack had probably wired them for motion and sound.

Looking around, she exhaled sharply. She didn't come this far to wait like a sitting duck for Jack to hand deliver her to Parr. She wiped her hands on her pants, her eyes traveling back to the egress window where she'd found the razors.

The opening was small, but promising. She could definitely wriggle through, if she could find a way past the noise of having to break the glass.

Lower lip between her teeth, Lily maneuvered her way up the wall, wedging her feet between two side beams, holding her breath the entire time until she was sure they'd hold. She hooked her hands onto the bottom sill and tried the window. Just as she'd thought. Stuck. Her head was pounding at this point. Tiny spots of light danced in her peripheral vision, and she frowned. *Now is when her concussion decided to kick in? I don't think so.*

Pushing the dull headache away, she squinted, and cocked her elbow. The aim was to tap the old glass. If the window frame was rotted enough, perhaps the entire pane would just give. "Please fall," she whispered to herself as she tapped at the edges and corners of the glass. The wood frame cracked, and a muffled pop at one corner sent her adrenaline spiking. Control was the key. Her breath hitched in her throat, and with her fingertips splayed evenly across the glass, she gave the thin pane a gentle push. Lily cringed waiting for the sound of shattering glass, but there was nothing but a soft thud.

Hoisting herself up, she peered over the back end of the sill, not sure what to expect. Fresh air washed over her face, and she looked down. The glass was intact, having fallen vertically into the winter-bare scrub growing along the side of the barn. If this wasn't life or death, Lily would have laughed out loud.

She shimmied out of the empty window, careful not to break the glass with her torso as she skimmed the sharp, spindly twigs and crouched beside the bushes. As far as she could see, there wasn't a soul around. The faint glow of the sun in the overcast sky told her it was well past midday, which meant she had a good three hours of daylight to help her find her way out of here.

A thick branch lay broken in half across rows of muddy tractor marks leading out toward a far field. Lily licked her lips, looking across both her shoulders before darting out to grab one of the halves. It was the perfect weight and length to do some damage, not to mention it fit perfectly into the palm of her hand. "Just a little longer than a Japanese Short Stick," she chuckled to herself, twirling it up and then down in a practiced motion.

"Hey! Hey you! What are you doing there?" A deep voice yelled from the corner edge of the barn.

Lily's head jerked toward the sound, and she stood motionless for a moment, trying to gauge if the man was a civilian or one of Parr's men.

He took a step toward Lily, his eyes bulging with fear. "Holy shit! Quinn, get Marcus or for sure we'll be Parr's newest lab rats! The girl got out!"

Lily took off running, but it was too late. Damn it. What was she thinking standing there like an idiot? The alarm had been sounded, and it would be only minutes before wolves would be snapping and growling behind her. A lot of good that stick would do her now. She couldn't outrun the wolves, and she was too outnumbered to fight, but if she could make it to the road, she might stand a chance.

"I've got her scent. She's headed toward the back pasture." One voice growled.

"Good, keep her moving that way, and I'll cut her off before she hits the milking shed and road east. If she hit's that, she'll be too close to the road and out of range."

East. The road was east of here. She stopped and squatted beside a broken down tractor, squinting up at the sky to get her bearings. Finding her position, she crouched, running as best she could through a fallow field toward what looked to be a barren orchard. At least the trees would give her some cover. "Thank you, boys," she muttered to herself.

Whoever they were, it was obvious they had phased to wolf form, but someone must have missed the memo that she could tap into the common shifter path.

Jack would be monitoring the telepathic traffic for sure, but he couldn't monitor everyone, the network was just too far-reaching to block. This time, she didn't need to work the averages. He'd monitor only those he knew could help her—Sean, Mitch, and the other hunters—Rissa, too. Lily smiled coldly. In his arrogance she knew he'd forget one very small, but very important detail. He'd never think to monitor Stephie.

Lily knew exactly how she would reach Sean. Now all she needed was to figure out where she was.

She hopped a low stone fence and headed into the orchard. The spread of trees wasn't that deep, only ten rows, so her cover wasn't going to last. She stayed low, running from tree to tree, and only stopping to check her bearings. When she reached the last row, she squatted down again to listen, using both her ears and her mind.

It was too quiet.

Cautious, she opened her senses to scan the area, but got nothing but static, just like she had two months ago, when Sean had first brought her to the Compound. Looks like Jack learned that trick as well from Volkmann's notes.

Underhanded bastard.

She straightened, but the sound of leaves rustling pulled her attention, and she glanced over her shoulder. A squirrel scurried along foraging in the leaves. She smiled at herself for being so jumpy and turned back, only to freeze in mid-motion.

Jack.

He wore his trademark half-smile as he leaned against one of the trees, his foot propped on a broken apple crate. She half expected him to tease her or break into a full on grin at her expense. He looked the same as ever, but the reality was the Jack she loved like a brother, was gone.

Quietly stunned, Lily's grin faded.

"What, not happy to see me?" he asked, pushing himself away from the tree, but his shift in weight sent his foot crashing through the rotted crate. He lurched forward, swearing and landed on his hands.

The scene unfolded in slow motion, and from the corner of her eye she noticed a stamped logo on the jagged edge of the crate. Bradford Farms Dairy. She finally knew where she was, but she wasn't going to stick around to verify it.

She took off running, heading out of the trees and down an embankment. One hundred feet ahead, she heard the sound of cars passing on the road. If she could just reach there before Jack caught up to her... He was shouting as he ran, and then there was nothing but the wind and the sound of his growls. He had phased.

Horns blared as Lily skidded into the street, breathless, with Jack on her heels. They swerved to avoid hitting her, but no one stopped, not with a large grey wolf menacing on the grassy shoulder. Jack lunged, sending a blue ford sliding across the wet pavement.

Tires screeched, filling the air with the scent of burning rubber and the sound of metal crashing against a utility pole. A man was thrown from the vehicle, and Lily ran towards the steaming wreck, but Jack's teeth sunk into her leg, and she screamed, hitting the pavement as he dragged her back toward the shoulder. People shouted from the other side of the road, some with cell phones in hand. Whether they were calling the police or filming the horrific seen, she didn't know. Either way, this place would be crawling with cops or television crews soon enough.

A black SUV skidded to a stop in the middle of the mess. Two men got out and grabbed Lily by her arms, shoving her into the backseat. Pain shot through her leg along with the warm, wet feel of blood slick on her skin. Fast and furious, they climbed in after her and took off, tires squealing on the pavement behind.

Jack howled once, and Lily watched as he raced across the road toward the woods. She turned from the window as the man next to her uncapped a syringe. "For the pain," he said, and stuck the needle in her thigh before she could protest. "Relax. It's only Demerol. You'll feel better in a moment."

In seconds, she couldn't focus, and her eyelids were weighted down. Dizziness hit, making the interior of the car swim, and then everything went black.

"Welcome back," Edward's smooth voice echoed in her ears before she could even open her eyes. Lily struggled to get her lids up, but they were so heavy.

"Give it a moment, my dear. I'm afraid you were given quite a large dose of Demerol. In fact, I had to take measures against my own men for causing you such distress." He sighed. "However, your constitution reminds me of my own. Sturdy and hard hitting," he said, with a prophetic undertone.

Lily swallowed and tried to move. She was lying down on a bed, that much registered, and her leg throbbed as she shifted position, but the pain was dull. She forced her eyes open, blinking to clear her vision. She was in a hospital room of sorts, and Edward sat in a chair to the right of her bed.

"Where am I?"

"You're in my lab," he answered matter-of-factly.

"Your lab?"

He nodded, pushing himself up from his chair. "Yes. There is a lot you don't know about me, but I'd like to share my story with you, if you're not in too much of a hurry," he said with a husky chuckle.

Parr walked toward the foot of her bed, then hesitated. "On second thought, why don't you tell me what you know about your-self, first?"

"Excuse me?"

He gestured with his hand, circling it encouragingly. "I want to know all about you, Lily. This past month has been interesting, to say the least, but this past week has proved most enlightening. I want to know what you know about your family history, where you came from."

Lily shook her head, perplexed. "Edward, I don't understand what you're driving at. I'm a twenty-six year old orphan. Both my parents died in a car crash when I was ten."

He nodded. "Yes, yes. This I already know. What I'm looking for is the extent of your knowledge regarding your parents."

Lily looked at him again. What was he driving at? "Edward, my parents? Really? They were just regular people."

His eyes hardened, and the thin line of his lips made the planes of his cheeks sharp and ugly. Annoyed, he pushed away from her bed, and she watched as he drew a deep breath before turning back around, his practiced veneer back in its place.

He smoothed the front of his navy double-breasted suit, his fingers following the lines of the tone on tone pinstriping. "I'm sorry, my dear. I didn't mean to confuse or frighten you. Perhaps you don't know more than what you've already told me. Pity, really."

"Edward, I'm not afraid of you," she said, fixing him with a cold stare. "I never have been, nor will I ever be. As to being confused, this whole business is what's confusing." She gestured toward him and the room.

He smiled at her bravado. "I've always admired your fire, and I'm glad to hear you're not intimidated by me. It makes what I am about to reveal all the easier, and yes, this nasty business is confusing. However, all will be made clear."

Edward walked to the desk against the far wall and picked up the phone. "Have someone bring in a fresh set of clothes and toiletries. Ms. Saburi is awake."

"Edward..."

He held up his hand. "You have been severely inconvenienced and abused by my people, all for an end that could have been settled with a simple conversation. The least I can do is try to make you as comfortable as possible. You're usually such a pretty, little thing," he said, his eyes sweeping her filthy clothes and hair.

At the look Lily shot him, he chuckled. "That's not to say, dangerous and clever. It's just I hate seeing you there bedraggled and dirty. I've had my nurses see to your wounds. They have been thoroughly cleaned, and I hope you won't mind, but I've taken the liberty of injecting you with an agent to prevent Jack's bite from turning you. I do apologize for his rashness, but it was understandable given the circumstances."

Lily's eyes widened. She didn't know which of his words to choke on first.

"Don't look so shocked, my dear. I have the utmost respect for you. As to the agent in question, well, I've my own set of researchers working for me here. Dr. Volkmann is a brilliant man, but he's not the only game in town—but I'll stop there as I'm getting ahead of myself."

There was a knock on the door.

"Ah. Come in," he said with a magnanimous smile.

A nurse walked in carrying a clean set of clothing and a travel bag. She nodded once to Edward and then put the items on one of the chairs across from the bed.

Edward smiled warmly and swept his arm toward the door on the adjacent wall. "There's a full bathroom, complete with shower. It may be hospital grade, but it will do. Please..." he said, offering his hand to help her out of the bed.

Both irked and uneasy, Lily raised one hand. "I appreciate the chivalry Edward, but I'm capable of taking myself to the bathroom."

He lifted an eyebrow, watching her carefully. "Very well, but I'll send the nurse back in just in case you need help."

Edward swept out of the room, and Lily swung her legs over the edge of the bed. "Help me. Yeah right. More likely to avoid my escape."

She stepped her feet onto the cold linoleum and shivered. At least she wasn't in one of those stupid hospital gowns. One of her pant legs was gone, and she could see the doctor's handiwork. "I guess Jack's bite is as bad as his bark, and he's going to need one of those teeth when I cut his balls off," she mumbled to herself, as she examined the wound. The stiches were tiny and precise, but there had to be one hundred of them holding her skin together.

The nurse came in and immediately hooked her arm under Lily's shoulder to help her to the bathroom. "Don't worry, sweetheart. I'll help you as much as I can. I used to work for Dr. V before Mr. Parr blackmailed me into working for him. My son was a vampire junkie, addicted to the rush that comes from them feeding on you. Edward threatened to expose the taboo and have us shunned, if I didn't leave the Compound and come here." Her voice barely rose above a whisper.

"Can you reach Sean or Mitch?" Lily asked, her eyes searching the woman's face."

She shook her head. "I'm watched too closely. But rest assured, you won't be given any more drugs. I'll see to that. I've been ordered to give you another dose of Demerol if you don't cooperate."

Lily sucked in a breath.

The nurse patted her arm. "Don't worry. The only thing I'm going to give you is a shot of B12. It'll help you get your energy back. You're going to need your wits about you. Trust me."

Lily threw her arms around the woman's neck.

"Thank you."

The nurse put her finger to her lips. "Just pretend to sleep and they'll leave you alone." She smiled. "Now let's get you cleaned up."

The hot water was delicious, and Lily scrubbed and sudsed, trying to wash away everything that had happened over the last twenty-four hours. She rinsed her hair and her body, stepping out onto the plain cotton mat the nurse had set out for her. The woman had left two white towels on the sink, and Lily quickly dried off, wrapping her body in one towel and her clean hair in the other.

She sat on the closed toilet seat and shut her eyes. Concentrating, she sifted through the familiar traces deep in her psyche, completely skipping the ones that led to Sean, Mitch, and Rissa. She ignored Jack's trace, squelching the urge to send him a mental bitch slap. She went further in, and beneath Rissa's trace, a faint line glowed at the back of her mind.

She had only used it once or twice while testing Stephanie's abilities. Her chest filled at the thought of how powerful a psychic the little girl truly was, and how easily she accepted it. She was unafraid, most of the time, anyway.

The day she and Jack had left for New York, Stephanie had tried to tell Sean that something bad was coming. She knew. She had seen it already, and Lily was just as guilty as Sean and Rissa for dismissing her fears out of hand, chalking it up to a bad dream. Certainly, something none of them would ever do again.

Lily would bet odds that Stephanie already communicated with her little brother, though he wasn't due to be born for another couple of months. The best thing Rissa did, though, was keep her daughter's talent a family secret. Lord knows what Parr would do if he caught wind of it, and what Jack knew of her only scratched the surface. Thank God.

Lily reigned her thoughts back in, and picked up the thread, giving the little girl a little mental tug. *"Stephie?"*

She could feel the child's sleep mottled answer. *"Lily? Is that you? Are you home?"*

Lily smiled. *"It's me, baby. But no, I'm not home... or at least I don't think so. I'm a little lost, and I need your help to figure out how to get home. You're the only one who can help me, but you cannot talk to mommy or Mitch about it with your mind. You can tell mommy and Mitch everything I say with your words, but I'm the only one you can talk to with your mind. Do you understand?"*

Lily waited, feeling the little girl trying to wrap her head around what she'd just told her.

"Lily, are you in trouble?"

Lily took a deep breath, couching her words very carefully. The last thing she wanted was to scare a four year old. *"Yes, sweetheart. I am. Uncle Sean can't find me with his mind, and whenever I try to reach him, I get a bad pain in my head. You're the only one I can talk to without feeling hurt. I need for you to wake up mommy and Mitch, and then we're going to play telephone. Okay?"*

"Okay. I like that game. We play it in school sometimes. I'll be right back."

Lily's shoulders slumped in relief. Mitch knew Maine like the back of his hand. From the outskirts of Bradford Dairy, they would be able to track her scent, and Rissa would make sure Stephie kept the trace open between them. Now all she had to do was wait and stay alive. She looked up at the ceiling, praying silently Sean did the same.

CHAPTER
TWENTY-ONE

Dressed, Lily brushed her hair out, letting it hang loose across her shoulders and back. After having it in a braid for so long, the idea of pulling it tight again made her head throb even more than her possible concussion. She opened the bathroom door, only to find Parr sitting in the chair near the bed opposite her.

"You look refreshed, and I'm glad to see the clothing suits you," he said with an appreciative gaze.

"Jeans and a tee shirt, how can you go wrong with that?" Lily answered with a shrug. She still couldn't get a handle on his generous benefactor bit. What was he after, besides Sean's status?

"Please, have a seat. I would very much like to continue our conversation." He got up and moved two chairs toward a window that overlooked the woods.

Outdoor flood lights illuminated the area, and Parr pulled up the blinds, giving Lily a full view of the barbed wire fence surrounding the perimeter of wherever they were. Passive aggressive. The man dripped with courtesy yet showed her the fence in case she got any bright ideas.

Lily sat down, careful not to jar her leg. "So, what is it you wanted to tell me, Edward?"

He cleared his throat at her direct stare. "Did you know I was originally from California?"

"No, really? That's gnarly dude," she said, mimicking a surfer's accent.

He smirked. "Yes, I was born into a very secretive cougar community in the Sierra Nevada's. My pride didn't believe in mixing with the outside world. It was detrimental to our growth in many ways, I'm sure you can imagine, but mostly it hindered our gene pool." He watched her closely.

"And?"

He chuckled. "Forgive me, if I watch you for signs of revulsion. It's very important to me that I make you understand."

Okay, Twilight Zone anyone? Flabbergasted, Lily just shrugged.

He cleared his throat again. "What I am about to say next is not something I'm proud of, it's just what we did to survive." He paused, watching her face again before continuing. "We had hunting parties, but we didn't hunt for food. We hunted for mates."

Lily raised an eyebrow, unconsciously pushing her chair back.

Seeing her flinch away, he waved his hands in front of him. "No, no, my dear. You haven't been brought here in that capacity...Lord no! I'm just telling you all this as background information."

Lily hmmphed. "Yeah, well according to your newest acolyte, Jack informed me that I now belonged to him. Part of the deal and all, for getting me here to use as bait."

Parr's eyes narrowed, and his face reddened. "He won't touch you, of that you can be sure. I'll kill him first."

She didn't know what to think, the man was acting like either her mate or her father. What was the deal here?

He dragged in a long breath. "Anyway, let's not dwell on how you got here. This is all about why you're here. Nearly thirty years ago, I was elected to this hunting circle. It's a cyclical pact, and only the males selected to breed can participate. Most of the women you read about that go missing in the mountains of northern California aren't mauled by cougars, they're taken by shifters. For breeding purposes."

He stopped and got up to pace. "There's that look of revulsion I was waiting to see," he said, pointing at her. "Please, try to listen with an open mind. Like I said, this was all in the past."

He turned and leaned on the side rail of the hospital bed. "I was lucky enough to be sent to the city on many occasions for things we needed that couldn't be found on the land. Over the years, I bartered not only for necessary items, but also for books. I taught myself everything, but what especially interested me was genetics. You see, Lily, I wasn't like the others of my community. I was a genetic throw back to our ancestors. An American Lion. Unfortunately, now extinct, myself notwithstanding.

"So, when it was my time to mate, I promised myself I would do everything in my power to ensure that my genetic anomaly, my line, didn't go extinct again. I studied and theorized and hypothesized, and then it came time to put those theories to the test, and the only thing I needed was a woman. One of my own, a shifter would have been best, but they were all claimed by this point. So, I had to take part in the hunting circle to carry out my plan."

He paused, pouring himself a glass of water, and offering one to Lily as well. She took the glass from his hand, nodding for him to continue.

"I managed to acquire a place in the Bay area, and stocked it, over time, with my books and equipment. I experimented with genetic mutation and DNA splicing, mostly." He stopped. "Don't look so horrified. I only experimented on myself, no one else."

Lily stood up, ignoring the pain that shot through her leg at the abrupt movement. "Don't look so horrified! You stand there and tell me you're some kind of shifter version of Dr. Frankenstein, and I'm supposed to be okay with that? I'm not stupid, Edward, I can see where you're headed with this, and it involves some poor woman you used for your own ends."

"Lily, please. Hear me out. Yes, it's true. I did abduct a woman, but she was homeless and on the verge of selling herself anyway. She was an illegal alien who barely spoke English when I took her. She lived with me, willingly. It's not like I tied her up." He glanced down at the red, puckered marks on Lily's wrists. "The one who did that to you is dead. I wanted you brought here, but not in the way it transpired, and for that I am sorry."

She flopped back down in her chair. "What do expect me say, Edward. Your lady friend may have chosen to stay of her own free will, but if she'd wanted to leave would you have let her? Would you let me?" Tony's words came back to haunt her. Make it easy on yourself, baby, and cooperate.

Parr ignored her question. "Where was I... *oh yes,* experimenting. The time came to put my experiments to the test. As you can imagine, my lady friend, as you call her, was surprised when I insisted on artificial insemination." He drew himself up, expanding his chest as if to prove his virility. "To my delight, it took on the first try and with twins, no less! I, of course, immediately packed us up to head back to the mountains. My children would be raised as full Shifters, regardless of their maternal line.

"Unfortunately, things didn't work out as planned," he paused as if caught in the memory. "Teresa, that was her name, didn't take well to life in the mountains, and being a human in a shifter dominated world—well, let's just say there were certain prejudices she had to endure. She ended up running away. I searched for her, but all I found were bloody clothes carrying her scent."

Lily looked at her hands. "So, as far as you know, she died while trying to escape?" Her words were a question mark, but her eyes were accusing. With the way the man clenched his jaw, she knew she'd hit a nerve, but his face was otherwise a mask. "Look, Edward. I'm sorry for your loss, truly, but what has this got to do with me?"

He studied her for a moment, his gaze so intense, he seemed to be examining her every feature. He stepped to her chair and stood over her, his fingers brushing beneath her chin as he lifted it. "It has everything to do with you. You are my daughter."

Lily stood up, knocking Parr's hand away. With the back of her legs she pushed her chair to the wall and scooted behind Edward to stand in the middle of the room. "I was right. You are delusional! My mother and father were my biological parents, I was not adopted."

Edward shook his head. "Perhaps they never told you, but there's no other explanation as to why you are immune to the virus I created. I made it using my own blood, so therefore the only people who would have any natural immunity to it would have to be of my bloodline! I have no idea what happened to Teresa or the other fetus she carried, but I know, YOU ARE MY DAUGHTER, and you will take your place by my side. My coup is almost complete, not just at the Compound, but I intend to be the Alpha of the Brethren for the entire country. My rule will be all encompassing."

"You did this? You caused all this death and pain? You're the one responsible for ruining all those lives, all those families?" Lily's fists balled in her palms.

He sniffed. "There is always collateral damage. I know you are my child because it's the only explanation why you survived, why your blood was a key to the serum Volkmann distilled. Every human I infected died within days, if not hours. And the vampires, well, tantalizing as they were, they degenerated to a base nature."

He waved his hands in the air. "It's immaterial now, anyway. I had the antivirus for the Shifters, you just came along to speed things up. It's karma, my darling child, can't you see that? You were brought here by something bigger than both of us. It was meant to be."

Lily paced back and forth. "Certifiable," she mumbled, her thoughts racing.

He chuckled. "It's a lot to digest at once, I know. It's taken me all week to come to terms with it myself. You see, I wanted you dead along with Leighton, but once I connected the dots, there was no way I could bring myself to murder my own child. Take a moment and think about it. I'm going to get us some champagne!"

Lily's eyes bugged out of her head. She had called him delusional before, but that was just rhetoric. Now she wasn't so sure. Champagne? Christ almighty, he's got me as some kind of heiress to the empire he's building in his mind! She chewed on her bottom lip. Nah. This had to be part of some elaborate ploy.

Her mind sorted through everything Parr had said. Genetic experimentation? On both humans *and* vampires? Parr had created some horrific shifter version of Nazi Germany and the sick human experimentations performed by Josef Mengele—and for him to dismiss the fallout as collateral damage—perhaps this wasn't just a ploy, and he truly was insane.

A thought registered and Lily slid down in the chair by the window. Stephanie's nightmare claimed the woman in her dream smelled like the people Volkmann was trying to help. She had to have meant the people infected with the virus, as that's the part of the hospital where Rissa had been staying while going through the antiviral testing.

Her mouth fell open as another puzzle piece fell into place. The redhead! She recognized Jack's scent as her mother's tormentor! That meant Parr had experimented on Améile! *Jesus.* It was him. He was indirectly responsible for all those deaths in the city.

The man's web and all the blood associated with it just seemed to widen, and Lily's skin crawled thinking about what else it might encompass.

Her nerves were on overdrive. She shot to her feet, pacing again. Is it true? Am I his child? She mulled his words over in her head. She shook her head, pressing her eyes shut at the prospect. No. She had her birth certificate, and her parents would never have knowingly lied to her, not when their best friends in the whole world had gone through it themselves. Beverly and Carl. They may have never gotten around to telling Terri, but Lily knew in her gut that Bev had told her mother. It was the kind of things best friends shared.

Lily looked at her left palm and the faint white line that traversed the center. Best friends. Sisters in everything but blood.

Her eyes flew open. Holy Christ! Terri was born in California, and she was a twin. Lily licked her lips, mashing them together. Yeah, but so were hundreds of other unfortunate kids.

The notion ran circles through her mind. What the hell was Terri's birth mother's name? Lily shook out her wrists, pacing even harder. She knew it, she heard it in the vision she had in the attic that day with Beverly. Oh God, it was Teresa! Terri's birth mother's name was Teresa.

Parr had just mentioned the woman who conceived his children was named Teresa. The timeline fit, and if Terri was half shifter, then that stupid blood sister ritual they did when they were twelve years old was what gave Lily her immunity.

Parr said the woman was pregnant with twins. What about Terri's twin? Lily's vision couldn't verify if the child survived or not. Think, Lily think...

She stopped pacing and sunk down on the edge of the bed. *Ryan.* It was the only piece that fit. He looked like Terri, and he was a half-shifter... a Werecougar! Holy Christ! Ryan was Terri's twin brother and Parr's son!

Parr walked back in, and Lily scrambled to wipe any sign of what she had just pieced together from her face.

The man's manner was not only celebratory, it was downright triumphant. He had two champagne flutes in one hand and a bottle of Dom in the other.

"A toast to my beautiful daughter, and my heir apparent," he said, raising the bottle high. He practically pranced to the side of the bed, sliding his arm around Lily's shoulder, and resting his head on hers. "Just think of it. Together we will bring the American Lion back to its former glory." He sniffed, almost overcome with emotion. "My darling girl, I am overwhelmed with my good fortune. I've even given the staff the night off!"

Lily sat there speechless, afraid to make any sudden movements.

"Don't you have anything you want to say to me? His demeanor flip-flopped, his eyes narrowing as if challenging her to disagree.

She ducked out from under his arm, moving toward the center of the room and a clear shot at the door. "Shall we open the champagne?" She cocked her hand on her hip.

"Ha! I so enjoy your nerve, my dear. Oh, Lily, we have so much to learn about each other, but I'm a firm believer in nature over nurture. My blood runs through your veins, so it's only a matter of time before you come around completely. That you sought revenge for your friend's death and taught yourself to hunt supes with no formal training, only proves my point." He let the silver paper from the top of the bottle flutter to the floor and untied the wire around the cork.

He walked to the door once more and returned with a white cloth. Draping it over the top of the bottle, he wiggled the cork until they both heard the loud pop. "May this be the first of many celebrations," he offered with a tender look.

Skepticism ricocheted straight into full blown alarm, and Lily pasted a smile on her face. This was no ploy. Parr had slipped a cog. He truly believed everything he said.

The flutes were on a small round table between the two chairs he'd placed by the window, and he filled the glasses, reaching into his pocket for sugar cubes. At Lily's raised eyebrow, he dropped one each into the glasses. "Sweets to mask the bitter bubbles." He smiled, handing her one of the flutes. Raising one high, he winked. "To us."

Sean slammed the car door behind him. He was tired of using a four year old as his intermediary. He wanted to hear Lily's voice himself, even if it was just in his head.

The police had been all over Bradford Farms Dairy. They found the rope and the razor, and the broken window, but still wouldn't offer the evidence as anything but suspicious, possibly coincidental. The only evidence they considered to be hard were the accounts given by eye witnesses, and those pointed toward an animal attack in the road, or at least that's what the police were leaning toward.

His hunters had her scent, but they lost it not far up the road, finding it impossible to track the scent of a single vehicle for more than a mile. There were just too many on the road.

Lily was okay at least that's what her last communiqué through Stephanie had said. Parr was acting crazy, and she was playing along until they found her. If he could only find Jack, then he'd have what he wanted in spades. Sean's hands itched to rip his former hunter's throat out. He was a dead man, regardless of the story he spun.

Sean's phone buzzed. "Leighton." He was in no mood, and his clipped tone spoke volumes.

"Sean, we've got Jack. He's been spotted in wolf form in the woods outside Bradford. He's been covering his tracks well. We must have been through that area three times. It appears he's been following the stream to camouflage his scent. Do you want us to move in?

Sean smiled. "No, Mitch, have one of the men send him a message along the Hunter's path. Tell him that Lily is still missing, and we have no leads other than the plates on the car that took her were from Maine. Say that I'm rallying the shifters for a full out search, and that I need my best officers by my side. Play it up, tell him that I'm distraught and that you're worried about my state of mind. That'll bring the cocky bastard in. If I know him, he'll think I'm easy pickings and lead me right where I want to go. Have one of guys do it now. We'll hold a fake strategy meeting in the library tonight. Tell him I want him there. No questions."

Mitch nodded. "You got it, boss. What if he says no?"

Sean's anger boiled just below the surface. "No refusals. Tell him it's mandatory or he faces abnegation."

JACK SNICKERED as he walked up the main path leading to the front door of the manor. "Like taking candy from a baby" he muttered to himself, pushing the heavy oak door aside and walking straight into the library.

"Hey," he said giving an offhand salute to the men standing around the room as he entered. He walked straight toward the table where Mitch and Sean were huddled over a map. Near the alpha's hand was a yellow legal pad with the names of hunter's listed alongside different regions from the State of Maine. "Am I late?"

Sean looked up and shook his head. "Right on time, as usual. Look, I've divided the map among the best hunter's we have, from there I've made teams of the lower personal, plus Ross Stanton has graciously offered to give us aerial coverage through his Avians."

"Great. What can I do to help?" Jack asked, the picture of compassion and friendship. He had to make this look believable, and overstated opinions or excessive enthusiasm were the quickest way to raise suspicion. This was the moment he'd been waiting for.

Sean looked at Mitch. My second-in-command here doesn't agree, but I want you both with me. He thinks I should have you managing the hunters and their regions, but this has shaken me up pretty bad, and I'll need you both to stop me from doing something I'll regret later."

Mitch gave Jack a knowing look. "He means he's afraid he'll go crazy and kill Parr before we have a chance to bring him before a tribunal. We want to handle this in a civilized manner. No bloodshed, just diplomacy."

"Of course. You can count on me. What's our plan of attack? Do we have a region of our own?"

Mitch shook his head. "No. We're heading back to Bradford. The police just got in the way when we were there, and we didn't really find anything. It looked on the surface as though the place had been sanitized, but if the three of us head out, we should be able to find something the others missed."

"Great idea. When do we leave? Jack asked, not wanting to sound too eager.

Sean just looked at him. "We leave now."

"Okay. Do I have time to grab a change of clothes? I'm feeling a little grubby."

Sean nodded. "Yeah. We'll meet down by the car in fifteen minutes."

Mitch and the others walked out, leaving just Sean and Jack in the library. Jack stood at the door, his hand on the oiled bronze handle. "Sean, I'm so sorry about this. I had no idea that Parr was working with the vamps. It's the only thing that makes sense, or else he wouldn't have gotten through me. I can't help but feel responsible."

Sean sighed. "I know, Jack. I know exactly on whose shoulders this lies and believe me—they're going to pay dearly."

Jack closed the door behind him, Sean's expression at his last statement giving him chills. He'd never seen the alpha so focused, not even when they were hunting Jerard. Could he suspect it was him who was truly responsible? *Nah*. He had all bases covered. The common shifter path was bugged, as was the Hunter's path, plus he had wiretaps on all the phones. He'd know the minute they doubted him.

He turned the corner and took the stairs up to his room two at a time. He'd grab a five minute shower and put on his camo. Really look the part. On the landing he ran into Clotilde, one of the old housekeepers, and they shared a look. She was one of Parr's moles. Why he felt it necessary to blackmail women was beyond him, but who was he to questions Parr's methods, when they seemed to get the job done?

"Hey," he said. "How's the boss doing?" He gestured down the stairs, so she knew he meant Sean and not Edward.

She clucked. "He's a mess. Yelling one minute and apologizing the next. You better find his lady soon or he's going to snap." She nodded then headed the rest of the way down the stairs.

A full grin spread across Jack's face. So, Mitch wasn't bullshitting. Sean was more pussy whipped than he'd thought. Edward would get a hardy chuckle out of this.

MITCH SAT in the back of the SUV as it cruised north, with Jack occupying the passenger seat next to Sean. They were quiet, with no one really saying much on the long drive. That suited Sean perfectly. With his hands on the steering wheel, he kept tabs on Jack from the corner of his eye, the scene from *Godfather II,* where Carlo Rizzi is garroted from the backseat by one of Michael Corleone's captains, playing over and over again in his mind as he drove. If only.

Truth be told, Mitch would strangle Jack in a heartbeat, but first they needed to find Lily. On the other hand, Sean wanted the pleasure of ripping Jack's heart out himself.

The silence grew, and there was a palpable tension in the car as the headlights marked the entrance to the farm, and its long gravel drive. Sean turned wide, bumping the side wheels into a large divot in the road. Jack's head smacked against the inside roof of the SUV.

"What the fuck, Sean? If you keep this up, I'm driving home," he complained, his fingers massaging the top of his head.

You'll be going home alright. In the trunk.

"Sorry, Jack. I guess I missed that one," he said, his face contrite, but chuckling inside. Sean glanced in the rearview and Mitch wore a wide smirk. Tearing this traitor to shreds was going to feel so good.

They pulled up to the ramshackle farmhouse and parked out front. The minute Sean stepped foot on the grounds, he knew they were in the right place. He could sense Lily, and this time it wasn't the old, faded scent they'd picked up when the police were here. This was new. She must be walking around. He inhaled again, and Parr's scent hit him as well. He didn't say anything, but he knew both Mitch and Jack sensed it too. Now he just needed to wait for Jack to make his move.

Smoke rose from the back behind the house, and Sean took off with Mitch and Jack on his heels. The barn was on fire, but the flames had already imploded the structure and were dying out. The wind had calmed, so the chance of the fire spreading was small, and even if it did, the buildings were abandoned and the property so far off the road, there was no danger of it spreading anywhere significant. If Sean knew Parr, he was well insulated from any danger from the fire, and if Lily was with him, then so was she.

"Well, so much for getting a better look at the barn," Mitch said, throwing a random stick into the embers.

"Bad luck, really," Jack interjected. "This whole thing has been nothing but a series of bad luck."

Sean's head snapped around. "Luck? Is that what you think this is? If anything, this whole situation smacks of precision planning," he said, stalking off toward the car.

Jack looked at Mitch. "I see what you mean about him walking a fine line. This isn't good."

Mitch just shook his head. "No shit Sherlock. Any other brilliant summaries or suggestions?"

Jack picked his way through the debris near the house to peer through one of the cracked windows. He smiled. "As a matter of fact, I do. Go get lover boy. I think I found something."

Sean came back around the house with Mitch. This was it. Bingo. Jack was going to make the second biggest mistake of his short life. The first, of course, betraying him and taking Lily.

"Mitch says you sense something. What is it? We went through all this earlier."

Jack snorted, and the familiarity of the sound made Sean want to shove his fist in his face. "Yeah. You went through this with a bunch of human cops trampling around like a herd of elephants, not to mention mucking up the scents. If you don't believe me, take a look for yourself," he offered, stepping to the side, a broad grin on his face.

Sean peered through the glass, and sure enough, on the mud floor inside were boot tracks leading to the front of a bookcase, Lily's boot tracks.

Sean looked at Jack. "Come on," he said, but then glanced over at Mitch. "Call the team tell them to meet us here. Lord knows who or what we're going to find around this place."

Jack led the way inside, with Sean following close behind. He sidestepped the ruined household items strewn about the floor and went straight for the bookcase. He knocked on one of the back panels like he was looking for a hollow sound.

"What are you doing? Trying to announce that we're here?" Sean whispered harshly.

Jack shook his head. "The bookcase is obviously the way in to some sort of secret entrance. Lily's boot prints end right in front, they don't turn around anywhere. Just get on the other side and help me lift it out of the way."

The shelves slide to one side, clattering in the silence like a bomb going off, but they managed to move the piece of furniture away from the bunker entrance, revealing a stairwell heading straight down.

"I'll go first," Jack volunteered, and he pulled a flashlight out of his pocket and flicked it on.

Sean bit the inside of his cheek. *You got that right. See you in hell, asshole.*

The staircase was metal, and they climbed down as quietly as they could, Jack flashing the light ahead and to the sides.

"Lily?" Sean tried their shared link, knowing better than to try the common path, but not hoping for much.

"Oh my God, Sean! I can hear you! Is Jack with you? He's been blocking me the whole time."

"Yeah he's here. I'm in the bunker. Are you anywhere near here, or have I just walked into a trap?"

"No, I'm here, somewhere. Edward has a secret lab here as well. He's behind the whole thing. The virus, the vamps, everything. If Jack's not blocking me anymore, then he must be hoping you'll follow my lead. Maybe you should pretend you still can't hear me."

"I picked up your scent up top. Has Edward changed location?"

"No. He blindfolded me, then led me around. Said it was for my own protection. He thinks I'm his daughter."

"What?"

"Yeah. The crazy bastard. Somewhere in all this he crossed that line between genius and insanity, so don't underestimate him. I'll tell you all about it later, right now just get me the hell out of here."

"I'm coming. Hang tight."

"Yeah, yeah. The last time you said that, I ended up half hogtied in an old barn!"

"I love you, Lily."

"Kiss, Kiss. I love you, too."

Jack looked at Sean, his eyes suspicious despite the hopeful trill in his voice. "What? Did you reach her?"

Sean shook his head. "Nope. Not a peep."

Confusion washed over Jack's face, and he coughed tilting his head away. "Do you want me to try?"

Sean shrugged. "Be my guest. It's gotta be me. I'm just too tense for telepathy right now."

Jack squinted, staring off into space. Sean knew he was bluffing. The only way he could possibly reach Lily was through the common shifter path since she didn't have access to the Hunter's pathway.

"Anything?" Sean asked, trying to sound hopeful.

"Yeah," Jack nodded. "Not much though. I think you're right. You are too tense, but the frequency seems jammed down here. I have a definite trace. Follow me."

Jack led him through a long tunnel to a back stairwell, and then up one level. The temperature evened out, so they must have surfaced somewhere on the property. Pausing by the inside door, Jack hesitated. "Do you want to try Lily again? The trace I'm following is starting to peter out."

Sean shook his head. "No, I've been trying all along and still nothing. Let's just go with what we've got."

"Lily get to Stephanie. Tell her to tell Mitch to hurry. I'm almost to you."

"Okay. I'm in one of the hospital rooms overlooking the woods. Careful, there's a barbed wire fence around the place."

"I think we're coming in via the underground. Get something you can swing, because you might need it once I go for Jack's throat. Parr is a 'puss in suits' so you won't have to worry about him, but our vampire friends will most likely prefer him intact. If you get my drift. So it would be nice if he didn't get away."

"Loud and clear."

Jack shoved at Sean's shoulder. "Come on, we're close. I picked up her trace again."

"Good. Just a little farther, right?"

"Yeah. Whew! Her scent. Can't you smell it? Even with what she's been through, she still smells amazing."

"That she is."

They walked at a fast clip down the hall. Sean quietly unclipped

328

Lily's 9mm from behind his back and palmed it at his side. He'd never felt the need to carry a firearm before, leaving that strictly up to her, but in this situation it felt justified.

"Sean!" Martinez called in a harsh whisper from the entrance to the hallway.

"What are you doing here?" Sean said, shock and annoyance dripping from his voice. "Who sent you?" Immediately suspicious, his hand closed over the gun's safety, ready to hit the release if necessary.

"Mitch sent me. I got to the Compound, and he knew exactly who I was. I guess you must have filled him in pretty well. I had my Harley, so I made it here before everyone else. They're on their way." He gave Sean a sheepish smile. "This shifter shit is pretty cool, now that I'm learning how to work it."

"Glad you're here, considering," he whispered, flashing a conspiratorial smile.

Martinez sniffed the air. "Hey, Lily's close. I can smell her," he said, obviously proud of himself.

Jack stalked back up the hall. "Yeah, no shit dickhead. We don't need you here, cop. So just scurry on back to your hole in the city. You've been a shifter for what, two days? Take a hike before you get yourself hurt," Jack sniped. "Sean, we need to move before Parr alerts his men that we've infiltrated."

Martinez snorted. "Oh, please. Don't use words you don't understand. In case you haven't noticed, smart ass, there's no one around, which means it's a trap and you're going to need all the manpower you can get."

Jack gave Martinez a hard glare, then turned on his heel. Sean winked at Ryan, clapping him on the arm for playing along. "Let's go get our girl."

The three of them stopped outside the last door. The plaque on the outside frame said, 'Recovery Suite'. Sean backed up to kick the door wide, when at that moment, Parr pulled it open.

"We've been expecting you," he said. "Haven't we my dear?" he asked, glancing over his shoulder to Lily.

Sean's eyes tracked Parr's, and it was all he could do not to charge into the room, but he wasn't going to put Lily in any more danger, not knowing what was waiting for him inside.

Jack walked in like he owned the place, all pretense of helping Sean fading with each step. Sean surreptitiously stuck the gun back in its holster, while Martinez walked in ahead of him.

Lily's eyes widened when she saw Ryan. She glanced at Sean, and shook her head almost imperceptibly, alarm rising in her scent.

It's okay, Ryan's in on it. He's backup.

When her expression didn't change Parr picked up on the little exchange. "And who is this, my pet?" he asked Lily, circling Ryan like he was an oddity. He sniffed the detective, and his eyes widened. "A WereCougar! How delightful! And obviously a friend of yours. Oh, don't you see my darling! It's fate." He beamed at her, clasping Ryan on the shoulder.

With a too wide smile, he leaned his head toward Ryan. "You'll have to forgive us, my friend, but there is still a little business I must take care of before my darling daughter can make the proper introductions."

"Daughter?" Jack replied. "Wait a minute, Edward. You never said anything about Lily being your daughter. And what about your promise? You said she was mine after we got rid of Sean."

Sean snarled, every muscle bulging with restrained anger, but the guttural noise that came from Edward was even more alarming.

Parr's expression turned ugly. "You aren't fit to lick her paws. I destroyed any claim you had on her, and that goes for you too, dog!" He looked down his nose at Sean. "Lily is as much a cat now, as she was the day she was born. She simply needs a little help finding her genetic way, and that's where I come in."

Gripping Ryan's shoulder even tighter, Parr grinned at Lily. "Now that you've found yourself a proper playmate, I see no further use for either of them." Parr let go of Ryan, and sipping his wine, waved them all off imperiously.

Ryan raised one eyebrow at Lily, then slid a sideways glance at Sean for help.

"Playmate!" Jack shouted at Parr. "Are you for real?" Glaring, he turned toward Ryan. "You fucking pig cop. You waltz in here and ruin weeks of planning! She's mine!"

"Watch out!" Lily called, jumping up from the side of the bed, but it was too late.

Sean lunged for Jack, his eyes yellow and his muscles rippling beneath his skin. Jack pivoted away and grabbed Ryan by the shoulders, tossing him into the window. The cop's head snapped back against the thick tempered glass. He was out cold, his head slumping over onto to his shoulder. Lily ran to the hospital tray for a wad of tissues to clean some of the blood trickling from his forehead to his face.

Jack planted himself in front of Lily, his arms folded across his chest, his face a picture of smug satisfaction. "Looks like your daughter's new playmate can't keep up with a real shifter. Maybe you'd better think twice about your choices for your little girl, Edward."

"Sean growled. You're a coward Jack. You think I'm a pussy because I won't put Lily in danger. But at least I don't hide behind a woman's skirts, or a woman's proximity. You're a dead man once I get my hands on you. At least Edward can plead insanity. You knowingly set up your friends and loved ones, people who trusted you. You're a disgrace, and it will be a pleasure to rip your heart out."

Lily's eyes were like daggers as she stared Jack down, as well. "That's if I don't get to him first."

Sean wasn't one for idle threats and Jack's eyes narrowed. He laughed it off, though, turning his attention to Lily. "Don't be too sure, sweetheart. "I've always admired your fire, Lily," he said, moving closer to where she stood between the bed and the window. "And when daddy dearest gives you to me, we're going to strike quite a match together."

Sean growled, but bit back on his urge to kill. The man was just too close to Lily, and he had no doubt Jack would use her in a heartbeat to protect himself. Lily was smart and skilled, but a threatened wolf at full strength would be no match for her.

"Ryan, are you all right? Can you hear me?" she asked, ignoring Jack, and squatting down next to Ryan's unmoving body, watching his eyes twitch behind closed lids. "He's probably going to need stitches, thank you very much, and of course I'm the one who's going to have to answer for this." Carefully, she lifted his hair away from his forehead, surprised to find the wound was almost completely healed.

"Dearest, it's not your fault you're so desirable that men fight over you. You take after me," Edward said with a laugh.

Lily's eyes narrowed, as she drew herself up to standing. "Listen to me you half crazed fuck. I am not your daughter! Teresa did get away from you, and she did give birth to your children, but she died in childbirth. I know, because I saw it. Your daughter was my friend, Terri, the one that Jerard killed. I saw everything the day I helped her adopted mother clean out her attic. I held Terri's baby blanket, the one they took from the hospital the day she was born. "YOU killed your own daughter, by starting this whole crazy mess. Your biological weapon is at the root of why your child is dead. As to her twin, he's lying right there unconscious. Ryan is Terri's twin brother, and he knows you for the power hungry madman that you are. Your dream of a dynasty is over Edward!"

Parr's face contorted, and his mouth opened wide. Large canines, as thick as a man's finger descended, and he lunged at Lily. "You bitch!"

Sean jumped forward, swinging the butt of Lily's gun down on the back of Parr's head, knocking him out cold. He slumped to the ground, a tiny trickle of blood dripping across his temple.

"Is he dead?" Lily asked.

"Nope. Just out."

Jack backed up, his body half turned to make a run for it, but he didn't get far. Mitch and the other hunters had arrived, blocking the doorway.

"Looks like we missed all the fun," Mitch said with a chuckle, looking at the two unconscious cats and Jack sandwiched in the middle between him and Sean.

Sean shook his head. "No. You're just in time for the finale. It's gonna be a rat killing."

Jack snarled menacingly, his eyes flashing yellow as he dropped to all fours, but before he had a chance to snap, crackle or pop a single muscle, Sean splintered his nose with one punch.

The young hunter's head snapped back, and on the rebound Sean grabbed his skull, crushing his head like a walnut. With a quick flick of his wrist and a muffled crack, the alpha snapped the younger wolf's neck as well, just to be sure.

Jack's body slid to the ground, and Sean stepped over him without as much as a backwards glance, gathering Lily in his arms.

It was over.

Ryan's eyes fluttered open. He moved his head slightly from side to side, wincing with the effort. "Lily?" he mumbled, taking a moment to breathe before bracing his palms on the floor and slowly pushing himself up to sit with his back pressed against the window. "What happened?" he muttered to no one in particular.

Lily let go of Sean, but he held onto her arm with one hand, while the other reached behind his back for her gun. He pressed the weapon into her hand, patting her on the butt before gently pushing her toward the window.

"Ryan? Look at me, can you hear me?" Lily asked. She tucked the gun into her waistband but kept her hand on it just in case. Concern was one thing, but Martinez was a trained cop who'd just been punked. He was more likely to shoot first and ask questions later.

"My ears are ringing, but yeah, I can hear you," he said, lifting his hand to his forehead. "My head feels a little spongy, though."

Lily reached down and hooked her arm under the detective's shoulder. "A little help here?" she said, looking across to the others.

Sean gestured for two of the hunters to help Ryan onto the bed. "I think he's going to be fine," he said, his eyes never leaving Lily. "I think we're all going to be just fine.

"Yeah," she nodded, her eyes misting over as her gaze locked with his. "Me too."

CHAPTER

TWENTY-TWO

They loaded Parr's unconscious body into the back of the SUV, his ankles and wrists cuffed for good measure. Turning him over to lie face up on the backseat, Sean's eyes narrowed at the tiny dart sticking out of the man's neck. He lifted a questioning gaze toward Mitch on the opposite side of the seat.

His second-in-command looked up, nearly bashing his head on the open door frame. "What?"

"That," Sean replied pointing at the dart.

Mitch shrugged. "God bless Dr. Volkmann and his toys." He grinned, pushing his jacket back, revealing the grip of a tranquilizer gun stashed on his hip. "It's the same make he used on us the day we went ape shit in his lab. If the drug worked on us, I knew it would work on this puss in suits."

Sean chuckled. "That's my line."

"Yeah," Mitch said, slamming the car door shut. "I know, and I plan to use it whenever possible."

The alpha snorted. "I always knew you were a poser."

Grinning wider, Mitch opened the rear hatch to stow his rifle bag in the floor compartment. "The doc said this sedative has a non-phasing agent that blocks our animal DNA from taking over. If you're tranqued with this stuff, you won't be able to phase even if you wake up. The drug is experimental, so Volkmann wasn't sure how long the effects last, but he promised at least twenty-four hours. The doc's been working on this in secret, just in case the virus got even more out of control."

Sean shook his head. "Scary, these scientist types. Are we going to have to keep an eye on him too?"

Mitch laughed. "Nah. He's a good guy. Definitely the king of the geek squad and believe me he's happy in his little realm."

"Are you two just going to stand there gabbing? Personally, I'd like to go home," Lily interjected with a smirk on her face and her hand on her hip. Ryan stood next to her holding an ice pack to his head.

"That headache from kissing the window with your skull, or from listening to her sass?" Mitch asked Ryan, with a chuckle.

Martinez grumbled. "It's a toss-up."

"Hey!" Lily complained but smirked at Mitch's answering wink.

"You okay to travel? It's a long drive," Sean asked the detective.

"I'm good as long as one of you has room for my Harley. There's no way I'm leaving it here."

Lily perked up. "How about I drive it home?" She fluttered her lashes at both Ryan and Sean.

Sean laughed. "In your dreams, wolf girl. You've given me enough grey hair to last a lifetime. You ride with me."

Lily walked up to him and rubbed her hand up and down his chest. *"What a great idea, as long as I get to ride with you between my legs and my arms wrapped around your waist. It might be fun to have all that horsepower rumbling beneath us."*

Sean groaned, his groin thickening. *"You're such a tease."*

She shook her head. *"Nope. I'm a promise,"* she told him, lifting onto her toes and pressing a quick kiss to his lips.

He cleared his throat. "Hey, Cougar, you have more than one helmet for that death machine of yours?"

"Yes!" Lily pumped her arm back and forth.

Ryan chuckled. "Yeah. In the saddle compartment. "Just be careful. I want them both back in one piece, and by both, I mean Lily as well as my bike."

Sean smirked. "Watch it, buddy. She's claimed."

Ryan climbed into the passenger seat of the SUV next to Mitch. "I know, but you can't blame a guy for trying. Hey, remind Miss Leather and Lace she's got reports that need to be filled out. I may be her partner, but I'm not doing her paperwork for her," he said with a wave, before closing the car door."

Mitch started the engine and rolled down the passenger window. "Meet you at home?"

Sean closed the hard saddlebag and handed Lily the spare helmet. "Yup."

"No detours, Sean. We have damage control to do back at the Compound, specifically with council members who backed the asshole passed out on my backseat. What do you think? Meet you in the war room in two hours?"

Sean glanced at Lily straddling the motorcycle and his cock throbbed, its head ready to burst. "Make it three."

LILY STOOD on the front porch of the manor house, her eyes watching the three-quarter moon at its zenith. She and Sean finally had a proper homecoming, and they would still be at it, if Mitch hadn't banged on the door for Sean to get his ass out of bed and to the war room. He'd been sequestered with the hunters and the defunct council for hours. The last time she'd caught sight of him was from the window in their bedroom, as he and two hunters carried Jack's body into the Great Hall.

"Penny for your thoughts," Ryan asked, his footsteps on the stone pulling her attention before he even spoke.

She smiled as he came up beside her.

He stood with his hands in his pockets. Pulling out a pack of Marlboro, he lit a cigarette, then lifting one leg to the railing, blowing smoke into the night air. He hooked his left hand into the front of his jeans and tilted his head her way. "I hope you know I was only kidding, earlier. A blind man could see you and Sean are meant to be together."

She smirked. "Guess the moon's spell really is broken," she said, sticking a piece of Nicorette in her mouth to squash the urge to ask him for a cigarette.

He looked at her strangely.

"The full moon," she said, gesturing toward the sky. "It's been the culprit behind all the physical cravings between us this week. Everything you felt, it was just the moon playing its monthly trick on the Shifters of this world."

He exhaled another lungful of smoke, his shoulders relaxing. "Thank God. I didn't know what the hell was happening with me. I've never been obsessed like that in my life. I wanted you so bad, I couldn't see straight! Do you know what it feels like to think you've lost your marbles? I don't even want to tell you what I did to myself to get through it."

Lily's cheeks flushed with heat, and she tilted her head, her hair falling in curls along the side of her face. "You don't say?"

"No. I don't say, or won't, anyway. I'd never be able to look you in the eye again and forget Sean...he'd kill me."

Lily glanced down at her hands on the railing. "No, he wouldn't. Not when I'm just as guilty," she looked back up at him, slightly embarrassed. "Though, based on the visual you just painted, I don't think I took things to quite the same extreme," she added, holding out her hand toward his. "Care to let me see?" She raised an eyebrow at him.

"Nope."

She laughed out loud, dropping her hand back to the railing. An awkward silence fell between them. Ryan looked out at the expanse past the circular drive toward the woods and beyond, the only sounds the wind in the trees and an owl hooting in the distance, punctuating the unspoken.

"Sean tells me you're leaving. Why?" Lily blurted out finally.

He inhaled the crisp air, flicking his cigarette to the wet grass past the gravel. He dropped his foot from the railing and stuck his hands in his pockets. "I have to," he said with a shrug.

"I don't understand. You just got here. This is where you belong if you're ever going to find out who you are," she argued.

He shook his head, but this time it was different. "Lily, I already know who I am. Finding out I'm a shifter doesn't change that. What we went through over the last forty-eight hours only proved the point to me even more. I have some things I need to take care of back in the city, but then I'm taking a leave of absence from the squad. I'll be heading west. I'm going to look for other cougars. Sean says it's something I need to do in order to phase."

She raised her hands in frustration. "Yes, but it's not something you have to do right away."

He grabbed her hands and brought them together in his. "I'm not. It's going to take some time for me to wrap up the whole vampire bloodbath thing with the department. We can both thank Sean for explaining the situation to Sébastien. The vampire provided more than enough evidence for me to give Shaw the report of his dreams, though I don't ever want to know how he went about it. Shaw will get a commendation for this for sure. It's not every day a cop gets to bring down a serial killer cult."

Lily's eyebrows shot up. "A cult? Really? Will they buy it?"

Martinez laughed. "Oh hell, yeah! And don't worry, I'm making sure to include how integral you were in catching all the nuances we missed. You should be up to your eyeballs in business after this."

Lily gently pulled her hands from his, her gaze thoughtful. "Thanks, but I'm giving up the lease on my apartment and staying here from now on."

It was Ryan's turn to raise an eyebrow. "Does that mean what I think it means?"

She nodded. "I think so, but I haven't discussed it with Sean, yet."

Ryan pulled himself up to sit on the railing, his legs dangling over the side. "I don't think you'll get much of an argument from him."

Lily laughed, pushing herself up to sit beside him. "Maybe, maybe not. I do tend to bring trouble with me wherever I go. You may have me knocking on your door yet, asking if you need a roommate."

He slid his arm around her shoulder and pulled her into a side hug. "Anytime partner, anytime, but I wouldn't bet on it."

"When are you planning to head back to the city?"

"Tomorrow afternoon."

Lily thought for a minute. "Us too...for the night. Maybe we could head in together. Sean can take the Ford F-150. We could secure your bike on the back bed. There's certainly enough room in the cab for all of us, what do you say? We could grab dinner together and talk about California and what you should expect. Maybe Sean and I could even fly out and meet you, you know, for moral support."

"Fine with me." He shrugged. "But why are you heading into the city for one night?" His eyes widened before she could answer, and he nodded slowly.

The vampires.

THE FIRE BURNED in the grate, just as it had three nights ago when they'd last met, only this time the fire seemed inviting and the ambiance in the room welcoming, almost grateful. The vampire adjudicators had been gathered again, and their chairs turned to face forward in tribunal mode. The large hearth rug had been removed, leaving only the grey concrete underneath, and a large copper drain the size of a dinner plate at the center of the space.

Sébastien poured a glass of cabernet into a wide mouthed wine glass and handed it to Lily. "How was your drive from Maine, not tedious I hope?"

"Fine. Luckily there wasn't too much traffic," Sean replied, putting a hand over his own glass when Sébastien moved to top it off. One glass was enough, considering. The task at hand was still distasteful, regardless of its justification, and the last thing Sean wanted was to participate in the party atmosphere the vampires had already set into motion. To them it was a celebration.

Rémy walked over. This time, his attire mimicked Sébastien's, having forgone his customary period clothing for a more GQ, Wall Street look.

"And how are you my little witch?" he asked, tongue in cheek, his eyes dancing as he waited for daggers. Only this time, his nickname for her was greeted with a beautiful smile.

Lily slipped one arm through his and raised her glass. "Rémy, I have decided from now until forever, I will be 'little witch' to you and you alone. Anyone else calls me by that name, and I promise their nether regions will get a visit from my boot."

At the look on Sébastien's face, they both burst out laughing. Lily inclined her head, mostly out of respect, but also to stop the wine from snorting out of her nose from laughing so hard. "Present company excepted, Sébastien, of course," she added quickly, wiping her mouth.

The master vampire flashed a dazzling, fang filled smile. "Only you, my lady. Only you..."

Across the room, Etienne motioned to Rémy that it was time. Lily dipped her chin once, acknowledging the vampire psychic, as Rémy took her hand to say goodbye.

"When this is all over, please come back and visit. What I see in your eyes makes me forget the monster I see in everyone else's." Then the vampire with the ruined face leaned over and gave Lily's cheek a sweet kiss.

He walked to his seat, as the others took their places as well. When they were settled, Sébastien motioned for everyone else to sit, except Sean.

"It has come to our attention that you have within your midst, a traitor responsible for acts of cruelty, injustice, and treachery against the vampire community. How do you plead, Sean Leighton, Alpha of the Brethren?"

"Guilty," he answered, "but only in that a shifter of my clan has caused said pain and suffering to the Vampires of New York, and to you, Sébastien, in particular. In retribution, I have brought the guilty party as promised. Do with him what you will. He has been abnegated by his own and is Werewolf no longer."

Sébastien rose from his seat and walked toward Sean. The two clasped arms and the master vampire put his hand on the alpha's shoulder. "We accept your offering of justice, and let it be known here and throughout my territory that no vengeance shall be harbored against the Alpha of the Brethren or any of his ilk. The matter will be settled tonight. Blood calls for blood, and blood shall have blood."

The other adjudicators nodded in agreement, as the master returned to his seat.

Sean remained standing and raised one finger, earning the floor once more. "If I may, Sébastien..." he said, and then paused to turn toward Lily who handed him a beautifully engraved wooden box. "May I approach?"

Sébastien waved him forward, and all eyes were riveted on Sean, their regard curious as he approached the master.

Sean placed the box in the vampire's hands. "You said blood calls to blood, and blood shall have blood. However, I promised you a heart for a heart, as well."

The master's eyes widened, and he ran his hands over the box's carved wooden edge. "Is this what I think it is?"

Sean nodded once. His face somber. "Yes. Jack Cochran was the puppet of the one responsible for this mayhem. He was the one accountable for Chen's death. His heart is inside the box."

A new appreciation for the shifters was evident in every face, and an air of respect filled the room. Even Abigail grudgingly nodded her approval.

"Perhaps the time has come for our species to have more than just a treaty of remoteness. Perhaps it's time for us to form a true pact. An alliance for all supernatural beings."

Sean looked thoughtful. "It would certainly be something for the ages," he replied. "And in the spirit of that notion, I vow that over the next week, a contingent of my hunters will be at your disposal to scour your shadow houses for others infected." He fixed Sébastien with a look of severity. "I expect their safety will be guaranteed, yes?"

The vampire spread his hands, as if the matter was *au fait accomplie.* "I will personally see to it myself." A shadow passed over Sébastien's face. "I am beside myself that so many of mine must be destroyed. Such a waste."

Sean exchanged glances with Lily, and Etienne nodded vigorously, catching Rémy's eye. "You have more information for us, Sean?" The older vampire asked, curious as to what made their own seer so animated.

"Yes, Rémy. The cure that may help save those whom you are loath to destroy lies in the blood." The Alpha's face was grim, as he gestured to the door and what lay waiting behind it.

The misshapen vampire smiled, the intact side of his mouth curving up as understanding dawned. "Thank you again, my friend. We will make sure not to waste a drop."

Curious whispers vibrated throughout the room, and Sébastien raised his hand. "It is time. Again, we are indebted to the Shifters for bringing us the one who has wrought such heartache." With a wave of the vampire's hand, Sean stepped back, and the master shifted his regard toward Lily. "My dear, you have suffered the most of any of us. Would you like Abigail to cleanse your memory and give you peace?"

Lily's eyes moistened at the considerate gesture, but she shook her head. "Thank you Sébastien. Your offer is kind and generous, but this is my world now, for better or worse. I accept it as it is, and I hope it accepts me for who I am in return. A friend once said, 'If this is my world, then I have to see if there's a place for me... as me.' And he was right."

A warm gaze and an even warmer smile beamed from Sébastien's face. "Clever girl. Oh, how you would make me smile every day if you would only share our blood." He sighed, "*Ah, c'est la vie,*" and with a lighthearted chuckle, drew himself up from his chair. "Perhaps one day we will be lucky enough to see you change your mind." He stepped forward, kissing Lily on both cheeks. "Until then, you are always welcome."

He then clasped arms with Sean once more, before returning to his seat. It was time.

Sean turned, motioning toward the steel reinforced door at the entrance. It swung open, and he gestured for his hunters. The men carried Edward between them, bound and gagged. He struggled, his feet scrapping across the concrete floor as they dragged him forward. The hunters dropped him in front of the adjudicators, as instructed, and then immediately turned to go. Not a word was spoken.

Lily hooked her arm in Sean's, and with a final nod, they were escorted out. She glanced over her shoulder once, and what she saw would haunt her for the rest of her life. It was the true face of the vampire, and it wasn't the polished, romantic image romance books love to paint. It was evil incarnate.

She jerked her eyes away, keeping her gaze straight ahead and glued to the vampire leading them out. As the door closed behind them, the sound of Edward's scream echoed through the hall. Justice had been served.

LILY PRESSED her cheek into Sean's chest as they sat arm in arm on the couch in her living room, her feet tucked up behind her. All she wanted to do was crawl under his shoulder and stay there forever.

She had given her landlord notice, and by the end of the month she'd no longer be a New Yorker. Her choice had been made.

"It's really over isn't it? Things can finally get back to the way they should have been in the first place, right?" she asked, her voice uncharacteristically small.

Sean pulled her tighter against his chest and kissed the top of her head. "I hope so."

"I feel like I could sleep for a week," she yawned.

Tilting her chin up, he kissed her mouth. "You're entitled. It's been a tough one, hasn't it?" She gave him a sleepy smile, burying herself even further into his chest.

He glanced around the room, his eyes centering on all the pictures of her and Terri. "Are you sure you want to leave? You don't have to, you know."

She looked up at him. "I know. And I'm not really leaving anything behind. Most of them are memories. Very portable."

"That's not what I mean, and you know it," he said, running his fingers through her hair."

"I know."

He shifted on the couch, pushing himself back so he could face her. "Did you mean what you said to Sébastien, that this is your world now?" he asked, drawing his fingers across her cheek.

She took his hand and placed it over her heart. "In my heart, your world has been my world from the beginning, but you know me. My brain is stubborn, and it takes longer for awareness to sink in," she said, tapping her temple with her other hand. "I want this, Sean. All of it. You, the Compound, everything."

"Does this mean what I think it means?" he asked, cocking his head.

She nodded. "Yes."

He just looked at her.

"What's the matter," she asked, suddenly nervous that her decision had come too late.

"Nothing. I just have something I've wanted to do for a very long time." He got up and went into the other room. When he came back, he sat on the end of the coffee table and took her hand in his.

Into her palm, he placed a ring. It was silver in color, but from the sheen, Lily knew it was either white gold or platinum. The sides were scrolled, engraved with beautiful lettering, and at the center glittered a large, square cut diamond.

"It's gorgeous, Sean."

"It's been in my family for over one hundred years. The lettering is an oath. It's in Gaelic, so don't ask me to pronounce it, but its literal translation is this—with my heart I love, with my body I protect, with my life I trade for yours, forever to keep."

"It sounds like a vow."

He closed her fingers around the ring, and then lifted her hand to his lips. "That's exactly what it is," he said, kissing her fingers. "It's very precious."

Lily kept her hand in his for a moment, not saying a word. When she gently pulled her hand back, she opened her palm and stared at the silver glinting in the light from the side lamp. The diamond sparkled like the tears in her eyes. "Maybe this should be in a safe place."

Horrified, her eyes widened the minute the words left her mouth, realizing how awful they sounded. She only meant this was New York and leaving expensive items like that in her apartment... oh crap. She swallowed hard, hoping he didn't take her meaning the wrong way.

His lips curled in a soft, closed lipped smile, and he took the ring from her left palm and slipped it on her finger. "It's right where it belongs."

She stared at the glittering stone on her hand for a moment, then looked at him. "How does this work? Is there a ritual or some ancient rite that has to be completed? I want to make sure we do this right."

Sean nodded. "Yes. It starts with a single question," he said, slipping down onto one knee. "Will you marry me?"

Heat rushed to her cheeks. "That's some question," she said, then threw her arms around his neck. "Yes!"

He pulled her to standing and cupped her face, kissing her deeply. "I love you, Lily."

"I love you, too." With a crafty smile, she pulled back from him, taking his hand. "Come on," she said, tugging on his arm. "I've got a sudden desire to be on all fours."

He lowered his chin, a playful smirk at the corner of his mouth "I thought you were tired."

"Yeah, but we've only got three weeks before the next full moon. Do you think you can have me ready to run with the moon by then? It might take some time and effort."

His smirk spread into a seductive smile and his eyes darkened with desire. With one fluid move he pulled her onto his lap on the couch. "Maybe," he growled, licking her bottom lip.

Straddling him, Lily ran her hand down his chest, hooking her fingers into the waistband of his jeans. His breath hitched, and the rumble at the back of his throat took on a dangerous, untamed tone.

"Make that definitely."

Acknowledgments

When an author publishes a book, whether it's their first or their five hundredth, it's nothing less than a defining moment in their life. Since I began this writer's journey, I've run the gamut in terms of emotion... from 'no excuses do the work' to 'what was I thinking?' to 'be careful what you ask for because you just might get it!'.

My unbelievably patient husband, Bill, for putting up with the insanity and verbal barrages that accompany being glued to my laptop for hours. Our three kids for knowing enough to leave Mom alone when she's writing, despite laundry piling up and pasta for dinner, yet again.

I need to send my undying gratitude to retired New York City Homicide Detective, William Mendez, for his many hours of counsel regarding the ins and outs of NYPD protocol, and the nuances of police department politics and its hierarchy. For his unfailing courtesy, and his generosity in sharing his recollections from case experiences, some of which so horrific it seems unfathomable they were forged from actual events. I also need to thank Officer Ronald Faivre, for his insights into surveillance and the daily life of an undercover street cop. Most importantly, I thank my readers. You made my dream happen. THANK YOU!

I hope you enjoy the book.

About the Author

Marianne Morea was born and raised in New York. Inspired by the dichotomies that define 'the city that never sleeps', she began her career after college as a budding journalist. Later, earning a Masters degree in Fine Art, from The School of Visual Arts in Manhattan, she moved on to the graphic arts. But it was her lifelong love affair with words, and the fantasies and 'what ifs' they stir, that finally brought her back to writing.

Have you joined my monthly newsletter yet?
Fun, Freebies and lots more!
www.MARIANNEMOREA.com

ALSO BY MARIANNE MOREA

The Wolf and the Rose

Torn Between Two Alphas

SYNDICATE CLAN SERIES

The Vampire's Daughter

Lady Wolfe

Queen's Gambit*

Rebel Witch*

*Releasing in 2025

WHISPER FALLS HOLIDAY

A Little Mistletoe and Magic

THE BLESSED

My Soul to Keep

CIA ROGUE OPERATIVE

Dangerous Law

CLUB VAMPIRE

Special Edition RED VEIL DIARIES Bundle

www.ingramcontent.com/pod-product-compliance
Lightning Source LLC
Chambersburg PA
CBHW072311020726
47501CB00002B/468